Forge Books by Elmer Kelton

Wild West

ELMER KELTON

A TOM DOHERTY ASSOCIATES BOOK | NEW YORK

WILD WEST

A Forge Book
Published by Tom Doherty Associates
175 Fifth Avenue
New York, NY 10010

www.tor-forge.com

Forge® is a registered trademark of Macmillan Publishing Group, LLC.

ISBN 978-1-250-16115-4

Our books may be purchased in bulk for promotional, educational, or business use. Please contact your local bookseller or the Macmillan Corporate and Premium Sales Department at 1-800-221-7945, extension 5442, or by email at MacmillanSpecialMarkets@macmillan.com.

First Edition: November 2017
First Mass Market Edition: November 2018

Printed in the United States of America

0 9 8 7 6 5 4 3 2 1

Copyright Acknowledgments

"A Heck of a Promise" originally published in *Ranch Romances,* Oct. 12, 1951, Vol. 167, No. 4

"Blind Canyon" originally published in *Ranch Romances,* Nov. 6, 1953, Vol. 181, No. 4

"Bullets from the Past" originally published in *Six-Gun Western,* Dec. 1950, Vol. 3, No. 5

"Climb the Big Rim" originally published in *Ranch Romances,* July 4, 1952, Vol. 172, No. 4

"Colt Size" originally published in *Ranch Romances,* Sept. 16, 1949, Vol. 154, No. 2

"Land with No Law" originally published in *Ranch Romances,* Oct. 4, 1957, Vol. 207, No. 2

"No Epitaph for Me" originally published in *Ranch Romances,* April 25, 1952, Vol. 171, No. 3

"One Son" originally published in *Ranch Romances,* Nov. 9, 1951, Vol. 168, No. 2

"Poison" originally published in *Triple Western,* Summer 1957, Vol. 18, No. 3

"Ride a Straight Road" originally published in *Ranch Romances,* Aug. 13, 1954, Vol. 186, No. 4

"Deadly Homecoming" originally published in *Triple Western,* Fall 1957, Vol. 19, No. 1

CONTENTS

Wild West

A HECK OF
A PROMISE

It happened and was over with so quickly that it was a moment before Chuck Sloan realized what had taken place. He had driven into the rodeo grounds and started around the arena toward the horse stalls, about half-angry because a flat tire on his old horse trailer had made him miss seeing Rosabelle Lee perform in the barrel race.

Not that he didn't know how it came out. Barring accidents, Rosabelle always won.

Then Buzz Whitney had come tearing toward him in his red convertible. Chuck glimpsed Rosabelle's laughing face beside Buzz. Water filled the ruts on the side of Whitney's car. The handsome cowboy swerved out toward Chuck to keep from splashing mud on his convertible.

Chuck whipped back to the right to avoid Whitney. He heard a woman's scream and the rending crash of splitting lumber.

Heart rubbing his Adam's apple, Chuck jammed on the brakes and jumped out. He caught a glimpse of

Rosabelle and Buzz looking back and laughing, then driving on.

Chuck's trailer had hooked onto a corner of a refreshment stand and ripped off the front of the flimsy structure. Splintered lumber lay across the trailer.

"Our stand, our stand," a girl's voice wailed.

"My horse," Chuck cried. Breathlessly he jumped up onto the trailer hitch and started shoving aside the broken boards.

"Oh, Tommy." he breathed with relief as he examined his nervous bay roping horse. "You're all right."

"Maybe your horse is all right, but you've sure made a wreck out of our refreshment stand," a girl's voice said angrily.

Chuck looked down at her. She looked to be in her early twenties, and she looked to be plenty mad. She stood with fists doubled belligerently on her slim hips. A tight apron revealed a figure that Chuck guessed would look good in a bathing suit. Even if her face was flushed with anger, it was sort of pretty. Not like Rosabelle's, of course. More like his sister, Jenny.

"I didn't do it, ma'am," he said apologetically. "Buzz Whitney pushed me over with that red convertible of his."

She kept glaring at him. He stepped meekly down from the trailer hitch.

"I didn't see any car but that heap of yours," she said sharply. "All I know is that the home demonstration club ladies worked all day yesterday getting this stand fixed up. Now look at it!"

Chuck fumbled in his billfold and came up with a ten-dollar bill and a five. "Reckon this'll patch things up?"

She glanced at the money and back at the stand.

"Well, it was just scrap lumber, covered with crepe paper. And you broke about a dozen pop bottles and a glass coffee pot. I guess this ought to do." She paused, then said, "But money won't help poor Mrs. Lockstetter. You've scared her out of her wits."

The girl nodded toward a portly woman who sat in a corner of the rickety stand, wailing to two ladies who were trying to comfort her. Spilled coffee dripped from her skirt.

Chuck timidly stepped toward her, hat in hand. "I'm real sorry, ma'am. If I'd . . ."

She took a look at him and screamed, "Cowboys! The most careless humans on earth! You ought to be in jail!"

Chuck jumped backward as if he were snakebitten. Red-faced, he turned quickly around and trotted back to the door of his car. The girl stood there. "She's right, you know," she said accusingly.

Chuck pleaded, "I told you how it happened. Now look—I don't want to leave a town and have a bunch of people there mad at me. I'd like to make this up to you some way."

She crossed her arms. "How?"

He studied her a minute. He couldn't help liking this girl, even if she did seem a little bit like a wildcat. "Well, I might take you to supper tonight."

He suddenly remembered what she had said about the home demonstration club. "Or maybe you're married."

"No, I'm not married. I'm the county home demonstration agent here. And I don't usually make dates with strangers."

Chuck waved his hand at the wreckage. "After all this, do you call me a stranger?"

She broke down and grinned. "No, I guess not. My name's Mary McIntyre."

It was a typical West Texas town and a typical West Texas cafe, with cowboy pictures painted on the walls and Mexican food cooked up by someone who had probably never been south of San Angelo.

Chuck didn't know why it was, but every time he started a conversation with a girl he wound up telling her all about Rosabelle Lee.

"Rosabelle's a real rodeo girl," he told Mary. "I've got me a little ranch up north of Big Lake, close to the Centralia Draw. Bought it when I got out of the Army. Of course, I had to borrow a lot, and the debt's still pretty heavy on it.

"Rosabelle's been wantin' me to sell it," he went on. "She says I'm made to follow rodeos and enjoy life like she does, not to be tied down to some little old place and work myself to death."

Mary McIntyre frowned. "There's a lot of satisfaction in having a place of your own and working on it. Rosabelle might be wrong."

Chuck leaned forward as if about to tell a secret. "I've asked her to marry me."

For just a second Chuck thought he saw disappointment in the girl's blue eyes. But he guessed he was wrong.

"What did Rosabelle say?"

"She just said we ought to wait a little bit. I think she's afraid she'll have to go out and live on the ranch. But she won't."

Chuck heard a girl's voice behind him. His heart warmed as he stood up and turned around. "Come on

over and sit down, Rosabelle. I want you to meet Mary
McIntyre."

He imagined he saw a cold look pass between the
two girls. But then he guessed he was wrong again.
They didn't have any reason not to like each other.

Chuck swallowed when Rosabelle leaned in front of
him to hang her wide-brimmed green rodeo hat on a
hook. Her blond hair tumbled smartly down about
her shoulders. A thrill went through him as her body
touched his for a second. He couldn't help noticing
how tightly her fringed leather jacket and her blue riding britches fitted.

"Buzz and I got the biggest bang out of you this
afternoon," Rosabelle laughed. "We thought we would
die laughing when you hit that refreshment stand and
all those old ladies started wringing their hands."

Chuck ducked his chin. He felt warmth creeping
into his cheeks as he glanced at Mary. He could tell she
was a little angry, but she kept quiet.

"I hear you won today, Miss Lee," Mary said finally.

"Oh, sure. I always do."

"You must have a very fine horse."

"Oh, Golden Lad's all right." Rosabelle frowned.
"After all, the rider's the main thing, you know."

He stood the silence as long as he could. Then,
"Rosabelle, I've been wanting to ask you . . ." He
glanced at Mary. It was awkward to be out with one
girl and ask another for a date. But with Buzz Whitney
around, he couldn't afford to wait. "There's a rodeo
dance tonight. I'd like to take you."

"Sorry." Rosabelle smiled. "Buzz has already asked
me to go with him tonight. We're driving over to the
next town. There's a swell night spot there. Why, here
comes Buzz now."

Chuck felt a sour taste in his mouth. He took one good glance at Buzz coming through the cafe door, his tailored Western suit pressed and his brown-and-white boots spotless. There was no denying Buzz was a top rodeo hand. But just three years ago he had had his name in a magazine's "deadbeat" column for skipping out on a hotel bill after a rodeo. Rosabelle, of course, didn't know that. She saw only his flashy surface.

It just happened that his father had been a tight-fisted old gent who saved ninety cents out of every dollar he made. He had had no one but Buzz to leave it to.

"Ready to go, Palomino?" Buzz asked. Annoyance tingled in Chuck as he noticed Buzz's hands placed familiarly on Rosabelle's shoulders.

The cowgirl bid Chuck and Mary good night, and headed for the door. Buzz held back a moment and leaned over close to Chuck's ear.

"Bad news for you, buster. Tonight I'm asking Rosabelle to marry me."

Chuck stood up angrily. But in a few seconds the couple was outside, and he saw them whiz by in the red convertible. Darkly he sank back down.

Mary watched him sympathetically. Finally she spoke. "Maybe it's better like this. If she tells him yes, you're saved from a marriage that wouldn't have worked out anyway. If she says no, you're still in the running."

Chuck doubled his fist. "If it wasn't for that ranch, we might be married now. But I know what it would be like for her. I grew up on one close to Rankin. Seemed the first thing my dad always did of a morning was to step out on the front porch and look for some sign of a rain. It was awful seldom he ever saw any. Rosabelle's never known that kind of a life. And

I won't have her working herself to death on a run-down place with a mortgage as heavy as a truckload of steers."

Mary frowned. "Did your mother ever complain?"

"No. I guess she kind of liked it. In fact, I did, too."

Anger flashed in Mary's blue eyes. "Then it's high time you quit feeling sorry for yourself, or for Rosa-belle. Hard work and debt didn't keep my mother and dad from enjoying life and loving each other. Dad had a place at Fort Stockton, irrigated a farm out of Co-manche Springs and ran cattle on grazing land.

"When I was a little girl it seemed like I spent all my extra time wading in the cold water and the mud with a shovel, helping my tired old dad irrigate. We worked from daylight to dark sometimes, then lit the lanterns so we could keep on working. We finally got the debt paid off, and we loved it." She paused, then went on, "If Rosabelle loved you, she wouldn't care if she had to live the same way."

Mary stood up, purse in her hand. "Now I think I'll go home."

Chuck reached across the table and touched her hand. It felt warm. "Please don't. No use to waste the evening. Won't you go to the dance with me?"

Annoyance showed in her eyes. "As your second choice?"

Chuck grinned. "We'll forget I asked anybody else. Just for tonight we'll forget there is anybody else. What do you say?"

Mary looked at him a long moment, her blue eyes somehow beautiful. She smiled and nodded. Chuck wondered why he felt warm inside.

She danced as lightly as any girl he had ever known, and it was a joy to hold her in his arms. She didn't squeeze up tight, maybe, as Rosabelle did. But then

Rosabelle did everything a little bit different from any-one else. Chuck couldn't get nearly so much dancing as he wanted, though. Seemed like everybody in town came by and had something pleasant to say to Mary.

"How long have you been here, anyway?" he asked her finally. "Looks like everybody and his dog knows you."

Her smile was good to see. "I came here two years ago, soon as I finished college."

"Why hasn't a popular girl like you gotten married?"

She flushed a little. "Too many fellows want excite-ment and adventure. I guess I just want a good home and a man I love. Besides, I promised Mrs. Malone I wouldn't get married for at least three years after I came here."

"Mrs. Malone? Who's she?"

"The district home demonstration agent. Boss of all us county HD agents. She never can get enough girls to fill the vacancies in her district. And she needs them to keep girls' 4-H club work going."

Chuck snorted. "Sounds like a heck of a promise to me."

When the dance was over, Chuck drove Mary to her home, one side of a small frame duplex house. A wind-mill out back creaked as its wheel turned slowly in the night breeze.

He stood on the front porch with her, holding one of her smooth, warm hands in his. He couldn't think how best to tell her good night. Somehow he didn't want to.

"Don't forget what I said about not feeling sorry for yourself or for Rosabelle," she said quietly.

He shook his head. "I won't, Mary. Do you think you could live on the ranch with me . . ."

He noted the way her eyes widened sharply.

". . . I mean, if you were Rosabelle?" he said quickly.

She lowered her eyes. "I'd go with you anywhere—if I were Rosabelle. Good night, Chuck."

She stepped quickly into the house, and before Chuck had a chance to say another word or ask another question, closed the door behind her.

Chuck was out at the fairgrounds early the next morning. He yawned as he poured out some feed and ran clean water into a bucket for Tommy. He must have rolled a hundred miles, just tossing back and forth in bed last night, he thought.

He had kept dreaming about Mary in Rosabelle's clothes and astride Rosabelle's Palomino. It hadn't seemed right. Then he saw Mary in her white apron, sweeping off the front porch of his little ranch house north of Big Lake. Rosabelle and Buzz had passed by in the red convertible and jeered at her, and Chuck dreamed she had gotten mad.

Crazy stuff, he thought, shrugging it off. Probably came from the Mexican food.

The thought of Buzz Whitney proposing to Rosabelle worried him all the time he was exercising Tommy. He kept watching the highway, hoping to see Rosabelle drive up. His heart leaped when Rosabelle's green sedan finally pulled in at the gate. Excitedly he spurred out to meet her. But his heart slid down again.

It was only her younger brother, Danny, come out to feed and curry Golden Lad. That was usually Danny's chore. Rosabelle didn't like to fool with horses much, except to ride them.

Despondently, Chuck rode over to Golden Lad's pen and watched Danny brush the sleek Palomino down while the horse munched oats out of a small galvanized bucket.

"Seen Rosabelle this morning, Danny?" he asked at last.

"Yep."

"Did she—did she say anything?"

Danny grunted. "Yeah. She said I'd have to take care of the Lad this morning."

Chuck's hands shook a little. "Didn't she say anything about last night?"

Danny snickered. "She didn't have to. I heard her come in myself—at four o'clock this morning."

His heart sick, Chuck turned and rode away.

A little after noon, Mary drove up to the rebuilt refreshment stand with three home demonstration club ladies. They started unloading hotdog and hamburger material for the afternoon crowd.

When Chuck could stand the temptation no longer, he started over to talk to her. He slowed up as he saw the portly Mrs. Lockstetter glaring at him. But the woman turned around, and he went on up to the stand.

Mary's face was composed, but somehow Chuck thought he saw joy in her eyes. A glow spread through him, and he couldn't think what to say.

"What about Rosabelle?" Mary asked. "What's her verdict?"

He shook his head. "Haven't seen her. It's time she was here."

Mary said nothing more for a little. Silently she sliced hotdog and hamburger buns and slipped them back into their waxed paper bags. A frown knitted her brow as she worked.

"Chuck," she said suddenly, "I—I've been wanting to say . . ."

"To say what?" he pressed eagerly.

She flushed and looked back down at her buns.

"Oh, nothing. I guess you'll—have to find out for yourself."

Buzz's convertible sped in at the front gate, leaving a trail of rolling dust behind it. Buzz braked to a quick stop close to the refreshment stand to let Rosabelle out. Then he spun the tires and sped on around the arena.

Chuck greeted Rosabelle nervously and bought her a cold drink at the refreshment stand. He dug the toe of his boot into the ground and felt his ears getting warm. "Buzz said he was going to ask you to marry him."

"He did."

Chuck swallowed. "Wh—what did you say?"

Rosabelle smiled and looked off to where Buzz's dust was just now settling. "I told him I'd think about it. You know, Chuck, he really shows a girl a nice time. Nothing cheap about Buzz. He doesn't have any old ranch to worry about."

Despair choked Chuck. He licked his lips and fought for strength. "I—I could sell the ranch, Rosabelle, if you really wanted it that way."

Another girl's voice broke in angrily. Chuck whirled and saw Mary standing there, warm red in her cheeks and fire in her eyes. "I didn't want to say anything," she said sharply, "but I'm not letting you do this, Chuck. Say you sold the ranch. It wouldn't take you long to spend the money on her!"

She turned heatedly to Rosabelle. "And just how long would you stay with him after all his money was gone?"

Rosabelle's face was dark, and her teeth showed a little more than they usually did. "That's pretty strong talk for a hotdog maker."

Anger made Mary breathe hard. "At least I don't

claim to be something I'm not. I don't paint myself up and wear clothes that make men whistle from two hundred yards away. And I don't try to spellbind them by making them think I'm a super-duper cowgirl when it's really my horse that does the job!"

Rosabelle bristled up at that. "I don't take any prizes I don't win. It's the rider that counts, not the horse."

"You bought Golden Lad after somebody else trained him," Mary declared. "It's him that knows how to barrel race. Without your own horse, you couldn't even win a booby prize!"

Chuck's throat was dry. He was afraid he would have to step between the girls.

"It isn't so! It isn't so!" Rosabelle screeched.

Mary held her doubled fists against her hips. "Maybe you'd like to ride a barrel race against me."

"I'd be glad to, sister! I'll show the world that no hotdog maker's in the same class with Rosabelle Lee!"

Chuck thought he saw triumph in Mary's eyes. "All right, then. Suppose you ride Chuck's horse. Chuck, has Tommy ever run barrels before?"

He shook his head. "Nope. Tommy's a specialist. Calf roping."

Rosabelle nodded assent, a mirthless grin spreading over her face.

"And," Mary added, "since the horse isn't important anyway, I'll just ride your Golden Lad."

Rosabelle's grin died like a match in a high wind. But Chuck knew she had gone too far to pull out now.

"All right," the cowgirl said. "I'll get the producer to let us match it off right after the regular barrel races this afternoon. He'll be tickled to give the customers a special treat—seeing a local hotdog girl get beaten by Rosabelle Lee."

Rosabelle strode off in long, huffy steps. She waved

to a couple of other cowgirls up near the chutes and yelled for them to wait. In a moment she was pointing back to Mary, and the girls were laughing.

Chuck wished he hadn't even come to this rodeo. He wished he didn't have to watch a nice girl like Mary humiliated.

"You oughtn't to've done it, Mary," he said quietly. "Your friends'll be laughing at you for weeks."

"Will you?" she asked. He shook his head. "No. But with me it's different."

She smiled. "I'm pleased to hear you say that, Chuck. And don't you worry. I told you my dad used to run cattle. I could ride a long time before I could read."

It seemed to Chuck to be the slowest rodeo he had ever seen. It felt like six hours between the grand entry and the girls' barrel race. One by one cowgirls from all over the Southwest spurred into the arena and wove their horses around three barrels spaced out evenly, then wove back again and galloped over the finish line.

Rosabelle charged out on Golden Lad for her regular contest ride and made the barrels in thirteen seconds flat. Best time of the day. In fact, best time of the entire rodeo.

As she came trotting out of the arena, Chuck worriedly watched Golden Lad's hard breathing. That would make it even harder on Mary, for the Palomino wouldn't be starting fresh when she raced him.

In a few minutes the last cowgirl racer came out of the arena. Rosabelle's time still stood untouched. Then the announcer was saying: "A real treat now, folks. A special race between Rosabelle Lee, cowgirl queen, and your own Miss Mary McIntyre.

The local crowd cheered and clapped at Mary's name. That warmed Chuck's heart a little. But it wouldn't be many minutes until they would be laughing at her, he thought.

Rosabelle was first. Quirt in hand, she took Tommy back far enough to get up good speed before she crossed the starting line. She pulled her hat down tight, nodded at the timekeepers in the judge's box.

Then she spurred and quirted Tommy in the same instant. He bounded forward like he always did when he left the roper's box on the heels of a calf.

Chuck watched his horse's speed and knew Mary didn't have a chance. But he leaned forward and sucked in his breath when Rosabelle reached the barrels. Tommy didn't know just what he was supposed to do. Rosabelle was reining him too hard, much too hard. He pulled out too far from the first barrel. The cowgirl jerked him back in time to go around the off side of the second barrel. But she had lost speed.

Tommy went past the last barrel, and Rosabelle tugged on the reins to turn him round.

"Light-rein him, Rosabelle," Chuck breathed. "You're pulling him too hard."

Rosabelle reined him heavily back around the barrels, then spurred and quirted him vigorously across the finish line. "Fourteen and three-tenths seconds," the announcer said.

Rosabelle was muttering as she came out of the arena. Still puzzled by this new task, Tommy stepped along nervously. Rosabelle jabbed him with her spurs. "Behave yourself, jughead!" she gritted sharply.

Mary smiled at Chuck, then trotted Golden Lad up to his place. Chuck smiled weakly back.

Then Mary shouted at the horse, and Chuck blinked away the sand that the Palomino's hoofs showered into his eyes. In almost no time Mary had gotten across the open space between the starting line and the barrels. She didn't try to rein Golden Lad. She just stayed in the saddle, shifting her weight as she anticipated the next move.

"She knows that horse savvies what to do," Chuck told himself.

Golden Lad rounded the last barrel, wove through them again, and pounded home. Mary shouted at him and fanned his rump with her hat at every step.

"Thirteen and five!" the announcer shouted.

Rosabelle sat there, slack-jawed, "It can't be," she breathed, color rising in her cheeks. "I've run those barrels a thousand times."

"You mean your horse has," Mary laughed. "He knows what to do. All you have to do is stay on him."

A couple of cowgirls walked by, grinning. "Hey, there, Rosabelle. Looks like that hick girl you told us about could give you some lessons."

Rosabelle's face was suddenly dark. She gripped her quirt until her knuckles whitened. She swung down from the saddle, cursing.

"It's this horse that did it," she shouted. "He's not fit for dog food!"

She lashed savagely at Tommy with her quirt. "Make a fool out of me, will you? I'll beat some sense into you!"

She swung at him again. Tommy reared and squealed.

Blood roared hot in Chuck's face. "Drop that quirt, Rosabelle!"

She swung at Tommy again. The horse flinched and jerked away from her. Chuck grabbed the quirt and tore it from Rosabelle's fist.

"I always thought you were a good sport," he said angrily. "But I guess I never saw you really get beat before. And you're fixing to get another licking right now!"

Grasping Rosabelle's wrist, Chuck sat down on a cowboy's rope can and turned the screeching cowgirl over his knees. The palm of his hand burned like fire as he gave her a spanking like she probably hadn't had since she had stopped playing with dolls.

A dozen cowboys and cowgirls stood watching, clapping their hands. Buzz Whitney trotted up, his face twisted.

"Take your hands off of her, Chuck Sloan," he shouted. "I'll whup the living daylights out of you!"

Chuck jumped up, dumping Rosabelle right on her hip pockets. "You better hire you some help," he roared back.

He tore into the fancy-dressed cowboy, pounding at his face and belly with all the fury that had built up in him for weeks. Buzz quickly folded up like a dry towel and sank to the ground. A grinning cowboy filled a bucket out of a faucet behind the chutes and splashed water at Buzz.

Buzz sat up, sputtering. But he didn't try to get to his feet while Chuck was standing there.

Rosabelle stood glowering, her blond hair hanging in strings. Her lipstick was smeared, and angry tears had sent her mascara trickling down her face in little black rivulets.

"You can keep your old ranch, Chuck Sloan!" she shouted. "Buzz and I are going places. You'll be hearing about us—in Cheyenne and Pendleton and Madison Square Garden. And I hope you stay on that ranch till you die!"

She lifted the swaying Buzz to his feet, then helped him stagger off.

An ache gnawed deep within Chuck as he watched

them go. It wasn't so much seeing Rosabelle go. It was the sudden, cold realization that something he had loved and believed in hadn't really existed at all.

Rosabelle's last words came back to him. It struck him that they were the only wise ones he had ever heard her say: "Stay on that ranch till you die."

Then he thought about Mary. She had known all this, and had braved ridicule to make him see it. A warm tingle ran through him. Pride, maybe. Or maybe it was something else. He remembered the dream he had had, of her sweeping off the front porch of his little ranch house. Suddenly he knew why the thought of her was so wonderful. He turned to find her.

She had tied Golden Lad to a fence. She was getting into her car, over by the refreshment stand.

"Mary, wait!" he shouted. But she didn't hear him. She drove away. He started to run to his car, to catch up with her.

Just then the announcer's voice came him. "Jim Todd next roper. Chuck Sloan get ready."

Sadly he turned back to Tommy and patted him on the shoulder. He swung in the saddle and trotted to the pen.

Even twilight didn't help the looks of the little duplex any. Chuck listened to the creak of the windmill as he stood on the front steps. He fancied his heart was pounding even louder. He knocked on the screen. In a moment Mary came to the door.

"Mary, I—" he stammered, "I've been wrong about so many things." He awkwardly twisted his hat in his hands.

Mary smiled and pushed open the screen door. "Come in, Chuck."

He tried to smile back as he walked in, but his face seemed to be frozen.

"Mary, last night you told me you would go with me any place, and live on the ranch with me—if you was Rosabelle. Well, would you do it now—being yourself?"

He thought he saw tears well up in her eyes, but he might have been wrong. They could have been his own.

"Am I second choice again?" she asked quietly.

"Not any more. Not since I got my eyes open."

He caught her in his arms and pulled her to him. The nearness of her body sent the blood roaring through him again. "Please, Mary, I'll need me a good home demonstration agent to make a home out of my place."

"B-but I promised Mrs. Malone . . ."

Chuck held her tightly and kissed her. She leaned her head back and looked happily into his eyes. Then she put a warm hand on the back of his neck and pulled his face down to hers. "But I guess she'll understand." She kissed him. "Like you said—it was a heck of a promise."

BLIND
CANYON

For a quarter of an hour Scott Tillman had hunkered on his spurs in the rough cedar brake, his stony gaze fixed on the smoke which drifted toward him from the new-built branding fire. The troubled plains wind brought him the smell of the dust stirred up by restless hooves, and the frightened bawl of the first calf to feel the burn of the hot iron.

Behind him he heard a man drumming big knuckles impatiently against the tough leather of high-topped boots. Tillman glanced back at the crouched figures of his own three men, and Bannock's five men.

The beginnings of an eager, grim smile began to work at big Clive Bannock's wide mouth. "We got us a job to do, Tillman. Let's get at it."

Regret weighed heavily in Scott Tillman as his glance returned momentarily to the pole corral half-hidden in the gathering of brush back down the canyon. He watched the man and the boy out yonder, burning a brand onto the thick hides of one struggling and loudly bawling calf after the other.

A futile wish brought a grimace to his thin face. He wished he could have kept this affair to himself and his own men. It was the devil's own luck that they had ridden into Clive Bannock and his Slash B crew.

"There'll be no shooting unless they start it, Bannock. I want no killing. Do you understand that?"

Bannock's eyes were cold. "We'll see," he said.

Silently the men moved back in a crouch to where two cowboys held their horses behind a shelter of thick brush. Scott Tillman swung into the saddle, his hard gaze lingering for a moment on Clive Bannock. Bannock limped heavily as he took his horse and maneuvered him around for an easy mount.

Tillman was younger by twenty years than big Clive Bannock. He was as tall, but he didn't have the great chest, the broad shoulders, the stout beltline that Bannock had. Everything about Bannock was big, even his broad, heavy face, and the bull neck that swelled his sweat-streaked collar. But it was the eyes that always ultimately drew a man's guarded attention. They were dark eyes, almost black, and hard as the flint of a Comanche spearhead. His ambition matched his size, for Slash B cattle were scattered across Winchester preemptions from the Canadian River down to the Caprock.

As for Tillman, he appeared to be just another cowboy, come north to the great buffalo plains from the thorny brush of South Texas. He was string-thin, so that his clothes always hung a little loose around his flat stomach. But there was strength in his gaunt, wind-whipped face. It was a strength that even Clive Bannock knew.

The riders were within fifty feet of the corral when the boy spotted them and yelped. The man dived toward a rifle he had left leaning against the pole fence.

Then he counted the horsemen, weighed the distance, and stopped with empty hands.

He met the riders with a forced smile instead of a loaded gun. "Get down. We can fix up a bucket of coffee while we finish branding this little jag of calves."

Relief eased through Tillman. There wouldn't be a fight, then. He had had his share of fighting a long time ago.

"Thanks, Owen," he replied, "I reckon not. We're just looking around. Good-looking bunch of calves. They show good breeding."

Owen kept his grin, but something was rapidly draining out of it. The boy behind him was scared. His hands trembled, and his freckled, fifteen-year-old face had blanched white. Owen kept talking.

"They got good mammies behind them. Good bulls, too. I'm always careful when it comes to choosing cattle."

Tillman nodded. "So I hear," he said with irony. He rolled a cigarette with tense fingers, alert for any sign of a wrong movement. "But the best of them gets careless once in a while. Even Jess Owen might make a mistake and put a brand on a calf that didn't match the one his mammy carried." He licked the cigarette paper and watched sudden red wipe across Owen's whiskered face.

The man eased a half a step closer to the gun. "Why, I could show you the mammies of these calves, if I hadn't already weaned them."

Tillman's jaw ridged. "Then I don't reckon you'd mind us bringing in a little bunch of cows we gathered back yonder and putting them in here with the calves."

He turned half around in the saddle and signaled. In a few moments he heard the bawling of cows behind him. The calves in the pen started bawling louder, crowding against the south end of the corral in an effort to see the cows.

Tillman didn't have to look. He'd already seen the cows with Wilma Dixon's Lazy D brand on their hips. A couple of his cowboys had found them hidden up a fenced-in canyon, apparently to be left there until they had forgotten their calves and could return to their home range without arousing some nosy cowboy's suspicion.

A Lazy D cowhand opened the gate. The calves spilled out among the bawling cows. They quickly began mating up with their mammies and hungrily making up for lost time. "Want to see any more, Owen?" Tillman asked.

Owen shrugged wanly. "Looks like we've seen enough. All right, I'll ride in to town with you. But you big fellows with your association don't think you can whip us little birds in our own court, do you?"

Tillman's mouth tightened. No, he admitted to himself, he didn't. Not a single conviction had the association managed to get, even against the most notorious of cow thieves like Curly Kirkendall.

The town of High Land had started with an adobe whisky post when the rolling plains had echoed to the slap of Sharps rifles in the rough hands of buffalo hunters. When the hunters and the buffalo were gone, great herds of longhorns had begun to drift up onto the broad buffalo plains. The settlement had grown into a wild gathering of saloons, gamblers, and doubtful women, where outcasts from the rest of Texas and from across the line in New Mexico could come and find others of their own kind.

But there was growing animosity among the cattlemen, both big and small. Had it not been for the

gnawing distrust which festered between the big outfits and the little ones, they might long ago have joined
forces and wiped High Land clean.

Even so, the town's denizens feared that the cow
outfits would someday form a coalition, organize a
county, and kill the town by law. So they beat the
ranchmen to the jump. Almost in secret, they had gathered a petition and gotten the county organized and
their own officers elected, before the cowmen stopped
sniping at each other long enough to realize how
serious the situation had suddenly become.

Owen laughed. "Still want to take me to town, Tillman? Soon's Judge Merriwether sees me, I'll be loose
again anyhow."

Big Clive Bannock nodded his great head at the
young man who rode beside him. Young Fletch Bannock edged his horse forward. "We ain't taking you to
town, Owen. We got our own court right here. And
the verdict is guilty. That cottonwood down yonder
by the creek looks just about right."

Quick anger whipped in Tillman as he whirled on
Clive Bannock's son. "There's not going to be any
hanging. I told you—"

A hint of grim laughter danced in Fletch Bannock's
wild gray eyes. He was a kid of twenty-one, with
his father's big frame but a quick, lithe movement like
that of a Mexican panther. The fuzzy attempt at a
mustache on his upper lip might appear ludicrous to
anyone who did not know about the two notches already carved on the well-polished gun which rode in
the kid's worn leather holster.

Fletch spat, "Shut up, Tillman. You're outvoted here.
If you don't like it, you better just take a little ride over
that hill."

Tillman stiffened to the cold pressure of a gun

against the small of his back. He knew it was Clive Bannock's.

Right hand upon his gun, Fletch Bannock loosened his horn string with his left hand and began to shake down his rope. He edged his horse a little closer to the ashen-faced Owen.

"Put your hands behind you, Owen, and take it like a man."

The thief slowly stepped backward until he was helpless against the pole fence. "It ain't right," he blurted. "A man's got to have a trial."

In desperation he dived for his gun. That was what Fletch Bannock had waited for. His own gun leaped into his hand and he fired. Owen slumped back against the fence and sagged down in a heap.

A helpless rage swelled in Tillman's throat. He turned to Clive Bannock and saw the satisfaction in the big man's face. "You had no call to do that, Bannock."

"Matter of opinion. Has working for a woman these last few years made a woman out of you, Tillman?

"Now what about this button here? He's old enough to know better than help Owen steal cattle. We might just as well take care of him, too, and show them small-time outfits that our association means business."

Trembling in anger, Tillman stepped down and stood in front of the quaking boy. "You won't lay a hand on him, Bannock. I'm mad enough to shoot you if you make one move toward him."

He thought he had seen the boy before, swamping out a High Land saloon. A drifting, homeless kid, likely. He was at an age where he might still become either an outlaw or a preacher, depending on which way he was shoved.

"What's your name, son?"

Stammering, the boy finally managed to say Chet Golightly.

"Now listen to me, Chet. You're mighty lucky to be getting out of this alive. If you were a little older, you'd likely be lying there with Owen."

He paused for emphasis. "Now, you catch your horse and head back east. Don't stop to tell anybody goodbye. Just get on that horse and go!"

Swallowing, the boy nodded. His freckles stood out darkly on his white-drained face.

His cowboys backing him up, Scott Tillman watched Bannock's men to be sure no one interfered with the boy. As the kid swung into his old broken-tree saddle, Tillman stepped up beside his horse.

"One more thing, son. Was there anybody else with you and Owen?"

The boy shook his head, "No, sir. Nobody but the woman."

Tillman swallowed. "Woman? What woman?"

"I don't know. I came out here only yesterday. She's back yonder in Owen's shack."

He pointed vaguely up the canyon. Then he hauled his horse around and, bare-heeled, kicked into a lope.

Scott Tillman leveled an angry glance at big Clive Bannock. There would have to be a woman!

"Let's put Owen's body across his horse and then go find that shack," he said darkly to his own cowboys.

As they rode out, he pulled in beside Clive Bannock. His jaw set, he nodded toward Bannock's son. The boy already was carving a new notch into his gun, extracting his full measure of grim pride.

"You're raising that boy into a man-killer, Bannock,"

Tillman said. "The day'll come when you'll wish to God you could start him over again."

Bannock shook his head. "No, Tillman. I want him tough. A man's got to be tough to carve himself a place in this country. He'll be as tough a man as I am. Tougher.

"You see, Tillman, my old man was a coward. Everything he ever got hold of somebody took it away from him. He was a great one for turning the other cheek. I hated the way we lived, and I got so I hated my old man. Soon as I was old enough to shift for myself, I ran off. I've never turned a cheek to any man. What I want, I get. And what I get, I keep."

It was a good canyon for a cowman. The curing grama grass stretched like a golden carpet from one side to the other, its flag tops bending under the constant wind of the high Texas plains. A meandering stream of cool, clear water split it down the middle. Gray jackrabbits leaped out of the grass at the approach of the riders and skittered away to pause again at a distance and listen, their black-tipped ears moving back and forth. Scattered up and down the canyon were a couple of hundred longhorn cattle, carrying good flesh. They raised their horned heads at the sight of the riders and eased away.

"By George," Bannock boomed, "I'm going to have this canyon. We'll split up the cattle. Like as not, they were stolen from us anyhow. Then I'm moving some of my stuff up here."

A hardness coiled in him, Tillman turned in the saddle. "Try it, and we'll run you out, Bannock. Owen's widow has still got first claim on this land. Any cattle we can't prove were stolen will belong to her."

The big ranchman savagely jerked his horse to a stop. "You haven't got any right to talk to me like that, Tillman. I own the Slash B. You're nothing but a foreman, a hired hand."

"That's right, Bannock. But Mrs. Dixon'll back me up. If there ever comes a time she doesn't, I'll leave. Till then, I speak for the Lazy D. And I'm telling you, leave this canyon alone."

Bannock's hatred flared alive in his broad face. It had been like this between them ever since the first time they had met on the rolling plains, three years before. Just up from the lower country, Bannock had tried to bluff Wilma Dixon into giving up one of the big natural lakes she needed badly for summer water. She had been a widow less than a year then, a very young widow, and Bannock had thought the bluff would be easy to pull.

But Scott Tillman had stampeded Bannock's herd before it ever got to the water. In the run, Bannock's horse had fallen on him. The big ranchman still favored the leg that had snapped under the smashing weight of the horse.

Scott watched in relief as Clive and Fletch Bannock rode away, their men trailing out behind them. It wouldn't be easy, explaining to Owen's woman. But maybe it would be a little less difficult with the Bannocks gone.

Jess Owen had built his shack of pickets, border style, and chinked it with mud. He had put it up toward the head of the canyon, where a spring bubbled forth the cool water that gave life to the plains and started the stream on its crooked course down toward the Canadian.

She came out of the shack's door and stood on the rock step, waiting for them. Tillman's mouth dropped open. He had expected to see a graying woman about Owen's age. Instead he found facing him a girl of eighteen or twenty, with a slender figure, smooth features, and long brown hair that drifted out over her shoulder in the easy plains wind. Tillman stepped down and took off his broad-brimmed hat.

Not yet seeing the body on the horse, she spoke first. "If you're Curly Kirkendall, Uncle Jess says tell you to unsaddle and wait. He's down the canyon. He'll be back directly."

Uncle Jess. Then she wasn't Owen's wife, after all. And if she didn't know Curly Kirkendall, she couldn't have been in this country long. Kirkendall had stolen cows from every ranchman in the high country, and not a one could prove it.

Crushing the hat clumsily in his work-roughened hands, Scott said hesitantly, "I'm not Curly Kirkendall, miss. And Jess Owen won't be coming back. He's dead."

She lifted a small hand over her mouth, and her terrified eyes saw Owen's body slacked across the saddle.

"Sorry, miss," Tillman spoke. "He was stealing cattle."

Tears worked slowly down her cheeks, but her brown eyes managed to shoot angry sparks. Tillman sensed that they were eyes unaccustomed to tears.

"And you killed him!"

"Fletch Bannock killed him, miss." He lowered his head. "But we were there."

She whirled around, her back to him, and covered her face with her hands. Tillman moved to place a hand on her thin shoulder, then drew it back. Gravely he glanced up at one of the cowboys and nodded toward Owen's body.

"Better find a shovel, Chuck."

When the grave was dug, Tillman went inside the

shack where the girl had fled. His hat again was in his hands.

"We can go down to Peace Valley and get a preacher for him, if you want us to. Otherwise, I reckon we're ready to bury him, if you are."

There were no longer any tears in her eyes, but defiance burned there. "I'm ready, I guess. I'll fetch a preacher up later."

Dick Coleridge was a quiet-mannered cowboy who never took off for town after payday for a round of women, cards, and whisky. Scott had him say a few words before the cowboys shoveled the dirt back into the grave.

Scott followed the girl down toward the rude picket shack.

"You can't stay out here by yourself, miss. You better come on along with us. Wilma Dixon owns the Lazy D. She'll be glad to have you stay at the ranch till you make some kind of arrangements."

Bitterly the girl shook her head. "Take favors from the people who killed Uncle Jess? I reckon there are women in High Land I can stay with."

"Women like Prairie Kate and Wild Mary Donovan? You don't look to me like you belong in that kind of company. We've got a lot to make up to you for. Why don't you come on along with us?"

Finally she shrugged her shoulders. "All right. But you're not doing me any favors. I'll pay for my keep. Is that understood?"

Helping her gather up a few of her clothes, he noted that Owen had turned over the shack to the girl. Owen's own bedding and clothes were in a small dugout shed down by the creek.

"Tell me what you were doing out here in the first place," Scott said.

"Jess Owen was my dad's brother. I reckon if I were honest about it I'd have to admit that they were both about the same caliber. My mother ran off from us when I was a little girl.

"We just kind of bummed around over the country. Dad did whatever he had to do to make us a living, and even then he generally gambled half of it away. Six months ago he was shot in a saloon. Uncle Jess had come up here. When he heard, he sent for me."

Defiance stood strong in her voice and in her brown eyes. "Maybe they weren't all they ought to've been. But they were kind to me; that's what counted. There haven't been many people that were ever kind to me."

Scott Tillman swallowed, and he dropped his gaze to the boot-packed dirt floor. There was a sudden stirring in him.

"You'll find other people can be kind, too, Miss Owen. I promise you."

Riding out of the canyon, they met another group of horsemen coming in. Scott counted six. And riding in the lead was Curly Kirkendall.

Surprise lifted Kirkendall's face as he reined up. Then the face settled into the easy grin it almost always held. "Howdy, Scott," he said. "Kind of off your range, ain't you?"

Scott nodded. "Maybe. But a cowboy's got to go where his cattle are. And lately a lot of ours've been getting off their range. I reckon you know as much about that as we do."

His tone was gentle, almost good-humored.

Kirkendall threw back his handsome head and laughed loudly and heartily.

Scott couldn't help smiling with him. They were on opposite sides of the fence now. There couldn't be any denying that. But there had been a time once, before Scott had realized he was riding up a blind canyon. And Scott never forgot that except for the wisdom of one man, he might be in Kirkendall's place.

"If you're going to Jess Owen's, Curly," he said, "you can save your time. You won't find him."

Curly's smile faded as the meaning soaked in. His gaze finally touched the girl. He took off his hat, revealing the curly mop of flaming red hair that had given him his nickname. "This is Owen's niece, I take it?"

Scott nodded "I'm taking her to Wilma Dixon, Curly. Mrs. Dixon will make a home for her till Miss Owen decides what she wants to do."

For a long moment Curly Kirkendall looked at the girl, his eyes soft. Then the outlaw said, "You go with him, miss. You can trust Scott Tillman, and Mrs. Dixon, too."

He donned his hat and rode on, his five men abreast of him.

John Dixon had built his ranch headquarters at a Comanche spring which swelled out of the grassy ground at the head of a long canyon. It was much like the location Jess Owen had chosen, except that it was far larger. The canyon walls helped shield it from some of the fury of the howling winter northers that burst down from the open plains above.

Even so, the plains wind always searched the place out, for the wind was a constant thing here on the Llano Estacado. It was a vibrant part of life, just as much as the endless, rolling land, the springs, and the snaky Canadian. Cool and pleasant, the wind brought the range to green awakening in the spring. With help of the hot sun, the toasting summer wind cured out the short grass that would be so desperately needed in the winter, when the same wind would come howling down with its dread chill, its ice and snow.

Riding by the rock barn, Scott motioned for his cowboys to pull in and unsaddle. With Nell Owen following him, he rode up the grass-covered slope to the main house. Like the barn, it was built of rock. John and Wilma Dixon had spent their first winter here in a dugout. That was the winter she had lost her baby. When spring came, Dixon and his cowboys built her the big house. But Dixon didn't get to live in it long. A horse dragged him down the side of a canyon, and Wilma Dixon was left to manage her ranch alone.

She wasn't really alone. Scott Tillman had owed John Dixon a debt that money couldn't pay. He stayed and took charge for Wilma. Instead of going under, as people had predicted it would when John Dixon died, the Lazy D grew into a bigger place than ever, second only to Clive Bannock's gun-won Slash B, which sprawled between its ragged boundaries down most of the way to the Caprock.

A bay horse was hitched to the fence on the shady side of the house. Scott knew it belonged to Doug McKinney.

"You can sit out here on the gallery," Scott said to Nell Owen. "I better talk to Mrs. Dixon first."

He helped her down from her horse and walked with her up to the porch. He pushed through the front door, with its oval-shaped, etched glass and the dust-catcher carving that framed it.

Wilma Dixon was still a young woman, in her mid-twenties. Hard luck and grief had matured her, but they had not cost her any of the beauty that had won cattleman John Dixon six or seven years ago. Now she owned thousands of cattle and controlled hundreds of sections of preempted land. But always in her deep blue eyes Scott saw a vague unhappiness, a deep loneliness and yearning. Scott always had been able to solve any problem that the ranch might give. But for her greatest need, he had had no answer.

Doug McKinney stood on the far side of the parlor, a cup of coffee in his hand. He was a hardworking man who owned a small ranch down the canyon, its borders touching the Lazy D on one side, Bannock's Slash B on the other.

He nodded at Scott Tillman, but there was reserve in his gray eyes. He never had really liked the Lazy D foreman. "Wilma tells me you thought you had the trail of some stolen cattle, Scott."

Tillman chewed his lip and looked at Wilma Dixon. "We did. We trailed them to Jess Owen's canyon outfit."

Distastefully, he told them about running into Clive Bannock, and Bannock's persistence in going along. He described the death of Jess Owen.

"We found out later that there was a girl at his shack. She's his niece. We brought her along, Mrs. Dixon. I told her she would have a home here till something else could be worked out. I hope that's all right."

There was sympathy in Wilma Dixon's voice. Tillman liked her for it. She had had grief enough of her own to be always ready to help someone else in need. "Please, Scott, bring her in."

Doug McKinney took a quick step forward. "Just a minute, Scott, before you do. There's something I want to ask you. You know Clive Bannock. You know what he is. Why do you keep working with him?"

Frowning, Scott said, "Because working together is the only way we'll ever clear this country of crooks and thieves. It's the only way we'll ever make it a decent place. You're right about Bannock. I don't like him, either. But it takes iron to fight iron."

McKinney made little attempt to hide his hostility. "I don't know that Jess Owen was a thief. I can only take your word for it. We've known for a long time that Clive Bannock has wanted to get rid of us small outfits. I've got a suspicion you'd like it too, Tillman. Is that why you and Bannock and four or five other big outfits armed your association, so you could squeeze us little men out? So you could call us cow thieves and run us off?"

Color flared in Scott's face, but he said nothing. This wasn't the first time.

Wilma Dixon sprang to his defense. "Doug, that's not fair, and you know it.

"The Lazy D has always been a friend to you. Why, you and I have known each other since I was a little girl. You threw your cattle in with John's, and we all came up here together. You don't think I'd turn against you now, do you?"

McKinney shook his head. There already were streaks of iron-gray in his hair, streaks that shouldn't be showing up for years yet.

"You wouldn't, Wilma. But Scott Tillman might." He reached out and took Wilma Dixon's hand. When McKinney looked at her, there could be no doubt how he felt about her, or why he had stuck with a hopeless ranch in the face of heavy odds, just to be near her.

"I've enjoyed the visit, Wilma. I'll come back when I can."

He paused at the door for a last word to Scott. "There are a good many of us small men, Scott. We can look mighty big in a fight. Remember that before you and your association undertake any high-handed murder."

When McKinney had gone, Wilma touched Scott's arm with her hand. "Scott, don't hold this against Doug. He's taken a lot of crowding from Clive Bannock. You can't blame him for being hard to get along with."

Scott shook his head. "No, you can't blame him."

He knew there was another reason for McKinney's not liking him, but it wouldn't do to tell Wilma Dixon. Maybe she sensed it herself—that she was the cause.

She still had hold of his arm, and the touch of her hand made him a little uneasy. "The girl is still waiting outside, Mrs. Dixon," he reminded her.

"Yes," she answered quietly. "Please bring her in."

There was a strong pride in Nell Owen. She stuck to her declaration that she would accept no favors, that she would expect to pay for her keep. Wilma Dixon finally gave up arguing with her about it and let her have it her own way. Inwardly Scott smiled. There was something he liked about this girl. He wasn't much surprised when, after only a couple of days of uncomfortable sitting around the house, Nell Owen decided to go back to her canyon. He knew by the determined set of her jaw that there wouldn't be any talking her out of it. But he tried.

"It's not the kind of country that a woman tackles alone," he warned her.

"Wilma Dixon made out all right," she said pointedly.

He rubbed his chin a little before he answered that one. "But John Dixon had the place well established before he died. And she wasn't exactly alone, even afterward. She had help."

Her brown eyes were stubborn. "Nearly everything

I've ever done, I've had to do without help. I've gotten by; I'll get by now. All my life I've had to be moving around. I've never had anything of my own, or a place I could look to as a home of my own.

"Well, now I've got a place, and I'm going to keep it. I'll not let anybody talk me out of it, and nobody is going to chase me away. If they think they can, they're in for a sad surprise."

She left the next morning. Somewhat against her will, he went with her to Peace Valley to locate a couple of trustworthy cowhands for her.

He watched her sell, sight unseen, enough of her cows to pay immediate expenses, and watched the way she bought supplies she would need for the ranch. There was no indecision or frivolity about her.

An admiration grew in him as he watched. And when at last she climbed into an old but sturdy wagon she had bought, he took off his hat with a grin.

"I think you're going to make it."

Her little jaw took on that determined set again. "You're doggone right I'll make it!"

She flipped the reins like a teamster and took the bouncing wagon north, her two middle-aged cowhands following along on horseback. Scott watched until they faded together as one tiny dust speck far out on the plains. All the way home he thought about her, and he wondered why.

Saltiest of the little ranchmen in the high country was leather-tough Jock Classen. An old bachelor, he was a short, stocky kind that had a banty rooster fire to him. One night a couple of years back, he and two Mexican ranch hands had run off a bunch of would-be cattle rustlers. It got to be an open secret that they were Curly Kirkendall and his men. And every time someone mentioned Jock Classen, Curly would duck his head and grin.

Jock had had a rousing run-in with Clive Bannock, too, and Bannock had left in a hurry, with Classen's shotgun boosting him along.

About a week after Jess Owen's death, a neighbor rode over to Classen's ranch and found Classen and both his Mexican hands dead. Classen had been shot in the back. His *gentes* had their guns out but evidently had never had a chance to use them.

Cold fury building in them, Classen's neighbors soon discovered that most of Classen's cattle had been rounded up and driven away. The job had been done two or three days earlier, according to signs. There was little use in trailing the cattle now, for they would be far across the New Mexico line before anyone could catch them.

The angry fingers pointed toward Curly Kirkendall. Yet there was puzzled uncertainty among the little ranchmen. Curly hadn't bothered them since the big outfits had formed their association. Most of them figured the rustler was laying off them to help discourage them from joining with the big brands.

But the bloody tragedy of Jock Classen gave Scott Tillman a burning new hope that he might be able to pull the big outfits and the little ones together. Maybe this was what they needed to show them that their only hope was in unity. At Scott's word, Lazy D riders spurred out all over the high country with word that there would be a meeting in Peace Valley after Jock Classen was buried.

Jock's funeral didn't last long. There weren't any relatives to mourn for him, and Jock had never given the minister a chance to get acquainted with him. So there wasn't much to do but read from the Book and lower the long pine box into the grave that had been cut down through the thick plains sod.

Anxiously, Scott scanned the crowd. Almost every ranchman in the high country was there—all of them but Clive Bannock. And he was one they would need most.

Doug McKinney's gaze, suspicious and half-hostile, had rested on Scott through much of the service. "All right, Scott, you've gotten us here. Where's your friend Bannock? Any agreement you make won't be worth a dime unless he's a party to it."

Worriedly, Scott looked back over his shoulder, studying the thin wagon trail that led off in the direction of Bannock's land. "He'll get here directly, Doug. He promised he would. What do you say we go on down to the meeting house?"

For an hour or more they waited there in the gentle shade of a cottonwood motte along the creek. The men whittled, spat, and talked in low voices. A restlessness began to move through them like the vague unrest that stirs a herd of cattle when it begins to sense a coming storm. Time and again Scott Tillman glanced up the trail for sign of Clive Bannock, but he didn't see him. It looked as if some of the men were about ready to leave.

Scott got up and stood in front of the group.

"I can't figure what's keeping Clive Bannock. He sent me word he'd be here. While we're waiting, we might as well go on and talk.

"This thing shocked all of us, big or small. It could happen again. The only way we can scotch it is to work together. Fighting separately, we can't stop it.

"I know a lot of you have been afraid of our association. You've thought it was a big men's trick to cheat you. But it isn't, I guarantee you that. Pull together, and we can clean out High Land and its thieves and throat-cutters. We can get us an honest government in this county, and we can make this country grow.

"Every man in this association will have an equal voice. Doesn't matter whether he has a hundred cows or ten thousand. Every association member here will vouch for that."

Doug McKinney frowned. "What about Bannock? Will you vouch for him?"

Hope was rising in Scott Tillman. In the faces of the men before him he could see the beginnings of agreement. They would get their association now, one that would be worth something. And because of it, the high country would be worth more, too.

"Yes, Doug, we'll vouch for him."

McKinney nodded, evidently satisfied. "All right, Scott. I guess it's the only way. Where do you want me to sign?"

One after another, the small ranchmen signed their names on the long, white sheet of paper. Scott and three other charter members watched, smiles carved deep in their wind-tanned faces.

Hoofbeats pounded along the wagon trail as the last men were signing. Clive Bannock rode in. Four of his men were behind him, and young Fletch Bannock rode at his side, the silver of his polished gun glinting in the sunshine.

Heavy Clive Bannock rested his big hands on the horn of his saddle. A dry grin spread across his wide face that was badly in need of a shave. "Looks like you're doing fine, Tillman. I'm right proud of you."

Irritated, Doug McKinney stepped forward. "I'd've thought you'd be here, Bannock."

The dry grin was still on Bannock's face. "That end

of the business I leave to Tillman. There's just one thing I wanted to tell you men."

Bannock's forced grin suddenly faded out, and Scott felt a quick, vague uneasiness.

Bannock said, "Jock Classen is dead. He didn't own his land; he just took it. So the way I see it, his place is open for the first man who steps in and pre-empts it.

"I've had my men moving my cattle over there today. I want every man here to know that Jock Classen's place is mine now. And I stand ready to back up that statement with whatever it takes."

For the space of time it takes a man's face to flare and his fists to harden into knots, there was stunned silence among the ranchmen.

Then Doug McKinney exploded into fury. He whirled first on Scott. "So you were going to vouch for him! Well, you have. You helped him get us all here so there wouldn't be anybody to stop him from taking Classen's land."

McKinney's hand fell upon the long sheet of paper the men had signed. He tore it in half and quartered it. Then he turned on Bannock.

"This time we'll stop you, Bannock. You've pushed us as far as we're going to go."

Fury rode Scott Tillman. But caution held a tight rein. He saw the cold spark that began to play in Fletch Bannock's hard young eyes, and sensed the easy downward movement of Bannock's hand.

"Do you think you're big enough to whip the Slash B, McKinney?" Clive Bannock demanded coldly.

"Not alone, maybe. But we can do it together. That's what Scott Tillman said. But we'll start our own association, Bannock. We'll whip all of you before we're done."

Scott saw the sudden clench of Fletch Bannock's

teeth a second before the boy spurred his horse forward. Fletch's big gray slammed into McKinney and sent him sprawling. The boy had his gun in his hand and was waiting, a steely grin crawling along his lip.

"Don't do it, Doug!" Scott yelled as McKinney's gun came out of the holster. He swung his booted foot and sent the pistol spinning out of McKinney's hand.

"Don't you see he's trying to kill you?"

But McKinney's face was flushed scarlet. He jumped to his feet, and with a rush spun Scott back against a cottonwood tree. Scott gasped at the driving weight of McKinney's fist high in his chest. He brought his own fist up, almost from the ground, and felt it jerk McKinney's head back like the popping of a whip. The ranchman sagged, clutching vainly for the tree to hold him up.

Scott turned on the Bannocks, his bruised hands trembling in anger. "Go on, Clive. Get out of here before this turns into a slaughterhouse."

Disappointment twisted Fletch Bannock's slick face. His lips curled under the fuzzy imitation of a mustache.

"Maybe you'd like to try something, Tillman."

Breathing hard, Scott met the kid's hostile stare.

"Come on, Fletch," said his father curtly. "We're through here."

Scott watched them go, his hopes dissolved, his skin flinching under the hostile stares of the small ranchmen who stood around him. Bannock had killed his cause, and had done it on purpose.

"You're through, all right." Scott muttered. "You may not know it, but you're through."

Scott Tillman usually knew where Curly Kirkendall could be found. Instead of riding straight back to the Lazy D, he angled west. The bitterness sank deeper and deeper into him as he rode. At dusk he drew rein before a carelessly built dugout that had been carved into the side of a hill and roofed over with sod. The front of it was made of mud-chinked poles, piled one on another in log-cabin fashion. A couple of wild-animal hides and a black-bottomed washtub hung beside the solid plank door, the prairie wind rocking them gently from one side to the other.

A man afoot suddenly appeared in front of Scott. He held a shotgun.

"Who are you, and what the hell do you want?"

Calmly, because he had been here before, Scott said, "I'm Scott Tillman. Tell Curly I want to see him."

In a moment the dugout door swung inward and Curly Kirkendall appeared in a frame of yellow lamp-light. "Get down and come in, Scott. Bryce, take his horse."

Scott shook hands and sat in a rawhide bottomed chair inside the musty dugout. Without saying much, he smoked a cigarette and studied Curly's laughing face.

"Well," the rustler said good naturedly, "what did you come for this time, Scott? To tell me again that I'm heading up a blind canyon and to warn me about the booger man?"

Scott shook his head. "No, I've done that enough already, and it never does any good. It's something else this time."

He leaned forward, snuffing out his cigarette on the leg of his chair and frowning darkly. "You know about Jock Classen, I guess."

Kirkendall's smile left him. "I know about it."

"Shot in the back, too. That didn't look to me like your brand of work, Curly."

"I didn't do it, Scott. None of my men had a hand in it."

Relieved, Scott leaned back again. "I didn't think you did. But I wanted to hear you say it. Do you know who it was?"

Cautiously Curly replied, "Maybe. But it ain't for me to say. There's too many people around High Land that know too much about me. Was I to go to working my jaw too much, they might start talking, too."

Scott argued, "Curly, I know we're enemies, theoretically. But we've been friends a long time, too. You know that whatever you tell me here tonight won't go any farther than this dugout. Lots of people think you killed Classen. If I knew who really did it, it might be of help to you."

Curly ran his hand thoughtfully through his unruly red hair, his indecision apparently painful to him. Then he said, "It was some of that High Land bunch. That's all I can tell you."

"But I thought you had High Land pretty well in hand, Curly. I didn't think you'd let anybody get away with something as bad as what happened to Jock."

Curly asked, "How long since you've been in High Land, Scott?"

"Four months. Maybe five. I carry all my business down to Peace Valley."

"Then maybe you ought to make a little run into High Land some day and get the sleep out of your eyes. You'll find out somebody else is dealing the hands there now. Fact of the matter is, it's got kind of unhealthy for me of late.

"Oh, it's the same old bunch, mostly. But they're listening to somebody else now. He tells them he's going to run this whole country, and if they string along with him, they'll all help sop up the gravy."

Scott Tillman cursed under his breath. The ugly shape of the thing was beginning to come clear to him now. He told Curly what had happened in Peace Valley.

"I've been blind, Curly. I've been figuring you for the worst enemy we had. And all the time I've over-looked one a dozen times worse. Doug McKinney has seen it all along, but it's too late for me to talk to him now.

"Bannock's playing it both ways from the middle. He'll whip out the little outfits first, and all the big outfits will get the blame; he'll see that you get some of it, like you did with Jock Classen. And when he's done with the little outfits, he'll have High Land's bunch with him to whittle down the big ranches."

Curly nodded, a grimness shoving aside his humor. "That's the way I see it." An ironic grin came to the outlaw's face. "Pretty picture, isn't it, Scott? You couldn't warn anybody now. After today there's no-body would listen to you.

"And if I was to try to warn them, they'd just haul me down to a handy cottonwood and make my neck longer."

Reining up at the Lazy D's rock barn, Scott unsaddled and turned his horse loose. He pulled the heavy watch out of his pocket and slanted it so the dim moonlight revealed the hands. Past midnight. But up in the big rock house a dim light still glowed behind the curtains.

Quietly Scott pushed open the door of the bunk-house and felt his way through the darkness to his bunk. He heard someone rouse and turn over in a cot back in the corner.

"That you, Scott?" came Dick Coleridge's sleepy voice. "Mrs. Dixon said tell you she wants to talk to you. She said it was important, and she'd wait up."

Scott hesitated. "Wonder what's the matter?"

Dick sat up in bed and rolled a cigarette. "I don't know. But Doug McKinney was here. He looked mad enough to bust."

Uneasily Scott walked up the slope to the big house and knocked on the door. Wilma Dixon's slender shadow fell across the curtain that covered the oval glass on the door. The door swung inward.

"Come in, Scott."

The pleasant smell of coffee was heavy in the room. Silently Wilma went into the kitchen and came back with a cup for him and a cup for herself. She didn't speak until she had sipped most of her coffee. But her deep blue eyes rested on him. There was a vague unhappiness in them.

"Doug McKinney was here today," she said presently, looking down. "He told me what happened at Peace Valley."

Scott put his empty cup on a small side table and stood up, looking bleakly across the room. "He can't believe I didn't help Clive Bannock plan that steal on Jock Classen's ranch, can he?"

Wilma shook her head. She rose to her feet. Scott saw her lips tremble. "No, Scott, he can't. And he gave me a pretty hard choice."

She walked toward him. There was a faint glistening in her blue eyes. She took hold of his arms and pulled close to him.

"Kiss me, Scott," she spoke softly.

He protested weakly. "But, Wilma . . ."

She said again, "Kiss me," and stretched up toward him. He folded his arms about her and kissed her with gentleness. She stepped back then, and he could see disappointment in her eyes.

"You don't love me, do you, Scott?"

He lowered his eyes. "I like you, Wilma. But that's all there is."

She nodded and turned half away. "I guess I've known it for a long time, deep down. But Doug loves me. And maybe I love him, too. I don't know. As long as you're around, I don't know anything for sure."

Scott picked up his hat, almost crushing it in his hands. His gaze was still on the door. "Then I guess you want me to go."

Wilma shook her head, her eyes brimming with tears. "No, Scott, I don't want you to. But I'm afraid it's the only way."

Stiffly she walked to the rolltop desk in the corner of the parlor and picked up a piece of paper. It was a check, filled out. It was a big one.

"This ought to take care of anything we owe you, shouldn't it, Scott?"

Nodding, he said, "Sure. I'll be gone in the morning."

Her voice was breaking when she called him at the door. "Scott, please don't hate me."

"No, Wilma," he answered tightly. "I couldn't hate you. There was nothing else you could do."

In the bunkhouse again, he sat down heavily on his bunk and stayed there a long while, rubbing his forehead, trying to decide what to do.

Dick Coleridge was still awake. "What's the matter, Scott?"

"I'm leaving in the morning," Scott answered flatly.

He heard Dick exclaim under his breath. After a moment the cowboy said, "I'm going with you."

Scott shook his head, although Dick couldn't see

him in the darkness. "No, Dick, you stay here. She's going to need help, good help. And you're the best I know of."

Dick was quiet for a minute. "Where'll you go, Scott?"

"I won't go far. I owe too much to John Dixon to go very far from her as long as everything's unsettled the way it is. If she needs me, I'll be around."

Next morning he was stirring before the cook was. In the breaking glow of dawn he gathered and packed his gear on an extra horse and saddled the horse he would ride. Under the baleful eye of the old bald-headed cook he ate a quick breakfast and got away before the rest of the cowboys were up. He didn't want to explain to anyone why he was leaving. He knew he couldn't if he had to.

By midmorning the steady gait of his horse had put a good many miles behind him. Scott knew where he was going. He slanted down over the rim of a canyon and into a wide, grassy valley where a cool blue stream worked its way down toward the Canadian. He watched the scattering of cattle which eased away from him as he approached. The sadness which had ridden with him since daybreak began to leave him. He liked this valley. Sometimes he wished he had set out to build his own herd instead of building someone else's. He might have taken up this valley himself, or one like it. But he had owed John Dixon a debt, and he'd wanted to pay it.

He almost didn't recognize the girl when he first saw her. She was wearing a loose, dirt-stained shirt and a pair of men's trousers, perspiration coursing down her young face as she tamped loose dirt around a fence post with the handle of a shovel. The two old cowhands stood farther up the line, digging post holes for a new corral.

She didn't see Scott until he spoke. Then her eyes widened quickly and she grabbed a gun which leaned against a stack of new-cut posts. She blinked away the stinging perspiration which had crept into her eyes, and laid the gun down again when she recognized the rider.

"Looks like you might need some help," he said.

She didn't reply at first. He couldn't tell from her eyes whether she was going to be hostile or not. She rubbed a sleeve across her face and left a brownish streak.

"Maybe," she said finally. "But I don't reckon the foreman of the Lazy D would soil his hands on a post-hole digger for a greasy sack outfit like this?"

He swung down and picked up the shovel. He tamped down the dirt hard as he could, then tested the post to be sure it was tight. It was.

"I'm not the foreman anymore. I'm looking for a job. Need another hand?"

Her eyes widened, then narrowed again in distrust. "There's bound to be a catch someplace."

Scott smiled. "No catch. I just want a job. I'll work cheap, and I'll work hard."

She stared levelly at him for a moment. He thought he could see a signal of laughter in her eyes.

"All right. Just throw your bedding in that little dugout shed where March and Pike have got theirs."

He unpacked the lead horse and turned both animals loose. After neatly stacking his gear, he went back to where the girl and the two elderly cowhands were working.

Before long his shoulders began to ache from the unfamiliar labor with the shovel and post-hole diggers.

He was used to hard work, but principally the kind that was done in the saddle. He watched the girl working as hard as if she had been a man. The way she did it, he knew such toil was a familiar thing to her. He guessed she wouldn't know how to stay in the house and be a lady.

He noted the deliberateness with which she removed a big rock from a post hole and heaved it away as if it had been an enemy. He knew that whatever she owned, she would fight for.

"How come you grabbed that rifle when I rode up?" he asked her once when he paused to ease the ache in his shoulders. "Is that the way you treat company?"

Her jaw stiffened. "I couldn't tell but what you might be one of Bannock's men," she answered, a hard determination in her eyes. "He sent me word he wanted this canyon to pay for the cattle Uncle Jess had stolen from him. I told him this valley is mine now, and that I'll fight to keep it."

There was work enough the next few days to keep everybody busy from daylight to dark. They built permanent pole corrals to replace the shaky ones Jess Owen had thrown up. He hadn't put much work into his, probably because he figured on leaving here in a hurry some time.

They improved and braced up the picket shack that Nell Owen lived in, rebuilding its roof so the water would no longer leak in when it rained. The men threw up a shelter for themselves to replace the dugout shed. There were cattle to work, calves to brand. Carefully Scott examined all the cattle for evidence of burned-over brands, so that any stolen cattle could be returned to their rightful owners. The Owen place was going to be on an honest basis from now on, Nell Owen said.

But Jess Owen had been slick. Evidently he had taken only unbranded livestock to burn his brand on, like the calves he had hidden far up the canyon. There was no way to determine which cattle had been stolen and which had been his own, or who any stolen animals might belong to.

"He wasn't a big-scale thief," Scott told the girl. "Nothing like Curly. Besides, half the herds in the high country were started by somebody with a wide loop and fast horse. Reckon you'd just as well claim all the cattle with the JO on them and start even."

The two saddle-stiff old cowhands soon came to accept Scott Tillman as their boss. They were good enough workers, but too many years had taken the starch out of them. Without anyone actually saying anything about it, they came to look upon Scott as the one who would give the orders. Even when Nell Owen told them to do something, often as not they looked at Scott to be sure it was all right.

It came about so naturally that Scott didn't realize it until it was accomplished fact. He thought the girl might resent it, but if anything, it seemed she was glad.

One day Scott rode far down the canyon, looking for a few head that had strayed out. He found them and pushed them back. On the way home he spied the broad white tail of an antelope out on the grassy flat. Fresh game for the table was always welcome, for it kept an outfit from having to kill much of its own beef.

His second shot downed the antelope. He had gutted the animal and was ready to swing it up on his horse when he heard the hoof beats racing up behind him. He glanced back and saw Nell Owen's frightened face as she slid her horse to a halt. She took a long look at the antelope, relief washing the color back into her cheeks.

"I heard the shots, and I saw your horse with an empty saddle," she said, her breath short.

Strange, he had never figured her as even capable of being scared. But here she was, scared as a rabbit— scared for him.

She was silent for a long moment, regaining her composure.

"I'm sorry I scared you," he said with sympathy. "But then again, I'm not. It's kind of an honor, knowing that you were scared for me."

She looked levelly at him. "Why not? You've been awfully good to me."

He replied, "I've had a lot to make up for."

"You've done that ten times over."

She dismounted and began to tighten the cinch on her saddle. Scott stepped down and knelt in the shadow of his sorrel.

"I can't figure out why you came here," she said. "There are plenty of big ranches down south that would pay you three times as much as I ever can."

Scott picked up a twig and began to poke at the ground with it. "Some things are more important than money, Nell."

Her brown eyes probed at him, and her lips were drawn inward worriedly. "Is it because of Wilma Dixon?"

He nodded, and caught the sudden disappointment that crept into her face before her stubborn pride covered it up.

"She'd be a good wife, Scott," the girl said, her voice strained. She turned away from him, her fist clenched white.

He stood up quickly. He reached out toward her, then changed his mind. "Look, Nell," he said quietly, "there are some things you don't understand. I don't love Wilma. She's a fine woman, that's true, but I'm not in love with her."

The girl was still turned away from him. "Why do you stay, then?"

Scott absently wrapped the bridle reins around his hand, knotting them against his knuckles, trying to figure out how to tell her. "I made a promise a long time ago to watch out for her. I've got to keep that promise, as long as she needs help. If it hadn't been for John Dixon, I'd probably be an outlaw today, like Curly Kirkendall. That is, if I wasn't already dead. Curly and I grew up together, down in the *brasada* of South Texas. We both came out of there as wild as Spanish ponies. We got in some pretty tight scrapes.

"One day Curly got the idea of robbing a bank. He figured that with all that money we could clear out of Texas and really live high someplace else. But John Dixon got wind of it. He tried to talk me out of it. When he couldn't, he bent a gunbarrel over my head."

"Curly got somebody else and tried it anyway. The other fellow was killed. Curly got away.

"That sobered me up in a hurry. I knew I owed John Dixon a debt that I couldn't ever pay him in money. I went to work for him as a cowboy. When he came up here, I came with him. And he never told anybody what I'd done, not even Wilma. Doug McKinney was the only one who ever knew. That's one reason he's never trusted me, I guess. I can't blame him.

"And that's why I've stayed, because I promised John Dixon I would. Wilma will marry Doug someday, and he'll be a good husband. Then I can leave. Till then, I'm always going to be around somewhere."

He had been looking far across the creek toward the distant canyon wall, as he told Nell the story. When he faced her again, he found that she was looking straight into his eyes. A smile played along her lips.

"I'm glad you told me, Scott," she said. "You know, we're a lot alike, you and me. Maybe that's why I've gotten so that I like to have you around."

Her face reddened in embarrassment for what she had said, and she quickly turned away. Scott put his hand on her shoulder and gently turned her around toward him again.

Something happened to him as he looked into her earnest brown eyes. She wasn't really pretty, like Wilma Dixon; there was even a plainness in her face. But there was something about her—some inner beauty—something that had nothing to do with a pretty face or pretty clothes. His hands on her arms, Scott felt his heartbeat quicken. He saw the softness come into her eyes and an unspoken word form on her lips. He saw the girl as he hadn't seen her before. He pulled her gently toward him. She came with eagerness, her face uptilted to his.

The people on the JO seldom saw anyone else, but news drifted in occasionally with a passing rider. There was a story about rustlers burning out a little ranchman up high on the rolling plains country, sweeping most of his herd along in a lightning raid. There was news of a gunfight—some said it was provoked—between another little ranchman and Fletch Bannock. In quick retaliation, Clive Bannock and his riders had swept down upon the place, run the ranchman off, and taken over the land. The cattle had been pushed off onto neighboring small ranches. There had been another brush when a group of the small stockmen tried to chase the cattle back from where they had come.

Scott and the two cowhands were building a good dugout shelter for themselves the day Fletch Bannock came. Nell Owen had almost decided the Bannocks had been bluffing. But here came the Bannock kid, trailed by five hard-looking gunmen from High Land. They reined up a dozen paces from the new dugout.

Scott felt the weight of the six-gun on his hip, where he had strapped it when he saw the riders coming. He glared at the slick-faced boy who sat in arrogance on a fine grulla gelding.

"You're not welcome here, Fletch," he said.

The boy gave him a lopsided grin and pushed back his hat. His eyes were the gray of granite. "Well, now, here's Scott Tillman. We about decided you run off to East Texas or someplace."

"I said you're not welcome, Fletch. Move on."

Fletch leaned forward, the grin suddenly gone. "No, Tillman. You move! We're taking this place for the Slash B, like we said we would."

Anger began to roil in Scott. He looked around him, but could see no more riders anywhere. Fletch evidently had thought there would be nothing to it, running off a girl and an old stove-up cowboy or two.

"Where's Clive?" Scott asked. "Can't he do his own dirty work?"

The youthful gray eyes were heavy. Fletch's fingers played ominously close to his gun butt. "Generally. Just thought I'd give him this valley as a surprise present. You better do like I told you, Tillman. I ain't in the mood to wait around."

Fletch's draw came so quickly that Scott barely saw it. Scott tried to reach for his own gun but stopped himself. It would be suicide, he knew.

Fletch grinned crookedly. "Pretty fast, wasn't it, Tillman? I could've blowed your brains out before you could get your hands on your gun. I got a good notion to do it yet."

Then Nell Owen stepped out of the picket shack, behind Fletch Bannock and his men. Scott saw her before the others did, raising a six-gun to eye level.

She sent the singeing bullet right across the rump of Fletch's fine grulla. The first wild jump of the squealing horse almost unseated the young gunman. Grabbing for the horn, he let the pistol drop. For a long moment, hanging low over the bucking horse's side, Fletch managed to keep hold of the rigging. Then he let go and went tumbling to the ground on his face.

The five men with him raised their hands at the sight of the furious girl and her steady gun. At her command they unstrapped and dropped their guns.

Trembling in rage, Fletch Bannock pushed himself up on his hands. Dirt covered his face and burned his eyes. A trickle of blood worked down from the corner of his mouth.

"Get up, Fletch Bannock," Nell Owen said evenly. "It's your time to start crawling. You're going back to the Slash B and tell Clive Bannock that a woman whipped you. You've had half the people in the high country scared of you—but they won't be any more. Everybody will know you're just a spoiled, bluffing kid." She motioned with the point of the gun. "Now git!"

Shame and fury flushed the young killer's face a crimson red. His lips were drawn back from his teeth as one of his men brought him the grulla horse, and he swung into the saddle.

Scott saw the Bannock rider reach into his boot top and hand something to Fletch. He heard Nell scream for him to look out. Then Fletch Bannock had whirled the grulla around and had the muzzle of the gun bearing down on Scott. Scott leaped to one side, stumbling as he heard the retort of the gun.

Somehow he jerked his own pistol out. Falling on his back, he looked up to see Fletch's face above him, his mouth twisted in rage beneath the fuzzy mustache. The gun was aiming down again.

Scott felt the sledgehammer blow strike him with the heat of hell.

With a terrible effort he squeezed the trigger. Young Bannock swayed in the saddle, his horse plunging in terror. Then the kid went slack and tumbled to the ground, almost at Scott's side. He lay in a twisted heap beneath the swirling dust.

Scott's right shoulder and arm were numb and useless. His left arm went around his stomach, trying to hold back the sickness that came with a rush.

"I didn't want to do it," he murmured painfully. "Why did he have to try?"

Eyes wide in fear, Nell passed her gun to one of the two old punchers and fell to her knees beside Scott.

"Scott, Scott!" she cried. "I tried to hit him, but the gun jammed."

The bullet burned in his shoulder with the heat of a blacksmith's furnace. He gritted his teeth against the grinding pain. He felt Nell tearing the shirt away, at the same time screaming to the five Bannock men.

"Go on, get out of here, before we kill the whole lot of you!"

One of the men braved the gun to step off and turn Fletch Bannock over. "Give me a hand here," he said to one of the others.

They lifted the body across a saddle. Then one man caught Fletch's grulla and got on him.

He looked down at Nell Owen long enough to say gravely: "You better get that fellow away from here, miss, a long way away. Old Clive will bust loose like a wounded grizzly when we take his son home to him.

He won't stop hunting till he's found Scott Tillman and killed him. He might even kill you, if you're in the way."

In a red maze of pain, Scott heard, rather than saw, the men ride away. He felt himself carried into the dugout. He groaned to the stabbing agony of a knife probing for the bullet. Then he gave in to unconsciousness under the searing of a cauterizing hot poker . . .

He awakened to the coolness of a wet cloth on his forehead, and the gentle touch of soft fingers on his face. "Scott," the girl's voice begged in desperation, "wake up. Wake up."

He forced open his eyes and tried to rise. He fell back in blinding pain.

"Scott," Nell persisted. "You've got to wake up. We have to move you."

He fought back the smothering blanket of unconsciousness. Nell Owen's soft lips brushed his forehead, and he saw the evidence of dried tears on her cheeks.

"I hate to do it, Scott," she said, "but we can't fight off Clive Bannock's whole bunch. They're bound to come."

Scott's head still reeled, and he struggled to clear his mind. "We can't leave, Nell," he said weakly. "They'll take the ranch. You'll never get it back."

"We couldn't hold it anyway," she argued. "It's not worth your life to try. We'll carry you to the Lazy D."

Scott shook his head. "No, that's the first place they'll look, and there's no use drawing Wilma into it."

Fear was beginning to choke the girl. "But where else can we take you?"

Again he tried to force himself up. This time, with Nell's help, he made it. He sat weakly on the edge of the bed.

"I know a place. Clive Bannock probably won't

even know where it's at. Even if he did, he'd never think to look there. We'll go to Curly Kirkendall's."

The ride took an eternity, an eternity of agony for the man who slumped in the saddle, the blood sticky inside the rude bandage. Nell Owen rode beside him, holding him in the saddle by the strength of her own lithe body. Most of the time Scott was in semiconsciousness, yearning to tumble from the saddle and yield to the beckoning comfort of the cool earth.

"You have to stay awake, Scott!" Nell pleaded with him again and again. "You're the only one who knows how to get there. You have to hold on!"

And somehow, long after daylight had surrendered to a pale sliver of moon, they found Curly's dugout.

Curly Kirkendall strode out to meet them in the dull silver of the night. He cradled a rifle on his arm. His jaw dropped as he recognized the half-conscious man in the saddle. "Scott!"

Nell's eyes pleaded gently. "Please, Mr. Kirkendall. I know he's been an enemy to you. But he needs help . . . needs it bad."

Curly barked the names of two of his men, and they came running. Together they gently eased Scott out of the saddle. They carried him to the dugout and ducked as they packed him in through the low door.

"My bunk, boys," Kirkendall said. Tensely he opened the shirt. "Bleeding some. Riding horseback that way could've killed him." His voice rose in anger. "Why didn't you at least use a wagon?"

Nell Owen's face was sick with anxiety. "Too easy to trail. They might track us anyway." Biting her pale lips as she rebound the bandage, she told Curly about the shooting of Fletch Bannock.

Gravely he nodded his head. "Don't you worry, ma'am. Clive Bannock will turn this country upside down, but he wouldn't think about coming here." He knotted his fist. "And if he was just to luck onto us, he'll wish to hell he hadn't."

Over in the corner a lank, black-stubbled man had been watching with sullen eyes. He dragged his feet across the dirt floor to Tillman's bedside.

"Looky here, Curly," he complained, "this Tillman has tried harder than anybody else in the high country to get us all sent off to the penitentiary. You mean you aim to keep him here now and protect him?"

Curly's voice was even. "When we're out shagging off Lazy D cattle, he's an enemy, Brycc. But right now, as long as he's in this camp, he's a friend—the best friend I've got. And don't you forget it for a minute."

Though her body ached with weariness, Nell Owen sat in a camp-built rawhide chair and kept vigil beside Scott. She sat in silence, holding his still left hand tightly in her own. On a small cast iron stove a pot of coffee sat untouched. Occasionally her sleepless eyes drifted to the men who slept on rolled up blankets at the back side of the long dugout. Her body cried for rest, but she wouldn't let herself relax. Scott might wake up. He might need her.

Near the back wall a blanket was flung aside and Curly Kirkendall stood up. She watched him with speculative eyes as he walked unsteadily to the stove and poured a cup of coffee. He frowned and ran his tongue along his lips.

"Cold," he said disgustedly, and threw the coffee against the side of the dugout with the indifference to cleanliness that takes hold of men in camp.

He walked up behind the girl with concern in his face. "He doing any good?"

She nodded. "He's resting all right."

Curly Kirkendall placed his rough hand gently on

her slender shoulder. "You ought to rest, too. I'll roust Bryce off his bunk and make him go over in the corner with the rest of them. I'll keep watch over Scott. I haven't slept worth a plugged two cents anyway."

Nell shook her head. "Thanks, but I'll stay."

Curly shrugged. "It's up to you. But you look as miserable as a Mexican sheep thief."

"I'll stay by him, Curly. He stayed by me."

Curly sat down on the edge of Scott's bunk. An ironic smile began to play on his lips. Presently he said, "He's lying there half dead, with the toughest man in the high country hunting him down to blow him apart. And yet I'd swap places with him in a minute, if I could."

Nell's eyes widened in question. Curly's gaze lifted levelly to her face.

"You bet your life, I'd swap with him. If I'd ever had anybody that thought as much of me as you do of him, I wouldn't be living in a dirty dugout and running off other people's cattle. No sir, I'd be the biggest man in the country, and there couldn't anybody ever stop me.

"Don't you ever leave him, ma'am. He needs you now, and he'll keep on needing you."

A faint smile brightened Nell Owen's weary face. "If he ever wants me, I won't be hard for him to find."

Scott Tillman awoke before daylight, a circular saw whirring in his head and a dull, hammering pain in his shoulder. He felt a weight lying across his legs. He eased up enough to see Nell Owen asleep, still sitting in the chair, her upper body fallen forward onto the edge of the bed.

He knew without being told that she had sat there all night. His heart warmed to her, and he half smiled as he looked at her now peaceful face. He dared not move for fear of awakening her. So he lay there looking upward, his eyes fixed on the sod roof. He tried to think, tried to plan, fighting against the throbbing ache in his head.

But he knew there was no use. There was no better place in the country for him than this, until he was again able to ride and use a gun.

And Nell had to stay with him, or Clive Bannock would find her. No telling what he might do to make her tell where Scott was hiding.

Through the next two days he felt his strength coming back to him slowly but steadily as the buildup of water in a mountain lake. He got off the cot and tried walking a little. Every time he moved, Nell Owen was there ordering him to sit down again, at the same time holding him so he wouldn't fall. It did no good to tell her he could stand alone. Anyway, he liked the touch of her hand, and enjoyed the quiet strength with which she held him.

"There's time enough for you to go walking around when that wound is healed," she said. "Right now, you'd better not try to get far away from me."

He grinned. "By the time I'm well, I probably won't want to."

From the first, he knew Bryce Fancher didn't like him. Even when he didn't see them, he could feel the man's hot eyes upon him. The showdown came after one of Curly's men, Wilkes, rode in from High Land.

"They say Clive Bannock's hunted this country high and low," the man reported. "He's been to every ranch and turned it upside down. Now he's offered a thousand dollars for whoever tells him where Scott Tillman is at."

Bryce Fancher whistled between his teeth and cut his eyes toward Scott. "A thousand dollars!"

A quick grin split his black-stubbled face, then gave

way to excitement. "Look, Curly, there's no need in us being fools. You don't owe this fellow anything, not after the way he's chased us around the last couple or three years. A thousand dollars! And all we got to do to get it is tell Clive Bannock where Tillman is."

Curly Kirkendall trembled in anger. "Shut up, Bryce."

Fancher's face darkened. "You're making a fool of yourself, Curly. But I don't aim to. I'm going to see Bannock."

Curly Kirkendall took one step forward and swung his fist so fast that Scott hardly saw it before Bryce Fancher's head jerked from its impact. The outlaw struck the packed floor on his back and rolled over onto his hands. Blood swelled into a ruby bead on Fancher's split lower lip.

"Get up, Bryce," Curly gritted. "Say another word about this and I'll lay your skull open with a gun barrel."

Fancher swayed to his feet and stiffly moved out the door, his eyes burning.

Curly jerked a thumb after him. "Better go keep an eye on him, Wilkes."

Wilkes sauntered out after Fancher.

Scott raised up onto his elbow, the cot groaning under him. "You don't have to fight my battles for me, Curly."

Curly frowned. "Are you in any shape to fight them yourself?" He grinned then, and slapped Scott on the good shoulder. "Anyhow, you skinned a wildcat or two for me, back yonder."

Nell Owen was working around the cast iron stove in the end of the dugout which served as a kitchen. Lying on his cot, Scott noticed how Curly's eyes softened as he watched the girl. Something of the wild, happy-go-lucky light went out of them, and a pinched, re-gretful look took its place.

Curly's mouth twisted in embarrassment as he caught Scott watching him.

"Scott," he said presently, "there isn't a girl from here to Canada that could beat her. I hope you know that."

Scott nodded. "I know it."

Curly's face hardened in self-condemnation. "In my time I've known more girls than you could count out of a gate in an hour. And yet, somehow, I haven't known a one. Maybe if I had . . ."

Bitterly, he said something under his breath and dropped his cigarette. He got up and stomped out the door.

Scott looked after him a moment. Then his eyes drifted back to Nell Owen. A proud smile touched his face as he eased his head wearily back down upon his pillow.

Curly's excited voice brought him up again. "Scott! Nell! You got to get out of here. Bryce Fancher's gone, and you can guess where he went!"

Nell Owen's face paled a second. Then she was over it. "March! Pike! Get the horses saddled." Her voice was as strong as it had ever been. "What do you think, Scott? Can you make it?"

"I guess so." Anger swelled in him. "But I'm getting tired of running like a scared rabbit. I'm half a mind to stay here."

Nell ripped off the old bandage and bound a new one in its place. "Don't argue with me, Scott Tillman. You're still not in any shape to stand up against Clive Bannock. Besides, if you stayed it would mean more trouble for Curly. I'd say he's got about all he needs."

March and Pike rode their horses up to the dugout

door, leading Nell's and Scott's. Scott glimpsed the man named Wilkes, being helped back from the barn, a bloody streak down the side of his head.

Boosted up into his saddle, Scott almost swayed off on the opposite side. Then he got his balance. The saddle and the feel of a strong horse beneath him settled him some and bolstered his confidence.

Curly looked levelly at him. "Scott, I got a notion you'll get your association now. What's happened the last few days ought to pull the ranches together against Bannock. They'll listen to you now.

"I want you to know that I'm fixing to leave this country. When all the ranches pull together, there isn't any room for me anymore. That's the way with the High Land bunch, too. When they see a strong association lined up against them, they'll clear out as quick as they can get their horses saddled."

Curly took off his hat. A lock of unruly red hair fell across his forehead as he turned to Nell. Without a word, he leaned forward and kissed her surprised face.

"Take care of our friend there," he said grinning, nodding toward Scott.

"I will," she said. Then to Scott, "Which way do you want to go?"

"The Lazy D."

Her face dropped a little, and he knew what she was thinking. Wilma Dixon. But she nodded and said, "The Lazy D it is."

Before the three men and the girl topped their horses over the rise and dropped down out of sight of the camp, Scott looked back. He saw Curly Kirkendall still standing there, watching them. Or, Scott thought, watching Nell . . .

Darkness was almost upon them when they heard the noise. It drifted in from behind them, so faint they could hardly catch it. Nell Owen stepped out of the saddle and stood listening. Her face was grave. "Gunfire," she said.

Scott's heart froze. "Curly's camp. Bannock!"

Without hesitation he reined his horse back around. Nell Owen tried to stop him. "Whatever happens, Scott, we can't get there in time to do any good. And you won't stand a chance against the bunch Bannock will have with him."

He wasted no breath in argument. "I'm going back."

Anguish was in her face, but she knew what a man had to do, and she said nothing more. She rode at his side as the four of them spurred back toward Curly's dugout, reeling the miles off behind them.

They found nothing but dead silence at the camp, a silence unbroken except by the faint crackle of flames inside the dugout.

Scott's teeth clenched. "He wrecked it all. He set fire to what would burn and tore up the rest."

There were bodies around the camp. In the darkness they managed to find three. All had been Curly's men. Scott and Nell called and searched but could not find the outlaw leader.

"He's lying out there dead someplace, and it's too dark for us to see him," Scott gritted. His left fist hammered in futile rage against his saddle horn.

"It was a massacre."

"Come on, Scott," Nell said quietly. "We can't do any good here."

He lowered his head. "No, I guess not. But it isn't over. Curly, I promise you, it isn't over."

The moon rode high above the big rock house of the Lazy D when Scott, Nell, and the two old cowpunchers kneed their horses between the high poles of the front gate and trotted them up to the yard fence.

Lamplight shone bright and welcome through the curtained windows.

Scott started to swing down by himself, but Nell protested quickly and caught his shoulder.

"You're already getting too big for your britches. You wait till we help you down."

She was smiling, but it was a thin smile that did a poor job of hiding anxiety.

Wilma Dixon answered the knock on the door. Her eyes widened in unbelief as the splash of lamplight spilled across Scott's face.

He saw her tremble as her gaze fell upon his tightly bound shoulder.

"Scott!" she breathed. Her blue eyes went to Nell. "Bring him in," she said quickly.

Inside, Wilma Dixon leaned against Scott and began to cry. "I thought . . . I thought . . . Oh, Scott, I didn't know what to think."

"I'm all right," he told her gently, his good hand on her arm.

Nell turned away quickly, but not before Scott saw the sick look in her eyes.

Footsteps thumped upon the porch. Scott turned toward them, and Wilma Dixon stepped back. Doug McKinney pushed through the door. His jaw sagged in surprise. His eyes made a quick sweep over Scott, Nell, and the two cowhands. They were hard eyes when McKinney wanted them to be. But right now there was no hardness in them.

He stood back uncertainly. "Scott," he said, "it's good to see you."

There was evident embarrassment in the way he stood stiffly, a wan smile creeping across his face. "It doesn't come easy to admit I've been wrong, Scott. But I was. I'd like to shake your hand, if you'll let me."

Scott shoved forward his left hand.

"Bannock burned me out," Doug McKinney said. "He's been like a wild man since you . . . since Fletch was killed. I've been afraid he might hurt Wilma, seeing as you used to be foreman here. So I moved my men over here."

"What about your own place?" Scott asked.

Doug shrugged. "Wilma's more important to me than anything else." The hardness came back into his eyes. "But I'll tell you, Scott, it's gone about as far as it can go. All the ranchers in the high country are ready to do something . . . anything. And it's going to have to be done quick."

Scott knotted his fist. His gaze moved from Doug to Wilma and then to Nell Owen. For a long moment he regarded her, his heart warming. Doug McKinney had abandoned his ranch to be able to protect Wilma Dixon. Nell Owen had left her own place to the heavy hand of Clive Bannock so she could save Scott.

Scott turned back to Doug McKinney. "You say the ranchers are all ready, Doug. Would they, come and come quick if we sent the word, if there was somebody to ride in front and know what he was doing?"

Sudden interest leaped into McKinney's eyes. "They would."

Confidence began to surge into Scott Tillman as he thought out his plan. "Then we'll start, Doug, now—tonight!"

He leaned forward, eagerness burning new color into the face that had paled from pain. "Here's how I see it. High Land is where most of Clive Bannock's strength is. That's where he gets the renegades to do his cattle-running and his burning-out. He's got the county law siding him because they think he's a cinch to come out a winner.

"But they're wrong. We're going to clean up High Land first. It'll be like cutting off Bannock's right arm. Then whatever we have to do about Bannock won't be half as hard. He knows he can cut us out one by one and whip us. But if we can all work together, he can't whip us, Doug. That's why he did everything he could to undermine the association and keep us fighting one another."

Enthusiasm was a spark that struck from a word and burst into bright flame among the group huddled in the lamplit parlor. Futile anger had been riding them all, and suddenly now they could see purpose ahead.

Only Wilma Dixon held back. "Scott, you've always been the one who was most against violence. Don't you know High Land won't give in easily? There'll be blood spilled in its streets, and some of it will be ours."

Scott shook his head. "I don't think so. Curly said something to me. He said that as long as the ranchers were fighting each other, he'd do all right. But if they ever got together, if they ever formed a real association, he was going to clear out as fast as he could get his horse saddled. And he said he wouldn't be the only one. I think we can run a bluff on High Land. I think we can whip it without having to fire a shot."

At midmorning the first cow outfit arrived in High Land. Turk Dedecker, cardsharp and occasional cow thief, was out behind his picket shack washing his face in cold water in an effort to clear his pounding, drink-swollen head. He heard the splash of horses wading across the boggy river and looked up quickly, wiping the water from his red-veined face with a dirty, frayed towel.

Dedecker's slack jaw dropped. His bleary eyes counted sixteen men—maybe seventeen. Every man carried a rifle as well as a belt gun. He caught the grim visage of the gray-haired man who rode in the lead. Suddenly Turk Dedecker's heart began to pound. His nervous tongue flicked cross dry lips, and he knew he needed a drink. He stumbled into his shack and slammed its door behind him. For some reason then, he picked up the heavy cedar bar and dropped it into place. His trembling hands groped under his bunk until they closed upon a bottle. He sat down wearily and drank from it, and wondered dazedly what had gone wrong.

An hour behind the first outfit came the string of riders from the Lazy F. Most of the hands had been sent out the night before to carry Scott Tillman's message to ranches all over the high country. But still there were an even dozen, counting the regulars and McKinney's punchers. And on the way they were joined by Dodd Jernigan's men from the Long J, and the brush-popping cowboys from the T Anchor down in the breaks, and old Charlie Merchant and his sons from their little valley spread.

Scott Tillman rode stiffly, a sharp pain jabbing him with each jolting step his horse took. But it wasn't as bad as yesterday, and there was little of the agony in it that he had gritted his way through on that awful ride from Nell Owen's ranch to Curly Kirkendall's. He would make it now, he knew. In grim satisfaction he looked back over his shoulder and recounted the men. There were little men and big men in the group, men who until recent days had known only distrust of each other. Now they rode together.

Beside Scott a slender girl rode sidesaddle, her eyes returning to him again and again in worry. He had tried to make Nell Owen stay at the Lazy D, but she had stoutly insisted that she was a ranch owner and had as much right to go as anyone. So he finally let her come along, and he smiled with a touch of pride.

A mile from town the fanned-out riders topped over a rise and rode headlong into another party. A chuck-wagon lumbered along behind it, two spans of mules straining in harness to keep up with the cowboys who rode ahead.

Tol Hervey angled over as the big groups merged into one. He raised a brown hand and showed stained teeth in a broad, mustache-framed grin. "Tickled to see you, Scott. With you back, we'll give them hell."

At just past ten-thirty they spanned out down the riverbank and splashed across toward the ragged scattering of picket shacks and adobes that was High Land. Scattered in an uneven circle about the town, riders from other outfits waited impatiently.

A smile broke across Scott Tillman's face. It wasn't a smile of humor, but rather one of satisfaction. There were fifty men here, maybe sixty.

That they had stirred up even the latest sleeping of High Land's denizens he had no doubt. He could see heads raised cautiously above the swinging doors of the Paradise Bar, and the side curtains pulled aslant behind the windows of Wild Mary Donovan's place down the street. At the adobe Plains Hotel a man stepped out the back door and looked apprehensively at the stable behind, as if wondering whether he ought to try to make it to his horse. Then, making up his mind, he trotted back into the building.

The whole thing had been Scott's idea. Now he could feel the eyes of all the men resting upon him, appraising him. Nervousness was tugging at him. And weariness was beginning to tell, too, for the price of his wound was still a heavy one.

Raising his left hand, Scott pointed toward the

largest building in town, a long T-shaped adobe which the High Land men had erected in smug triumph after their furtive theft of the county seat.

"We'll meet at the courthouse." He spoke as loudly as he could.

At the door he swung down joltingly, the weakness bearing heavily on his shoulders. The door groaned inward on its hinges, and a stringy man with black mustache and angry black eyes walked out onto the wide stone step. The tarnished badge on his grease-spotted vest blinked in the morning sun.

"Now look here, Scott Tillman," he said, shaking a stubby finger, "I don't know what you're about, but I'm giving you fair warning. This is a peaceful town. We won't stand for no . . ."

Studiously Scott ignored the hot words. "You got the keys to the jail cells, Sheriff?"

"Sure I have, but I don't see . . ."

Scott's voice was cold. "Give them here."

The sheriff jawed half a dozen more angry words before his lips began to tremble and the words died in his throat. He handed over the keys. Scott slipped the gun from the man's slack waistband and turned him around.

"Let's get to the cells."

He unlocked a cell at one corner of the combination courthouse and jail and pushed the sheriff in. He slammed the door shut.

The sheriff's voice was almost a wail. "Tillman, I'm an officer of the law! You can't . . . you can't . . ."

"Where's Judge Merriwether?"

The lawman's stubby fingers clasped tightly the iron bars. "Over at the hotel. Now, boys . . ."

Tillman turned away from him. "Tol, how about you taking three or four of your boys over and getting the judge? Drag him out of bed if you have to, and pull him over here in his nightshirt. Make as much show of it as it's worth. It'll let everybody know we're here for business."

Five minutes later the men were back, pushing in front of them a pudgy, red-faced little man who held his checkered pants up with one hand and his plug hat on with the other. The judge was panting with every step and hurling epithets whenever he had the breath.

"Throw him in there with the sheriff," Scott said sharply. "Whatever we decide to do with them, they'll both take it together."

One of the cowboys had a rope in his hand. He shook out a loop in it. The judge stopped cursing, his red face suddenly drained white.

Outside again, Scott Tillman addressed the horseback group. "I want all the ranch owners to meet with me here at the courthouse. I want the cowboys scattered out to every part of town.

"Eight or ten men go into every saloon and watch. Don't drink with anybody and don't play any cards. Just stand along the wall and watch. If anybody asks you what we're doing here, tell them we're organizing a cowmen's association. Tell them we're going to handle our own law and punish our own criminals. Tell them we're drawing up a list of all known murderers, cow thieves, crooked gamblers, and any other deadbeats we know of. And when we get the list made up, we're going to start dealing out a little justice."

He held his breath as he watched the cowboys spread out over the town. He half expected some scared citizen to start shooting, but the thing went off quietly.

In a few minutes the town was covered with grim

cowboys who watched and waited, guns in their hands and ropes on their saddles.

Out on the riverbank two wagon cooks had started shoveling out places for cook fires. This might be a long day, and cowboys had to be fed.

The ranch owners tramped into the courtroom and sat in the rawhide chairs that were scattered over the packed-earth floor. There were a dozen of them—thirteen counting Nell Owen. There were far more stockmen than this in the high country, but they hadn't all gotten here yet. Probably not all had even received the message. But this was enough to do the job that faced them today, Scott thought.

The weakness pulling him down, Scott sat in a chair behind a table at the front of the room and faced the group. "There's been a lot of talk about an association in the past. Some of you liked it, some of you didn't. But I don't think there's any doubt among you now that we need one. If you didn't think so, you probably wouldn't be here. So I guess the first thing to do is to sign up."

Nell Owen stood up. "I'll be the first one."

So the meeting went, with every man in the room signing the charter roll. Then came discussion of an association name. Next came the rules under which it would operate. Each member was to be assessed according to the number of his cattle to pay for range detectives; no member was to hire a known cattle thief; no member was to hire a cowboy fired by any other member for drunkenness on the job, gambling on the ranch, or cruelty to horses. No member—and this hurt some—was to kill any animals other than his own for beef.

And meanwhile, throughout the mud-built little town, the tension drew taut as a guitar string.

Turk Dedecker was the first one to break. The lank gambler sat in the Paradise Bar, where he had fled for company after realizing how utterly alone he was in his mud-chinked picket shack. His fingers, usually nimble, seemed to stumble over the deck with which he played solitaire. He tried to keep his eyes from lifting to the six hard-faced cowboys who stood with their backs to the adobe wall. He thought he remembered one of the men from a poker game a good while back. As he recalled, he had won a month's pay in an hour's time. He usually did.

For the fifth or sixth time he attempted to smile their way and said weakly, "A little game, anybody? I'll buy the drinks."

A half dozen pairs of hard eyes bored at him, and no one spoke a word. Hands trembling, Dedecker poured another drink and dashed it down.

Apologetically he arose and swayed toward the door. "If you boys don't mind, I got business . . ."

He was surprised they didn't move to stop him, but he didn't pause to ponder over it. He left the building in a heavy trot and didn't stop running until he had reached the livery stable. Under the watchful eyes of five cowboys he flung a saddle on his horse and swung up. But as he started to ride away, one cowboy stepped forward and gripped the reins.

"We better go ask Tillman about this jaybird," he said.

They led the quaking Dedecker to the courthouse. Tillman walked out and raked the gambler up and down with a hot glare. "Let him go," he said finally. "But if he ever comes back, he's liable to stretch a rope."

Turk Dedecker spurred out of town in a high lope

and didn't slow down until he had put High Land out of sight behind him.

A hundred pairs of anxious eyes watched him go. Before long, dust began to rise above stables and barns around the town. First it was one or two men riding out furtively, saddlebags bulging with what little gear they felt worth saving, blanket rolls tied behind their saddles. Then they left in groups of three and four, riding in every direction. The cowboys noted that in almost every instance they rode out slowly enough. But as soon as they had reached the opposite bank of the river, they spurred up and disappeared over the hill in a lope.

Shortly before noon a couple of cowboys came into the courtroom and announced that the hotel was virtually empty. There wasn't a single person left in the Paradise Bar, either, except the owner. And he had approached a couple of the cowboys with a proposition to sell the place, stock and all, cheap.

Mary Donovan hadn't given up, but three of her girls had left town in their fancy rig, headed south.

A cook began to clang on an old iron bar hanging from one of the chuckwagons lined up along the river. The cowboys filed down to the river to eat, a handful of them at a time. In a group, the owners left the adobe courthouse and walked down to the river. Scott Tillman was with them, and Nell Owen stayed close by his side.

A weak sickness still stirring in him, Scott ate little. Most of his meal he took from the coffee pot. Sitting in the river bank sand and leaning heavily back against the wooden spokes of a wagon wheel, he watched the single rider who had left the town in a slow trot, looking back over his shoulder.

Dick Coleridge walked up and sat on his heels beside

Scott. "That's the only one in the last half hour or so. Looks to me like all of them that are going have already left."

Scott frowned into the tin cup. "Many holdouts left?"

"Yeah. Hard to tell exactly how many, but there's a bunch of them gathered over yonder in that big adobe, the one with the smoke coming out the chimney. They've been scooting over there with their guns and all the grub they could carry under their arms. Looks like they might make a stand."

"Any others around town?"

"Some. But most of the rest don't act very excited. Reckon they figure they're in the clear and don't have much to worry about. The really bad ones have left or are over in that adobe."

Scott glanced around toward Doug McKinney. "What do you think, Doug?"

McKinney rolled a cigarette, his narrowed eyes on the holdout adobe. "I think we could take them, Scott. But it's up to you."

His weight still against the wagon wheel, Scott gazed at the big adobe building. He could feel the speculative, apprehensive eyes of the crowd upon him. He said finally, "It'd be expensive, Doug. Too expensive."

He pushed himself up onto his feet. "Dick, we'd just as well pull the boys out of the other places. Put all of them around that one building, back far enough that nobody'll get hurt, but close enough that whoever's in there will know there's a party outside waiting for them. We'll just sit back and let them do the sweating. They can't stay there forever."

That seemed to suit most of the cowboys. They weren't too keen about getting shot at if they didn't have to be. Disappointment drooped the shoulders of a few, however, especially the youngest.

"I thought we came here for some action," one of them grumbled, loud enough so Scott would hear.

In quick irritation Scott turned to him. "The man we're really after isn't here. He'll get here soon enough. Then you'll have plenty to do."

A cordon was set up about the holdout building, a cordon bristling with guns. From inside the building came sounds of shuffling feet as the besieged men prepared for what they expected to be a storming of their stronghold. But the storm never came. Watching from outside, Scott Tillman could almost feel the tension build within the trapped men. Outside, the cow outfits waited in patience that must have been nerve-wracking to those who sweated and fumbled with their guns in the adobe.

When at last he thought he had waited long enough, Scott Tillman arose and walked out in front of the cordon. He saw the sudden fear flash into Nell Owen's face. A dull dread gnawed at him, the realization that one of the men inside might shoot him down. But it was a chance he had to take.

"How about it?" he shouted. "Are you all about ready to come out?"

There was a moment of heavy silence, then a voice answered, "To what, a hanging party? If you want us, you know where we're at."

Scott sensed the ragged edge of fear in the voice. He called: "I'll make a deal with you. Come out without your guns and we'll let you go—provided you leave town in ten minutes. We want no killing if we don't have to have it."

He waited for an answer. It didn't come. For a good three minutes he stood there in the open, alone, waiting.

Then, in disappointment, he walked back to the waiting line of his men.

Relief washed over him as he sat down again. The whole time he had stood there, he was braced against the possibility of a tearing bullet. Now he relaxed, and he was surprised to find his hands trembling a little. The shoulder was aching, too.

Quietly, Nell Owen sat down beside him. She took his hand, and he noticed the unnatural whiteness of her face. She didn't speak, but she didn't have to. Her eyes said all there was to say.

Half an hour they waited. Occasionally there came a hint of the buzzing of voices in the building.

Scott's heart leaped as he saw the heavy wooden door inch inward. "Get ready," he called quickly, jumping to his feet. "It may be a break."

But just one man stepped out. Anxiously he looked across at the guns that faced him. His searching eyes fell upon Scott Tillman.

"That deal you promised. Does it still hold?"

Scott nodded.

Resignedly, the man said, "You win, then. Mind you, we wouldn't give up if we thought there was a chance. But there's not a man here that wants to commit suicide. They're coming out now, all of them. They won't be armed. Mind that none of your boys gets itchy fingers."

One by one the men filed out of the adobe building, hands over their heads. The cowboys lined them up in a double row. There were eighteen of them. Three punchers took a quick look inside the building.

"That's all," they said.

Grimly, Scott Tillman faced the surrendered men of High Land. Among the bunch were gamblers, a few known thieves, and some men who were strangers to him. But he was reasonably sure that most of their names could be found on sheriffs' dodgers in the courthouse, if the sheriff hadn't burned and rented out his bad memory for a reasonable price.

"The deal is that you get out of town in ten minutes. You'll be watched, every one of you. You've got just enough time to catch your horses and leave. And remember this. Any man who ever comes back to this part of the country takes his life in his own hands. Now move out."

One by one the men rode out over the hill. None of them carried their guns, and few carried any belongings except what they wore on their backs. Silent cowboys rode along with them to the hilltop and stopped there, watching them until they passed out of sight far across the next rise.

A slow grin built on Scott Tillman's face. "Well," he said to Nell Owen, Dong McKinney, and whoever else was listening, "that just about takes care of everybody but the sheriff and Judge Merriwether."

He walked to the courthouse, a dozen men behind him. At the door he turned and said, "A couple of you bring your ropes in. We want to make sure our county law gets all the show it paid for."

Judge Merriwether stood up and grabbed the bars of the cell door, blustering like a March wind. "Now see here, Tillman, I demand that you turn us loose. You'll be dealt with to the full extent of the law for this."

In exaggerated concern, Scott half turned and motioned toward the ropes held by two cowboys. "Under the circumstances, Judge, I'm afraid you better stay here for your own good. We've got some boys around here that are plenty riled. I might not be able to stop them if they were to get some fool kind of a notion."

Merriwether sagged. His tone suddenly changed to one of pleading.

"What is it you want, Tillman? The sheriff and I have always been fair men. We'll try to do anything you want, so long as it's honest and just."

With his good hand Scott Tillman thoughtfully rubbed his jaw. "Well, there's one way I might be able to talk to the boys. If I could show them a written resignation from the two of you, and told them you weren't ever coming back, there's just a chance they might let you go."

"Resign?" There was a note of outrage in the pudgy jurist's flabby face. But his bluff crumbled and his shoulders sagged. "All right. We'll sign."

He hadn't even looked at the sheriff. But it was clear that there wouldn't be any argument from the stringy lawman.

In satisfaction Scott leaned against the courthouse and watched the deposed sheriff and judge spur their horses into a stiff trot and disappear over the hill.

"We'll call another election," he said. "And there won't be enough votes left in High Land to keep us from getting some honest government for a change."

From down toward the riverbank he heard a sudden stir. Then half a dozen cowboys came riding up to the courthouse. Between them sagged another rider. Scott heard Nell Owen's muffled exclamation as her hands came up in front of her mouth. Scott's heart took a sudden glad leap.

"Curly," he breathed. "Curly Kirkendall!"

"We caught him riding in across the river," a cowboy spoke. "He said he wanted to talk to you."

Curly Kirkendall looked half dead as he eased down out of the saddle and leaned weakly against his horse. Scott grasped his hand.

"We heard the shooting last night and went back, Curly," he said. "But we couldn't find you. We thought you were dead."

Curly's eyes rested upon Nell Owen. They softened. "You went back for me?" She nodded, and he smiled weakly.

Inside the courthouse, after a drink to clear his head, Curly told his story. As he spoke, his eyes were on the girl, a bright fondness in them.

"When Clive Bannock rode in yesterday, we walked out and met him like we didn't know there was anything wrong. He didn't say a word. He just pulled his gun, and his men opened fire on us.

"Bill and Shorty fell in the first blast. They nicked me, but I managed to get back in the dugout. We stood them off till dark. By then there weren't but three of us left. Shug Gatlin was pretty hard hit.

"We tried to slip out of there in the dark. Shug and I made it, but they killed Wilkes. We were close enough to hear them when they busted into the dugout. Bannock roared like a lion when he didn't find you, Scott. They searched through the dark but couldn't see us. Finally they rode off toward the Slash B. But I heard Bannock say he'd find you all right, come morning.

"We headed out afoot, trying to get to the Lazy D, but Shug never made it. He died before we was halfway there. I finally got there, but you were already gone.

"Mrs. Dixon fed me. I was there when Bannock rode in, looking for you. She's a real woman, that Mrs. Dixon. She hid me and then stood there with a gun under her sleeve while they searched the house out for you. I would've killed Bannock right there, if I'd ever got a chance to get close to him."

His tired face twisted in hatred. "There was only

one good thing about the whole business, Scott. I got Bryce Fancher. I saw him fall." He added gravely. "Clive Bannock won't be long in getting here. I met a good many of the people you ran out of town. The first one of them that runs into Bannock, he'll come to get you, Scott."

Scott nodded. "I know. That's why we're waiting."

It was sundown when the wait ended. A cowboy came splashing across the river and spurring up the dirt street to the courthouse.

"He's coming, Scott. I counted twelve with him."

Scott's mouth hardened into a grim, colorless line. "All right, Dick," he said, turning to Coleridge. "Spread out like I told you."

The cowboys split off into two groups and fanned out away from the courthouse into two long, gun-bristling skirmish lines. The head of each line was near the river, and both lines ended at the adobe courthouse.

Clive Bannock's men hit the river and forged across it without hesitating. Then, on the town side, Bannock raised his hand for his men to stop. He looked at the stern lines of horsemen who faced him.

At the distance Scott could not see the man's face. But he knew what would be in its heavy features— stolidness, hatred, a grim determination.

Bannock hesitated for only a moment. Then he raised his hand and dropped it in a forward arc, motioning his men on. Sitting up in his saddle, straight as a rifle barrel, he came riding in between the two lines of armed men who formed a deadly lane about him. There was apprehension on the faces of the men who followed him, but there was nothing in Bannock's face, nothing but a black hatred.

Twenty paces from the courthouse door, he reined

up. In hostility he glanced around him and back of him at the cow outfits.

"My men are out of it," he said loudly enough for all to hear. "I got no quarrel with anybody except one man. Scott Tillman! I want you to come out!"

Slowly the cowboys began to pull back. Bannock's men pulled away, too. There was no fight in them now, not after the sight of the cowboys who outnumbered them so badly.

"Tillman," Clive Bannock called again, "this is just between me and you, nobody else."

He sat there on his horse, his face dark and heavy, his manner like that of a black-robed judge passing down the sentence of death.

"Everything I've ever tried to do, it's been you that stopped it, Tillman. It was you that broke my leg and put this lameness on me. It was you that stopped me when I tried to make my ranch bigger. It was you that killed my son. Now it's going to be either you or me. I want you to come out, Tillman, and face me."

Despair sank deeply into Scott Tillman. Somehow he had known it would be like this. It had had to be. He tried to lift his right hand, but it was no use. His bullet-torn shoulder was heavy as lead, and the fingers hardly moved. With his left hand he reached across and drew his gun. He thumbed the hammer and raised the pistol experimentally. The left hand was shaky and uncertain. He knew it would fail him, but he knew there could be no other way. He took a step toward the door.

Nell Owen rushed in front of him, her eyes brimming. "Scott," she cried, "I've never begged anybody for anything in my life. But I'm begging you—don't go out there."

Despairing, he drew her to him. "Do you know any other way?"

There was no answer, no answer except the wracking sobs that came from deep within her as she held tightly to him. Gently he pushed her back.

Curly Kirkendall grabbed his arm. "If you won't think about yourself, Scott, think about her," he said, pointing his chin toward the girl. "Let me face him! I've got as much to hate him for as you have—a whole lot more."

Scott smiled weakly, shaking his head. "Watch out for Nell, will you, Curly?"

Then he moved out onto the wide stone step, the gun in his left hand. His heart thumped dully within him. He tried to force back the fear which struggled in him, the fear that choked him and brought a tremor to the futile hand which gripped the gun.

He stepped down. Everything seemed to melt away from in front of him, and he saw nothing but Bannock's eyes, the iron-hard eyes that gazed at him in hatred.

Scott heard the footfall behind him. Too late he turned around and felt the gun jerked out of his hand. He grabbed at it and saw the hard fist which drove at his chin. He sprawled out in the sand and lay there, trying to push himself up on his elbow.

He heard Curly's voice like a coil of barbed wire. "It's not a crippled arm you're facing now, Bannock. It's me, Curly Kirkendall. You tried to get me blamed for it when you killed Jock Classen. You burned out my place last night and killed five of the best men I ever had. Now here you are, ready to kill a man who isn't able to fight for himself. But you're facing me, now, Bannock. Kill me, if you can."

Clive Bannock's arm flashed up with lightning

speed, the same kind of speed Fletch Bannock had had. His gun belched flame before Curly's did. Curly buckled, the breath gusting out of him. He fired once as he fell, and Bannock jerked. Bannock gripped the saddle horn to steady himself, and arched the gun downward once again.

Doubled in pain on the ground, Curly brought up his gun with both hands. The guns thundered together. Bannock slumped forward over the neck of his plunging horse, and the pistol slipped from his fingers as he tried desperately for a hold on the mane. Then he tumbled to the ground and lay crumpled in a heap, a handful of the horse's mane gripped tight in his dead fist.

Scott was on his feet as Nell Owen and half a dozen ranch owners burst out of the door. Scott knelt beside Curly. His heart swelling in his throat, he tried to lift Curly with his good hand.

"Quick," he cried, "somebody help me carry him inside."

In pain Curly said, "No, Scott, don't move me." He struggled hard for breath. Nell Owen knelt beside the young outlaw, lifting his head gently into her lap.

Scott found it hard to speak. "You're a fool, Curly."

A thin smile broke across Curly's knotted-up face. "Always was, Scott. Always was."

He coughed. "I think I've found the end of that blind canyon you've always been talking about, Scott."

With a terrible effort Curly lifted his hand and placed it on Nell Owen's arm. He raised his eyes to hers. "Take care of her, Scott. She's one in a million."

Scott tried to answer, but he couldn't. Then there wasn't any use, for Curly wouldn't hear . . .

Under the broad noonday sun, the gentle wind of the buffalo plains, stirring in their faces, Scott Tillman and Nell Owen reined up at the head of the JO canyon and looked down upon what had been the ranch headquarters.

The corrals were there, but the timber which had been snaked down from the hills for the building of more pens had been piled up and burned. The picket shack was nothing but a heap of cold, gray ashes, rapidly being whipped away by the constant wind. Here and there the improvements that had been built by sweat and strain and muscled backs lay scattered and broken by vengeful hands.

Scott glanced at the girl and saw her momentarily harden in anger.

"A pretty bad mess, isn't it?" he asked her.

She nodded. The anger left her, a healthy determination taking its place. "But we'll build it back, better than it ever was. We'll build the corrals first, because we'll have lots of cattle to brand, Scott."

She swung to the ground, and he dismounted with her. She led her horse along toward the charred ruins of the house.

"We'll build the house back, only this time we'll build it of stone. We'll build it so it can grow as we need it, Scott. And we'll build it strong, so it'll be here for our grandchildren and our great-grandchildren to see."

Smiling, Scott took hold of her arm. "Are you proposing to me, Nell?"

Her face colored in realization of what she had said. Then she smiled too. "Well, so I was. What do you say?"

He pulled her toward him, and she came with quick eagerness. The prairie wind caught his answer and carried it along to be lost down the silent, green canyon.

BULLETS
FROM THE PAST

Big Andy Webb looked regretfully at the old doctor who stood just inside the front door of the saddle shop. Straightening his tall frame, he laid aside the bridle he had been making and rubbed his hands on trousers that had been worn out long ago.

"I hate to keep puttin' you off like this, Doc, but I haven't got a thing to pay you with."

The young saddlemaker glanced quickly at his little son, a sandy-haired youngster who sat on a bench, tongue on his upper lip, while he laboriously platted a quirt.

"You know how I stand with the bank, now that old Eli has come out and took it over. Next week Jimmy and I won't even have this shop, the way it looks now."

Doc Brooks nodded. "Sure, Andy, this drouth's been hard on everybody." He blinked away sand in his eyes, blown there by a dust devil on the dry, powdery street.

"But I've got a chance to buy some new medical equipment and set up a better office. It might let me save a few lives that would be lost otherwise. Like your wife's was, Andy. If I could collect even a third of the bills owed me I could have what I need, Andy," the wrinkled old doctor went on. "If things lighten up for you, I'd sure appreciate you payin' what you can." Doc Brooks hated asking for his money, but circumstances forced him to.

When the old man had hobbled back out onto the rickety plank sidewalk, Big Andy went to work on the bridle again. A dry, hot breeze brought him the listless music of a tinny piano in the saloon next door. His gaze kept returning fondly to little Jimmy's freckled face, clean, honest, and eager. It hadn't been so many years since Andy had been Jimmy's size. He was glad his son would never go through the same kind of boyhood. Andy had grown up motherless in outlaw camps up and down the Texas Panhandle. His father's name had been blazed on reward notices and dodgers all over the country. Andy was only fifteen when his dad's horse had trotted into camp alone, saddle empty but smeared with blood.

The orphan had become a skilled cowboy, but with other people's cows. Then, when Andy was only twenty, a man had died in a blaze of gunfire. It wasn't Andy's gun, but Andy had gotten the blame. He had headed south in the dark of the moon.

Always expert with leather, he had become a harness and saddle maker. Eventually he had learned to love a girl and had married her. Fine craftsmanship had made his new name known all over West Texas. Then Alice had died, and the drouth had begun. Rains had failed. Hot winds had turned grassland into powder, breaking ranchmen first, then townsmen in turn.

Now here Andy was, hardly thirty, awaiting the foreclosure that would put him and his eight-year-old out on the trail. He was wistfully watching the youngster smooth out the quirt when a shadow fell across the floor. It was a big shadow, a round one.

"Better get a lot of trinkets ready for the rodeo crowd that's coming in tomorrow, Webb."

Hot, angry blood rose in Andy as he recognized the insolent voice of banker Eli Fuller. Defiantly he stood up and faced the sharp Easterner who had come to profit from the drouth.

"Get out of here, Fuller," he gritted, "or I'll cram that cigar down your fat throat!"

Little Jimmy stood up in alarm, then darted out the door.

"Now, don't get mad, Webb," the banker mocked. "I just wanted to see how my shop is getting along."

Andy bristled. "It ain't your shop yet. Now drag your fat carcass out of here!"

Fuller smiled condescendingly, his teeth bearing down on a long cigar which stuck up out of his mouth at a jaunty angle. "You shouldn't talk like that, Webb. If you'd be reasonable, I might even keep you on as an employee."

Outlaw heat surged through Big Andy. He lunged at the banker and drove a hard fist into the man's soft belly. The cigar dropped from Fuller's thick lips and rolled down his bulging vest, showering ashes and fire. The banker held up his soft hands defensively as Andy grabbed his collar.

Then a young woman burst through the door. "Stop it, Andy. For heaven's sake, stop it!"

Big Andy had doubled his fist again, but he slowly loosed it. The woman's alarmed blue eyes were opened wide. She gripped Andy's arms.

"Let him go, Andy," she pleaded. "Things are bad enough without you getting yourself in jail."

The fury in him began to subside. "All right, Mary," he said. "But Fuller better not come back in here."

The banker slowly backed toward the door, face flushed and belly bouncing a little over his low-slung belt.

"You won't be so independent next week, Webb," Fuller threatened, a tremor in his voice. "If you stay in this town, I'll see that you starve!"

An angry, helpless curse in his throat, Andy stepped forward. Mary Wilson gripped his arms again. Excitement had put scarlet in the young woman's cheeks and given her blue eyes a deep color. Her oval face seemed beautiful as she looked up at him pleadingly.

"My dad's in the same shape with the bank as you are, Andy," she said. "But even Jimmy knows you can't afford to fight Fuller. He came after me. And it's certainly a good thing he did."

Any other time Andy would have grinned. "He always knows right where to go, doesn't he?"

She smiled faintly. "Even if I am his schoolteacher, Jimmy likes me."

Big Andy put his hands on her slender shoulders. A new, tender warmth rose in him. "So does his dad."

There was something familiar about the tall, rugged man who strode into the shop and stood squinting at Andy. The saddlemaker frowned unbelievingly at the scarred face, then murmured darkly: "Rocky! Rocky Mertzon!"

The tall man smiled thinly, a black gap showing between his tobacco-stained teeth. "Howdy, Andy. Haven't seen you since you left the Panhandle on a fast horse." He extended a weather-roughened hand. Andy hesitated a moment, then took it with cool civility.

"Thought you were in the pen," Andy ventured carefully.

"I was, a long time ago," Mertzon said, a smile twisting his wind-whipped face. "But I got tired of it."

Big Andy watched suspiciously as Mertzon's darting black eyes took in the shop. "I was hopin' I'd never see any of that old bunch again, Rocky. I'm sorry you found me."

Mertzon grinned crookedly. "Nice setup you got here, Andy. Too bad you're goin' to lose it. I've heard all about it. And I been figgerin' out a way to help you and me both at the same time."

Andy paused uncertainly. He picked up his son's unfinished quirt, then put it down on the bench while Mertzon built a cigarette.

"Those old days are behind me, Rocky. If it's somethin' crooked, I don't want any part of it."

The outlaw frowned. "You ain't in much shape to bargain. Look here, Andy, you got a bank on one side of you and a saloon on the other. A perfect setup. With the rodeo that starts tomorrow, there's apt to be a lot of money layin' around in that bank. And with the crowd that'll be here, the sheriff ain't goin' to pay much attention to one stranger."

Mertzon's slitted gaze probed big Andy's eyes for a sign of interest. "I'll wait around on rodeo day till there ain't any customers in the bank. Then I'll clean the place out and leave through the back door. You'll have your back window open, Andy, and I'll pitch the loot through it as I run by. Then I'll go in the back door of the saloon and be mixed up with the crowd before anybody has a chance to git after me."

The outlaw grinned. "That fat banker has a standin' reward of one thousand dollars for any bank robber, dead or alive. When I git through, he won't have that much!"

Eagerly Mertzon leaned forward. "I'll give you a thousand out of whatever I git, Andy. And all you have to do is leave your back window open."

Temptation boiled in Big Andy. A thousand dollars! That would more than pay what he owed Fuller, if he could figure out a way to explain where he got it. And he could pay Doc Brooks the money he had owed him ever since Alice had died.

But Big Andy shook his head. "I quit that kind of business a long time ago. I'll go hungry before I take a chance on leadin' my son through the kind of life I had!"

Mertzon scowled. "Maybe you'd like me to spread the word about the old days in the Panhandle. That'd really fix your kid up!"

An old fear made Andy's heart beat faster. "I've spent more than ten years tryin' to live that down. I've worked up a reputation that Jimmy could be proud of. You wouldn't take that away from me, would you, Rocky?"

Mertzon looked up with a cruel grin.

"The Weaver brothers up around Tascosa are still wonderin' what became of you. They got a funny idea it was you that killed Tom Weaver."

Andy's heart jumped. "That's a lie! You shot Tom Weaver! I wasn't even there!"

Mertzon still grinned crookedly. "Sure, but the Weavers thought it was you. Still do. Maybe you'd like a chance to prove to 'em different."

Pulse racing and his face stove-lid hot, Andy dived for a drawer in which he knew would be a pistol. But even as his sweaty hand touched the gun butt, he felt Mertzon's .45 poking him in the ribs.

"That's a fool play, Andy," Mertzon growled. "You been goin' straight too long. All you would've done was make an orphan out of that kid."

Defeated, Big Andy slowly settled back against the work bench. His heart thumped rapidly. His mouth was dry.

"I'll pull the job tomorrow," Mertzon said. "Have that window open. And if you git any ideas about crossin' me up, just remember the Weavers."

He holstered his gun, stepped out into the street, and was gone.

The next day, standing in the front door of his shop, Andy watched the occasional tiny dust devils whirl across the powdery street. A small but steady stream of riders kept a thin haze of dust hanging in the air. The rodeo was bringing its crowd. Andy's hands were wet with nervous perspiration, and a nameless tension tied his innards in a knot. Where was Rocky Mertzon? If he had to pull his robbery, why didn't he come on and get it over with?

Andy watched as his son and a group of boys romped gaily down the dusty street, playing cowboy. There was a fresh patch in the seat of Jimmy's worn trousers. No question about who had made the repairs, Andy thought with a twinge of conscience. Mary Wilson mothered the boy like he was her own.

His heart warmed then as he saw the young school-teacher coming down the wooden sidewalk. Her pretty face beamed.

"Dad did it, Andy!" she exclaimed. "Dad did it. He found a buyer for his cattle. He had to cut way down into his breeding herd, but he got enough money to pay off Tiller's note on the ranch."

He managed to grin with her. "What did Fuller say when you all paid him off?"

"He wasn't in. We deposited the money with the teller. We'll pay Fuller later."

Andy's grin faded as a sobering thought struck him. What if Rocky Mertzon robbed the bank before Mary's father could pay the debt? He would get the Wilsons' money, and the mortgage would still stand. Fuller would take the ranch.

Sick at heart, Andy moved to his bench and sat down. It wouldn't be just the Wilsons, either, he told himself. The bank money didn't belong to Fuller only. It belonged to depositors from all over the area—friends of Andy's—who were trying to pay their debts and still live like human beings.

Andy could see old Charlie Wilson across the street, joyfully slapping Sheriff Bronson on the back. He thought of Jimmy. What if the truth were guessed, and Andy had to go on the dodge? What about Jimmy?

Despairingly the saddlemaker watched fat Eli Fuller swagger past on his way to the bank. Nerves tingling, Andy rubbed his sweating hands against each other for what seemed like hours. He couldn't let this go on. He had to stop it!

He reached into the drawer, hauled out the six-gun, and shoved it into a boot-top, out of sight. Then he strode firmly out onto the sidewalk. He spotted Rocky Mertzon sitting on a bench in front of the saloon. Big Andy gestured at Mertzon with his chin, then walked back through the shop into the rear room. As Mertzon came in a minute later, Big Andy lifted his foot and snaked out the gun.

"You're not goin' through with it, Rocky," he declared, the gun leveled at Mertzon's chest. "I'll leave town tonight. I'll risk my name being smeared, and I'll risk the Weavers. But you're not robbin' that bank!"

Angry red flamed in Mertzon's eyes. "You're mighty

righteous for a feller whose old man robbed half the banks in Texas." For a heated moment hatred glared from his narrowed eyes. Then he slowly turned around, as if giving up. Big Andy lowered the gun a little.

Suddenly Mertzon whirled back and grabbed at the gun. In a second he wrenched it from Andy's hand. Big Andy threw a hand up defensively as he saw the glint of the slashing gun barrel. Something exploded in his head. He dropped to his knees, the shop reeling before his eyes.

"You're not fast enough for me, Big Andy," Mertzon snarled. "You never was!"

There was a second of blinding pain as the gun barrel struck him again. Then there was only darkness.

He became conscious of soft hands wiping his face with a wet cloth. His head throbbed dully, and he grimaced at a sickening taste in his mouth.

He forced his eyes open and saw Mary kneeling over him. Painfully he lifted himself up onto his elbows. He could see a red stain on the wet cloth.

"What happened, Andy?" she asked in alarm.

"Somebody slugged me," he told her. "Help me up."

As he struggled to keep his feet, Mary quickly told him that Jimmy had come back to the shop to get his quirt for play. He had found his father in the back room, unconscious. His first thought had been to run to Mary.

"We've got to get you to Doc Brooks," she said with concern.

Andy shook his throbbing head. "No, I've got to see the sheriff. Right now!"

Leaning on the slender girl for support, he started for the front. Then two shots exploded in the bank next door. Despair choked Andy like a giant hand clasped around his throat. In his excitement he felt his

strength returning. He and Mary got to the bank a few
seconds before the sheriff did.

Acrid gunpowder stung his nostrils. The room was
cloudy with choking smoke, which slowly swirled upward toward the high ceiling. The back door was
open. Then Andy saw the excited bank teller kneeling
beside fat Eli Fuller. Moaning, the banker lay sprawled
on the floor, one flabby hand clutching at a bleeding
shoulder. A chewed-up cigar, one end still smoking,
lay beside him.

"The back door!" boomed Sheriff Bronson's voice.
Andy moved to the door ahead of the lawman and
stepped out into the alley. No one there!

The old lawman cursed. "Got clean away, Andy! He
must've had a plenty fast horse!"

Guilt lay heavy in Andy as he followed the somber
sheriff back into the bank. The ashen-faced teller was
gesturing nervously and recounting the incident to the
gathering crowd.

"Mr. Fuller seemed to lose all reason when the
masked man took the money. He grabbed at a gun,
and the robber shot him!"

Doc Brooks hobbled through the huddled circle of
men and ripped the banker's vest and shirt away from
the wound. A low, disappointed murmur ran through
the crowd as the doctor announced that the wound
wasn't too serious. A little sick, Andy started for the
door. Mary came to him, her face stricken.

"Oh, Andy," she sobbed, "we didn't even have a
chance to pay Fuller. He'll surely take the ranch now."

Andy sympathetically put his arm around her shoulder and led her outside. The sheriff was swearing in
volunteers for a posse.

Andy looked vainly for Mertzon. He hoped the outlaw hadn't had time to get back to the saddle shop.

Tension gripped him as he realized what he had to do. There wasn't much time. He held Mary's hand tightly and called: "Wait a minute, Sheriff. I don't think you need to do that. How about comin' into the shop with me?"

The sheriff stared quizzically, then followed him. Mary gazed at him in puzzlement.

It wasn't any trouble to find the bag of stolen money under the shop's back window. As Andy handed it over he told Mary, the sheriff, and half a dozen possemen the whole story—about his boyhood in the Panhandle, about Tom Weaver, and about Rocky Mertzon.

"Rocky probably figgered I wouldn't wake up till it was all over, and then I'd be scared to say anything. If Jimmy hadn't found me and Mary waked me up, I'd still be lyin' here. I guess this means jail for me now," he concluded darkly. "Mary, I wish you'd take care of Jimmy."

Sheriff Bronson snorted. "Nobody's goin' to blame you for this, Andy. Maybe you should've come to me in the first place, but just the same, you tried to stop it. You like to've got your skull bashed in. Folks'll be grateful to you."

It turned out he was right. Andy was dead tired by late afternoon, when people stopped coming around to shake his hand. Eli Fuller hadn't sent any thanks, however. The banker had growled that it was all a plot of Andy's to get him killed. He sent word that he was taking over the shop the minute the note fell due.

His ranch secure now, old Charlie Wilson asked Andy to come help him run the ranch. No drouth ever lasted forever, he argued, and this one had about run its course. Besides, it would be handy to have a cow-wise son-in-law, he hinted.

But Andy couldn't forget the Weavers. No sign of Mertzon had been found. He knew the angered outlaw would eventually keep his threat, to tell the Weavers where Andy was. If Andy stayed, it meant more gunplay. So there was only one thing to do—pull out.

As he closed shop that evening Andy found his pistol and shoved it into his boot. Turning to go, he picked up Jimmy's unfinished quirt. He fingered it fondly as he headed home for the last time. It was dark when he climbed the front steps of the lonely house. Jimmy met him at the front door. The boy's eyes were wide with alarm.

"There's a man here to see you, Daddy," he said excitedly. "He says he's a friend. But . . ."

Raw fear cut through Andy as he saw Rocky Mertzon standing there, not two paces in front of him. The outlaw's hands hovered over his gun butts. The gap between his teeth showed black behind the twisted, cruel lips, making Andy feel this man's ruthlessness.

"I changed my mind about the Weavers," Mertzon snarled, "I'll finish this job myself."

Andy felt cold sweat popping out on his forehead. Gripping the quirt handle tightly, he realized he couldn't beat Mertzon to the draw.

Suddenly Mertzon's hands moved downward. Andy shoved the boy to the floor. A million needles pricking his skin, he lashed out with the quirt and slashed it across the outlaw's face. The man bellowed with rage and pain.

His guns thundered, but Andy was between them, lashing madly at the outlaw's hands. One gun clattered to the floor.

Then the years rushed back, and Andy was twenty

again, untamed, hard as a man can get only on the outlaw trails. Breathing hard, he threw himself desperately on Mertzon. Frantically, he tried to wrench the other gun out of the man's hand.

Teeth clenched, straining and sweating, the two men struggled for the weapon. For a second the muzzle grazed Andy's stomach.

Then slowly he twisted the gun back toward Mertzon, every muscle in his body aching with the effort. Beads of sweat stood out on the grunting man's forehead. Andy grimaced at the robber's hot breath in his face. The gun boomed then, and Mertzon went limp. Andy swayed dizzily a moment. Through the swirling gunsmoke he could see the outlaw lying twisted on the floor. He also saw Jimmy streak out the door.

A moment later half a dozen men, led by Sheriff Bronson, crowded into the room.

"There's your . . . your bank robber," Andy breathed heavily.

Bronson examined the outlaw. "Wanted to get even, eh?"

Andy nodded, his breath still short. The sheriff instructed the men to carry Mertzon's body outside. Then he turned back to the weary Andy.

"Doc Brooks'll get enough out of Fuller, takin' care of that shoulder, to buy the equipment he's been wanting. And Fuller'll sure throw a fit when you pay him off with his own money, the reward money. The thousand dollars he's always offered for a bank robber, dead or alive!"

Then Mary ran up the steps and into the room, followed by little Jimmy. Seeing Andy on his feet, she sighed in relief, then almost fainted.

Holding her, Andy felt all the tension leave him, replaced by a warmth he hadn't known in four years.

"Jimmy sure knows who to go to," he told her softly. "But from now on he won't have to go hunt you. He can find you right here."

CLIMB THE BIG RIM

It was a raw, thorny, man-killing country that even the devil wouldn't have. For two days Wade Massey had worked his way across it, cursing the bare stretches of rock and sand, the tangles of clutching chaparral. Now, his ride almost done, he reined up a moment.

He took off his broad-brimmed hat and wiped his sweaty forehead on a dusty sleeve. He squinted against the glare of the hostile sun and let his gaze sweep again the broad panorama of the desert.

The land was choked up with mesquite and catclaw and ironwood, and worst of all there was the cholla cactus that seemed to reach out and grab at horse and man. No, sir, he told himself, even the devil wouldn't lay claim to a country like this.

But there were people fool enough to want to, and there were bankers fool enough to lend them money to try it.

Wade looked down at the Rafter T headquarters, huddled around a spring that fed a narrow little stream. The bankers must have been caught on their warm side when Price Stockton and Glenn Henry, brothers-in-law, had talked them into making a loan so they could bring cattle into this country, Wade reflected. But their warm side had gradually taken on a chill when the years started slipping by and the cattlemen hadn't even been able to pay interest on the loan.

Looking at the country, Wade couldn't understand why the partners hadn't given up and turned their cattle back to the bank long ago. Particularly, he couldn't understand why Price Stockton had kept on going even when his partner died in agony after a smashing accident on the slope of a rocky hill.

But what the hell. He shrugged as he swung back into the saddle and jogged on down toward the huddle of rock buildings and pole corrals. It wasn't his job to be wondering why. The banking firm of Underwood & Watson had sent him to get their money back or take over the ranch. They didn't care which.

He stopped again a couple of hundred yards from the ranch buildings. The thought struck him that no wagon could ever get in here. The country was too rough. The rocks for the buildings had been moved by hand, or by pack mule. He glanced over the pole corrals. The rails had been snaked down from the higher timber country, most likely.

A lot of hard labor and pure guts had gone into the building of this place. The thought set a worry to nagging at him again. Underwood & Watson hadn't sent any word to Stockton. They were going to let Wade break the news.

"There's no way of knowing how he's going to take it," Oliver Underwood had said. "But I can guess.

"That's why we're sending you. You know cattle, horses and the ranch business as well as anybody. And you're young enough and husky enough to take care of yourself in a fight."

Wade was hot and tired and thirsty when he swung down beside the little shoveled-out stream, a few yards below a fence which kept livestock away from the spring. He loosened the cinch and let his horse lower its head to the cool water. Wade moved a couple of steps closer to the spring, dropped to his belly, and began to drink of the good, running stream.

He didn't see the woman walk up on the other side of the spring. He didn't become aware of her until he rose onto one knee and wiped the water off his mouth and looked up.

He saw first that she was young and slenderish and wore a slat bonnet. Then he saw that she held a small hand up to her mouth in surprise and that the color had drained from her oval face. She dropped the wooden bucket she carried.

Awkwardly Wade got to his feet, crushing his hat with one hand and rubbing his stubbled chin with the other. He hadn't shaved in three days. He probably looked like an outlaw.

"I didn't go to scare you, ma'am," he said apologetically.

She swallowed. "You didn't scare me," she said weakly. "It was just that you—you looked for a minute like someone else, a fellow who used to ride in and stop at the stream and drink from it the way you just did."

Wade couldn't help staring at her. He liked her full, slenderish figure, the way the lacy top of her full-length dress swelled outward as she breathed rapidly. Her face wasn't beautiful like some he had seen, but it was soft-looking and warm, with fine features. She wasn't a girl any more. She was a woman.

"This man," he said cautiously, "is he somebody you're afraid of?"

She quickly shook her head. "Oh, no," she replied, "it wasn't that." He could see a sign of pain in her blue eyes. "He meant a lot to me. He's been dead a long time."

Wade nodded and dropped his head. It was then that he noticed the golden rings on the third finger of her left hand. He swallowed once in disappointment. But, he told himself, he should have known. A rose like this couldn't bloom on the desert and not be appreciated by some man.

"I came to see Price Stockton, ma'am. He around?"

She smiled then, and the pain left her face. Her lips were like a pale rose. "He's out riding the east line. He'll be back for supper. But if you're looking for a job, I'm afraid it's been a long ride for nothing."

Wade still couldn't keep his eyes away from her. Price Stockton had chosen his wife much better than he had chosen his ranch, he thought.

"I'm not hunting a job," he said. "I'm here on business, Mrs. Stockton."

Her eyebrows went up a little, then she smiled again. "Mrs. Stockton is at the house. I'm Bess Henry. Price is my brother."

Wade took in a sharp breath. Bess Henry. So she was the widow of Stockton's partner. Oliver Underwood had said Glenn Henry was killed two years ago when he roped a steer and was jerked down the rocky slope of a steep hill. Wade felt sorry for the woman now. But somehow he felt a little relieved, too.

"There's grain in the barn," she said. "Unsaddle your horse and come on to the house. We've got a pot of coffee on the stove."

Wade took a straight razor and a bar of soap out of

his saddlebags and shaved in the cold water before he went to the house. Bess Henry didn't mention it, but he could tell by her eyes that she appreciated it. She called Mrs. Stockton into the kitchen.

Stockton's wife was a jovial, plump woman with hair already beginning to gray. Wade placed her at forty. Stockton must be twelve or fifteen years older than his sister, he thought.

After they had had coffee, he stood in front of the rock house with Bess Henry and watched the sun sink into a splash of brilliant red beyond the bald rim which jutted up high and wide far to the west.

"One thing I can't understand," he said, "is why you stayed on here. It looks like too hard a country for a woman. Too hard for a man, I'd say."

She shook her head. "It's not an easy life," she agreed. "Life comes hard here sometimes. But when you have to work and fight for something, you appreciate it all the more. At times it seems like the devil himself is against us. But look at it now."

She swept her hand out toward the blazing sunset, the rolling mountains, the high, wide, formidable rim. "Have you ever seen anything grander? You look at it this way and you can forget the heat and the rocks and the thorns. That's why Glenn loved it so much, I guess. That's why I've stayed here even though he's gone. He's part of it now. So am I."

No one could ever explain just how love works. One man can know a woman for years before he finally realizes she is the one he wants. Another can be with a woman only an hour and know even then that he is in love with her.

That's how it was with Wade Massey. Long before Price Stockton finally came in at dark, Wade knew he had fallen in love with Bess Henry. It took all the strength he could muster to keep from reaching out and grasping her hand, or even pulling her to him and kissing those pale rose lips.

His heart was like a heavy rock inside of him. Before he finished his job for Underwood & Watson, she would probably have to leave this country she loved. And he knew she would leave hating him.

Price Stockton was a strong man, maybe six feet tall, about the same as Wade. His brown, leathery face showed he had spent the better part of his forty years out with the cattle in the hot dry wind, the blazing sun, the biting cold of winter. But the crinkly turkey tracks at the corners of his eyes showed he knew how to grin.

He came in afoot, leading a horse that limped on his left forefoot.

"Stumbled and fell up in the hills," he told his sister. "The foot is pretty badly twisted."

Wade noticed that Stockton was skinned up a little, too. But the man never mentioned it.

"I didn't want to turn him loose up there in the shape he's in," Stockton said. "We can rub that ankle with salted grease a few days and maybe it'll come down."

Right then Wade knew his job was going to be twice as hard. He liked Price Stockton right off. Maybe Stockton wasn't the best ranch manager in the country, but he loved stock.

Through supper, Wade forced himself to joke with Price Stockton and miserably felt the warmth of Bess Henry's smiles. He tried to figure some way he could break the news easily.

He didn't get the chance. About the time he was finishing his last cup of coffee, the kitchen door opened and a cowboy walked in, spurs jingling.

"Say, Price," a gruff voice spoke, "Slim says he seen that big brindle bull—"

The voice broke off suddenly. It was a voice that rubbed up Wade's spine like a wood rasp. He turned quickly around in his chair and almost let go his coffee cup.

The cowboy dropped his hand to his hip as if forgetting he didn't have on a gun. His brown eyes were panicked. Then he turned and bolted for the outside.

Wade knocked over his chair as he jumped up and beat the man to the door. The puncher stopped and stood there, his muddy eyes wide, his quick breath ragged. Wade didn't reach for his gun. He knew he wouldn't have to.

"Lodge Agnew!" Wade said, his own breath coming fast. "I've hoped for a long time I'd run into you again. But I never really expected to."

Agnew was trembling. "You're a long way from New Mexico," he breathed. "You wouldn't drag me back, would you, Massey?"

Price Stockton had shoved his chair away from the table. He stepped up beside Agnew. "What's going on, Lodge? Is this man an officer?"

Agnew shook his head. "The last time I seen him he was working for a bank. He closed out a ranch."

The cordiality suddenly disappeared from Stockton's face. The lines in it hardened. "A bank?" He peered keenly into Wade's face. "You're working for a bank?"

Wade swallowed. There would be no breaking it easy now. "That's right, Stockton. I work for Underwood & Watson. I came to take up the loan they gave you and Glenn Henry."

Stockton's back stiffened. Wade glanced at Bess Henry. She blanched. Then her eyes turned to ice, and she looked down at the table. Plump Mrs. Stockton was about to burst into tears.

Wade felt little and mean. But it was his job. He had had to do it before. Usually the ranchmen were glad to turn the whole mess over to the bank and let someone else worry about it a while. But occasionally there was a case like this one, and Wade hated to look at himself in the mirror.

Price Stockton's voice trembled a little. The yellow lamplight made the lines of his face deep and harsh. "If they'd just sent us word—but no, they sent you sneaking in here like a coyote."

Agnew glanced at his boss, and his muddy eyes were desperate. "He's just one man, Price. You could run him out of here," he said hopefully.

A tremor of excitement played through Wade as he could see Stockton mulling over Agnew's suggestion.

"You could, Stockton," Wade agreed flatly. "But I'd be back. And I'd bring along a sheriff and maybe a couple of deputies next time."

Angrily Stockton studied Wade's face. His eyes looked as if they could strike sparks. But gradually Wade could see the ranchman giving up. Finally Stockton asked, "All right, then, what do you want me to do? Any choice?"

Wade nodded. It was going a little easier now. He slipped a tobacco sack from his shirt pocket and rolled a cigarette.

"You've got a choice. But first I'd just like to know what the trouble is. Why can't you make the place pay?"

Stockton shrugged. "The country's good enough. It keeps the cattle in good shape. But we've never been able to drive enough of them to the railroad to pay expenses. We can't get a whole herd through that brush country. But you'll find out for yourself, soon enough. Now, what's the choice you were talking about?"

Wade took a long drag on the cigarette and watched Stockton. "You can turn the whole outfit over to the bank, lock, stock and barrel, and wash your hands of it."

That hit Stockton right between the eyes. The fury rushed back into his face.

"Or," Wade went on, "we can try to get enough cattle to the railroad to pay what you owe the bank. I'll ramrod the roundup and the drive. But they'll be your cattle till they sell.

"The market's not any too good right now. It might take every hoof on the place to pay off the debt. On the other hand, you may have had enough increase the last few years that you'll still have some cows left when the debt's squared. If you have, that'll give you something to start out new with. But I wouldn't count on it much."

He looked again at Bess Henry and miserably accepted her hostility.

"The choice is up to you, Stockton," he said. "Personally, I'd give up this godforsaken country. I'd be glad to get shed of the whole mess."

Stockton's eyes were hard. "I like this country, Massey. It's wild and it's rough. But it's mine, mine and my wife's and Bess's. If we've got to fight you and the bank every step of the way, we'll keep it."

He didn't try to prevent his hatred from showing. "Now that we got that settled, what's the first thing we do?"

Wade said, "The first thing is to get a real crew of cowboys in here. If the rest of your bunch is like Lodge,

I don't wonder that you've never been able to get your cattle out."

"And the next?" Stockton asked.

"The next thing is that I'm taking Lodge to jail."

There was a look in Agnew's muddy eyes like that of a scared rabbit. He had been a coward back in New Mexico. He still was.

But Stockton didn't like it. "What's Lodge done?"

Wade explained. Over in New Mexico a couple of years ago, someone had been stealing a ranchman blind. The stockman had a good cow country, but it was a good rustler country, too. He had fought until he was whipped down.

"He finally threw in his chips and turned it all over to the bank," Wade said. "I went to liquidate the outfit. Then I found out Lodge and his brother were mainly responsible for the stealing.

"We got them cornered in a canyon with a bunch of stuff they were changing brands on. We wounded Lodge's brother. Lodge lit out. He abandoned his brother, left him lying there bleeding to death. We never did know how Lodge got away.

"We managed to save his brother's life. He's in the pen now, and not claiming Lodge as kin. But he's going to have company right soon. I'm taking Lodge to town."

Firmly Stockton stepped in front of Agnew. "Lodge has done nothing wrong while he's been here. He's always been a good hand. You're no officer, Massey. Even if you was, you'd have to get the say-so of the territorial governor to take him back to New Mexico. Lodge is my man. He stays."

Wade felt anger surge up in him, then let it burn out. He knew Stockton had him there.

Presently Wade said, "I'll start for town tomorrow,

then, and bring out some cowboys. If there's any chance in the world of getting that herd out for you, we'll do it."

A steady hatred kindled in Stockton's steely eyes. "It's easy for you to say that. What've you got to lose?"

Wade glanced once at Bess Henry, then back at Stockton. "I've got plenty to lose."

Several days later he was back again with a group of hand-picked cowboys. Among them was Snort Shanks, long-legged, long-thinking cowhand from over in the Mogollons; Blackie Hadden, dark, squat puncher who seldom opened his mouth but was always out in the lead when the pinch came; two Mexican vaqueros, Felipe Sanchez and Ernesto Flores, who would chase a runaway steer down the bald face of a cliff just to see which one could rope him first.

There were three other cowpunchers cut from the same cloth. Wade had never worked with them before, but he knew the breed. They'd move cattle off the Rafter T or leave scars that would show for the next fifty years why it hadn't been done.

He saw Bess Henry standing in the doorway of the rock house, watching them as they rode in to the barn. But when her eyes met his, she stepped back into the house. Bitterness touched him. After all, he was just doing a job he was hired for. But he could understand how she felt.

Price Stockton and his own cowboys were ready to go next morning when Wade's men saddled up in the predawn darkness. Wade had brought out a string of pack mules. These stood ready in the corral, packed with bedding and food and cooking utensils, and grain for the horses. It would take grain to keep the herd in shape to outrun the wild Rafter T cattle.

Stockton sat his saddle, tight-lipped and aloof.

Wade had it on his tongue to say again that he would save Stockton and Bess the ranch if there was any way to do it. But faced with Stockton's coldness, he swallowed the words and motioned the men to start.

Bess Henry and Mrs. Stockton stood in the doorway, watching them move out in single file. Wade studied the younger woman's face for some trace of kindness. All he found there was silent hostility.

All right, then, he told himself bitterly, he would take their hatred as a challenge. He'd get those Rafter T cattle to market if he had to do it in spite of Bess Henry and Price Stockton—and Lodge Agnew.

It was past noon when they set up camp alongside a little creek down in the rough country to the south. It was rougher than anything Wade had seen on his ride from town. There seemed to be nothing but steep, rock-scattered hillsides, deep gullies and box canyons. But this was where the cattle were.

Now and then on the trail out, they had seen some of them, but seldom for long. Usually there would be just a quick glimpse before the cattle would clatter down a slope or over a rocky hill with their heads wild and high and their tails arched. There was still lots of old longhorn in them, although most showed the sign of blood from some of the new breeds that were being brought into the country, here and yonder.

The rest of the day the punchers spent throwing a barricade across the front of a small box canyon that had grass and water. They left enough opening for an extra-wide pole gate. Wade and Hadden snaked the pine poles down from the hillsides.

As the men sat down to supper prepared by Chili, Stockton's hostile-eyed, big-mustached cook, Wade outlined his plan to them all.

"This canyon will be our corral. This is where we'll

bring them until we've got enough cattle to try making a drive to the railroad. We're going to gather in everything. There's six- and eight-year-old bulls in these mountains that've never felt a branding iron or a knife. We'll catch them if we've got to climb up and down the cliffs to do it."

He glanced at Price Stockton, then back to the men. "From now on till we're through, I'm the boss. And any man who's afraid to chase a steer down one of these rocky slopes as hard as his horse can run had better leave now."

He peered sharply at each of the Stockton men. There was only one who worried him, outside of Lodge Agnew. He was a small, middle-aged puncher named Corey Milholland. Wade could see the nervous twitching of the man's hands, the dread that crept into his eyes. It seemed to Wade that Milholland was a little fragile for this country.

"How about it, Milholland?" he asked. "You want to leave?"

Price Stockton whirled around from the coffeepot where he had been filling his cup. "You leave Corey alone, Massey," he warned. "He's been with me for years. He's staying."

Wade bit his lip. "Have it like you want it, Stockton. But I'll be watching him. He better keep up."

They headed west from camp next morning. Eight or ten miles away he dropped the riders out in a wide semicircle and started pushing back toward the box-canyon corral.

It didn't take long for the action to start. Wade jumped a little bunch of mixed cattle in a valley. At the sight of him they lifted their tails and struck out in a high lope for the south. Wade followed behind until he knew they would pass in front of the next rider to him. He reined up on a high point and watched in satisfaction as they bounced off of Snort Shanks and moved on to the next man. They would be run down by the time they reached the outside of the drive. The outside man would bring them in.

Sitting on the point, Wade gazed out across the rocky hills ahead of him. They were rugged and perilous, mean and hard. But there was a majesty to them, he realized, a wild beauty that made a man want to stop and drink in a long look. Maybe if he stayed here long enough he could learn to like the country a little, he admitted to himself.

The drive went on about the way he had expected. Now and again he could hear the loud shouts of a cowboy or two as they raced to head off a bunch of runaway cattle. He had a good many of those races himself. More than once he spurred down a steep hillside after a big steer. It was all a man's heart could stand to watch his horse's flying hoofs slipping, sliding, down those treacherous slopes.

It was always a relief to see Snort down there at the bottom, waiting to pick up the steer and push him on. Snort had lucked onto a fairly gentle little bunch of cows and calves. These made it easier for him to catch and hold the waspier cattle.

Along toward the middle of the afternoon, Wade stopped on a hill and took a long look around him, giving his horse a chance to get its wind after chasing two bulls for about a mile.

On another hill half a mile away he could see a rider spurring hell-bent after an animal that had broken in the opposite direction from the roundup. The rider was in easy roping distance of the steer, but he didn't swing his loop. The steer plunged down off the slope.

The cowboy reined up and stood on the rim of the hill, watching the steer get away.

Anger flared through Wade. He recognized the horse as the one Corey Milholland had been riding. Any other puncher in the outfit would have gone down after that steer. Well, there'd be retribution tonight, when the day's drive was done.

The first day's gather was a good one, everything considered. The count was close to a hundred head. The cowboys pushed most of them into the box can yon trap, roping and dragging in those that wouldn't be driven. Wade and Hadden dropped the poles into place in the gateway.

The cook was finishing supper. Wade stopped close to the cooking fire. "Milholland," he called, "come over here."

Nervously the bent cowpuncher walked up to him. Price Stockton followed suspiciously.

"I saw you let a steer get away this afternoon, Milholland," Wade said severely. "He took off down a hill and you didn't even make a move to stop him. You remember what I told you last night?"

Silently the cowpuncher shook his head.

"All right, then," Wade spoke, "get your gear together. You're leaving in the morning."

Stockton stepped up beside Milholland and stood there angrily, his face dark. "Maybe you need to remember what I told you last night, Massey. Milholland's my man. If you fire him, you've got me to whip first."

Anger blazed in Wade. He glared at Stockton a moment. "If you want me to save your outfit for you, you've got to let me run this roundup."

He thought he might stare Stockton down. But the

ranchman held his ground. "You're running the roundup, Massey. But you're not firing my men."

Wade had to give in. "You're winning this hand, Milholland. I'm letting you stay against my better judgment. But from now on you're riding with me. You'll make a hand if I've got to drag you."

As they rode out the next morning in a different direction, Wade got a chance to move his horse up next to Stockton's. "Milholland's out of place here, Stockton," he said quietly. "Why keep trying to protect him like he was a little boy?"

Stockton gazed straight ahead. "You think he's yellow. But he's not. He was with Glenn Henry the day Glenn roped a big steer and got jerked down off a bluff. Glenn wound up on a ledge about forty feet below the trail, tore half to pieces. His horse was dead.

"Corey Milholland crawled down to that ledge and worked Henry back up onto the trail a few inches at a time. It took guts to do it, Massey. If he had slipped he could've fallen back down the bluff and been killed along with Glenn.

"He was afraid to leave Glenn alone up there, so he got him onto his own horse. Corey led the horse home, him walking along, holding Glenn in the saddle half the time. It took him nearly six hours to make it. Glenn died anyway, but it wasn't Corey's fault. He did his best and risked being killed."

Stockton took a deep breath, then went on, "So you see why he didn't go off that hillside after the steer yesterday. He remembers what happened to Glenn. And you see why I'm keeping him, even if I've got to whip you to do it . . ."

The next few days the cowboys spent in drives similar to that of the first day, each time covering new ground and bringing in seventy-five to a hundred or more cattle a day. By the time all the ground had been covered, there were around eight hundred head on grass and water in the canyon.

During the drives Wade kept Corey Milholland close to him. The puncher was a little slow in following when the riding got tough, and occasionally he wouldn't follow at all. Had it been up to Wade, he would have let the man go.

Lodge Agnew worried him, too. It wasn't anything he could put his finger on, but every time Wade turned his back on Agnew, he felt a tingling sensation up and down his spine. He knew that with him around, Agnew could still taste the threat of the penitentiary.

Lodge made no attempt to get along, either with Wade or with Wade's cowboys. He was especially contemptuous of the two Mexicans. One night he called big Felipe Sanchez a *pelado*, which in Spanish was like calling a man trash. Felipe jumped to his feet and whipped out a long-bladed knife. Before Wade could grab the vaquero and pull him away, blood dripped from a three-inch gash along Agnew's cheek and spread into his week's growth of beard.

Wade took Felipe out away from the campfire, calmed him down a little and gave him a long lecture. But a new dread edged in with all his other troubles. He knew the fiery Felipe wouldn't be content to let the thing lie as it was now. And he knew Lodge knew it.

But Felipe never got a chance to carry the fight any further. He didn't show up next afternoon at the end of the drive. When the day's catch of cattle had been put in the canyon, the cowboys went back to look for him.

They found his riderless horse first, with rope missing from the saddle. A little later they found Felipe at the bottom of a washout. His neck was broken. There were rope burns on his battered and torn body.

"Dabbed a loop on something and then got tangled up in the rope," Snort Shanks surmised.

They took Felipe back to camp and dug a grave for him at the edge of the canyon. Stockton silently stood beside Wade as the last dirt was being shoveled into the hole.

"Interest on that loan is beginning to run pretty high," Wade commented quietly.

When the job was done, he called the crew around him. "The cattle have got to get used to being herded if we're going to have any luck driving them out of here. This is as good a time as any to start. We'll set up guard shifts now, and we'll start night-herding them."

Agnew grunted. The reddish light of the campfire reflected from the bandage on his cheek. "They can't get away long's they're in that canyon. Looks to me like you're just trying to give us some extra work."

Wade said, "As long as I'm bossing this outfit, you'll do what I tell you and you'll shut up about it."

Agnew grumbled, "Maybe you won't be boss very long."

The cowboys started scouting over the ground they had worked before. There were still a number of outlawed cattle there that would have to be roped and dragged down out of the hills. Wade didn't want to move camp until the area had been cleaned up.

For three days the cowboys scouted and brought down cattle that had gotten away from them. The going was much slower now, for a cowboy might spend a couple of hours catching just one steer or one tough old bull.

In some cases they would tie a gentler animal to the wild one, slowing the fire-eater down so he could be handled. Some of the outlaws had to be roped and thrown and wooden clogs tied to a foreleg. Then every time the animal tried to run away, the long clog would get tangled with his feet and throw him for a loop.

By the end of the second day they had picked up only about forty cattle. Wade was beginning to think about the long drive to the railroad.

The afternoon of the third day he almost met a fate similar to Felipe's. Wade was working his way along a steep mountainside that had a sheer drop off the edge of the trail. Corey Milholland trailed along behind him.

Corey had almost quit trying to make a hand after Felipe's death. When the chase got perilous, he would hold up and pick his way along. He let many an animal get away.

It didn't do Wade any good to talk to him. He had about decided to start leaving Milholland in camp, to help the cook.

The first sign he had of danger was the sound of rock striking rock. Jerking his head up, he saw big rocks bouncing down the mountainside.

"Get back, Milholland!" he yelled. He spurred hard, trying to get away from the rocks.

He was almost in the clear when his horse stumbled and went to its knees. Before Wade could move, a rock the size of a washtub slammed into the animal's shoulder and knocked him off the trail.

Wade choked off a cry of panic as he felt himself falling over the sheer edge. He grabbed at the shale and rocks as he slid. They broke his nails, tore his hands. Big rocks and little ones bounced off of him as he rolled, fell and slid.

But at last he stopped. He wasn't on any ledge. It

was merely a little jut in the steep slope. If he held still, he might hang onto it. If he tried to move, he would probably fall some more.

Fire burned a hundred places on his body. Pain lanced through him, seeming to pin him against the slope. His hat was gone. His shirt was ripped to shreds. Only his leather chaps had kept his legs from being torn as his arms were. Sweat burned into his skinned face as he slowly lifted his head and looked upward toward the trail. He figured he had slid thirty or forty feet.

In a moment the frightened Corey Milholland peered over the edge. Relief swelled over his face as he saw that Wade was still alive.

"Hang on," he called. "I'll pitch you my rope."

But the rope didn't reach. The end of it dangled a good ten feet above Wade's head.

Wade tried to inch up toward it, but he slipped and dropped another couple of feet down the slope.

It was all up to Milholland now. Wade wouldn't have given a plugged nickel for his chances in the cowpuncher's hands. He could see doubt and fear play across the man's face. Finally Milholland spoke.

"I'll try to work down there to where the rope will reach you. There's a big rock I may be able to tie on to."

Hugging the slope, Wade could feel his heart hammering while Milholland carefully worked down off the trail. He closed his eyes once as the puncher's foot slipped and a shower of dirt and pebbles came down. He expected to feel Corey's body slam into his and knock both of them on down the slope.

But somehow Milholland caught himself. In a few moments he had worked down to where a large rock stuck up out of the slope. He tied his end of the rope to it, then pitched the other end of it to Wade.

Reaching out for it, Wade felt himself slip. He grabbed the rope just as he started to slide on down it. Hitting the end of the rope sent new pain tearing through him. But the rope held, and Wade held to it.

Painfully he started working upward, hand over hand. It seemed it took him an hour to get up to the rock. Milholland pulled him up to its temporary safety, then untied the rope.

"I'll climb back up to the trail and pitch you the rope again," he said. "In your shape you couldn't climb that slope any other way."

Milholland went up, then helped Wade work on back to the trail.

Wade sat there, panting, wincing at the pain and staring down at his dead horse far below.

Finally he looked up at Milholland. "For a week now, Milholland, I've been calling you a coward. I hope you'll let me take it back."

Wade shoved out his hand. Milholland took it.

Next day Wade was too stiff and sore to go chasing wild cattle with the rest of the crew. He decided it was time to begin hunting for a new trail to the railroad. He loaded a pack mule with enough supplies to last a week, then struck out northward. He took Corey Milholland with him.

There were only two directions the herd could go— west or north. The railroad swung up in a northerly direction when it reached a point about even with the ranch headquarters. To try getting to the road by the east would mean an extra hundred or hundred-fifty miles of driving over country as rough and violent as that in which the cattle ranged. The cowboys were sure to lose the biggest part of the herd in a stampede sooner or later.

To the south lay nothing but more rough country, and, ultimately, the Republic of Mexico. To the north was the desert he had ridden over between the ranch and town.

"We've tried that way before, a dozen times," said Milholland as they sat beside a water hole, resting the horses. "The desert always licks us. They'll stampede every time. First thing we know, most of the cattle are right back down here where they started from. We're left with a little handful, just enough to take on in and sell for what things the ranch can't do without."

He pointed to a cholla cactus. "It's them things as much as anything else that causes us trouble. A steer swings his tail, gets it tangled up in one of them chollas and stampedes the whole outfit. The stuff's like a jungle out yonder in the desert. There's no way of getting around it when you take the trail north."

Wade let his gaze range over the land to the west. Over there, long miles away, the great rim stretched as far as the eye could see. Its sheer walls jutted almost straight up from the floor of a valley in which a river moved slowly southward.

"Ever tried taking them over the rim, Corey, and moving them to a loading point farther west?"

Milholland shook his head. "Over that rim? It'd take a mountain climber, and a good one at that, just to get over it afoot in most places. Only way you'd ever get a herd of cattle over it would be to take them out one at a time on a pulley, like drawing water out of a well. There ain't anybody that foolish."

Wade couldn't take his eyes off the rim. "Ever tried it?"

"Never even been over there. You can tell from here it's impossible."

Wade still wondered. "How long would it take to move a herd to it from here?"

Milholland's eyes widened. "Five days. Maybe six. But I'm telling you, there ain't any use studying about it. It won't work."

Wade swung back into the saddle. "Just the same, Corey, we're riding over to have a look."

It was after sundown almost a week later when they got back to the roundup camp. Wade caught his breath up short as he saw Bess Henry standing beside the cook. Firelight reflected in her oval face. Her slender figure in full-length riding skirt was silhouetted brilliantly against the darkness.

Wade hoped for a smile from her, a word of greeting. He got only her level stare. Disappointed but not really surprised, he tipped his hat and rode his horse on out to unsaddle him.

As Wade walked back into the firelight, Price Stockton looked up from his supper plate.

"We'd about decided you weren't coming back, Massey."

Lodge Agnew stood with hands shoved into his waistband. His turbid brown eyes held something like laughter, but Wade knew there wasn't any humor in him. The cut on the man's cheek still showed through his whiskers. "Yeah, we figgered maybe that little avalanche the other day scared you off."

Wade had all but forgotten about the avalanche while he was busy looking for a new trail. The memory of it came back to him and sent a little chill running up his back.

He stared at Agnew's dark, stubbled, cowardly face. A sudden suspicion bobbed up for the first time and became almost a certainty with him. It hadn't been cattle that had started the rock slide.

Agnew. Wade was sure the man wouldn't shoot him in the back so long as there were other cowhands around. But what if he got another chance to make it look like an accident?

Wade tried to shake off the chill by turning away from Agnew and facing Bess Henry. He touched his hat brim again and felt a thrill running through him.

"You're a long way from headquarters, Mrs. Henry."

"They're half my cattle, Mr. Massey," she replied flatly. "At least they are till they reach the railroad."

He felt his cheeks turn warm and hoped the firelight would hide the color he knew flooded his face.

It wouldn't pay to try to talk to her. She would have a sharp answer every time. He wished that, for once, she would again be like she had been that first day he had seen her. But he knew she wouldn't. Not anymore.

He turned to Price Stockton. "How's the gather been since I've been gone?"

"Pretty short. Twenty or thirty a day. Couple of times we lost them all."

Wade rubbed his chin and looked out beyond the firelight. "We ought to have thirteen or fourteen hundred in that canyon. That's enough for one drive. Tomorrow we'll cut out what we don't want to take. The next day we head for the railroad."

Squatting on his heels, Price Stockton grinned crookedly and sipped at his coffee. "We won't get across the desert with them. We'll hit that cholla country and in two days most of them will be right back here where they started from."

"No they won't," Wade said. "We're not going through the cholla. We're taking them over the rim."

Stockton spilled half his coffee as he jumped to his

feet. The rest of the camp was suddenly quiet as an Indian graveyard.

"You're crazy," Stockton thundered. "Nobody's ever taken cattle up that rock. Nobody ever will."

Wade had expected this, but he couldn't hold down the tremor of excitement that rippled through him. Hands on his hips, he said, "I'm going to, Stockton."

Stockton pitched the rest of his coffee into the fire and dropped the cup. The coals hissed. The ranchman swung his angry eyes back at Wade.

"They're still our herd, Massey. I'm not letting you lose a thousand head of cattle for us."

Wade noted the way Stockton's right hand inched down toward his gun butt. A cold shiver passed through him as he moved his own hand into place.

"I'm taking those cattle over the rim," he repeated. "With you or without you."

He could see in Stockton's face the debate that went on behind the man's eyes. A hot mixture of hatred, distrust and fear. But finally the ranchman dropped his hand away from the gun. Wade could hear sharp breaths sucked in by half a dozen men. His own heart had picked up its beat.

"It's your hand this time, Massey," Stockton breathed. "But I'm warning you now. If you lose that herd for us, I'll kill you."

In his own heart Wade could feel the desperation that must be gripping Stockton as the man turned and walked out away from the firelight to hold solitary council. He couldn't help sympathizing with him.

He turned and found Bess Henry's level eyes boring into him. "Tell me, Massey. Just what are you getting out of this?"

He bit his lip hard, then answered, "Two hundred dollars a month."

That took her by surprise. But the doubt quickly returned to her face. "I don't believe you ever intend for these cattle to reach the bank, Massey. I just wish I knew what you've got up your sleeve."

So that was it! It wasn't just that he was going to take most of their cattle—maybe all of them—to pay a loan. They had a suspicion that somehow he meant to take the herd for himself, and leave them just as deeply in debt as they had been before.

"You're wrong, Mrs. Henry," he said quietly. "These cattle are going to reach market, and they're going to apply against your debt. I promise you."

She stared at him a long moment. He thought he could see her eyes soften a little, and he knew it must be his imagination. But even the thought made his heart pump faster.

"I wish I could believe you," she said. She turned away from him and walked out toward her brother.

They bunched the cattle in the back side of the canyon. Wade and Price Stockton rode into the herd and started cutting the cattle that weren't to make the trip—cows with calves and the best of the young cows. These, and others like them in bunches to be rounded up later, might form the nucleus of a new herd for the Rafter T. Might, if enough other cattle could be taken out to liquidate the debt.

But if there were heavy losses on the trail—and Wade feared there would be—these cattle would probably have to be rounded up again and taken to market anyway. Then there would be no nucleus, there would be only a violent country of rock and cactus, jagged cliffs and rimrocks—and some broken dreams.

Wade knew these thoughts were eating at Stockton, too. He could feel the ranchman's silent hostility whenever the two of them chanced to come close together in the herd.

By midafternoon about two hundred and fifty cattle had been cut out to stay a while longer. The rest, older cows, steers and outlawed bulls, were kept in a bunch. A thousand head, more or less. Not a big herd, as trail herds went. But with them would go the fate of the Rafter T.

As the little bunch of cows and calves was being pushed out of the canyon to scatter back into the hills, Wade managed to ride up beside Bess Henry.

"It's a pretty long ride back to headquarters, Mrs. Henry. Don't you think you better get started? It's liable to be dark before you get home."

She looked directly into his face. He could see a firmness in her eyes, but there was no longer any sign of hatred.

"I'm not going home. I'm staying with my cattle."

A dozen protests immediately rose up in him, but he choked them off.

"It's going to be a long, hard drive. It's liable to be dangerous, too," he spoke quietly. She kept looking into his eyes, to his discomfort. "They're still my cattle."

The crew was up long before daylight. As the first streaks of light began to play above the broken mountains to the east, cowboy yells rose in the sharp morning air, and the herd began moving uncertainly.

By the time the sun had risen to throw its light down across the canyon rims, a long, thin line of cattle was stringing through the rocky, broken hills. The point was moving westward. And it was moving fast.

"Keep crowding them," Wade ordered the crew. "We've got too much wild stock in here to trail-break them easy. The first couple or three days have got to be hard and fast."

It was a fearsome land to take cattle through. There were sheer canyon rims to skirt, steep washouts to cross. Always wherever the terrain was the roughest, some of the mossyhorns would make their break.

A few got away. Most of them came back at the end of a rope, bracing their legs vainly against the power of the horses that dragged them in. It was fearsome, sure. But it wasn't impossible.

Wade wore down one horse after another, the way he kept riding back and forth, up and down the herd, keeping the cowboys pushing, helping drag back runaways, going out in front of the point men to find the best way through.

Occasionally he would pass Bess Henry, riding at one side of the herd, about halfway back from the point. She worked as hard as any of her cowboys.

Once he brought back a steer that bolted out from behind her, and she smiled at him. It was the first time she'd smiled at him since that day he had ridden into headquarters. She caught herself, and the smile faded quickly. But at least there had been one for a moment. Maybe later there would be others.

Toward nightfall Wade found a small box canyon. There was a good chance they would stampede tonight, if anything happened to set them off. In a box canyon, though, the chance of stopping them was much better. They wouldn't run far up a steep canyon slope.

But the herd was thirsty. It had watered only once, shortly before noon. Now cattle's tongues lolled out, and they walked with heads low.

Wade found water at the foot of a canyon. The walls were steep, but not too steep to climb. It was no trouble getting the cattle down to the water. But it took until dark to fight them up the other side after they had drunk their fill.

Finally the herd was bunched in the box canyon and the cook started unpacking his mules. The cattle started bedding down fairly easily. They were tired.

Lodge Agnew flopped down on the ground and sighed heavily. "I'm going to lay right here till daylight. There ain't nobody going to get me up."

Wearily Wade walked up beside Agnew. "I will, Lodge. We're standing a double guard tonight."

Wade felt the eyes of the crew swinging around to him.

Agnew raised up onto one shoulder. "Hell, Massey, this bunch is wore out. We got to have rest."

Wade knew. He was having a little trouble staying on his feet. "I'll be right out there with you. That herd's still not trail-broke, Lodge. I'd give you odds it stampedes. We've got to be ready to stop it."

Agnew's dust-reddened eyes smoldered. "You're not getting me out for no double guard, Massey. You better not try."

Wade looked at the regular Stockton hands. From their faces he could tell they felt the same way. He listened a moment to the quiet stir of the cattle. He wasn't going to lose that herd now because men wanted to sleep.

"You'll stand your guard, Lodge," he declared, "if I've got to tie a rope around your feet and drag you out there. That goes for everybody else."

He could feel the hostility of the Stockton men, even where he couldn't see their faces. But every man rolled out and stood his guard duty that night. Even Lodge Agnew. And the herd didn't run.

It was a sleepy group of cowboys who huddled

around the cook fire for a silent breakfast the next morning. Everyone had stood guard but the cook and Bess Henry. By tradition the cook was exempt from that job. And by tradition Bess Henry should not have been with the herd in the first place.

Wade helped her mount her horse. He noticed how stiffly she swung up onto her sidesaddle. She was as tired as the rest, maybe more.

"It's still just a short day's ride back to headquarters when you haven't got any cattle to slow you up," he said. "Why don't you go home?"

She shook her head. "I'm beginning to think you're going to make it to market after all, Massey," she answered quietly. There was no longer any hostility in her eyes. "I want to stay and see."

Again the herd snaked out toward the west. There wasn't any trail. Wade had to make one—Wade and the point men. As in the day before, he worked back and forth down the line, pushing men and pushing cattle.

They were tired, but they would have to get a lot tireder. He was going to walk the legs off this herd if he had to, to keep them from stampeding and getting away at night.

Today fewer cattle tried to break out. Of those that tried, all but one were brought back.

There wasn't any box canyon that night. The cattle were bunched in a valley along a dry creek bed, where they could run either of two ways. But they were tired. Wade had hopes they wouldn't stampede.

The sun sank below the bald rim. Wade found the rim holding his gaze more and more now. It looked a lot closer than it had back yonder at the roundup ground. But it appeared even more formidable.

Wade saw Stockton looking at it, too. In the ranchman's eyes were doubt and dread. And as he turned to glance briefly toward Wade, the younger man could see something else there, too, the same grim warning Stockton had voiced before the drive began.

A full moon came up that night. In its gray light the rocky hills softened and took on beauty. There was something in them now he hadn't felt before. A grandeur, and even a peace.

But the peace didn't last long. Even though the herd was tired, it didn't bed down the way it should have. Many of the cattle stayed on their feet, milling around aimlessly. There wasn't anything Wade could put his finger on, but there was a tension in the herd, like a metal wagon spring bent back almost to the breaking point.

He never knew what started it. Maybe a steer stumbled and fell. Maybe one bull hooked at another and boogered the rest of the herd. Whatever it was, it made the cattle jump to their feet and take out in one hard, mad clatter of hooves.

Three or four cowboys yelled at once. Wade spurred his horse into a hard run. He heard a voice shouting at the cattle and realized with a start that it was his own.

They headed north down the dry creek bed. It was a wild run, a combination of panic and plain outlawry.

Wade spurred hard to get up to the lead, but he couldn't make it. There wouldn't be any turning them back now, not until they had run themselves down. They might go two or three miles. But they were tired. They couldn't keep it up too long.

Spurring along beside the stampede, he could feel his horse gradually slowing up. He could tell the cattle were slowing up, too, and stringing out farther and farther behind him. Near-panic edged through him as he watched the rough, tricky ground fly by under his horse's hooves. He realized it was bad business to look at the ground.

He didn't know how long it took before the cattle up front finally began to falter. He spurred a little harder and passed them. Gradually he slowed them down until he was able to turn them back and get them to milling.

Soon another cowboy joined him. It was one of Stockton's men. The puncher looked at him a moment before he finally grinned. "I thought I was doing some tall riding. But here I find you were ahead of me all the time. You're a real hand, Massey."

Wade enjoyed the warmth that went through him. It was the first time in days any Stockton hand except Milholland had tried to be friendly to him.

They started pushing the cattle back. Run down now, the cattle handled fairly well. Gradually as they moved back down the creek bed, the herd grew larger. Now and then a cowboy would join the bunch, bringing along some cattle he had managed to keep hold of.

It was hard to tell, even in the bright moonlight, but Wade thought he had most of the herd back already. In the morning they would scout and get the major part of the rest. Tired and sore, Wade couldn't help feeling pretty good about the situation.

But then Lodge Agnew joined the bunch, not far above the original bed grounds. He brought no cattle with him. A sudden suspicion grew in Wade, so strong he couldn't keep from voicing it.

"You didn't try to help us stop them, Lodge," he accused. "The hard run threw a booger into you, and you dropped out where nobody could see you. If we didn't need every man we've got, I'd run you right out of camp."

Agnew bristled. "You've been throwing it into me every chance you get, Massey. I'm warning you, one of these days you'll get a bullet put through you."

Wade wanted to knock Agnew right out of the saddle, but he gripped his saddle horn to keep from doing it. "If you do the shooting, Lodge, that bullet'll be in my back."

It took another hour to account for all the men. After sunup the cowboys started scouting up and down along the creek bed for scattered cattle. By noon the count was only about fifty head short.

"They'll be halfway back to their old stomping grounds by now," he told Snort Shanks. "They'll be around when we round up the second batch. Let's head out."

Shanks scratched his chin as he looked across the wide expanse of desert ahead, this side of the rim. "You told me it's still a three-day drive. You sure there's water?"

Wade nodded. "Milholland and I found one water hole when we came to look this country over. But there'll be some thirsty cattle before we get to it."

Shanks and one of the Stockton hands took the point again, and the herd strung out. There was still some devil in part of the cattle. Wade could only hope he could walk it out of them. He issued the same orders he had given out the first day of the drive. Push them hard. Wear them down.

It was a question, though, who wore down more—the cattle or the cowboys. As the afternoon dragged on and the sun began dipping low over the rim, Wade knew the fatigue that worked through the men. He could see it in their tired, dusty faces, their sun and wind-cracked lips, their reddened eyes. He could feel it right through to the marrow of his own bones. But they kept pushing until the moon rose.

When at last the herd was bunched and most of the cowboys pulled into camp, they unsaddled their horses and flopped wearily down on the ground. Some never even ate supper. They slept like the hard, immovable rocks of the rim.

Next morning they got up still tired and irritable. Words were short as the men saddled fresh horses and went back to the cattle. One puncher sleepily let his horse bump another rider's leg, and Wade thought he would have to drag the two men apart.

The cattle were getting thirsty, thirsty enough to set men to worrying. Wade thought about the water hole and hoped they wouldn't be many hours in reaching it.

But they didn't reach it. Before noon he struck out far ahead of the herd and tried to locate the place. But one canyon looked like another. One stretch of rock and sand and cactus was no different from a dozen others.

Wade rode his horse down, but he couldn't find water. Returning to the herd, he picked up a fresh horse and got Milholland to come along with him. All afternoon they searched. But the hole could not be found.

"Like I told you," Milholland explained apologetically, "I never had gotten over this far west before, and I didn't know the country. There ain't any landmarks hardly that a man can go by.

"The hole's out there someplace. We know that. But we could walk the cattle to death, trying to find it."

So they rode back to the herd.

Biting his dry, cracking lips, Wade reined up beside Snort Shanks. "Keep leading them, Snort, straight on for the rim. There won't be any water tonight."

Shanks's mouth dropped open. For the first time Wade could see silent disapproval in the cowhand's eyes.

"No water? But the whole outfit's dried up. How long have we got to go till we do get water?"

Wade lowered his head. "Till we get over the rim."

The lanky cowboy stared incredulously at him. He blinked his dust-bitten eyes and rubbed a big hand across his parched lips.

"All right. There ain't much we can do except try it. But if you know any prayers, you better dust them off."

When the word passed on down the line, it brought near-rebellion. Far behind him, Wade could see Lodge Agnew talking and gesturing bitterly with Price Stockton. Wade knew what he was up to. He was working on Stockton's anger and distrust.

Finally Stockton rode up toward Wade. Lodge followed a full length behind him. Bess Henry came along a little behind Agnew.

Stockton's eyes were blazing. "You can't do it, Massey. No telling what another couple of days without water might do to this herd, or to the men, for that matter."

Wade tried to stare him down. "What had you rather do?"

"Anything besides keep going this way, without water."

Wade rested his hand on his saddle horn and noticed it trembled a little. He was mad. "Maybe you'd like to turn back and call the whole thing a failure. Maybe you'd like to turn your whole herd over to the bank and let them worry about getting their money out of it. Maybe you'd like to leave this country and admit it whipped you."

He knew instantly that he had hit a soft spot there. Price Stockton might not be the best manager in the world, but he wasn't a quitter. And he wouldn't let anything make him out as one.

"I can last as long as you can, Massey. Longer. Keep driving, then, and be damned. But just remember what I told you. If this herd doesn't reach the railroad, you'll never get there either!"

Stockton jerked his horse around and headed back toward the men in a long trot. Agnew followed him. Wade knew Lodge was still talking to him, firing him up.

Bess Henry stayed. Wade sat his horse as she rode on up to him. Dust streaked her face, and her long hair strung out windblown beneath her wide hat brim. Her clothes were dusty and grimy, and ripped in places. But she was still pretty. She still stirred his blood just as she had the day he first rode up to the Rafter T.

"It looks like you need a friend, Massey."

He nodded and forced a thin smile. "I haven't got many around here right now."

She smiled back at him. "You have at least one. Me."

Wade's heart drummed. "You've changed a lot, then. You weren't having much to do with me."

Her smile faded, but there was earnestness in her blue eyes.

"You've worked hard these last few days. You've ridden hard and you've worried yourself sick. I'm getting more convinced all the time that you're not doing it for the bank. You're doing it for us. Price still thinks you're trying to beat us out of our cattle. But I think he's wrong. I'm betting on it."

Wade's eyes were on her face. Even with the dust, it was lovely to him. He wanted to reach out and touch her. He felt his own face coloring, and he swallowed hard.

"Thanks," he managed. "I'll try to see that you win your bet."

They bunched the cattle by moonlight, but they never did get them bedded down. The cattle were restless and irritable, hooking at each other and bawling. By the end of the first guard shift Wade knew there was no use trying to make them rest.

"They're all up and walking anyway. They might just as well be walking on toward the rim," he told Snort Shanks. "We'll get the men up and head them out again. The more we move, the sooner this outfit reaches water."

He thought he would have to whip half of the crew to get them up and into their saddles. Even the cook, who hadn't been saying much, acted as if he wanted to take the bottom of a skillet to Wade's head.

Price Stockton rode along stolidly with Lodge Agnew beside him. Even in the moonlight, where he couldn't see Stockton's face, Wade could feel the hatred that seethed through the ranchman. Wade could almost reach out and touch it.

Sunrise found the herd plodding along a good four or five miles from the bed ground. The cattle's heads bent low. Saliva dripped from their muzzles and trailed along the ground and in the short, dusty bunch grass. All up and down the line, proddy cattle hooked at one another, kept each other at a distance.

The hours dragged numbly on and on. Heat and thirst had settled over his weary body so long ago that Wade was hardly conscious of them anymore. He was hardly conscious of anything.

The horizon bobbed up and down as a vague, wavy, unreal picture he had seen in restless dreams. His tongue was stuck to the roof of his mouth. He couldn't have spoken if he had wanted to. Occasionally he snapped himself out of the trance long enough to see the other riders were going through the same thing.

It was a nightmare come true, a fiendish dream born of misery, a devilish ride he would never be able to remember clearly because his senses had dulled to a blunt edge. He was hardly conscious of the long, aching miles that dragged by, or of the fact that the sun had reached its peak and had started down again.

Suddenly there it was, right ahead of them. The enemy they had seen and dreaded so long. The rim!

Wade snapped himself out of his trance. He looked at the rim—tall, forbidding. His burning eyes eagerly scanned the bottom of it. Sure enough, there was the pile of rocks and the scattering of stunted desert brush that marked the trail he and Milholland had found.

They had missed the water hole. But they had come to the right place on the rim.

Wade motioned for the men to bunch the herd right below the rim. While the cattle were being pushed together, the cook rode up with his string of pack mules.

"How about it, Chili? Got enough water left to give every man a good long drink of it?"

The cook nodded. "That's just about all I got left. But what'll I fix supper with?"

Wade pointed his chin upward. "There's water a little piece over the rim."

The cook took a long look at the rim, Adam's apple bobbing as he stared, cut his eyes back to Wade, and they held a look that said the trail boss was crazy.

Punchers rode in one by one and watered out. Wade watched Bess Henry. She tried to sip the water in a ladylike manner. But she was too thirsty. She gulped it down like the men. Watching her, he enjoyed the easiness that gradually came back into her dusty, burned face.

He waited until every man in the outfit had had water before he dismounted, picked up the last canteen, and drank as much as he felt was safe. The thought came to him that water never got all the credit it was due. Right now he wouldn't trade a cupful of it for the stocks of every saloon in town.

He became conscious of Price Stockton standing in front of him, afoot. Lodge Agnew stood behind the man, and a little off to the left. He could feel the storm brewing up in Stockton.

"All right, Massey," the ranchman said acidly, "you've got them this far and almost killed them. What're you going to do now?"

Wade motioned toward the rim. "We're taking them on up."

Stockton scowled. "How? You going to fly?"

"There's a trail," Wade answered curtly. "Milholland and I found it, and rode up on it. It's rough. It's got some dangerous spots. But we can do it."

Lodge Agnew spoke up, and Wade began to see what he was up to. "It can't be done, Price. He brought your herd all the way out here to see it die, just the way I told you. Then you won't have a chance of squaring your debt. The bank'll take over. And our friend Massey will make himself a bankful of money—on your cattle."

Stockton's face was flushed dark. Wade could see that the heat and the thirst and the misery had gotten to him. He wasn't thinking straight. He was hardly thinking at all. He was taking Lodge's words and accepting them for truth.

"Lodge's right, Massey," Stockton breathed. His hand dropped down to the butt of his gun. "You've got us here where we can't help ourselves. We can't fly our cattle up the rim. We can't take them back. This herd is as good as dead. You've killed it. But you'll never live to make a nickel off of us!"

Stockton started to pull his gun. Wade dropped his own hand to his gun butt.

"I can beat you, Stockton," he said quickly. "Don't pull that gun. I don't want to kill you."

Stockton hesitated, but Wade knew from the wild look in his steely eyes that he wouldn't hesitate long. Wade took a step toward him, another, and another, talking all the while.

"It'd do you no good to kill me, Stockton. The bank'd send another man, and it'd send a sheriff, too. You'd lose your ranch and cattle, Stockton. They'd haul you in for murder."

The ranchman was still paused, the gun half out of his holster. Wade kept moving toward him. Three more steps. Two.

"They'd hang you, Stockton, hang you!"

With a wild curse the ranchman jerked the gun free. Wade jumped in and grabbed it with both hands. For a moment the two men wrestled, twisting and jerking at the pistol. It thundered suddenly. The sound hammered painfully in Wade's ears. The gunsmoke pinched his nostrils. But the bullet had gone wild.

He wrenched the gun from Stockton and pitched it away. He glimpsed Blackie Hadden picking it up. Then Stockton stepped in wildly, his big fists flailing.

Wade's anger, the misery and worry he had been through, cut loose in him then. It was no longer of importance that Stockton was Bess Henry's brother. It mattered only that Stockton had hated him, had made a tough job tougher every chance he had, had taken Wade's help and offered nothing but hostility in return.

Wade more than matched the ranchman's blows, giving two for every one he took. He was doing it automatically now, without thought, swinging savagely and without remorse.

Then the anger and bitterness was drained out of him, and Stockton lay on the ground, beaten.

Shame crept back into Wade as Bess Henry stepped up quickly and knelt beside her brother. She had a canteen in her hand. She poured water over a handkerchief and began touching it to Stockton's face.

"I'm sorry, Bess—Mrs. Henry," Wade said quietly. "I lost my head."

She looked up at him without any anger in her eyes. "You could've beaten him to the draw. Most any other man would've killed him. You kept your head long enough that you didn't do that. I'm grateful to you, Wade."

Lodge Agnew's voice cut into him like the sharp teeth of a saw. "You haven't heard the last of this, Massey. He'll get you yet."

Wade whirled on the man. The anger came roaring back to him.

"You caused this, Lodge. You've been digging at him, working him up to it, hoping he'd kill me so you wouldn't have to. You knew that when this job was done I'd take you back to New Mexico or kill you trying. You tried to kill me by rolling rocks down the slope of that hill and knocking me off the trail.

"And I don't think Felipe Sanchez died by any accident, either. I'd bet ten years of my life that you waylaid him, roped him out of the saddle and drug him to death. Then you tumbled him down that bank and made it look like he had got himself in a jackpot. I never would be able to prove it, Lodge. But I know!"

He paused, all the fury welling inside of him. "I wouldn't draw on Stockton awhile ago. But I'm itching to draw on you. Go on, you back-shooting coward. Pull that gun!

Agnew's face was almost purple with rage. His hands trembled as he started to reach for his gun. But he caught himself.

"Go on, Lodge," Wade shouted, his voice raw. "Draw it."

Agnew swallowed hard. He lifted his hands level with his chest. "I ain't drawing against you, Massey. I ain't no fool."

Rage seethed through Wade. He wished Agnew would try to draw. He wanted to beat him and pump slugs into the coward's body until his gun was empty and then stand over him and watch him die as Felipe had died.

But disappointment seeped into him. He knew Lodge wouldn't draw. He would kill if he could, but not this way. Not when the other man had an equal chance.

"All right, then," Wade breathed bitterly, "roll up what gear you got and move out. It doesn't matter where you go. When this job is done I'll come looking for you, Lodge. And I'm going to kill you."

Almost the entire crew was there, watching. Wade turned on them angrily. "We haven't got time to be standing around. We've got to get those cattle up over the rim and on to water tonight."

Even the foot of the trail looked tough. Wade was a little bit glad the cowboys couldn't see all of it. There were places ahead that would scare an eagle. It was an old Indian trail, ten to twenty feet wide in places, two feet wide in others.

"From the looks of it," he told Snort Shanks, "I'd say the Apaches used it for years before General Crook finally rounded them up. I'll bet white men have never found it."

Shanks eyed it like one fistfighter eyeing another. "Well, if the Apaches could take horses up it, we'll take cattle."

Snort's confidence put Wade back in the best humor he had been in since yesterday. "I hoped you'd see it that way. I'm letting you lead the first bunch up. I'll follow them with Ernesto."

They cut out about fifty head of the thirsty cattle, choosing mostly cows that weren't apt to give much trouble.

"You ready, Snort?" Wade asked. His heart was beginning to pound.

The cowboy looked up at the rim, swallowed, then glanced back at Wade with a nervous grin. "Nope, but I won't be ready at this time tomorrow, either. Let's go."

Corey Milholland reined in beside Wade. "Massey," he said quickly, "how about letting me ride along with you on that first bunch?"

Wade was puzzled. "Well, it's all right with me. But it's liable to be dangerous, going up with the first bunch. What do you want to do it for?"

Milholland's face was earnest. "You thought I was a coward, Massey. Well, I was. Maybe I still am. Pulling you back off that steep slope was something I had to do. There wasn't any way around it. But I want to see what I can do when I don't really have to. I want to see if I'm still a coward, or not."

Wade put his hand on the old cowboy's shoulder.

"You're no coward, Corey. But if you want to prove it, come along."

He signaled Ernesto Flores to stay behind. The vaquero grinned. He didn't mind that order.

Snort Shanks started up the tortuous, twisting trail as point man. Wade and Corey Milholland began pushing the thirsty, fighting cattle. The proddy ones didn't want to start the climb. Wade and Milholland had to whip them along with ropes to crowd them onto the trail. Once the cattle had started up, the two kept close behind them.

"Don't push too hard," Wade cautioned. "Let them pick their own pace."

It was a scary trail, every bit as boogery as he had thought it would be. In spots it wasn't a trail at all— just a place that cattle and horses could pick their way across in single file.

Up and up they toiled, barely inching along. Many times Wade's heart bobbed up into his throat as cattle lost their footing. They always got it back, though. All but one old cow. She didn't stop falling, bouncing and sliding until she was a hundred and fifty feet below. The life was gone from her long before she came to rest.

But there could be no turning back. Wade and Milholland kept pushing just hard enough that the cattle wouldn't stop.

Then they came to a place where rushing rainwater had gouged out a part of the trail. It had left a steep furrow that the cattle had to cross. One slip would carry them down the mountainside like timber in a log chute.

Snort Shanks paused only a moment. He stepped down and led his horse across, then he remounted while the cattle began picking their way over. Wade realized that he had hardly taken a breath from the time Snort had started until the last cow had made it.

He turned back to Milholland. "You ready to try it, Corey?" Milholland's face showed fear, but he managed a sick grin. "I made it before, when you and I came up here by ourselves." He swung down and walked across, leading his horse. Wade felt pride welling up in him.

At last they reached the top. Wearily Wade took the first deep breath he had taken since he had left the bottom of the rim. He turned and looked back down. He almost wished he hadn't.

The cattle lifted their heads, sniffed the air, then struck out in a long trot. Wade felt the faint breeze fan his face. Water! The cattle could smell it ahead.

"Let them go, Snort," he called. They followed the half mile or so to the water hole.

After Wade and Snort Shanks had watered their horses, they left Milholland to hold the first bunch of cattle and help hold up those that would come later. The look in Milholland's face as the two punchers left him filled Wade's heart with warmth. The old cowboy had made peace with the world.

There was joy on almost every face when Wade and Snort reached bottom.

"There's water at the top, plenty of water," Wade told them. "But get ready for a hard climb before you get to it."

They cut off another small bunch of cattle. Again Snort Shanks led out. At intervals of a few minutes, Wade would start a cowhand or two up with another bunch. So long as the cattle could see others of their kind ahead of them, they went up fairly well.

So it went, one little bunch after another, winding upward in single and double file like a string of red ants on the desert. He could hear cowboys above him, shouting and whistling, moving the starved cattle on.

At last the big herd had been whittled down to one little bunch. There was no one left but Wade, the cook, Price Stockton, Bess Henry, and the wrangler with the remuda of horses.

Stockton had regained his senses but was still shaky. Bess and the cook had helped him into his saddle. He leaned heavily over the saddle horn. Wade looked worriedly at him, then at the woman.

"Ready, Bess?"

She nodded. He started the last bunch of cattle up the trail. Bess followed, leading her brother's horse. The cook came next, his string of pack mules following along behind him. Last would be the remuda.

When they finally reached the washout, Wade turned to Bess Henry.

"Pretty dangerous here. You want me to lead Stockton's horse?"

Her face paled beneath the dust, but she shook her head. "I'll make it."

Wade felt proud of her spunk and went on, watching over his shoulder and holding his breath. She made it all right.

Far below, Wade could see the bodies of three or four cattle that hadn't made it. Bess Henry had not looked down. Wade was glad she hadn't.

When finally they reached the top, Bess rubbed her arm across her face and murmured, "Thank God."

Wade reached out and touched her hand. "It was tough. But it's not so bad the second time."

She smiled at him and gripped his hand. Warmth flooded him. She must have felt it, too. Her lips parted. Wade almost leaned forward and kissed her. He caught himself and leaned back in the saddle. He thought he could see a trace of disappointment in her eyes. Slowly she relaxed her hand.

But the beating of Wade's heart did not relax. He had to look away from her to slow his racing pulse. He had been in love with her for weeks now, but there had been a time he might have left, and, eventually, possibly forgotten her. That time was gone. He knew he would never forget her now. He might leave, but nothing would ever be the same.

Cattle were strung out for half a mile or more, running, bawling, madly heading for water. The cowboys were not trying to hold them. It was a sight to make a man glad he had been to hell and back, seeing the way the cattle and horses enjoyed that water.

Cows, steers and old bulls waded out to where they stood up to their bellies in water before they even stopped to drink. The unridden saddle horses drank their fill, and many of them laid down in the cool water, rolling and splashing.

The sight of it brought joy to Bess Henry's eyes. She seemed to shrug off much of the weariness. Watching her, Wade was glad.

He glanced at Price Stockton. The ranchman had stepped weakly down from his horse and loosened the cinch so the mount could drink in comfort. Now he stood watching the cattle and horses. The heavy lines in his face seemed to soften. The anger and hatred drained from his eyes. A silent peace began taking their place.

Wade looked a little way up and down the river. There was grass here, grass enough to hold the cattle for weeks. Lord knew they needed a rest. The cowboys needed it, too.

"We'll set up camp here, Chili," he told the cook. "Looks like we've found the promised land."

Next morning Wade found Bess Henry sitting her horse on the bank of the river, contentedly watching the herd scattered loosely out over a quarter-mile square of grass. A few hundred yards away sat Price Stockton, watching the same scene.

"How is he, Bess?" Wade asked. "How does he feel now that we've got the trip whipped?"

She smiled. "He's feeling all right, Wade." She reached out and touched his hand.

She continued, "He knows now that you were trying to help us. He's wanting to make some kind of amends. He'll tell you himself, Wade, when he's found the words he wants to say."

She looked warmly into Wade's face. Her eyes were soft and beautiful. "I owe you a lot too, Wade. I want to make it up, some way."

Wade gripped her hand, gripped it tight. "This is all the payment I'll ever need, Bess."

He reached for her, pulled her close to him. He kissed her and found her lips eager. He kept holding her tightly while she leaned her head against his shoulder. She murmured his name, so softly he could barely hear it.

Later he told her, "It's a good day's ride on in to town, when you don't have a lot of cattle to slow you up. I'm going in today. I want to check on the market and send a wire to Underwood & Watson.

"I'll try to locate a grass lease, too. These cattle ought to have a month or two of grazing before they're shipped. And we'll need to have grass waiting for the next bunch we bring up."

She held his hands and looked worriedly into his eyes. "Be careful, Wade. One of the boys told me that while he was on guard last night, he saw Lodge Agnew come by. He was heading for town, too. He won't give you an equal chance."

The morning of the third day, Wade started back from town. He was feeling good. He had found a fine grass lease with plenty of water. The market wasn't the best he had ever seen, but it was better than he had expected.

Best of all, he had a message in his pocket, and it held the Underwood & Watson signature. He had wired Oliver Underwood that he was bringing out the first bunch of Rafter T cattle. At present market prices, he had said, they should pay well over half of the interest due. Another herd like it would finish up the interest and pay off some of the principal.

Moreover, he had found a new trail to market and believed that from now on the Rafter T would be a good financial risk.

COLT SIZE

As dusk closed in, Tom Binford glanced at the little boy huddled beside him on the springy buckboard seat. A trace of tears shone in the kid's eyes again.

"We'll be home pretty quick, Danny," Tom said tenderly. "Your grandad'll be glad to see you. And there's a mighty pretty girl who'll fix a warm supper for us."

Looking down at the child's freckled face, Tom remembered the boy's mother, pretty Lora Summers. Tom had once thought he loved her, when he was a cowboy on her father's ranch; but that was before Barney Driscoll had swept her off her feet, and talked her into eloping with him. Only after the marriage had Lora realized Driscoll had wanted nothing but her inheritance.

Driscoll, though, had defeated his own purpose. After six years of living with his drunken cruelty and hatred, *Lora* had died.

She had left Driscoll nothing but a four- year-old son whom he didn't want.

Now, two years later, the boy's grandfather lay dying. Old Frank Summers had been smashed up by a runaway team which had wrecked his wagon on the crooked road that led to Rocky Wells.

Feebly he had asked Tom Binford to find his grandson and bring the lad to him.

After two weeks of following Driscoll's sign from one West Texas town to another, from saloon to saloon, Tom had found the boy, hungry and lonely, shut in a dingy room above a rank-smelling bar.

Angrily Tom had led the youngster down to where his father was sitting on the losing end of a poker game. Eyes blazing, Driscoll had risen drunkenly and slapped the youngster across the face.

"I told you to stay in your room!" he snarled. "Now git up there!"

Blinding anger had run through Tom, and he had piled into Driscoll, swinging, pounding, smashing. Then he had stood swaying over the half-conscious man, his bruised fists clenched.

"You're not fit to have a son!" he had said. "I'm takin' this boy back to his grandad. And if you ever come after him, I'll kill you!"

Maybe Tom hadn't realized then what he had said, but he knew now. When old Frank died the boy would inherit the ranch, and Barney Driscoll would be sure to try to take it for himself.

In the darkness that gathered ahead, Tom could see the ranch. A warmth rose in him as he thought of the way Della Graham would smile when the buckboard pulled in. Maybe she had finished her wedding dress while he had been gone.

But a doubt tugged at him as he considered her reaction to Danny. What would she think about their starting life together with a six-year-old foster son who belonged to neither of them—particularly when she remembered that Danny was the son of a woman Tom had once hoped to marry?

His heart was beating faster when he pulled up at the kitchen door of the frame ranch house. Della Graham stepped out, her blond hair shining like gold in the yellow light of the lamp behind her.

Tom climbed down off the buckboard and kissed her warmly. "How's Frank?" he asked her then. "I've got his grandson here."

Della sadly shook her head. "You're too late, Tom. He wanted to hold out till you got back. But he died a few hours ago." Tom couldn't say anything.

Della reached for the frightened boy. "Come on, fellow," she said tenderly. "We'll take care of you til your daddy comes to get you."

Quickly Tom found his voice. "His dad won't ever get him again. We're keepin' him!"

Della looked at him, her eyes wide with surprise. Tom carefully lifted Danny down, heat roiling within him. "See those bruises on his face? See how he trembles when you speak to him? You think I'll ever let him go back to a dad who'd treat him like that?"

Della's lips moved, but she said nothing. Still burning inside, Tom tried vainly to read what was in her eyes. Finally she spoke again.

"Then you'll likely have to fight, Tom. Old Frank told us he was leaving everything to this boy. You think the father won't try to get Danny back?"

In the days that followed the funeral, Danny seemed to lose his fear. He followed Tom, and Della's father, the retiring foreman, all over the ranch. He was interested in everything he found—the doggie calves in the milk pen, the half-wild cats that stayed in the barn, the chickens Della kept to furnish eggs for the ranch.

Tom grinned when he saw the youngster shine up his new brass-toed boots, or spied him proudly watching his shadow as he road along on the paint pony Tom had given him.

But Tom always watched the road from town— watched for Barney Driscoll. And he worried about Della. Though her father was about ready to leave the foreman's job to Tom and move to his own little ranch, Della hadn't said a word lately about the wedding. What if she didn't want to keep the boy?

The small ranch crew was having its noon meal one day when a buckboard came ratting up in front of the house. A moment later big Sheriff Will Yarby stepped through the door.

"Howdy, folks," he greeted pleasantly. "Sorry to bust up your dinner, but I got a little business." Another man walked in, and a sudden tautness went through Tom. It was Barney Driscoll!

"I've come to get my son," Driscoll announced grimly. He smelled strongly of liquor. "And I've made out charges against you, Binford, for kidnappin'."

Raw anger rising in him, Tom stood up and shoved his chair out of the way. He glanced at Danny, and saw the youngster shrink back, terror in his eyes.

"You're not taking him!" Tom declared hotly. Then he turned to the sheriff. "Will, you can't give this boy to him. All Driscoll wants is the ranch Frank Summers left. He'll mistreat Danny just like he always did!"

The lawman sadly shook his head. "Sorry, Tom. He's the boy's daddy, and I got a warrant for you. I got to take you in."

Driscoll smirked. "Maybe you'd like the inheritance for yourself, Binford. Or maybe its's because you were in love with Danny's mother!"

Tom choked back a hot reply and fought a blinding

urge to smash Driscoll's face. He shot a quick glance at Della, but her eyes betrayed nothing.

Yarby muttered angrily, "Shut up, Driscoll. Just because you got the law on your side is no excuse for you to blow off that way." Then the officer turned to the girl. "Get the boy's things, Della. And, Tom, you'll have to come with us."

Fury rode in Tom as he waited. Then he glanced at a shotgun propped up in the nearest corner. He caught Mort Graham's eyes and winked.

Moving swiftly, Tom shoved the table forward. Driscoll grunted and buckled as it hit him in the stomach. Tom grabbed up the shotgun. It wasn't loaded, he knew, but neither the sheriff nor Driscoll would want to take a chance.

Catching his breath, the lawman grinned. "Might's well sit down, Driscoll. Looks like we'll have a long wait."

Face livid with rage, Driscoll exploded, "You'll pay for this! All of you!"

Della' blue eyes were wide with excitement as she came out and gave the boy his small bag of belongings. Tom handed the shotgun to Della's father and signaled for Danny to follow him.

"Dump some food in a sack for us while we saddle up," he yelled back at Della. He grabbed Danny's hand and quickly led the boy to the barn. A moment later their horses were saddled and the rest of the mounts had been chased off into the pasture. Della came running out with a canteen and a sackful of food.

Her eyes glistened as she stopped in front of Tom. "Are you sure this is right?" she asked.

"Maybe not, but it's better'n lettin' Driscoll get the boy back," Tom replied. "We'll hole up in that old nester dugout on the south side of the ranch. And, Della, see if there isn't somethin' Judge Matlock can do."

From the house came frenzied sounds of a struggle. Tom quickly kissed Della, lifted Danny up into the saddle, and mounted.

Driscoll burst out of the kitchen door, a gun in his hand. Tom slapped Danny's pony on the rump and spurred away. He saw flame spout from Driscoll's gun and heard the buzz of the bullet. The gun spoke again, and Danny gave a startled cry. He dropped his bag and swayed over the saddle horn.

Dry-lipped, Tom caught the boy and held him in the saddle as he spurred on toward the protecting line of brush. Panic surged through him as he saw Danny's face whiten, and felt warm, sticky blood on the boy's sleeve.

He knew the bullet hadn't been meant for the boy, but he swore bitterly against any man who would be so careless with his son's life.

Moments later, in the protection of the thick mesquite, Tom pulled up and dismounted. He lifted the frightened youngster out of the saddle and tore open his sleeve. The bullet had passed through without touching the bone—but Tom knew the boy would soon be sick from shock.

When the wound was bandaged, he put Danny back onto the saddle and headed for the dugout. The sun was low in the west when he lifted the weakened lad down again and carried him into the dark, musty old dwelling. Tenderly he put Danny on a cot.

Danny's forehead was hot, and his eyes were a little glazed. Shock had sapped his strength.

Anxiety was like drying rawhide around Tom's

heart and he built a fire to boil some water. The youngster never whimpered as Tom carefully cleansed the
wound.

It was a long, painful night for Tom as he sat on the
edge of the cot, watching the boy's chest in its faint,
irregular heave and fall. Time and again he felt the
warm forehead, and swore softly when he caught himself dozing off.

Shortly after dawn, Danny awakened and tried to
sit up. But he sank back with a weak cry.

"Where's Della?" he asked softly. "Why isn't she
here?"

Tom gripped the boy's hand.

"We'll see her before long," he assured Danny, and
felt pleasure when the youngster smiled. Then he took
the bandage off.

A new fear assailed him—the wound was turning
blue!

Sick at heart, Tom bandaged the arm again, and
walked to the low door of the dugout. The boy had
to have a doctor, but the minute they showed up in
town . . .

Slowly he walked back and looked down at the
boy's white face. If they stayed here, the youngster
might die. If they went to town, Tom would be shoved
into jail and Danny given back to Driscoll.

Tom fought the tightness which clutched at his
throat. There wasn't any choice. They had to go to
town!

He turned the paint pony loose and held Danny in
front of him on the saddle as they headed for Rocky
Wells. It seemed hours before they turned into the
crooked, winding road that was the last lap of the way.

Sleepiness stung Tom's eyes, but he held grimly onto
the boy. They passed the spot where the runaway team

had piled up old Frank Summers' wagon. Then the town of Rocky Wells pushed up out of the rolling rangeland. Riding along the dirt street toward the doctor's house, Tom sadly looked down at the white, young face which lay against his chest.

This is the end of the line for us as a team, Danny, he thought grimly.

Then he carried Danny into the house and the baldish, gray-bearded doctor examined the boy's arm.

"Good thing you brought him in, Tom," the medical man said. "He might've gotten gangrene if he had stayed in that dugout. You used good sense, son."

A few minutes later Sheriff Will Yarby walked in. "I heard you'd come back, Tom. Guess you know I've got to arrest you," he said apologetically.

Tom nodded. "Let's go, Will." Little Danny raised himself up on his good arm. "Tom," he said weakly, "you're not gonna leave me, are you?"

The heavyset sheriff stood uncertainly, his face softening. He studiously rubbed the back of his neck. Then he said, "No sonny, he's not goin' any place."

Softly he said to Tom, "I'll leave you with him, if you promise not to try running off again."

Tom agreed.

Will Yarby paused in the doorway. "I'll send Della over right away. I'll have to bring Driscoll over, too. Don't you go losin' your head."

In a few minutes Della came running in and threw herself into Tom's arms "Oh, Tom," she cried, "why did you come back? You haven't a chance now."

"I had to," he told her quietly. "Danny's hurt."

Her face went pale, and she stepped quickly to the bed where the boy lay. She took his hand and smiled weakly down at him as the lad opened his eyes.

"How bad is it?" she asked the doctor.

Tom moved to her and put an around her shoulder. The doctor told her the boy would be all right, if given good care. Tom felt a warm glow inside as he saw the way she looked down at Danny. She did love him, he was sure.

The door swung open and Driscoll stalked in belligerently, followed by Sheriff Yarby and Judge Matlock. Driscoll reeked of whisky, and his bloodshot eyes were full of hatred.

"So you brought him back," he snarled. "Try and get that ranch away from me, will *you* ? I'll have you sent to the pen for so long you'll never get out!"

He turned to the physician and demanded, "Wrap that kid up. I'm takin' him out of here!"

Alarmed, the doctor protested, "He's in no shape to travel. He's got to stay here and rest."

Driscoll cursed. "Stay here so they can steal him again, you mean? They think if they can keep the kid they'll get the ranch. Now bundle him up! I got a buckboard outside."

Angrily Tom stepped toward Driscoll, fists clenched. The sheriff grabbed his arm. "Hold it, Tom. You're under arrest, you know."

Judge Matlock reached inside his huge coat and pulled out a document. "Just a minute, all of you. Since there seems to be so much worry about who's to get the ranch," he said, looking coldly at Driscoll, "maybe I'd better read Frank Summers' will again."

Della's hands gripped Tom's arm as the judge read aloud. Tom caught the jurist's emphasis on the part which said Judge Matlock was named administrator of the estate.

The big man cleared his throat. "Now, in view of the fact that I haven't time to run such a ranch myself, I'll have to appoint someone to manage it for the boy, in a regular foreman's capacity."

Driscoll grinned. "That's me. I'm his father."

The judge glared at him. "It'll be whomever I choose to name. A few minutes ago you were willing to risk the boy's life to carry him away from here, to make sure of getting the ranch. That shows you have no interest in the lad's own welfare.

"I know someone else who loves the boy, though, loves him enough to risk losing everything he has to save the youngster's life."

The judge turned to Tom. "Tom, I'm appointing you to manage Frank Summers' estate."

Tom squeezed Della's hands and looked happily at Danny.

"It's a trick!" bawled Driscoll, his face crimson. "You're tryin' to cheat me out of what's mine, but it won't work!"

In a flash he reached under his coat and snaked out a six-gun.

"As long as you don't have the kid you can't take the ranch. And the brat's goin' with me!"

His bloodshot eyes were ablaze, and his gun hand trembled dangerously from the effects of his drinking. Keeping everyone covered, he stepped back to the bed. Danny whimpered with pain as his father picked him up.

"The man is drunk—crazy mad!" Tom breathed, a million fires blazing within him.

Backing out the door, Driscoll heaved the youngster onto the buckboard seat. Climbing up, he flipped the reins, and the team surged forward. The buckboard veered crazily and skidded around a corner on two wheels.

"He doesn't even know where he's goin'!" Tom shouted excitedly. "He's headed for the road that killed Frank Summers!"

His heart thumping, Tom dashed for his horse, swung into the saddle, and spurred after Driscoll. Wind whipped in his face as he slowly closed up the distance between him and the buckboard. Then Driscoll was on the treacherous, crooked road. The buckboard bounced, skidded, and cut corners.

A prayer was on Tom's lips as he watched Driscoll whipping the team for even more speed. He had to get Danny off that buckboard before Driscoll killed them both.

Bending low over the saddle horn, he spurred again and again. Dust boiling up from the bouncing vehicle stung his eyes, Driscoll started shooting at him. Heart pounding dully, Tom heard the bullets zip by. Then the gun was empty, and Driscoll hurled it back at him.

Tom closed in, and finally pulled up alongside the racing buckboard. As he reached out to grab Danny off the seat, Driscoll cracked a whip at him. Tom smothered a cry of pain as the lash burned across his shoulders. Driscoll cursed and drew back for another swing

Quickly Tom caught Danny and pulled him off the buckboard. Face livid with fury, Driscoll tried to jerk the racing team around. They turned sharply. There was the rending, crushing sound of splintering wood as the buckboard's coupling pole snapped. The front wheels jerked loose, and the vehicle seemed to stand on its side a second.

Driscoll's cry was cut short as the buckboard heaved over and crashed down on him. Then there was only the sound of the spinning rear wheels, and the panicked team galloping away.

Danny began to cry. Tom carefully swung down and

put the lad on the ground. Dropping his reins, he trotted over to the wrecked buckboard—but there wasn't any use. It had fallen on Driscoll before his body had straightened out. His neck was broken.

His mouth dry from the choking dust, Tom turned and walked slowly back to the sobbing boy. He put his hands on Danny's thin shoulders and turned the lad around to face the back trail. A billowing cloud of dust showed where another buckboard was moving rapidly toward them.

"Everything'll be all right, Danny," Tom spoke gently, leading the boy forward. "We're goin' home to your new mother."

LAND WITH NO LAW

The hot July sun hammered down on the four riders as they slow-walked their mounts into the main street of Lofton, their shoulders slumped with weariness. Not a breath of wind stirred the manes of the scattering of horses hitched up and down the way, and dust raised by the plodding hooves hung listlessly in the dry air.

From the heat-dried adobes and the sun-darkened frame buildings, people moved out into the street to watch. This was a quiet afternoon, and the movement of the riders was quick to catch the eye. People saw the four horsemen first, and then their gaze dropped back to the fifth horse. It carried on its back a slack bundle wrapped in a dusty woolen blanket. The riders drew rein in front of the sheriff's office. One of them stepped down stiffly, so tired that it seemed he would fall to the ground. He turned back to the man behind him, and only then did it become apparent that this man's wrists were in handcuffs.

"All right, Nichols," said the sheriff, "you can get down."

Several men moved out hesitantly from the board-walk and looked at the bundle on the fifth horse. One of them asked worriedly, "Who is it, Mark? Who did they get?"

Sheriff Mark Truitt took a deep breath and leaned heavily against a hitching rail. His blue eyes were bloodshot from endless hours of riding without sleep, and from the bite of alkali. His face, although young, looked old now through a matting of black whiskers, grayed by a powdering of dust.

"Chip Tony," he said after a long moment. "They got Chip Tony."

The sheriff's smarting eyes moved along the rapidly gathering crowd and picked out a young cowboy. "Harley, I wish you'd go find Will Tony. Better take somebody with you, and break it easy. His sun rose and set on that brother of his."

Another man took the reins of the led horse and asked gravely, "Want me to take care of Chip for you, Mark?"

The sheriff nodded, and there was pain in his voice. "I wish you would."

He looked then to the two weary men who still sat their horses. "Homer, you and Joe put the horses up, then go get some sleep. I can handle it from here."

They nodded. One of them pulled his horse back. The other hesitated a moment. "Mark, get Doc Work-man to look at your head. That's a bad lick you got there."

"I'll be all right. You go get some rest."

Mark Truitt caught his prisoner's arm and motioned him toward the door of the combination office and jail. The prisoner, an unshaven cowboy in his mid-twenties, took a long look at the gathering crowd. Fear chilled his eyes.

There was no one in any of the three jail cells, not even a drunk sleeping one off. Truitt found one of the cell doors half open. He unlocked the handcuffs and motioned Nichols into the cell. He locked the heavy barred door with a key from his desk, then turned back toward the front porch.

More men were gathering, and soon there was a large crowd out front. Truitt knew he owed them some kind of explanation. He took off his hat and pitched it back against the wall. He stood in the doorway, one hand braced on the jamb to help steady himself against his bone-weariness.

"We didn't have any trouble finding the trail of the stolen cattle," he said. "We followed them south, into the brush. The thieves were getting close to the river, and we had to jump them quick or they'd be across the border. We thought we had them, but somehow everything just seemed to go wrong.

"They killed Chip, and they shot the horse from under me. We got one of them"—he nodded back toward the cell—"when Homer Brill shot his horse and it fell and pinned him down. We had to let the rest of them go. There was nothing else we could do."

An angry hum of conversation lifted to him as the crowd talked it out. Someone asked, "It was the Rankin brothers, wasn't it?"

Mark Truitt nodded. "Yes, it was the Rankins. We saw them—Edsel and Floyd both."

Some of the men slowly began to disperse then, but many of them stayed there, talking and gesturing sharply among themselves. Truitt caught the angry tone of the talk. He knew some of it was aimed at him.

"He got a good man killed, and he didn't even catch those cow thieves," he heard some say. "It's sure time for a new sheriff, I'm telling you."

"There'll be one," someone replied hotly, making sure he was loud enough for Truitt to hear. "Wait till the election's over tomorrow."

Mark Truitt hadn't thought about the election in two days. Now it came back to him. Turning, he saw the placard some nervy soul had tacked beside Truitt's own door: "Elect Dalton Krisman Sheriff." He let it stay there.

Truitt moved back into his office. He wanted to drop into the big chair at the desk, but he didn't allow himself that yet. He reached into a drawer at the bottom and took out a bottle and glass. He didn't use liquor much, but once in a while he felt the need of it.

He downed a stiff drink and then set the glass and bottle on his desk. He walked across to the washstand and poured the basin full from the tin pitcher. He splashed cool water over his dirty, bewhiskered face, rubbing hard with a wet rag to get some of the dirt off. Funny, he thought, how much it helped relieve a man's weariness just to wash his face. He was careful how he used the wet rag against the side of his head. An angry red place still remained where his head had struck the ground as his horse went down. It was tender to the touch, and it throbbed without letup.

Finished, he turned and found two men waiting. They were both cowmen. One was well into middle age, the other one not far from it. Both were gray from a life of hard work and worry.

"Mark," said old Sam Vernon, "we just heard. Is there anything we can do?"

The sheriff shook his head. "There's nothing anybody

can do now, Sam. We've lost Chip Tony, and one cow thief isn't much trade for a kid like Chip."

He glanced at the other man. "We didn't even get your cattle back, Luke." Luke Merchant was a wagon boss of the big LS outfit. He had been a Ranger once. Merchant's eyes kindled as he looked back into the cell where the prisoner sat, with his head in his hands.

"I wouldn't have brought him back alive."

Truitt eyed him evenly. "Yes you would, Luke."

The wagon boss dropped his gaze and made futile, angry gesture with his hands. "Yeah, I reckon I would." That was why he had quit the Rangers. He had come to hate guns and violence with a passion that a man can develop only after he has been through the hell of battle.

Sam Vernon added, "Bad break, Mark. Mighty bad. It looked for a while as if you weren't even going to get back for the election."

Truitt shrugged. "It might've been better if I hadn't."

"Krisman's really been making the rounds while you've been gone, Mark. The things he's been saying— and people are listening to him. It looks bad."

Truitt eased down into the chair and looked hopelessly at the papers piled up on the rolltop desk, papers and letters that needed attention he hadn't been able to give them. He rubbed his hand across his eyes, trying to ease the burning in them and knowing he couldn't. He wished they'd talk about something else besides the election. He was too tired to care about it, one way or the other.

"It was kind of a joke when Krisman first announced he was running for office," said Luke Merchant. "He never made much of a go of anything in his life; he just talked loud. I never took him seriously."

"We've got to take him seriously now," Sam Vernon

declared. "He has folks uneasy and beginning to want a change. Sometimes they'll make a big mistake, Mark, just because they get anxious for a new deal."

Truitt shrugged. "I'm too worn out to care. If they want Krisman in, they're welcome to him."

Sam Vernon argued, "He's not sheriff material, Mark. In the first little crisis he'll break to pieces. The Rankin boys would eat us up."

Truitt said bleakly, "Looks as if they're doing it now."

"You'll get them, Mark, if folks'll give you time. You've crowded them plenty. Without you they'd have been a lot worse. But if Krisman wins, it'll be an open invitation to them. The only thing that could stop them then would be vigilantes, and we don't want any of that."

All Mark wanted right now was to go in the back room, throw himself across the cot, and not wake up for a week. But he wondered if he could sleep, if the picture of Chip Tony's broken body wouldn't keep coming back to him.

"What're you going to do, Mark?" Sam Vernon pressed him. "Are you going to get out there and work for the vote?"

Truitt shook his head. "I'm going out there tomorrow and try to find somebody to go with me after the Rankins again."

Sam's eyes were black. "Then you'll lose, Mark. And the Rankins'll be rid of you."

A girl stood in the doorway, a tall, pretty girl with worry in her blue eyes. "Mark," she said in a strained voice, "are you all right?"

He looked at Betty Mulvane, and for a moment he couldn't speak. How much he had thought of her these last few days! He wanted to reach out to her and hold her close, but he couldn't with these men here to watch.

So he said simply, "I'm all right, Betty." He knew she understood everything else he wanted to say.

She took a step forward, conscious of the other two men but looking only at Mark. "They said you were wounded."

"Just a lick on the head. It doesn't amount to anything."

They stood looking at each other and Betty's eyes were soft. "T.C. said I should tell you he'll be over in a minute to watch the jail for you. Don't you want to come and eat?"

He shook his head. "Later, maybe. Right now I'm too tired to eat."

She nodded, her voice gentle. "All right, Mark. It'll be there, whenever you're ready."

He heard the clump of feet on the boardwalk and looked past Betty toward the door. Dalton Krisman marched in. Five or six others followed him. Krisman was a large man, good-looking in his way, still a few years shy of middle age.

He was a little soft, for he seldom did much hard work. He always dressed neatly, without ever quite overdoing it to the point that people would scoff at him behind his back. He could even be a likeable sort when he wanted to be. Right now he wasn't trying to make Mark Truitt like him.

Krisman took off his new hat and bowed toward Betty Mulvane. "Hello, Betty. I should have known you would be here."

She colored, for it was hard to know just how Krisman meant it.

Krisman turned then to Mark. "I understand you've

failed again, Mark." His voice was loud enough to carry to anyone who might be listening outside.

Mark Truitt eyed his opponent warily, knowing Krisman was playing this for political advantage but not knowing exactly what he could do about it.

"We didn't get the cattle back," Truitt conceded.

Krisman's voice sharpened. "Edsel and Floyd Rankin are still at large with a hundred and fifty head of LS cattle, and the blood of Chip Tony on their hands."

"We got one of their men," Truitt said stubbornly.

"Some cheap outlaw," Krisman said, glancing back to the cell. "Some worthless cowboy gone bad. The Rankins can find another just like him and not lose a day. One cheap outlaw to make up for the loss of a fine young man like Chip Tony? You've made a sorry mess of this, Mark Truitt."

Krisman was standing near the desk. He picked up the bottle and held it high, making a show of reading the label. He didn't say anything about it, but his inference was plain enough.

Truitt knew Krisman was deliberately baiting him in front of these men, but he couldn't prevent the flush of heat in his face. "You never had any use for Chip Tony while he was alive, Krisman, and he never had any use for you. I won't have you using his name in a cheap political move."

"Maybe you'd like to tell us just what happened," said Krisman.

Mark Truitt shook his head. It ached. It had ached ever since he had taken the fall. "Right now I'm tired, and I want to rest. I'll give a full report on it later."

He knew he was in no condition to stand up to Krisman's sharp tongue. Krisman could cut him to pieces.

"I think we're entitled to a report now. Here's Scott

Southall. He's delayed publication of his paper a whole day to see what report you'd bring in. I think readers all over the county will be interested."

The sheriff frowned, seeing the newspaper editor standing behind Krisman. Southall was a short, thin man who looked as if he would blow away in a good west wind. For some reason, Southall had never liked Truitt. Maybe it was because Truitt took people as they came, and he let them take him the same way.

He never was one to go out of his way to slap a man on the back and tell him a lot of things he didn't mean, the way Krisman did. And Mark Truitt hadn't spent much money in Southall's paper, either, advertising his candidacy. He hadn't had it to spend. But Krisman had.

Mark could visualize the story on the front page of Southall's weekly if he didn't take time now to tell what had happened:

"The sheriff refused to tell the people of Lofton County the details of the ill-starred chase after the notorious cattle thieves, the Rankin brothers, although candidate Krisman demanded such an explanation."

Southall would make it strong.

Truitt shrugged futilely and sat down at his desk. "All right, I'll tell you what happened. We trailed them south, deep into the brush. They had left a good trail. It didn't seem as if they cared much. They were going fast anyway, and it wasn't far to the river.

"We hoped they'd stop somewhere, and we could get them easy. Once they hit the river, there'd be nothing we could do, because they'd be over the border. Pretty soon we could tell they weren't going to stop, and we had to get them the best way we could.

"Something went wrong—we never did know just what. We thought we'd surprise them, but when we made the run at them, we found they were ready. The first shot knocked my horse out from under me. The others went on. That's when they killed Chip Tony."

Dalton Krisman's eyes widened with interest. "You mean, Truitt, that you weren't even with your men when the boy was killed?"

"The fall stunned me. I couldn't get up."

Krisman had his chance now. He pounced on it like a cat on a mouse. "Couldn't, Mark, or wouldn't? Could it be that you didn't want to, that it was the shooting that stunned you, not the fall? That you lay there, scared, and didn't lift a finger to help the others?"

Betty Mulvane exclaimed, "Krisman, you're a liar."

Trembling with anger, Mark Truitt pushed to his feet and eased Betty aside.

"You know better than that, Krisman."

"No," said Krisman, "I don't. It looks logical enough to me. You got yourself in a situation that was over your head, and you knew it. Even after your horse went down, you could have kept on shooting at the rustlers to help cover your men as they went in. But you didn't, Mark. You panicked. You lay there and left them to their fate. You let Chip Tony die!"

Truitt's fist came up so fast that Krisman never even saw it before it sent him reeling back into the thin arms of Scott Southall. The surprised editor couldn't hold him. Krisman went down heavily. Rising up on an elbow, he shook his head and rubbed his jaw. There was triumph in his eyes, and a trace of a grin on his torn lip. He had done even better than had expected.

"Now you fight, Mark, now that there's no one shooting at you. I won't cheapen myself by brawling in here. I'll do my fighting tomorrow, when the voters come in. And I'll beat you, Mark Truitt."

Scott Southall helped Krisman to his feet. Krisman

staggered out the door, his hand on his jaw so anyone who was outside would know what had happened. Suddenly he was a martyr to truth.

Southall jotted rapid notes on a folded sheet of paper. Presently he looked up, plainly pleased. "Anything else you'd care to say for the readers, Sheriff?"

"Get out!"

The editor scampered out. Sobered, Truitt stared after him. Sam Vernon stood sadly behind him, saying nothing. Truitt was angry with himself. He knew he had given Krisman what he came for, and probably a lot more. He gritted something under his breath, then turned and walked into the back room. He flopped down across the cot and dropped off into a fitful sleep.

Some movement in the room finally awakened him. He raised his head and saw that it was dark. He had slept through the afternoon, and into the early evening. A match flared. Betty Mulvane stood with the lamp chimney in one hand, the match in the other. She lit the lamp and put the chimney back on. Then she turned the wick down to where there was no smoke.

"Hello, Mark. I brought you some supper."

He swung his feet over the edge of the cot and sat up. His head still throbbed a bit, but was no longer as bad as it had been. "Thanks, Betty. I didn't intend to sleep so long."

The sleep had helped, though. He fingered his chin, feeling the scratch of whiskers and knowing he looked half outlaw.

"Don't apologize," she told him softly. "I don't care if the whiskers are a foot long, just so you're safe."

She pointed to the tray she had set down on a small table. "Now you come on and eat something. You need it. I told T.C. to go along and have his supper, that I'd wake you up."

He reached out, caught her hand, pulled her to him and kissed her.

She smiled and pulled back a little. "People are talking enough already."

He felt a stir of resentment. "Not about you, I hope."

She shrugged, keeping her smile even, though it somehow looked hollow. "When a single girl insists on staying in a town like this and running a cafe all by herself, feeding fifty men a day, they're bound to talk a little, I guess. And when she's seen so often in the company of the sheriff, and nothing is said about marriage, they'll talk a little more."

He clenched his fist. "They can say all they want to about me, Betty, but I won't stand for their talking about you."

"You can't very well throw them all in jail, Mark." She lost her smile then. "Sam Vernon didn't exaggerate. They're saying plenty about you, and it isn't good."

"Krisman?"

"He starts it, and it gets bigger as it goes along. The paper came out a while ago. Southall gave you both barrels."

She handed him the paper. "I wasn't going to give this to you till you'd finished your supper, but I guess you might as well read it."

In one column was a story about the battle with the Rankin brothers. In the adjoining column was a story about the incident in the sheriff's office. Truitt glanced at the large headlines.

SHERIFF A COWARD?
CANDIDATE KRISMAN CHARGES
TRUITT PANICKED, DID NOT FIGHT
SHERIFF ASSAULTS OPPONENT

Glancing down the story, he caught Betty Mulvane's name. "One Betty Mulvane, proprietress of an eating establishment here and constant companion of Sheriff Truitt, hurled epithets at candidate Krisman."

Truitt threw the paper down. He felt himself trapped. What he wanted more than anything else was to pick up both Krisman and Southall bodily and throw them in the creek. But he knew he couldn't do it.

Betty said, "Don't let it worry you. Southall will be in the cafe someday, and I'll drop a little lye soap in his coffee." She was smiling again, and she managed to coax a little smile from him. "Now eat your supper."

Mark Truitt watched her as he ate supper and sipped his coffee. She was a pretty girl, and maybe that was what caused most of the talk, when you really came right down to it. When a girl looked like Betty Mulvane, it seemed as if folks just couldn't leave her alone.

In the lamplight her hair seemed almost red, but in reality it was brown. She kept it combed back tightly and rolled up in a bun, so it was out of her way. Truitt had never seen her let it down, but he imagined it must reach nearly to her waist.

There was comfort in sitting here like this, close to Betty, not thinking for the moment about anything else, or anybody else. They were a pair, Mark Truitt and Betty Mulvane. Neither one had any family, any place they could really call home. Maybe that was why they had been drawn together in the beginning.

What she'd just mentioned, that nothing had been said about marriage, had set him thinking. He'd done a lot of thinking about it of late. He had meant to ask her—had really wanted to ask her—but he didn't have much to offer. The only things of value he owned were two saddle horses and a gold watch. He had a little money in the bank, but it wouldn't go far in setting up a business. Or in setting up housekeeping, for that matter.

He didn't want to ask her until he had something to show. And from the way things were going, that might be an awfully long time. There was something else, too— the Rankin brothers. Until they were out of the way, he did not know what might happen, when he might ride out and not come back. He didn't want to leave a wife behind to the agony of a wait that would never end.

T.C. stepped in through the front door and went on to the back room. Rail thin and getting along in years, he limped heavily. Rheumatism had knocked him out of a saddle job and set him afoot, and now about all he could do was tend the jail.

Now T.C. was excited. "Mark," he said, "some of the boys down at the Big Chance are getting likkered up. There's talk of taking your prisoner out and hanging him."

"Serious talk?"

"Drunk talk. It could get serious."

Mark frowned. "Who's in on it?"

"Some of the cowboys. Most of them are friends of Chip Tony's, or Will's."

"Is Will Tony over there?"

T.C. nodded. "He's sitting in a corner by himself. He's been there all evening, they say, drinking alone. He wasn't taking part in the lynch talk, as far as I could tell. But he's a man who can pack a lot of hate. I reckon that if they came he'd come with them."

Mark Truitt stood up, reached for his gun belt, and

buckled it on. "You'd better get along. Betty. I'm going over to try to clamp the lid on it. If I don't get it done, this won't be any place for you."

"Mark," she said anxiously, "don't take any chances. He's not worth it."

"He's my prisoner. If he were Edsel Rankin himself, it would be my duty to protect him."

He unlocked the gun case and checked the rifles there. The best thing in a situation like this was a good shotgun, and there were two in the case. He broke them open to make sure they were loaded.

"Grab you one of these, T.C., and keep it in your hands. Stay just inside the front door. The other one's for me, if I come back needing it."

T.C. gulped. "Think you will, Mark?"

"I hope not. I'm going to try to stop it right where it's started."

He cast a quick glance at the prisoner. Nichols was pretty much an ordinary cowboy, in appearance. There was nothing about him to stamp him as an outlaw, the way there was with some of them. He probably was just a weak-willed man who had wandered into out-lawry with empty pockets and had stayed at it because he got spoiled by the easy money.

Nichols was watching them, his face drawn with worry.

"I'll do what I can," Mark told him.

Nichols's voice was shaky. "Damn the Rankins, any-way. They could have come back and gotten me. They just let me lie there and get caught. It's them these fell-ers really want to hang, not me."

Mark Truitt could hear the angry voices before he got to the wide-open front door of the Big Chance Bar. They were loud voices, calling for the blood of the out-law in the jail, the one who had helped kill Chip Tony.

It was the liquor talking, the sheriff knew. Deep down, the men wanted to do it, but there was something—maybe fear, maybe guilt—that held them back. So they went to the bottle to drown that fear, or that guilt. Now they were getting dangerous, for their half drunkenness left nothing to hold them back.

Mark Truitt stopped just inside the door. One by one, men saw him, and the sharp talk frazzled out to silence. Truitt studied the faces, trying to decide who the leaders were, whether any leaders had yet developed.

"I hear you boys are talking about taking my prisoner," he said evenly. "That kind of talk will get you in trouble. I want it stopped."

A belligerent cowboy with a freckled face took a step forward. "Maybe you think you can stop it."

"I can, and I will. I'll do it peacefully, if I can. If that won't work, I'll do it some other way. But I'll do it."

"There are too many of us here," the freckled one said. "If we made a move, you wouldn't try to stop us, any more than you tried to stop the Rankins when they killed Chip Tony."

The cowboy began to edge forward. Mark Truitt knew that if this one hadn't been a ringleader up to now, he had just declared himself one. "Stop it right there, Speck," Mark said. "I don't want to hurt you."

"You're not going to hurt me, Sheriff. You're yellow. You lay down on Chip. You won't try to stop me."

He kept coming, his shoulders hunched. He was drunk and angry. He was going to knock Truitt aside to show the others he could. He never got the chance. Mark Truitt's hand blurred upward, his six-shooter in it. With a solid thump, the barrel struck the cowboy's head. Speck sank like a sack of oats. The men gasped in surprise.

"There's not going to be any lynching," Mark said again, his voice firm. "If anybody else thinks he can walk over me, now's the time to try."

An angry murmur moved through the men, but they stayed still. Truitt glanced at Will Tony, who sat by himself at a table in the corner, just as T.C. had said.

"How about it, Will? You're not in on this, I hope."

Will Tony stared at him without answering, and Mark could read nothing in his eyes.

The freckled cowboy stirred. Mark Truitt gripped him under the armpits, helping him to his feet. "Come on, Speck," he said. "You've got a bed for the night. And there's one waiting for anybody else who wants to try anything against my prisoner."

He didn't think there would be, now. He thought he'd scotched the thing for good. But to help be sure, and in an effort to bring some reason into the men, he added, "In the first place, it's my duty by law to protect my prisoner. In the second place, he's not a Rankin. I doubt that he's even a very good cow thief. But it may be that I can get him to talk. If I get lucky enough, he might even lead me to the Rankins. He sure can't be any help hanging from a limb. Now think it over, and break this up."

He turned to the bartender. "Frank, I think you'd better close for the night."

Frank nodded solemnly. Truitt thought the barman was relieved.

T.C. stood in the door of the office as Truitt came back, supporting the sagging Speck. He said nothing, but his eyes were wide as he opened the door, then looked back down the street to make sure Truitt wasn't being followed. The prisoner, Claude Nichols, stood in the cell, gripping the iron bars nervously.

"You can relax," Truitt told him. "It's over with. This is the headman of your reception committee."

Nichols eased and breathed a long sigh. He dropped back onto his bunk, trembling a little. He ran his hands across his face. His color was gone.

"Thanks, Sheriff," he said presently. "One thing about you, you stood up for me. The Rankins ran off and left me."

"It's not all for nothing, Nichols. I've been hoping you'd lead me to the Rankins."

Nichols stared at him, then shook his head. "Not in a million years."

"I'll make a deal with you. Lead me there and I'll turn you loose."

Nichols thought a little; then he shook his head again. "No trade, Sheriff. I couldn't run far enough to hide from them."

With Speck locked up, Truitt pitched the keys on the desk and sat down heavily in his chair. He kept remembering the way Will Tony had looked at him. They had been friends for a long time, he and Will. They had ridden together, hunted together, worked together on some of the cow outfits before Truitt became sheriff.

He wondered if Will Tony believed the stories Krisman was putting out. The thought bothered him.

The polls opened at eight o'clock. There was already a good stirring of people by then. By midmorning families were arriving from points far out in the country, the men to vote, the women and children to visit and buy provisions. There were other county offices on the ballot, but there was little competition for them. Only the sheriff's race stirred any talk.

By law, Mark Truitt could have closed all the saloons on election day. But he didn't want to. For the men of this country, the saloon was more than just a place to get a drink. It was a social center, a place to sit and talk with friends, just about the only place there was to pass time. So Mark let the saloons stay open, with the one restriction that they couldn't sell liquor until after the polls closed.

Wherever he went, he felt the eyes of the bystanders following him. Sometimes he could hear men talking low after he passed by. He could feel the growing hostility.

He walked past Southall's newspaper office. Scott Southall stood in the doorway, enjoying the coolness of the morning before the onset of the day's heat. At sight of Truitt, however, he turned back into the shop and busied himself at tearing down the type that had been set up for yesterday's paper.

Mark paused, watching him through the open doorway, wishing there were some way to even up with him for those snide lines about Betty. But he couldn't touch the little printer, and he knew it.

Even though sales were cut off, there was no shortage of liquor. Men knew enough to bring their own on election day. They gathered in the saloons, or along sidewalks on the shaded side of the street, or under the cottonwoods down at the creek, playing cards, drinking, telling windies and waiting for the votes to be counted. As long as things didn't get out of hand, Truitt left people alone.

At noon Betty Mulvane had all the crowd she could handle in her cafe. Expecting this ahead of time, she had cooked up two huge roasts, which made for faster serving. Betty and a Mexican girl who helped her were running their legs off, getting the crowd fed.

Betty gave Mark a special smile, but that was the only preferential treatment she had time for. Later, as he passed by again, she motioned him in. The place was finally empty.

"There are still some biscuits left, and I brought some wild plum jelly out of the cellar after the crowd was gone. Still hungry?"

He shook his head. "I could use some coffee, though."

He toyed with the spoon in the cup, wanting talk more than anything else. "You've probably heard as much talk from as many people as anybody in town, Betty. What're they saying?"

Her eyes were troubled. "It isn't good, Mark. You've still got friends, but lots of folks are turning in the other direction. They're stirred up over the Rankins; you haven't caught those two yet. Then there's that story in the paper, and the things Dalton Krisman is saying. I've even noticed them looking at me a little oddly, Mark. I'm hurting your chances."

"Don't say that, Betty."

She shrugged. "It's the truth, though. If I've heard it once, I've heard it a dozen times today. 'Where there's smoke, there's fire,' they say."

Mark sipped his coffee, his eyes narrowed in thought. So Krisman was going to win the election. And he was dragging Betty down to do it.

Somehow Mark had known yesterday that he was going to lose, but he had been too tired to care. Now rested and thinking clearly, he could understand better what Sam Vernon and Luke Merchant had been driving at. Krisman could make a good speech, but he would never in a hundred years make a good sheriff. Talk was all there was to him. The people of Lofton County would be more vulnerable to the Rankins and their kind than they had ever been before.

The Rankins were a hard pair. Edsel, the older, was

cold and scheming, as dangerous as a javelina boar. Floyd, the red-haired younger brother, was wild and daring and as ruthless as they came.

These two weren't like some cowboys who went wrong because of a grievance, or just because of a search for easy money. They had grown up at outlawry, had been taught thievery and violence like other boys are taught reading and writing and arithmetic. Their father had been a cow and horse thief before them, an early day wolf poisoner who had been left over when the times moved on. Mark Truitt had seen the old man once, before somebody finally killed him. Old Harper Rankin had what the early cowmen called the "coyote eye."

And it had been his legacy to his two sons. They'd preyed on this country in a two-bit way for ten years, mavericking a little, or stealing ten or fifteen head and making off with them, when they could get away with it. The boys grew up learning how to work a running iron in one hand while holding a rifle in the other.

They hadn't really cut loose the wolf, though, until about two years ago. A Lofton County ranchman had caught Harper Rankin with twenty good young heifers, heading in the wrong direction in too much of a hurry. When the smoke cleared, Harper Rankin lay dead.

Three nights later the Rankin boys had ridden up to the rancher's house and cut the man to pieces with pistol fire, on his own front porch. They killed one of his Mexican cowboys for good measure.

Word eventually worked back that the boys had sworn to ruin every cowman in Lofton County before they were through. Working out of the thorny tangle of the brush country down south, they made periodic sorties into Lofton County, always getting a hundred

to three hundred cattle at a time, and sometimes killing
a cowboy or a rancher while doing it. Then they would
jump back across the border into Mexico, taking the
cattle with them into the huge country below.

Folks said old Harper had picked up many of the
wolf's habits while poisoning lobos back in the early
times. Now he had passed them on to his sons, in
spades. There would be no peace in Lofton County
until the Rankin brothers were dead, or packed off to
the penitentiary, never to return. But Dalton Krisman
was not the man who could do it.

Most times, on election day there would be an im-
promptu horse race. Or somebody would bring in a
mean horse or two, and there would be bets on
whether one good rider or another could stay on him.

There was none of that today. The mood of the
people was against it. Mark Truitt could sense the futile anger that grew in the crowd in town. It was impossible to vent that anger on the Rankins, even though
they were the cause of it. So people began to look for
something or someone else to take it, and Dalton
Krisman was helping them find the man.

He was all over town, working like a ferret. By noon
there was hardly a home where he had not at least
stood on the front porch and talked with the people
inside. He had been in every saloon, every store, half
a dozen times.

He had been down along the creek bank where
groups of ranchers, cowboys, and families whiled away
time in the shade. He had been down in the Mexican
end of town, where hardly anyone ever voted. Dalton
Krisman wasn't missing anybody.

Three o'clock came, and time for Chip Tony's funeral. Mark Truitt put on the only suit he had and
brushed the dust off his boots. He had hardly stirred

out of the office since noon. Maybe he needed to get out a little more. Maybe, like some of his friends said, he was losing to Krisman by default.

It wasn't Truitt's way. He liked people, but not in bunches. And he hated trying to sell anyone something, even himself. He had always known he would make a poor drummer.

He went by the cafe and found Betty ready to go. "Are you sure we ought to go together?" she asked him.

"Let's go," he said.

It looked as if most of the county was there to see Chip Tony buried. Chip had been a likeable kid, and a mighty good cowhand. He had had a lot of friends. But many of these people hadn't known him. They were here out of curiosity, and because this was about the only thing there was to do.

The funeral itself went off quietly enough.

There were a couple of hymns, and a short eulogy by the preacher. Betty Mulvane stood beside Mark. Once, when he felt his throat tighten and the tears come burning to his eyes, Betty gripped his arm a little, and it became easier for him. He looked down at her, grateful for her presence, wishing she could always be there.

He glanced several times toward Will Tony, wishing he knew what was running through the man's mind. But Will never looked at him, so far as Mark could tell. Then he must believe what Krisman had been saying. Mark closed his eyes tight. The thought that Will Tony was against him hurt worst of all.

At last the funeral was over. Chip's close friends filed by, each to shovel a bit of earth into the grave. Then came the explosion Mark had feared all day. He heard someone say, "It's all over now for Chip, but they shot the wrong man. If they were going to kill somebody, it ought to've been the sheriff who went yellow and let the kid die."

The voice was loud, purposely so, and the crowd which had been moving away from the cemetery stopped, waiting. Mark Truitt saw them all eyeing him curiously, waiting to see whether he would take it up or let it lie like that.

He looked behind him, searching for the man who had said it. He found him, a tall, bull-shouldered rider named Jase Duncan. Duncan had been with Krisman yesterday at the sheriff's office. Now he stood a little in front of the crowd, letting Truitt know it was he who had spoken. Duncan was a poker-playing, beer-drinking friend of Dalton Krisman.

It was not hard to see where this trouble had come from, Truitt thought darkly. But he was in a squeeze, and there was no getting out. He walked toward Duncan with slow, determined steps. Two paces from him, he stopped and stood rigid.

"That's a lie, Duncan. Jim and Homer were with us down there in the brush. They'll tell you it's not so."

He wasn't speaking for Duncan, because he knew Duncan probably didn't care, one way or the other. He probably knew the truth, just as Krisman did. But he was willing to warp the truth if it suited his purpose. Jase Duncan loved to fight.

Jase said, "Jim and Homer are your friends. You had them deputized. They'd lie for you. For all we know, they may have held back, too."

Truitt flinched. Jase had scored with that one. He had insulted Truitt's friends. Now there could be no compromise. Any attempt at one would brand the sheriff a coward, sure enough.

"A cemetery is a place of peace," Truitt said slowly. "We can't fight in here."

Jase Duncan grinned in anticipation. "It's not far to the gate."

He turned and walked toward the opening. Truitt followed after him, resignedly taking off his coat as he went. He hung it across the wooden gate, and placed his hat atop a post.

He looked back apologetically at Betty. Then he turned to face Duncan and found the man almost on him. Duncan's fist bludgeoned into Truitt's face, staggering the sheriff back against the gate.

Pain roared through Truitt's head. For a second or two he saw only a whirling bright flash. Instinctively he dropped down. Duncan's second blow struck him on the shoulder. Truitt came up with his own fist, still not seeing clearly, but knowing Duncan must be there.

His fist connected solidly. Duncan grunted. Truitt had hit him in the throat. For a moment, then, it was a standoff. Both men warily pulled back to recover and try again.

Mark Truitt hated fist fighting; he always had. He had seen a little boxing a time or two, and he wished he knew something about it, wished he knew how to spar and duck an opponent's fists while at the same time making his own connect where they were intended to. But he didn't. He had no style other than just to try to hit a little harder and a little faster than his opponent, and see if he could outlast him.

There was no style about Jase Duncan, either. He just came in swinging. If he happened to hit you just right, the fight was over, then and there.

This was a poor show, even a sordid one, two grown men standing there swapping licks, slowly, painfully, wearing each other down until neither could do more than stagger around, trying to get up strength for another swing.

Jase Duncan's nose was bloody. One of his eyes was swelling shut. His breath was coming slow and hard, with a desperate rattle like that of a steer that had been roped around the neck and dragged too long.

Mark Truitt was little better off. His face was bruised and cut, and a smear of red edged across the ridge of his cheekbone. His shirt was half gone. It was all he could do to pull himself along, one step and then another, and try to get strength enough for one more good punch.

Jase Duncan finally went down and stayed down. It wasn't so much that one man was a better fighter than the other, but simply that Mark Truitt had a little more stamina, had somehow outlasted him.

Truitt sank to the ground and leaned heavily back against the gate post, sweat and dirt and blood streaking his face as he opened his mouth wide and tried for a deep breath. Betty Mulvane knelt beside him, anxiously looking him over, her fingers gently searching his sore face.

"We've got to get back to town and take care of this," she said.

The crowd began melting away, and some of its members looked ashamed. They'd had all of this show they wanted. Joe Franks and Homer Brill and some of Truitt's other friends gathered around him. They didn't say much; there wasn't much to be said. But just having them here was worth a lot to Truitt.

Then Will Tony came up and stood looking down at him. Truitt couldn't tell what he was thinking, for Will's eyes were dark and grieving. Will Tony turned away and caught Dalton Krisman by the shoulder. Krisman had been kneeling by Duncan.

"Krisman," he said bitterly, "I don't want you ever to speak Chip's name again. You've been using it, making it cheap, trying to get yourself into office with it. If you do it again, I'll make you wish you'd never heard of Chip Tony!"

He gave Krisman a shove that landed the surprised candidate in the dirt.

Will Tony came back and stood by Mark Truitt again, his hands shoved deeply into his pockets. "They're trying to cheapen you, Mark. And they're cheapening Chip, too. I'm glad you fought Jase. It may not have helped you any, but it did me a world of good."

Relief came to Mark Truitt then. He tried to stand up, but he couldn't. He sank down again but lifted his hand to Will Tony. Will took it.

"I wish I'd hit that Jase Duncan a lick or two myself," said short Joe Franks.

Homer Brill, tall and thin, said, "You're so stubby you couldn't have reached him with a four-foot elm club."

"You're so skinny you couldn't even've picked the club up," Joe shot back.

These two old friends were always sniping at each other. Mark knew that right now it was for his benefit, to cheer him up. As long as he had a few friends like these left, and Will Tony didn't blame him, he could take whatever else came along.

"What're we going to do now, Mark?" asked Homer Brill.

"There's not much we can do," Joe put in. "I got the word straight from one of the election judges a while ago. They've been sneaking a count. Krisman's carrying."

Mark Truitt nodded. He had expected nothing else.

Sam Vernon leaned on the fence and said sadly, "They'll be swearing him in Monday morning, then, and we can give the country back to the Indians. The Rankins'll take us."

Mark Truitt pushed himself to his feet, holding to the gatepost. He had his breath back now, although a hammering pain had him worried at first that Duncan had cracked one of his ribs.

"I'm not quitting without one more try," he said grimly. "I'm still the sheriff here tonight and all day tomorrow. I'm going back into that brush. This time I'm going over that river after them, border or no border."

Betty was dismayed. "Mark, you can't do that. You're not in shape for it. Besides, they wouldn't let you. Your term's too nearly up. The judge wouldn't allow you to go."

"He won't know till it's too late to stop me. Once I get down into that brush, it won't matter if I take a day or a week. Nobody will come there after me."

"How'll you know where to look for the Rankins?" asked Joe.

"By taking the prisoner along. One way or other, he'll talk. He may not want to, but he'll do it."

Little Joe Franks stood up. "Well, sir, you're not going without me."

Homer Brill frowned. "If you're going to take that kid along, I guess I'd better go, too, and help you nursemaid him."

"Thanks, boys," Mark said gratefully. "I hoped you would."

Luke Merchant, the ex-Ranger, had been squatting, tracing cattle brands in the sand. He looked up. "It's been a long time since I rode out on something like this. I quit the Rangers because I'd had a bellyful of it. But I didn't throw my guns away, Mark. I can be a lot of use to you, if you'll have me."

Sam Vernon wanted to go, but Truitt had to turn him down. "You know why, Sam. Ten years ago, maybe, but not now. It's going to be a long, hard trip. We can't have any riders on our hands who might give out."

"No," Sam agreed reluctantly, "I reckon not. The best of luck to you."

Will Tony had been standing, listening, saying nothing. Now he lifted his gaze to Mark Truitt. "Mark, I'm going too."

Truitt looked at him dubiously. "Will, are you sure you want to—after Chip, I mean?"

Will Tony said firmly, "I'm going, Mark. If you don't let me go with you, I'll follow after you. I'm a good tracker, you know. I can even outshoot you. You'll need me."

Truitt nodded then. "I'll be tickled to have you."

He wound up with five men, all ones who would do to ride the river with. They were level-headed men he could trust to do what he wanted, to be where he needed them, when he needed them.

"We'll travel light," he said. "We'll take a spare horse apiece the first part of the way, so we'll have a fresh horse to change to. We'll drop the extras off out at George Frisco's ranch, this side of the river.

"Joe, you and Homer arrange for the horses over at Milt's stable. Milt will keep his mouth shut. Remember two extra horses for Claude Nichols. Betty, I'll let you get the grub because you can do it without anyone's catching on. We'll meet at your place after dark. We'll eat a good meal there, and it may be the last we get for several days. We'll travel all night so there won't be anybody catching up with us and bringing us back.

"We've got to keep it quiet. In the first place, the Rankins seem to know as much of what's going on around here as any of us do. I don't know who's spying for them, but I do know he's pretty good at it. In the second place, we don't want Krisman crossing us up. So don't tell anybody you don't have to."

But, hard as they might try to keep it a secret, Truitt knew there was a fifty-fifty chance the word would leak out anyway.

With Betty Mulvane, Truitt started the short walk back to town. He moved slowly, stiff and a little sore from the fight.

Worriedly, Betty said, "Mark, you don't have to do this."

"I do, Betty. I've got a responsibility to the people of this county."

"Your responsibility ended when they turned you out today. Let their new sheriff handle it for them, if they think he's so good."

"He can't, Betty. You know that. I don't even know if I can. But I've got to try it once when I don't have a hand tied behind my back, when I can go over the river after the Rankins."

"Lots of men wouldn't care what happened after they were voted out."

"But I care, Betty. This town is home to me. I have lots of friends here, friends who've backed me whether I won or not. Before I turn the job over to a counterfeit like Krisman, I've got to make one more good try, for them."

They turned in at the sheriff's office. T.C. stared at Mark's battered face, but he made no comment. T.C.

had had to miss the funeral so he could stay and look after the prisoner.

"I'm going out for a little while, if you're going to be here, Mark," T.C. said.

Mark nodded. "Go ahead. I'll be here."

He wondered where T.C. was going, until he saw the jailer hail Dalton Krisman on the street and limp over to talk with him.

Mark grinned with what little humor was left in him. "I guess T.C. knows how the election's going. He wants to be sure he's still going to have a job."

Betty poured fresh water in the washbasin and fetched a clean cloth to wash the dirt and blood from Mark Truitt's face. "I'll worry about you all the time you're out, Mark. But I want you to know this—I'm proud of you for going."

She leaned down and kissed him.

They gathered at Betty's cafe, one by one, soon after dark. There were Homer Brill and Joe Franks, as inseparable as beef and beans. They would argue and needle and insult each other all the time they were out, but if one of them ever got his foot in a trap, the other would get him out or break his neck trying.

There was Harley Mills, a good-natured cowboy who had never said a cross word to anyone in his life, as far as Mark knew. But you couldn't walk over him. When he got real quiet, you'd better watch out, because he might be fixing to stomp you good.

Luke Merchant was the old hand of the bunch, quiet and efficient, gray-haired now but still rawhide tough. He could have been sheriff any time he had wanted the job. Last was Will Tony, grim, taciturn, carrying his grief and his hatred wound up inside him tighter than a watch spring.

Betty had supper ready for them, fried steak and potatoes, with hot biscuits and red beans, and plenty of coffee. She watched soberly while they ate, and a sparkling of tears showed in her worried eyes.

Mark broke the silence only once to ask, "Did Nichols eat much?"

She nodded. "He put away a good supper."

Mark said, "He's going to need it. He's in for a surprise."

Finishing up, the men rolled cigarettes and sat smoking them, looking down at the table, or out the window into darkness, dreading the start and putting it out of their thoughts as long as they could. Every man knew the danger he was getting into, and he knew he might not come back. Chip Tony was fresh on their minds. Yet, because of Chip Tony, not a man was ready to call it off.

There was a sound outside, and Betty looked up quickly. "Uh-oh. Trouble."

Dalton Krisman pushed the door open and stood there looking at the possemen. Behind him was the dried-up publisher, Scott Southall. "What do you think you're doing, Mark Truitt?" Krisman demanded. "You heard the final count. I beat you, two to one. Where do you think you're going, now that you've got to turn in your badge?"

Innocently Mark Truitt looked at the men around him as if to ask if any of them knew what Krisman was talking about. "Who said I was going anywhere?"

"You've got saddle horses waiting over in the livery barn. I saw them myself. I know what you're up to, Truitt, and I'm here to stop you. I'm the new sheriff around here."

"This is Saturday," Truitt reminded him coldly. "The last I heard, you won't be sworn in till Monday morning."

"The wish of the people has been made known. There's nothing left but a formality. You're through, Truitt."

Firmly Truitt said, "I still have the badge on. Till I take it off, I'm the sheriff."

Krisman's face reddened. "The judge can stop you, and he will. I've sent Jase Duncan to fetch him."

A moment of despair came to Mark Truitt. This was a sorry way for it to end. He sat down and turned his back on Krisman, as if he had given up.

"Betty," he asked, "you do still have some of that good plum jelly down in the cellar?

"I've got some here on the shelf," she said, not understanding.

"It's been open too long. I want some fresh. Lend me the key."

When he got it, he drew his six-shooter. "Krisman, you and Southall come along with me. We're going to get some of that jelly."

Krisman blustered. Truitt poked him in the belly with the gun muzzle, and Krisman stepped sharply to the door. Joe Franks and Homer Brill grinned like a pair of Cheshire cats and followed along behind.

The cellar was in back of the cafe, with ground-level double doors that opened flat. Mark unsnapped the padlock and swung one of the doors open. A set of steep stairs led down into the dark, cool hole.

"Go ahead, Krisman. You too, Southall."

The muzzle of Homer Brill's gun prodded the man down the steps in a hurry. "Hurry up there, Sheriff," he said sarcastically. "Can't keep the press waiting." He turned back to Southall. "You next, Editor."

Mark shut the door behind the pair and snapped the padlock in place. He could hear them shouting, but the earthen walls of the cellar absorbed most of the sound. It would not carry far. Unless someone just happened to be walking down the alley, it was unlikely the two would be heard.

Mark walked back into the cafe and handed Betty the key. "You might want to take a look in there tomorrow morning," he said.

She smiled a little, understanding now. Then the smile was gone. He saw the tears she was fighting back. "Be careful, Mark."

He took her hand. "I will." He didn't want to let the hand go. He leaned forward and kissed her. "Betty," he said hesitantly, "when I come back—"

He paused there, and she asked, "What, Mark?"

He gripped her hand tightly. The words somehow slipped away from him. "I'll tell you then," he said, and moved out into the night.

The possemen held the horses in the darkness behind the jail, while Mark Truitt went in the front. He paused, looking in the window first to be sure the judge wasn't there. Then he hurried through the open front door and took the keys off his desk. T.C. looked up from a newspaper he was reading.

"I'm taking the prisoner, T.C.," Mark said.

The crippled jailer stood up worriedly. "They're not working up a lynch mob again, are they?"

Mark didn't answer. He swung the cell door open and motioned with his chin. "Come on, Nichols."

Mark locked the handcuffs on Claude Nichols' wrists and handed the man his hat from a nail on the wall. "Let's go."

He paused at the door. "Blow out the lamp, T.C. As far as anybody needs to know, Nichols is still in here."

The light winked out and T.C. stood on the porch.

"You'd think they'd have given up this lynch talk. You never can tell what people are going to do."

Just at daybreak they rode up to George Frisco's little adobe ranch house deep in the dry, thorny stretch of brush country that lay north of the big river. Two dogs came bouncing out, barking and raising cain around the horses' heels. A couple of the horses shied away and kicked at the dogs.

The old rancher poked his gray head out the door and squinted at the riders. He came out, but kept his gnarled hand on the door until he was satisfied who the visitors were.

"Mutt! Shep!" he shouted at the dogs. "Git away! Git!"

The dogs drew back, still barking to show that they remained on guard.

"Mark Truitt," old George said. "I couldn't tell who you were at first, you fellers coming along in front of the sun that way. Get down and come in. The coffee's still hot, and if there's not enough, we'll make some more."

"Thanks, George. We were hoping you'd ask us."

He had known the rancher would. In this broad, lonesome country, as seldom as people saw each other, the old man probably would have invited the Rankin brothers themselves in, if they'd happened to come riding by.

He'd already had his breakfast—probably had eaten two hours ago—but he poured fresh coffee for the riders, emptying the pot. He put in a few fresh grounds along with the old, added more water, and set the pot back on the stove. He sliced some bacon and made up biscuits out of a big crock of sourdough.

"No eggs," he apologized. "I used to keep some chickens, but there weren't enough of them for me and the coyotes both."

Truitt was grateful for the coffee after the long night ride. It was strong enough to float a six-shooter, the way an old bachelor ranchman like George usually made it. Living alone like this, most men hated to cook. Breakfast and one other meal usually got them by. They made up the rest on strong black coffee.

George stared at the prisoner, and at the handcuffs that still clamped his wrists. He didn't ask any questions. Chances were he had the situation about half figured out anyway.

"The election's over, I reckon," he said. Truitt smiled wanly. "It's over. I lost." George swore softly. "Lost? To that Dalton Krisman? Why, I never thought he'd get more than one vote, and that one his own. People get crazier all the time. That's why I moved way out here, so I wouldn't have to put up with a lot of their foolishness."

He shook his gray head, as if he still couldn't believe it. "Krisman. Now, ain't that a joke." He changed the subject then. "You fellas look as if you had a long ride. Why don't you stretch out and sleep a while?"

They needed it, Truitt knew. But he glanced at the prisoner.

"Don't worry about him," George said pointedly. He pulled a pistol out of a holster hanging on the wall and shoved it into his waistband. "He's going to take a nap too . . ."

Nichols hadn't said much during the whole ride. At first he had been eager, for he had assumed, as T.C. did, that the move was to get him away from a lynch mob. As the hours wore on, he had become more and more worried.

Now, an hour after they had saddled their fresh horses and headed south from George's adobe house, he asked, "What do you want with me, anyhow?"

"You're going to take us to the Rankins," Truitt told him flatly.

Nichols shook his head. "I told you once that I'm not going to do it."

A chill was in Truitt's voice. "You'll do it."

Mark Truitt had been afraid he might not easily find the place where Chip Tony had died, but now here it was, a big opening in the aimless, endless tangle of mesquite and brush and prickly pear. Ugly, red-necked carrion birds flopped their awkward wings and lifted themselves grudgingly into the air, settling back yonder a ways. Here lay two horses, dead now for several days.

Tony had ridden quietly, drawn apart from the others, his thoughts his own. Now he pulled over to Truitt, a bleakness in his eyes. "Is this the place?"

Mark nodded, and Will said, "Show me where they killed him."

Will Tony stood there a long while, an angry glaze coming over his eyes. He turned upon Nichols then, danger in the grim set of his jaw.

Sensing trouble brewing, Mark said, "We'd better get moving."

He led off quickly. Will Tony remounted his horse and fell in behind, looking back over his shoulder.

Even after so many days, the trail was not hard to follow, for the Rankins had not tried to hide it. The river was not far ahead. Beyond it was sanctuary. They had had no reason to hurry, or to worry about pursuit.

The seven riders reached the border in about an hour. Here it was, a broad, muddy river hardly deep enough, in most places, to swim a horse. But it might as well have been an ocean, for it was the national boundary, a legal barrier a lawman did not easily breach.

"Too many times I've sat here grinding my teeth," Truitt told the possemen, "knowing they were right over yonder and not being able to go after them."

Now he had brushed aside all thought of law. His badge meant nothing across the river, and he was losing it anyway. "The river used to look big," he said, "but now it looks mighty little. Let's get across it."

He splashed out into the muddy water, in the lead. The others strung out behind him. They were far out from the bank before they reached water deep enough to make the horses swim. Within moments the hooves found solid footing again, and the riders were across the river.

Stopping on the far bank to let the horses shake themselves off, Mark Truitt looked back across the river with a strange sense of jubilation. Swimming it had been in a way like striking a long-awaited blow at an old enemy. There was no telling what people would do to him when he got back to Lofton. He'd worry about that some other time. Right now he didn't care. What mattered was that he had crossed the river.

"Your badge doesn't mean much now, does it, Mark?" commented Luke Merchant. He'd crossed a river or two himself, in his time. "We're on our own."

"We always were," Mark replied.

He turned to Nichols. "Now comes your part, what we brought you for. You know where the Rankins stay when they're over here. You're going to take us to them."

Nichols tensed. "You might just as well take me back to your jail, Truitt. If I were to tell you, my life wouldn't be worth a counterfeit Confederate dollar."

"It won't be worth more if you don't." Truitt's voice was firm. "We're going, with or without you. The bargain I offered you still goes. Lead us to the Rankins, and we'll turn you loose; you'll have your freedom. If you don't lead us there, we can't afford to be tied down to you. We'll have to get rid of you." His hand lay on the rope tied to his saddle.

Nichols's face was pale. His tongue ventured out over dry lips. "It wouldn't be legal, Sheriff."

"We stopped being legal when we crossed the river. Make up your mind. Which are you most scared of, the Rankins or us?"

Nichols's gaze swept over the six men around him, and he found no comfort in the stony faces. Will Tony's right hand worked the hornstring loose from his saddle. Grimly he began shaking out his rope.

"You say you'll let me go?" Nichols queried anxiously.

"That's our agreement," said Mark. "Your freedom for the Rankins." Nichols looked at Will Tony once again, watching Will finger the rope. For a moment death brushed him with its cold hand. "All right," he said weakly, nodding his head. "I'll take you."

"Lead out, then," Mark said firmly. "And just remember this—one wrong move and you're dead."

For a time they moved along the trail left by the stolen cattle. There had been no rain to alter it. Wind had scoured away much of the loose sand, but the ground was still visibly scarred. Eventually, however, the tracks were lost in a general scattering of cow trails.

"They turned the cattle loose down here," Nichols said. "The Rankins have a mighty big herd now, and most of them wear brands from north of the river. The Rankins just about took over this stretch of country around here. Some of the people work for them, and the rest are too scared to put up a fuss.

"When they get a little short of cash they round up a few head and sell them farther west, back over the river. But I imagine the big part of all the cattle they've stolen are still right down here, scattered from Cape Cod to Hickory Bend. Edsel has some big notion of being the biggest cowman in northern Mexico someday."

"What about young Floyd?"

"As long's he has plenty of whisky and pretty women, he doesn't care whether school keeps or not."

Keeping the lead, Mark Truitt stayed in the brush. His eyes searched the skyline for signs of other riders. Above all, they had to get across this dry and baking land without being seen.

Once he spotted a man half a mile to the east, pushing a horse along in a slow lope. Quickly Mark stepped out of the saddle, and signaled the others to do the same.

"Think he's seen us?" asked Homer Brill.

"He might have seen you," Joe Franks said, "sticking up there like a telegraph pole."

"I don't imagine he saw us," Mark told them. "We've got a good cover of brush. I just wish I knew who he was, and what he's doing down here." He turned back to Nichols. "How much farther?"

Nichols shrugged. "We might make it by dark. At the rate we're going, we're not getting there very fast."

"It's better to stick to the brush and get there slow than break out in the open and have them waiting for us," Mark replied.

The afternoon sun pressed down on them with all the deadening power that July can have in the dry brush country. Even at a slow trot, the horses sweated heavily. Mark rubbed his sleeve across his face, tasting the salt of perspiration on his lips and the burn of it in his eyes.

It was hotter here even than at Lofton, because the elevation had dropped. Lofton was considered dry country, but here, beyond the river, the annual rainfall was much less than that north of the border. It showed in the stunted brush, the sparse, coarse grass, the thick scattering of pear and cactus. It was outlaw country in every way, Mark thought. Even the land itself seemed forsaken.

Now and then they began running into cattle. The animals were as wild as deer down here in this big open country, where they had to walk a long way to get enough to eat and drink.

"Look there, Luke," Mark said, pointing to the LS brands on the hips of a bunch of cows, before the cattle clattered away.

Luke Merchant nodded grimly. Many a time, as LS wagon boss, he had counted up the losses after the Rankins cut a swath across his company's range.

Nichols was tensed up like a man waiting for the hang rope. Mark knew why. If anything went wrong now, if the Rankins should come upon them, they would know Nichols had led the posse here. It wouldn't go easy with him.

"We're getting closer," Nichols said thinly.

"How close?"

"An hour or so, I reckon, at the rate we're going."

Mark looked to the west. The sun was not far above the skyline any more. It was losing some of its awful heat. In an hour it would be sundown. He wanted time and light to look the situation over.

"Let's ride a little faster, then," he said.

Harley Mills was humming a tuneless something

half under his breath, behind Mark. Harley never spoke unless he had to, but that humming was always there. It had never bothered Mark before. Now, in this building tension, it grated on his nerves. *Easy now*, he told himself. *Go easy or you'll bust a spring.*

Working out to the edge of the brush, they came in sight of the Rankin headquarters just before the sun reached the top of the rocky hill off in the west. It was an old adobe-built outfit, and some of the out-buildings were crumbling because of neglect. The only half-decent building left was the main house itself, a square brown structure squatting in the sun amid a loose scatter of mesquites and prickly pear and gua-jillo brush.

Behind the adobe sat a low-built jacal made of mesquite poles and thatched with the thin, sharp blades of the bear grass. The corrals, of crooked mesquite trunks and branches, leaned one way and the other, needing attention. The only thing resembling a barn was an arbor of mesquite posts, the top piled high with brush for shade. All four sides were open to the scorching winds and the rain, when there was any rain.

"That's it," Nichols said with a quiet desperation. "Now I've held up my end of the trade. You fellers have to turn me loose."

Mark said, "We'll turn you loose, but not just yet. You might decide to redeem yourself by running down there and spoiling everything we set out to do."

They all dismounted and squatted on the ground to look over the dusty Rankin camp. Luke Merchant pointed. "There are horses in the corral, Mark. It looks as if they're home."

Mark nodded. "Somebody is." He watched a man walk out of the adobe house with a bucket in his hand and dip it into a water barrel, then go back into the house.

"Lupe Aguilar," said Nichols. "He cooks for the outfit."

A moment later another man walked out to the corral.

"Shark Fisher," Nichols whispered. "Edsel Rankin never goes anywhere without him."

Mark's voice was tight. "Then the Rankins must be there."

He studied the building, looking for the best way to get in. There was too much open ground to cross to rush in from here. The Rankins would spot them too soon and would have time to put up a defense. But if they could get in close, and overrun the camp in a matter of seconds . . .

"Is that arroyo yonder deep enough to hide a horse?"

Nichols nodded. "It's six feet or so along this end. Floyd Rankin fell in it one night when he was drunk. He almost broke his neck."

Mark grunted in satisfaction. "Is there any way to get a horse out of it, down there close to the house?"

"The bank's caved back just below the corrals yonder, where that brush comes in so thick. You could get horses up over it there."

Mark looked back at the men behind him. "That's the way, then. We'll go into the arroyo here in the brush, leading our horses. We'll stay in it, out of sight, till we get down below the corrals. We'll mount up then and rush the house before they have time to get ready for us."

Will Tony broke his somber silence. "Do you want prisoners, Mark?"

"We'll take them if we can. But remember this—we

may never have another chance like this at the Rankins. If we can't take the Rankins to prison, we don't want to leave them alive."

Will Tony's mouth went flat. "That suits me fine."

Nichols was trembling. "What about me?"

"We can't leave you out here. You'll have to go in with us."

"But you made me a promise."

"And we'll keep it. After this thing is done."

He motioned the others to follow him. Working carefully through the thinning mesquite, they led their horses until they came at last to the arroyo. They had to hunt awhile to find a place where the banks were caved enough to get the horses down.

Mark moved out in front, six-shooter in his hand, picking his way cautiously along the gravelly bottom of the arroyo. This section was a near stranger to rain. Yet, when it came, it often fell in a violent downpour that sent great sheets of water cascading along to slash and erode the land and leave angry gashes like this red arroyo as a further blight to disfigure the appearance of an already blighted land.

It was almost dark now, and he knew this would be a race against time. He could smell the wood smoke that drifted out from the chimney of the adobe house. They might be eating about now.

There might never be a better time to catch them. It occurred to him that he hadn't eaten anything since he had left George Frisco's place this morning, except for a tin of sardines he had split with Will Tony. But he felt no hunger. The rising excitement took care of that.

He felt his heartbeat quickening. He had been in tight places, but he felt that never before had he been in one as tight as this, or important. He glanced back at the men behind him. Their grim, nervous faces showed they were feeling the sense of strain just as he did.

Scared? Sure, he was scared. He always had been when he got in a situation like this. He had never been ashamed to admit it. But despite the tug of fear, he went on. He always did. And he knew that the men behind would follow him.

They moved carefully up the arroyo, with the air still and close and stifling hot. Occasionally Mark paused to move aside a rock that might make a horse stumble. He wished time and again that he could afford to risk a look out over the top of that bare rim.

A foreboding came to him then, a sense that something would go wrong, or perhaps already had gone wrong. He wanted to dismiss it, but the experience of past years told him to heed. He had to look out over the top now. He found a little niche for a foothold and cautiously raised up.

He saw horsemen sweeping toward the arroyo from out of the cover of brush.

"Look out," he shouted, "It's a trap!" He triggered a quick shot at the horsemen.

"Mount up and run!"

It was hopeless to stay here and put up a fight. They would be like quail caught on the ground, hemmed between these narrow red banks.

He heard a sharp cry as a bullet struck one of the possemen. But in the space of two or three seconds every man was in the saddle and spurring back down the arroyo.

Their trap sprung seconds too early, the outlaws pressed in closer. Guns crashed. Red dirt spat from the arroyo rim as bullets dug in. The outlaws were pushing along even with the possemen, keeping up a running fire. The lawmen were firing back, all of them but stocky Joe Franks. He bent low over the horn, clutching a wounded arm. But he was spurring as hard as the rest.

Through the dust and the smoke, Mark glimpsed Edsel Rankin. In desperation he leveled a shot at him, but knew he had missed. He fired at another rider, though, and he didn't miss. The man toppled from his horse and rolled over the edge into the arroyo, dropping heavily to the gravel floor.

Heart in his throat, Mark spurred hard, bringing up the rear and keeping the fire going, holding the Rankin bunch off as much as he could from the rest of the men up front. Once again he caught sight of Edsel Rankin, but he couldn't get a clear shot at him. He looked for Floyd Rankin. He saw him nowhere in this group of riders.

With Will Tony in front, the possemen reached a break in the arroyo wall and put their horses up out of it. Claude Nichols's horse stumbled on the treacherous footing and went down on its knees. Nichols spurred anxiously, giving the animal its head.

From out of the dust, Edsel Rankin shoved up on the far bank of the arroyo. He shouted Nichols's name and fired. Nichols slumped over his horse's neck. Mark triggered another shot at Edsel, and the outlaw pulled back. Nichols's horse got its footing and went up out of the arroyo. Harley Mills grabbed Nichols in time to keep him from sliding out of the saddle.

Mark came out of the arroyo last, turning back to fire once more as he reached the level ground on top. He heard wild bullets whine out into the brush. Will Tony was down on the ground, kneeling with his saddlegun in his hand, ignoring the fire around him to take slow and careful aim. Every time he pulled the trigger, a man or a horse went down on the opposite side.

"Come on, Will," Mark shouted. But Will seemed transfixed. He kept on firing.

Mark pulled his horse up beside him, leaned down and grabbed Will's arm. "Come on, Will," he shouted again. "We've got to find better cover. They'll be over in a minute."

They pulled back into deeper brush, with Harley holding the wounded Nichols in the saddle. The Rankin crew had found a place where they could jump their horses over the arroyo. They continued swapping fire with the possemen, but they kept a respectful distance. Neither side's fire was effective.

"The only thing we can do now is wait for dark, so we can slip out of here," Mark said.

He turned to see how badly hurt Joe Franks was, and found Homer Brill already wrapping Franks' arm. Tight-lipped, but forcing a grin, Joe said, "A dog bit me worse than this, once."

"How long did he live?" Homer asked.

Claude Nichols was hard hit. Blood oozed from a hole high in his left shoulder. They had a hard time stopping the bleeding. Nichols lay groaning, his face the color of paste, cold sweat standing on his forehead.

"They smashed his shoulder," Harley said. He had sure and gentle fingers when it came to a thing like this. He was wrapping the wound. "He'll die, just lying here."

"Let him," Will Tony growled. "He's one of them."

"No." Mark shook his head. "We can't just let him die without a chance. You've got to admit he kept his end of the bargain."

"Did he? They were waiting for us, weren't they? He must've gotten word to them somehow."

Luke Merchant spoke up. "They got their word all the way from Lofton, Will. Didn't anybody see him but me?"

"See who?" Mark demanded.

"Jase Duncan. He was with Edsel Rankin a while ago."

"Then Krisman's tied up with the Rankin boys," Will said bitterly.

"Maybe," Mark Truitt replied. "But more likely they've been using him, and he just didn't have sense enough to see it."

He bent over Nichols. "Nichols, can you hear me?"

Nichols nodded weakly. "I hear you." His voice was raspy.

"We've got to get you out of here. We'll help you, but you've got to ride. Can you make it?"

Nichols nodded again.

Mark said, "Where's the closest place we can take you where you can get some care?"

"A little town called Rosita. I have a girl there. She'll help me."

"Where is it?"

"Ten miles west."

"Do you have enough strength to help us find it in the dark?"

"I'll try."

Darkness was not long in coming. Under its cover, and before the moon could rise, the seven men moved out as quietly as they could, making a wide circle to avoid the Rankin bunch. When Mark thought they were in the clear, he struck a straight line west, guided by the stars.

They finally came across a pair of ruts worn by wagon and cart wheels. Nichols indicated that these would take them into Rosita. It was well they did, for he lapsed into unconsciousness and was useless from then on. They took turns holding him in the saddle—all but Will Tony. He made it plain that he thought they ought to leave Nichols right there in the road.

Luke Merchant pulled in beside Mark. "What do we do now, Mark—go back?"

"I don't know. I can't seem to figure anything out. It depends, I guess, on what you men want to do. But I'm not ready to give up without one more good try."

It was near midnight when they suddenly came upon Rosita. Every dog in town seemed to notice them and run out to bark around the horses' heels. The horses were too tired to pay much attention.

Rosita was a haphazard collection of adobe buildings and rude jacales, most of them long since dark. Only in one, far down the street, could Mark see light. He heard the listless plunking of a guitar from that one.

The barking of the dogs made Nichols stir. Mark shook him gently. "We're in town," he said. "Which house?"

Nichols groaned.

"Which house, Nichols?" Mark pressed him.

Nichols roused himself enough to point. It was an adobe, with most of the plaster gone and the mud blocks disintegrating from lack of care. Mark knocked on the rough wood door. There was no sound, so he knocked again. Presently a dim light glowed through cracks in the door. He heard a bar being lifted out of place. The door swung open and an old Mexican man stood there in nothing but his pants, holding a flickering candle.

"*Que pasa?*" he asked sleepily.

"*Tenemos un amigo aqui,*" said Mark. "We have a friend of yours here. He's wounded."

The Mexican held the candle to Nichols's face, and then woke up abruptly. "Maria! Maria!"

Mark and Homer Brill carried the wounded man into the house and laid him down on a blanket on the dirt floor, where the old Mexican evidently had been sleeping. A girl came in from the other room of the small house, tugging at a loose cotton dress.

"*Quien es, Papa?*"

She recognized Nichols then, and her hand went up to her mouth. "Claudio!"

For a moment she swayed in shock. Then she got hold of herself and knelt by the man's side. Mark helped her turn Nichols over on his stomach. She tore away the shirt and saw the wound. She shouted orders at the old man. He brought a bottle of tequila, and she began using it to clean the wound. Nichols was in the hands of a good nurse, Mark figured. There was no need of their remaining here any longer.

"One thing," he told the girl. "He's hiding from the Rankins. If they find out he's here, they'll come and kill him."

The old Mexican's eyes widened. "Rankin? But the *rojo*, the little Floyd, he is in town now. He drinks at the cantina."

"Are you sure?" Mark demanded.

"*Si, señor.* All day he has been there, drinking tequila. He makes my son Pepe play the guitar for him. Pepe has not yet come home."

Will Tony's face clouded. "We don't have to go home empty-handed, then. We can get one Rankin."

Mark said, "That we can, Will. We might even get two Rankins before this is over. Let's go."

They remounted and moved up the street, if it might be called a street. It was a meandering trail, worn more by convenience than by plan. Only one building showed a light, and the lone guitar still strummed inside. Even without seeing the crude lettering on the front, Mark knew this had to be the cantina.

He saw two horses standing hipshot in front, hitched to a post. They were gaunt. They probably had stood there like that all day, without anyone's bothering to feed or water them.

The cantina had an open window. Sometime in the past there had been a pane, but the glass was long since gone. Mark leaned low in the saddle for a glimpse inside.

He saw a man, an American, slumped asleep in a chair at a table, an overturned bottle lying in front of him. Another man, a Mexican, half asleep, listlessly fingered a guitar. And in a corner sat red-haired Floyd Rankin, holding a plumpish, dark-skinned girl on his lap. He was kissing her hungrily, his hand roving up and down her back.

He stopped once to drink from a bottle. It tipped over as he set it down on the dirt floor. He laughed foolishly, caught it, and set it up again. Then he went back to kissing the girl.

"Wake up that guitar, Pepe," he shouted. "How can I make love without music?"

The guitar music livened up for a moment, then slowed again. Pepe was tired and sleepy and wanted to go home.

Mark pulled back and dismounted. The others followed suit. "Here, Joe," he said. "You'd better hold the horses. The rest of you come in with me. No shooting unless we have to. I want Floyd Rankin alive."

He pushed the door open and moved well inside, gun in hand. The possemen fanned out on either side of him. Floyd Rankin's gun belt hung from a chair by his corner table. He jumped to his feet, dumping the plump girl unceremoniously on the floor. He reached for the gun.

"Don't do it, Rankin. We'll kill you!"

Too drunk to reason, Rankin hesitated. Mark took two quick steps forward and grabbed the gun belt. At the last second Floyd Rankin lunged for it, and sprawled out drunkenly on the dirt floor. Mark pitched the gun belt back to Harley Mills.

He took a quick glance over the room. There had been only three men in it besides Rankin—the guitar player, a nodding old man behind the plank bar, and the sleeping American at the table. All of them were awake now.

The American was slow in coming around. When at last he perceived what was taking place, he made a grab at his hip. But Homer Brill had already relieved him of his gun.

"Just sit there and keep still," Mark said roughly. "We're not interested in you."

To Rankin he said, "Come on, Floyd. You're riding with us."

Rankin was sobering quickly. "That badge doesn't mean a thing down here, Truitt. Besides, they tell me you were going to lose that election. You're not the sheriff any more anyhow. You have no right to take me back to jail."

"Correct," Mark said coldly. "I have no right, so I'm not taking you to jail. I'm going to take you back and turn you over to the ranchers. They'll know what to do with you."

It was a lie, but it served the purpose. Folks said the Rankins were fearless, but there was fear in Floyd Rankin's eyes now. Even the coldest of them was likely to feel sick at the thought of rough hemp drawing tight around his neck.

"The ranchers? That'll be a lynch mob, Truitt. There won't even be a trial."

Mark shrugged. "I don't imagine there will. You've never given anybody a trial before you killed him. Let's move out."

Will Tony protested, nodding toward the other American at the table. "What about this one? He's part of the bunch."

Mark replied, "We probably couldn't prove it. We've got a Rankin, and one prisoner is enough. Let that one go."

Will Tony hesitated, looking for a moment as if he might shoot the outlaw anyway.

"I said let him go," Mark gritted.

The outlaw swallowed hard, his face gone pale. He was suddenly cold sober. The plump girl began shaking her fist and cursing the possemen. She scooped up an empty tequila bottle from the floor and hurled it at them. She rushed at Will Tony, her sharp fingernails reaching for his eyes. Will slapped her so hard she fell to the floor.

They hustled Floyd Rankin out the door and slammed it behind them.

"Which horse is yours, Floyd?"

Instead of replying, Rankin tried to make a run for it. Mark stuck out his foot and tripped him. He pounced on him, dropping his knee on the man's stomach hard enough to knock the wind out of him.

"You can just get that kind of business out of your head."

He took out the handcuffs he had used on Nichols and clamped them on Rankin's wrists.

"Which horse, Floyd?"

Rankin gasped for breath. When he got it back, he said weakly, "The dun."

They put him on it and rode out, heading due north. They crossed the big river before they stopped to rest the horses, and then only because Mark was afraid the animals couldn't make the remainder of the trip unless they halted awhile. The riders dismounted stiff and weary and hungry, and most of them flopped down upon the ground.

But Will Tony sat upright, a lingering resentment in his face. He hadn't spoken since they left Rosita. Now he glared at Floyd Rankin. Mark knew Will was half hoping Rankin would try to run again, so he could have an excuse to shoot him.

"What's eating you, Will? You've been in a black mood ever since we left that town."

"It's that other one, the one we let go. We ought to've shot him like a snake. We oughtn't let a single one of them get away."

"I didn't just let him go, Will. I turned him loose for a reason."

"What reason could there be?"

"To tell Edsel Rankin what happened. To put him on our trail. If he thinks we're going to turn Floyd over to the ranchers for a hanging, he won't waste any time coming after us."

"And what do we do when he does?"

"We'll just try to be ready."

Mark had never seen a chained wolf act meaner than Floyd Rankin was acting now. "You won't get away with this, Truitt," Floyd said, snarling. "Edsel will eat you up alive."

"We'll see." Truitt decided to try his luck getting a little information out of Floyd. "Edsel's pretty smooth, having Jase Duncan in Lofton to spy for him."

Floyd grinned gloatingly. "So you finally found out about Jase. It took you long enough."

"You even had Dalton Krisman on your side."

"Yeah, only he's too dumb to know it. Edsel sent him campaign money to beat you, but he didn't let Krisman know where it came from. Jase would give it to him and tell him he collected it among friends who wanted to see him put you out of office. He beat you, too, didn't he?"

"He beat me," Mark said.

"Edsel's smart. He'll fix your wagon. You just wait and see."

They rested until well past sunup, then started out again. But the horses were still tired. The riders had to go slow to keep from wearing them out. Every so often they would get off and walk awhile, leading, saving the horses.

Mark Truitt kept watching the back trail for dust. He didn't think Rankin could be on them this soon, but he couldn't be sure. One thing a man had to admit about the Rankins, they would do just what you thought they wouldn't. Rankin would have fresh horses, and the trail the posse was leaving was clear enough for a ten-year-old boy to follow.

The long, hot day sapped them of strength. They needed sleep, and the heavy hands of fatigue were on every man's shoulder. Hot and miserable though he was, the grimy sweat working into his eyes and down his collar, Mark found himself dozing occasionally as he rode.

He had a rope around Floyd Rankin's neck, the other end tied to his own horn, so Rankin could not run away. The sun was well into the brassy western sky when they caught the welcome sight of old George Frisco's adobe ranch house. The horses were barely going to make it.

As before, the dogs met them, setting up an awful

racket, but now it disturbed the horses not at all. George Frisco hobbled out from his open-front adobe barn and waved his hand.

Mark half fell off, he was so tired. George hurried to him and steadied him. The old man said with concern, "Don't you fellers ever know when to quit? Get down, all of you, and rest yourselves. I'll hustle you something to eat."

He noticed Floyd Rankin then. His gray-bearded jaw dropped. "Looks as if you made you a haul. But where's the other one?"

Mark said, "He'll be along directly, I expect." He shook his head. "You may not like what we're fixing to do to you, George. I'd have asked you first, if I could. There's liable to be a mighty big fight here after a while. I think you'd better ride off out in the brush and wait till it's over."

George frowned. "You mean Edsel's coming after this young heathen?"

Mark nodded. "He's our bait."

"How many men will Edsel be bringing?"

"There's no way of telling." The old man lifted a rifle off a pair of pegs on the wall, and opened the breech. "Then one more on your side won't hurt you any. Hell no, I'm not going to ride off into the brush and hide."

While George Frisco hurriedly prepared something for the hungry men to eat, Mark walked out to scout around the house, hunting places that would provide good cover. By the time they had all eaten, a pinpoint of dust was showing up to the south, along their back trail. "I'm going to stand here on the porch and draw them in," Mark said. "I have places picked out for the rest of you. If Edsel Rankin can set a trap, so can we."

Joe Franks, with the stiff arm, took a saddlegun and moved out behind an old wagon which lay upended, one wheel off. Homer Brill found a shovel and scooped himself a shallow hole behind a green clump of prickly pear. Harley Mills squatted beside a half dugout which once had been a home for somebody, before the adobe was built, and now was used for storage. Luke Merchant and old George Frisco took opposite ends of the barn.

"There's a little ditch right over yonder, Will," Mark said. "It's got enough brush to hide you, and it'll let you cover the front of the house."

"You mean you're going to stand out on the porch here, in the open, and let them ride right in on you, Mark?"

"Somebody's got to decoy them, Will, so the rest of you can get a good shot."

"And what if you don't get time to duck back through that door when the shooting starts?"

Mark didn't answer that. "Get on out yonder, Will, while there's still time."

Mark took a final look inside at Floyd Rankin. He had handcuffed him to a heavy woodstove. He had wadded a rag into Rankin's mouth and tied a handkerchief across Rankin's face to keep the gag in and prevent him from making any outcry.

"Just you keep quiet now," he warned.

There wasn't much else Rankin could do.

Mark stepped out onto the porch, the saddlegun in his hand. He left the door wide open and stood in front of it, so he could jump back inside when the shooting started. He had little hope that the trouble would end without shooting.

The pinpoint of dust had grown greatly. Presently the riders showed up through the brush. They paused a moment, just out of firing range of the house, cautiously looking the situation over. Mark hoped everybody was well out of sight.

The outlaws studied the adobe house. A man pointed at the corral, with all the horses in it. Then Mark could feel the eyes all fasten on him. He braced, hoping they wouldn't shoot him right now. But he reasoned that they wouldn't, at least until they knew where Floyd Rankin was.

He counted thirteen men. Unlucky for somebody, he thought. Who?

Edsel Rankin led them, riding a high-strung bay horse and jerking it violently, cursing when it fought its head. Holding a six-gun, Rankin made a motion with his hand. His men fanned out on either side of him. Some were Americans, some Mexicans. Every man bore the stamp of an outlaw. All of them had guns out and ready.

Rankin drew rein twenty paces from the house, warily eyeing the windows. He looked at Mark Truitt then, and his gray eyes stabbed with hatred.

"I want my brother, Truitt."

"So do I," Mark replied.

Rankin's face was dark and twisted. "Send him out here, Truitt, and we'll ride away. You know we've got you outnumbered. Hold back and we'll pull that house right down over your ears."

Inside the house, Mark Truitt could hear Floyd Rankin stamping his feet. The bare earth would make no sound, so he must have twisted around to where he could stamp against the side of the cookstove. Edsel Rankin heard the noise too, and Mark knew the outlaw sensed that it was his brother.

Mark said, "You can't afford to do any wild shooting, Edsel. He's in there, and you might hit him."

He could see this realization reach Edsel Rankin and feed his anger.

Mark said, "We want you too, Edsel. You may have us outnumbered, but we've got you surrounded. You can't get out of here."

Edsel Rankin's head jerked desperately around as he tried to seek out the men waiting in ambush.

"Mark Truitt," he breathed, "I'll nail you to the door!"

His gun muzzle came up.

Mark dove back inside the door. He hit the dirt floor on his side and went rolling. Half a dozen bullets buzzed after him like angry hornets, and he felt one graze his leg with a touch of fire.

Knowing now that they were in a trap, some of the outlaws wheeled their horses around and spurred out. In an instant, guns roared around them. Three men fell in the first volley. One got up again, but two of them never would.

Edsel Rankin screamed something and spurred out toward the barn, his men right behind him. Gunfire from George and Luke turned them back. Rankin's Mexican sombrero jerked away. One of the men behind him bounced half out of the saddle, then caught himself and held on weakly, while his horse stampeded past Luke Merchant. The rider bobbed a time or two and fell rolling.

Rankin wheeled his horse back and tried to run straight out the way he had come, firing blindly as he spurred. Mark Truitt's saddlegun crashed. Rankin's horse stumbled and went down. Rankin rolled in the sand. He came up fighting, shooting in Truitt's direction and grabbing at the reins of a panicked horse that had just lost its rider.

Guns roared. Fire spat from every direction. Heavy

smoke drifted across the wild melee. Horses squealed in terror. One horse went down, and then another.

All this time Rankin was shouting and cursing and firing wildly at everything he saw move. None of his men were listening to him. Gripped by fear, they moved blindly one way, then another, firing at anything or nothing.

Mark saw a familiar figure then. Jase Duncan was one of the few still on horseback. He spurred toward the open door, hoping perhaps to kill Truitt and get to safety inside. Mark raised the saddlegun and held it steady. When Duncan was almost to the porch, he squeezed the trigger. Duncan dropped like a sack of lead.

All of Rankin's men were afoot now, crouching to provide less of a target. Their horses were tearing wildly back and forth, hunting a way out. Some of the men were pleading for mercy, raising their hands. Rankin was cursing them, calling them a hundred kinds of yellow coward. But they were through, and he could see it.

"Give up, Rankin," Mark Truitt called. "You can't get out of this alive." Edsel Rankin grabbed the reins of a panicked horse. He fought to get a foot in the stirrup, then swung up. Spurring viciously, he headed the horse straight for the door, straight at Mark Truitt.

Mark brought the saddlegun up again. Rankin's six-gun fired. Mark felt the saddlegun take the impact of the bullet. The gun splintered in his hands. The force of it drove the gun back into his stomach, knocking the wind out of him. He stood there stunned, unable to move.

Edsel Rankin was almost on him, the six-gun leveling again. Helpless, Mark could only stand and look into Rankin's twisted face, to see the rage and the hatred that surged up there.

Then he saw a movement behind Rankin, saw Will Tony raise himself up out of the ditch. He saw flame belch from Will Tony's gun. Edsel Rankin buckled. His horse stopped abruptly. Rankin's body pitched forward, over the frightened horse's head. It landed on the porch and went rolling, coming to a standstill at Mark Truitt's feet.

The shooting was over now. The Rankin bunch, what was left of them, stood with their hands up, in the stifling swirl of smoke and dust. Mark saw his own men break out of their vantage points and come hurrying toward him.

He knelt and looked at Edsel Rankin's body, then straightened again. He saw the question in Will Tony's eyes as Will came up. He nodded, and a look of satisfaction came over Will Tony. Mark had done what he came for. The Rankins were through.

Probably there wasn't a person in Lofton who missed seeing the posse come into town. By the time the horsemen pulled up in front of the sheriff's office, there must have been fifty or sixty people crowding around to watch Mark Truitt and the others step down and hold guns on seven weary, beaten outlaws.

Young Floyd Rankin was handcuffed. The rest had their wrists bound to their saddle horns. Mark Truitt moved from one to another, cutting the rawhide strings that held them, so they could dismount.

The word swept across town like a whirlwind. "They've got Floyd Rankin down at the jail!"

Betty Mulvane rushed from her cafe and ran down the street. She shoved her way through the crowd and threw her arms around Mark. She didn't care who was watching. She couldn't speak, but she didn't have to.

T.C. stood in the doorway. "Unlock the cells, T.C.," Mark said.

They moved the outlaws inside. Mark followed them, his arm around Betty.

Just then Dalton Krisman came pushing through. "Make room here," he shouted. "Make way for the law."

He bustled through the office door, a gun in his hand.

"Hands up, Mark Truitt," he barked. "You're under arrest."

But shortly behind him came the balding old judge. "Put that gun up, Krisman. Haven't you any sense at all? They're already trying to laugh you out of town for throwing that girl in jail, even before you got your badge. Can't you see Mark's got Floyd Rankin, and some of the rest of the outlaw gang?"

Flinching under the judge's sharp tongue, Krisman looked about him and saw people snickering. Ridicule was one thing he could not take. He shoved the gun back into the holster where it belonged.

"All right, T.C.," he said unnecessarily, "lock them up."

Unnecessarily, because T.C. already had done so.

Even the old jailer was grinning a little, taking a chance on being fired.

Mark Truitt couldn't resist a little sarcasm himself. "When you get time from your duties, Sheriff, there are three more men out at George Frisco's place. They were wounded too bad to bring in."

"And Edsel Rankin?" the judge asked.

"Dead."

Mark took off his badge, which had remained

pinned to his shirt. He extended it past Krisman and handed it to the judge. "Property of the county," he said.

It was obvious that the judge hated to have to take it. "I'd like a full report on this thing," he said. "After all, I have to know how you've been spending the county's money. What say we go over to Betty's and have some coffee?"

The crowd parted and made room for them. By the time they got to Betty's cafe, Sam Vernon was with them. Luke Merchant had come along, too. Mark told them the story. What he left out, Luke put in.

The judge nodded gravely. "I can guarantee you one thing, Mark; there won't be any more of this talk about cowardice. They've been rawhiding Krisman till his back is sore, about being locked in Betty's cellar overnight with Scott Southall. People didn't take it very kindly when he put Betty in jail, either. They didn't let her stay in there but about an hour.

"I expect when the story gets out about the Rankins financing his campaign, Krisman'll catch it sure enough. He'll ride out of town some morning and not come back. We'll have to hold another election."

Sam Vernon said, "Mark, you say you think most of the cattle the Rankins have stolen from us are still down there, and we can go down and bring them back?"

Mark nodded. "It's a mighty big country, and it would take some time. But I think it can be done."

Sam pondered a while. "Seems to me you'd be the right man to take charge of the roundup. I'd be willing to give you, say, ten percent of my cattle that you recover. I think I could get the others to make the same deal. It'd give you a start, Mark. A good herd of cattle would help you build something while you're sheriffing. Think it over."

Mark smiled. "I won't have to think it over. I'll take the offer."

He thought they would never finish their coffee and leave. But at last he was alone with Betty Mulvane.

She touched his hand. "Just before you left, you said you were going to ask me a question."

He nodded. "I was. I was going to ask you to marry me. I haven't much in the way of property right now, but maybe someday I will have. If you were to think it over and decide to gamble along with me . . ."

She leaned her head against his shoulder, smiling. "I won't have to think it over," she said. "I'll take the offer."

NO EPITAPH FOR ME

On the offside of the hill, two of the three shivering riders swung down from their saddles. Stiff-fingered, they tied their split leather reins to winter-bared mesquite limbs swaying in the chill morning wind. Hunching over against the cold, they trudged up the hill.

The third man stayed in the saddle. He was bent low over the saddle horn, clutching with a gloved hand the dried crimson blotch that spread down from the shoulder of his thick woolen coat. His pinched young face was almost blue. His struggle against pain had left ugly tooth marks on his lower lip.

Reaching the top of the hill, Clay Forehand crouched low. He glanced a moment at the heavy gray clouds and grunted in satisfaction. There was a smell of rain in the air, freezing rain that would chill to the bone. But it would wash out tracks. Zack Bratcher crawled up behind him. "See them anywheres? They coming on?"

The wind was blowing straight down from the

wide-open plains of the Texas Panhandle. Forehand blinked the wind-bite from his eyes and peered anxiously over the back trail. "There's a little speck down there. Can't tell if it's moving or not."

Awkwardly, because of the cold, he reached his sheep-lined coat and pulled out a six-shooter. He slipped it into the crotch of a stout mesquite, near the ground where the wind couldn't move it. He worked it around until the sights were aligned on the speck. Blinking again, he concentrated on the front sight. The spot moved slowly from the top of the sight and off to the left.

"They're heading up the river," he said.

Zack Bratcher chuckled, a chuckle that came from deep in his thick throat. A grin showed stained teeth through the black stubble that covered his wolfish face.

"Then we've shook them, by God. It's took us two days, but we've shook them."

Clay grunted. "If they don't circle back and cut our sign before it rains. Now let's put some more miles behind us so we can find shelter for Allan."

He trotted down the hill, enjoying briefly the warm tingling of blood circulating through his saddle-stiffened legs. He wasn't a big man, this Clay Forehand. But though he was hardly more than thirty, he already had a way of carrying himself, a stern set to his stubbled jaw, that made men walk around him.

Untying his own horse, Clay led him up beside the wounded man's mount. "How you making it, boy?"

Allan Forehand swayed over the horn. He mumbled an unintelligible answer through his chattering teeth.

Attempting a show of cheerfulness, Clay rested his hand on his brother's knee. "Hang on, boy. We'll be finding you a house and a warm bed directly."

But, he pondered darkly as he swung into the cold saddle, it had better not be too long. The jogging ride might start the wound bleeding again. Allan had spilled too much blood already, this side of the San Angelo bank.

The rain started, as he had hoped. First it fell in scattered droplets cold as ice. Then it was a deluge, spilling off the flattened broad brim of his hat, soaking his pants legs and filling his boots, working its chill through to the marrow. But muddy brown rivulets poured off the hillsides, taking all tracks with them.

Long, cold, sodden hours added up the miles. But Allan was falling back. Clay slowed down to stay beside him. Irritably Bratcher drew rein and pulled around to face them.

"Come on, come on. Let's get moving." Warmth rose on the back of Clay's neck. "The kid's doing the best he can. You keep your mouth shut."

Bratcher's muddy eyes glowered. He chewed his thick lips. "The kid didn't have any business being with us in the first place. If he hadn't been so chicken-hearted he wouldn't've got shot."

Clay kept hold of the boy's arm, steadying him as they rode. "He can't kill people the way you can, Zack, like they was rabbits. Even when he saw the button aim the six-shooter at him, he couldn't make himself kill a youngster like that."

Zack grunted. "There wasn't nothing kept me from shooting."

Clay swallowed down a hard taste that came to his mouth. The picture was still sharp in his mind, Zack Bratcher swinging his gun down into the horrified button's face after Allan had been hit. The face had all but disappeared.

Zack squinted his eyes and frowned. "Now if you

don't hurry that kid up a little, I'm taking my share of the money and riding on."

A threat of real anger rode up and down Clay's throat. He wanted to say, "Go on and be damned to you." There'd come a time, maybe, when he would. But now he might need Bratcher.

It wasn't long until they pushed out of a mesquite thicket at the head of a draw and saw the little cow camp snuggled against the long, rocky foot of a table-top hill. Brownish smoke trailed with the wind as it curled out of a tin chimney that shoved crookedly up from the roof of a small rock house near the hill base.

Relief warmed Clay, tightly he gripped his brother's shivering arm. "Come on boy, we've found you a bed."

Zack Bratcher held up his big, hairy hand. "You hold up a minute, Clay. We was careful to keep our faces covered when we hit that bank. When we pull out of this place we can't leave anybody alive to be describing us and getting us identified. You got that?"

Clay looked at his brother's pale, drawn face and nodded immediately. "Sure, sure, we won't leave any-body. Now let's get to that house."

A little brown dog trotted out to meet them. He barked loudly, then dashed in to nip at the ankles of Zack's skittish horse. Cursing, Bratcher jerked at the reins and pulled out his pistol.

"Put that gun up, Zack," Clay said stiffly. "We need their help and killing their dog ain't going to make them friendly."

Muttering, Bratcher holstered the gun. The solid plank door of the rock house swung inward, and a young woman stood in the doorway. She was wiping bread dough off her hands onto an apron of cotton sacking. She gazed open-mouthed at Allan, who was swaying in the saddle.

"We got a hurt man here," Clay said. "We got to get him to bed."

She paled. She had an attractive face Clay noted involuntarily. With the care town girls could give it, it could have been a pretty face.

"Bring him on in," she said uncertainly, gripping the door edge a little fearfully.

To Clay, watchfulness was ingrained, result of years of riding and looking back. As the pleasant wood-fire warmth of the one-room house enveloped him, his sweeping gaze took in every corner. One bed. A big, iron kitchen stove, with dry mesquite wood piled high in a box behind it. Pantry in one corner. Table and cabinet of rough pine lumber. Quirt, rope and battered hat hanging on pegs stuck in the plaster of the rock wall.

Poor as sheepherders, he thought disinterestedly. But snug and comfortable, a man could bet his boots.

Clay, put his brother down on the one bed. "Boil us some water and get us some clean cloth for a bandage," he ordered the woman.

Quickly she poured a bucketful of water into a pan and set it on top of the big iron cookstove. She shoved some more wood into the fire. Then she picked up the bucket and started for the door.

Bratcher stepped in front of her and caught her roughly. "Where you think you're going?"

She trembled. Her voice shook. "Just to get some water out of the well."

Bratcher took the bucket out of her hand. "I'll git it. You stay here."

Carefully Clay took the heavy coat off of Allan. He unstrapped the boy's gun, looked for a place to put it, then shoved it far under the bed.

He tried to take off the shirt, but the dried blood had stuck it to the wound. He waited impatiently while the water heated. Then, gingerly, trying to keep from scalding the boy, he soaked the dried blood and pulled the shirt away.

Looking at the raw wound, he swallowed hard. A deep blue color had already spread far outward from the bullet hole. The smell of rotting flesh pinched Clay's nostrils, made him pull his head away.

He tried to shut his ears to his brother's ragged breathing. He blinked at the stinging in his eyes. Not a chance in a hundred now. Dazedly he went on trying to cleanse the wound, but his hands shook. He felt the woman's arm brush against his. She took the wet cloth from him.

"You'd better let me do it," she said. She seemed to have found her voice again. With only a little hesitation, she finished cleaning the wound. She started putting on a bandage.

Watching her, Clay noted that her lips were drawn thin and pale as she worked. But her fingers were sure. He noted a slight trembling in her slender throat. He let his gaze settle on her figure, fully rounded down to where it was lost in the fullness of a skirt that trailed the floor.

"What's your name?" he asked her. "Who lives here?"

"I'm Mary Sloan. There's just my husband and me. He's out looking at the cattle."

"When's he coming in?"

"For supper, any time now. Maybe ten minutes, maybe an hour."

Zack Bratcher shoved through the door and set down the bucket. He took off his hat and shook the water from it. "I put the horses out there in a corral and gave them a little of the feed I found. They'll be handy in case we got to leave."

He looked toward the unconscious boy. "Wish he'd hurry up and do whatever he's going to, so we could shove on."

Clay jumped to his feet, face hot, fists clenched. He caught himself and tried to force down the hatred that edged through him. Some day, Zack, he thought, you 'n me will find out which one is the fastest. But it won't be today.

Clay sat back down on the edge of Allan's bed and anxiously watched the boy's face. After a while he became conscious of Zack seated on a hide-bottom chair in a corner, his gaze following the woman as she worked at the stove. A hunger began to look out of those muddy eyes. The woman walked over next to Zack and reached up to get a can of coffee down from a shelf.

Zack shoved up from the chair and grabbed her. He crushed her body to his and eagerly sought her mouth with his thick, stubble-rimmed lips. She cried out in fear and anger.

Clay jumped up. He grabbed Zack's big arm and pulled it away from the woman. She jerked out of Bratcher's grasp. Choking, she grabbed a quirt from a peg on the I wall and lashed it across the outlaw's dark face once, twice, and a third time.

Clay shoved Bratcher back into the chair so hard that the man's head bumped against the rock wall. He wrested the quirt from the woman's trembling hands.

"Get this through your thick head, Zack," he roared, "we want this woman's help with Allan. That's all we want from her. You got that?"

Bratcher rubbed his hairy hand across his face and felt the raw welts rising beneath the black beard. There was poison in his eyes.

"All right, you wench," he gritted. "When we leave here, you'll pay for that."

"Shut up, Zack!" Clay snapped. But he saw sudden dread wash across the woman's face.

Clay jerked his head up. From over the drumming of rain on the roof he thought he heard a halloo. He listened intently. It came again, from up around the foot of the hill.

"Jim!" the woman gasped. She ran toward the door.

Clay caught her. "Your husband?" She nodded in fear.

Gun in his hand, Clay took position by the small, many-sectioned window to watch the rider coming in through the rain. "Open the door so he can see you," he commanded. "But don't let on there's anything wrong."

The tall young horseman reined up thirty yards in front of the house. His leather chaps flapping, he swung down and yelled a greeting as his wife opened the door.

Then she screamed. "Keep away, Jim! For God's sake, run!"

She darted out the door and into the rain. Catching a sharp breath, Clay bounded after her. He caught her and jerked her roughly to a stop. Instead of running away, the cowboy hurried toward them, anger in his face.

He stopped short as Clay brought up the gun. "What is this, anyhow?" he asked quickly. Clay noted with satisfaction that the puncher wasn't packing a six-shooter. He let the woman run to her husband and throw her arms around him, sobbing.

"You better come on in," Clay said. Inside, out of

the rain, the young woman clung tightly to her husband. Zack was grumbling. "If it'd been me, I'd've shot them both out there."

Clay flicked Zack a hard glance that told him to shut up. Looking at the woman, and not knowing why, he felt something like pride rising in him. She had courage, that one did. He found himself envying the cowboy. Clay had never known a woman who would risk a bullet in the back for him. Some of the kind he been around would have put a bullet in his back, if they thought there was money enough in his pockets to make it worthwhile.

"You'll both be all right as long as you don't go acting foolish," he told the couple. "Now I think we need some supper."

Clay managed to get a little broth down Allan's throat. But Allan never regained consciousness enough to eat. Clay could feel fever rising in the boy. Cautiously he looked under the bandage. The blue was spreading.

What about our milk cow?" Jim Sloan asked after supper. "We've got to go milk her or her bag'll spoil."

Clay looked at Zack. It wouldn't do to take Sloan out and leave the woman alone with Zack. It wouldn't do to leave Sloan with Zack, either. Bratcher's gun hand was too itchy today.

So Clay followed both the Sloans out toward the cow pen and left Zack to watch Allan. Clay felt a strong respect growing for Sloan as he looked at young ranchman's corrals.

Half the fences were made of mesquite limbs and trunks. The rest were of piled rocks. This far from town, and this far from timber, plank corrals were too expensive. But the rock was here. All it took was labor. Sloan had put in plenty of that. Clay thought unpleasantly of his father. All Pa had ever worked at was meanness.

While Jim Sloan unsaddled his horse the woman turned a big heifer calf in with the milk cow. She left her a few minutes then put a short rope around her neck and led her off to a smaller pen. Jim started milking.

"That heifer calf's about big enough to butcher," Clay remarked as the woman returned with the short rope.

She shook her head. "Oh, no saving her for a cow. When our baby gets here, we'll need more milk."

Clay's eyes opened a little wider. "Baby?"

She nodded. "It's due in the spring."

He glanced at Jim Sloan. He caught the pride in the cowboy's eyes. Clay wondered, and unwelcome memories crowded to his mind, memories of his boyhood.

His parents had had a deep hatred for each other. They had never really wanted him. It had been a long time ago. But sometimes even yet in a nightmare Clay could imagine Pa was hiding him with a razor strap, taking it out on the boy for something the old woman had said.

Clay had saddled an old plowhorse in the dead of night and headed west before there was any fuzz on his face. He had never gone back but once, years later. He had found Pa and the old woman treating Allan like they had treated him. Clay stole his brother away and took to the rough country with him. Anything was better for the kid than staying with the folks, he thought.

Now Allan was dying an outlaw's death, and Clay wondered. He let his eyes brood on Jim and Mary Sloan. Things would be different with their baby. These folks weren't like Pa and the old woman. Trouble was, the baby would never be born. Like Zack had said, when they pulled out of here they couldn't afford to leave anyone behind them.

After nightfall the rain drummed intermittently on the roof. Allan's breathing became more labored. Fever burned in his face. In delirium he turned his head from one side to the other, mumbling in coherently.

Clay's throat grew tight and his pulses quickened. Wasn't there something somebody could do for the boy?

Mary Sloan did all she could. She put cool cloths over the boy's burning forehead. She tried to keep the wound clean. By midnight she was dragging her feet. Jim Sloan stood quietly behind her, helping whenever he could.

Zack Bratcher had taken a couple of quilts and thrown them on the floor in another corner. Once in a while he would turn over, grumbling.

After midnight Clay let the Sloans spread blankets on the floor and get some sleep. He sat up alone with Allan, keeping the fire going, watching the fever mount, feeling the life ebb lower.

At daylight all were up again. Zack was grouching about being hungry and muttering that Mary Sloan had damn well better get to work at the stove, if she knew what was good for her. But first she came over to the bedside and looked at Allan.

Clay swallowed and blinked his eyes that burned from worry and anguish and lack of sleep. He hasn't got a chance, he thought woodenly. It's just a question of time.

Zack was rummaging around in the little pantry next to the cabinet. "I'm starved plumb to death. Where's the beef?"

Mary Sloan said, "We used the last of it for supper."

Zack glared at her, mumbling in his beard. He stomped outside and shoved the door shut behind him.

While Clay sat on the edge of the bed, running his fingers through his hair and blinking back the sleep from his eyes, Mary Sloan re-cleansed Allan's wound. Her face paled as she worked. She knows it too, Clay thought bleakly. The kid hasn't got long to go.

Presently Zack came back in, lugging a heavy hind quarter of fresh-butchered beef. "Now, woman," he growled, "we'll have steak for breakfast."

Mary Sloan's slender hand went up to her pale mouth. Her eyes widened. "Our calf," she cried. "You butchered the calf we were saving for our baby!"

Angrily she stepped toward him. Quickly Jim Sloan grabbed her. "Stop it, Mary. Don't be a fool. He'd shoot you for no reason at all."

She sobbed. "It was our baby's heifer—our baby's."

Zack grunted. "Shut up and start cookin'. When we leave here you won't be worried about calves or babies or anything else."

Clay stood up angrily. "Damn you, Zack, can't you keep that blabbing mouth of yours shut?"

Mary Sloan choked. "Jim, they're going to kill us!"

Sloan's face turned a shade whiter. He gripped his wife's shoulders. "Get hold of yourself, Mary," he said in a moment. "I'll put some wood in the stove and we'll get breakfast."

Sloan went to the woodbox and took out a couple of big sticks of dry mesquite. Zack hovered over the stove, an expectant grin on his whiskered face as he looked at the quarter of beef. Sloan shoved the wood in the stove and settled the coals with a long poker.

Suddenly he swung the poker up and brought it down across Bratcher's skull. The gunman fell heavily to the floor.

"Get out, Mary," Sloan yelled. "Run!" The woman dashed in desperation toward the door.

Clay was on his feet and grabbing at his gun. Sloan rushed him, the poker swung back over his shoulder. He brought it down just as Clay pulled up his gun hand. The poker struck the bone of the wrist, and sharp pain lanced through Clay. The gun clattered to the floor.

Throwing his weight against Sloan, Clay managed to knock the cowboy off balance and tumble him backward. In an instant Clay scooped up the fallen gun with his left hand and swung it at Sloan's head. The cowboy went limp.

His wrist burning like fire, Clay jumped to the door and shoved outside. Mary Sloan was running for the barn. Her long skirts were tripping her, and the deep mud was slowing her down. Clay caught up with her and grabbed her arm. She struggled a moment, then gave up. All hope in her eyes slowly died.

Getting his breath back, Clay said flatly, "Can't say as I blame you for trying. But it was foolish."

The feel of her soft, slender arm under the heavy grip of his left hand sent a peculiar but pleasant tingle through him. Not hard to see why Sloan had married her. For a moment he felt an impulse to pull her to him, to know the thrill of her body against his own.

But that was the way Zack Bratcher did things. Clay fought down the urge and led her back toward the little rock house.

Jim Sloan was struggling to push himself up off the floor. With a sharp cry, Mary Sloan ran to him. She dipped a cloth in cool water and tenderly washed his face. As he came around, she put her cheek to his and hugged him tightly.

Watching them, Clay swallowed, real folks, these two. If Pa and the old woman could have been that way. . . .

Zack Bratcher was on his hands and knees, straining to get to his feet. Once up, he steadied himself on the stove's guardrail. He blinked his muddy eyes, Memory came back to him and he reached shakily for his gun.

Clay's voice had the edge of whipsaw. "You put that gun up, Zack!"

Bratcher's brownish eyes were hard as rock. His hand wavered only slightly. Clay could feel his heart beat quicken. He let his own hand ease down toward his gun.

Allan's feverish voice made Clay whirl around. The boy was threshing about deliriously. Heart in his throat, Clay caught the boy's arms and pushed him back down onto the bed. Allan struggled another moment. He relaxed then, and the heavy breathing stopped.

Unbelievingly, Clay shook Allan, cried for him to breathe again. He was suddenly caught up in a roaring black storm. He cursed himself, he cursed the San Angelo bank, he cursed Pa and the old woman. But there was no use. It was over.

After a bit, Clay made himself look at the other people. He could see dread in Mary Sloan's eyes and pity, too.

Zack Bratcher's voice was brittle. "Well, now that it's all done, we better be riding."

Woodenly, Clay shook his head "Not yet. I want to bury him first." The rain had stopped. They wrapped Allan in a patchwork quilt and carried him three hundred yards from the house, at the foot of the long hill. There Jim Sloan dug a grave and Allan Forehand was laid to rest.

Sloan had brought along a short plank. As Clay was finishing filling the grave and and noticing dully the growing stiffness of his wrist, Sloan took out a pocket knife and began to carve on the wood.

"What's that for?" Clay asked abruptly, laying down the shovel. Sloan looked up in surprise. "A headboard. You want to mark the grave, don't you?"

Clay jerked the board out of Sloan's ands and hurled it away across the rocky slope. "No!" he cried. "You think I want people saying here's the grave of Allan Forehand, shot down while robbing the San Angelo bank?"

He tried desperately to keep his voice from breaking.

"It wasn't the kid's fault he ended up like this. I caused it. Me, and Pa, and my old woman. It's better for us to leave him here without a trace than to bury him with an outlaw marker over his head."

Sloan didn't argue. Quietly he picked up the shovel and finished filling the grave. Cooling a little, Clay felt strangely grateful. The cowboy had wanted to help.

The job done, the group started back toward the little rock house. Jim and Mary Sloan walked in the lead, the cowboy holding his arm around his wife's shoulder. Clay was next, stumbling along, his head down, his eyes blurred. Behind him stalked Zack Bratcher, itchy hands rubbing the butt of his six-gun.

As they reached the house, Bratcher's voice called out harshly, poison as a snake. "Turn around, you Sloans!" Clay blinked hard and raised his head, the

Sloans had stopped. They had their arms around one another, waiting for Bratcher to squeeze the trigger. There was fear in their faces, all right, but they weren't running and they weren't begging. They were staying together right to the end.

A sudden thought struck Clay. Where might Allan be right now if he had had folks like these instead of Pa and the old woman? In his mind he could see again Mary Sloan working until she was dead on her feet, trying to ease Allan's pain. He thought on Pa's shift-lessness, and on Jim Sloan's rock house and rock corrals. He heard again the cursing and bickering of Pa and the old woman, and he looked at the young couple in each other's arms.

Before he realized it, he had his hand on his gun. His wrist was still stiff.

"Keep your gun in your holster, Zack," he said sharply. "They're not going to die."

Bratcher's muddy eyes cut furiously to Clay's. "The deal was that we left nobody alive. You backing down on that, Clay?"

Clay's voice was firm. "I'm saying we owe more than we can pay them. We're leaving them alone."

Bratcher snarled, "I owe them nothing but two slugs. I'm paying that debt if I've got to cut you down first, Clay." The wolfish look came to his face. "If I beat you, I'll be three times as rich as I was yesterday. And I'll never again have to listen to you tell me what to do."

Clay could feel his heartbeat quicken. For a long time he had known this would come, if he stayed with Zack too long. Now here it was. The butt of the gun under his hand was slick with cold sweat.

He was aware of the Sloans moving cautiously toward the door of the house. Then he saw that sudden warning in Bratcher's eyes a split second before the outlaw's hand jerked upward with the pistol. Clay pulled his own gun.

Sharp pain stabbed through his wrist, slowed his draw. The lick from that damned poker, he thought desperately. Bratcher's first slug spun him half around. He thought he heard a door slam. Falling, he squeezed off a wild shot at Bratcher and knew it had missed.

Another slug ripped into him. Flames roared through him. His head reeled. The gun slipped from his stiffened fingers. He tried to push himself up from the ground and felt cold mud ooze around his hands.

He raised his head painfully and blinked away the haze. Bratcher was stepping cautiously toward him. The whole scene was swaying back and forth. Bratcher leveled the gun again. Clay tried to make himself search for his fallen pistol, but he could do nothing.

A shot echoed in his ears. The thought came to him that Zack had missed. He blinked again, and saw Bratcher sprawled out facedown in the mud.

Clay's arms gave way under him. He could feel the wet ground under his whiskered cheek. Someone caught hold of his shoulder, turned him over onto his back. It was Jim Sloan. Mary Sloan stood over him.

"You—you shot Zack," Clay managed to say to Jim. "But where'd you—find a gun?"

It was Mary Sloan who spoke. "Allan's gun. When you brought him in, you pitched it under the bed. You forgot to take it out."

Now it was Jim Sloan who was speaking. "We're grateful to you, Forehand. We wish there was something we could do."

Weakly, Clay shook his head. No, there wasn't anything anybody could do now.

"There's one thing," he said painfully. "When that

baby comes, you treat him right—give him a chance. He won't end up—like the Forehands . . ."

And so it was that another grave joined Allan's there at the foot of the rocky hill. Like the first one, it was left without a marker. But Clay and Allan Forehand were to have a monument just the same, a living one.

The spring rains had come and the grass had risen green when Jim Sloan hitched the team to the wagon and took Mary down the long, dim trail to town. When he brought her back a few weeks later, there was someone new in the wagon, wrapped in tiny blankets and carried in its mother's lap.

They named him Clay Allan Sloan.

ONE SON

Leaning back against the front fender of the ranch pickup truck, Matt Cooper absently fumbled with his horsehead watch fob and watched the door of the doctor's office with a patience that came from spending a lifetime in the saddle.

He wished old Foster Harbison had let him go along when he went in to the doctor. But Foster was a proud old West Texas ranchman who seemed to feel that there was something disgraceful about letting the infirmities of age creep up on him.

Presently the door opened, and Foster Harbison moved out onto the front steps. Matt started to step forward, then stopped abruptly. His heart dropped as he studied the dark lines of despair in Foster's kind old face. Matt knew what the doctor's verdict had been.

Without a word, Harbison ambled slowly over to the pickup and got in, his head down. Matt felt a catch in his throat. Sliding behind the steering wheel, he wanted to ask Foster how much time the doctor had given him. But he didn't.

"Any place you want to go?"

Foster shook his grey head sadly. "I just want to go home, Matt."

Matt started the motor and backed out of the parking place, hoping Harbison wouldn't see the mist in his eyes. But Harbison wasn't looking anyway. He still had his head down.

Matt felt an ache deep within him. It just didn't seem right that Foster might go. For thirty years Matt had been Foster's foreman. They had worked together, eaten together, suffered together, raised their kids together. No stranger would have been able to tell which one was boss.

Now Matt realized his own age as if for the first time, and the jolt of it was like a kick in the stomach. He was as old as Foster. It could have been his own heart as easily as Foster's. And if Foster went, might it be long before Matt went, too?

He tried to shake these thoughts from his mind. He remembered something he had seen when he went to pick up the ranch's new power cattle sprayer. Now he made a detour off the main road leading out of town. No use letting Foster see young Wade Harbison's car parked in front of that Lone Star honkytonk.

As an excuse for making the detour, Matt pointed to a new house on the right-hand side of the street. "There's Bill Scott's new home that he's built so his kids can be close to school."

Some of the despair left Foster's face, and a hint of a smile showed there. "Good kids, Bill's are."

Then the sadness came back. Presently he began to talk. "I wouldn't mind going so much, Matt, if I knew I had a son like Bill's that was going to take up the ranch right where I left off. But Wade . . ."

Harbison was silent a moment. "I had hopes that

when Wade got back from the war he'd marry your daughter Molly, and that I'd have me some grandchildren to sit on my lap and tell stories to before I finally—had to go. It looked for quite a while like it was going to work out that way. Then something happened. I don't know what came over him."

Harbison sat there gripping his hands together until the knuckles were white. "If I had it all to live over again, Matt, I wouldn't settle for one son. I'd have me four, or maybe five. You know, it wasn't till the day they brought me the telegram that Wade was missing in action—it wasn't till then that I realized I just had one son.

"God was with me then, and He brought my son back. But it seems like He's looking the other direction now. In a way it's almost like Wade was missing again."

Matt swallowed down the catch in his throat. "Wade's going to be all right, Foster. The way I see it, it's just that the war took him so young. It robbed him of those wild years me and you had just before we got to be men. Now he's kind of making up for them. Something'll happen one of these days, like it did to us, and he'll get his feet on the ground."

Foster nodded. "Maybe so. I hope it won't be too long."

Matt's daughter Molly was waiting for him at the front door after he let Foster out and had the cowboys help him unload the power sprayer from the pickup. Matt's heart warmed at the sight of her. Standing there in a crisp new cotton dress, she looked as fresh as a new calf on a spring morning. But despite her smile, he could see worry behind her dark blue eyes.

"I could tell by Foster's look that the doctor's report wasn't good," she said.

Matt looked down at his box-toed boots. "The doctor says he's got a chance only if he'll sit back and take it easy, and has nothing to worry him. Otherwise, it's just a matter of time, and not too much time at that."

Molly's eyes were suddenly clouded. "He would sit back, if only Wade would take hold and run the ranch. But like it is, Foster'll work and worry himself to death. I've got a notion to tell Wade just what I think."

Matt lifted his hands in alarm. "No, Molly, you can't. Foster made me promise not to tell Wade. If Wade's going to reform, it's got to be because he wants to. It can't be just because his dad is sick."

Anger darkened Molly's cheeks, and Matt saw a hint of tears in her eyes as she turned away from him. He watched her a long moment, gathering courage for what he was to say.

"We've got to bring Wade back to his senses, Molly. For Foster's sake, we've got to. And I think you can do more than anybody."

Slowly she turned back around to face him. "Why me?"

Matt gripped his knuckles nervously. "You're still in love with him, Molly."

She started. The tears welled up, and she leaned back against a chair, her head bowed a little.

"I guess a blind burro could see that," she admitted, the hurt plain in her voice, "but what am I supposed to do, throw myself at him and tell him I'm his if he'll settle down and quit acting like a half-grown kid?"

Matt shook his head. "Not exactly like that. But it was you that broke off your engagement after he had thrown one too many wild parties with that rodeo gang of his. Maybe if you'd just kind of let him know you still feel the same way about him that you used to, he'll finally break down and ask you to give him another chance. He's three years older now. If you love Foster, you've got to try, Molly."

She nodded. "All right, Dad. We'll see."

All the rest of the afternoon Matt kept glancing at the road that led in from town, hoping to see the trail of dust that would mean Wade's car. But when suppertime drew near, there was still no sign of the boy.

Since Matt's wife had died, Molly did most of the cooking for the small Harbison ranch crew. Foster always came over to the Coopers' house to eat. Molly would set out a plate for Wade, too. But the last three years he was seldom around.

Just as the cowboys settled down to eat, Wade's car pulled to a stop outside, an empty horse trailer rattling behind it. The two punchers glanced out the window at him, then at Foster. They looked down at their plates as Wade strode gaily in and let the screen door slam behind him.

Matt studied the young man a moment. No one could ever deny that Wade was a handsome lad, the kind that nice old ladies always wanted to introduce their daughters to. Nor did he lack ability.

He could ride just about the saltiest ranch bronc that might be led out to him. If he didn't ride the first time, he would keep getting back on till he finally did ride. Throwing a rope was just as natural to him as throwing a baseball. And he could judge the value of a cow just about as well as his old daddy could.

For the first time in Matt didn't know how long, Molly smiled at Wade. "Better late than never," she said. "I was about to use your plate to feed the dog in."

Wade stopped and stared at her as if he couldn't believe it. He finally grinned. "Now, you wouldn't want to poison a dog, would you?"

All through the meal, Matt saw Wade stealing puzzled glances at Molly. A wild hope rose in the foreman. Maybe Wade, too, felt the way he had used to.

After supper Wade hung around the dining table, struggling hard to find new topics of conversation with Matt while he actually kept stealing glimpses of Molly. Matt went out on the front porch alone and sat down to smoke his pipe. Presently he glanced back through a window and saw Wade helping Molly with the dishes.

A warm new satisfaction spread through Matt. By dogies, it looked like it might work.

After a while Wade came out and strode toward the barn. Matt knocked the ashes out of his pipe and followed him.

"We've got three pastures of calves to brand, Wade," Matt said. "According to the almanac, the signs'll be right in a couple of days. Kind of hoped you'd want to be here to help."

Wade shook his head. "Looks like you've forgotten about the rodeo coming to town, Matt. You couldn't hire any extra help. And as for me, I've already promised some of the boys I'd be around for the roping events."

Matt choked down the disappointment. "Seems like there's always a rodeo or a matched roping or some doggone thing someplace when we've got work to do here," he said pointedly.

He saw a sign of irritation rise in Wade's face. "I'm sorry it's that way, Matt."

The boy turned to go, then stopped a moment. "I

asked Molly to go to the rodeo dance with me the last night of the show. She said she would. That all right with you?"

Matt grunted. All the disappointment hadn't left him. "Sure, Wade. It's all right with me."

Next morning Wade ate breakfast with the rest of the crew and followed the cowboys out to the barn. Maybe he would make the morning ride, Matt thought. Old Foster hobbled out to the barn with them, and Matt noticed him glancing hopefully at the boy.

In the corral Matt shook out a horse loop in his rope. "What do you want to ride this morning, Wade?"

Wade shook his head. "Afraid I haven't got time to go along this morning, Matt. Got to work on my rig and get it ready for the rodeo."

Matt gripped the rope tightly. He glanced at Foster and saw disappointment wash across the wrinkled face. Foster hesitated a minute, then said, "Catch me old Packrat. I'm going along."

Matt hefted his rope doubtfully. "Don't you think maybe you ought to stay around close for a while, Foster? You got to have rest."

Foster shook his head irritably. "There's been mighty few days since I've had this outfit that one of the Harbisons hasn't been along to help. And that policy ain't going to change as long as I'm able to see a cow."

Matt purposely missed the first loop, hoping Wade would speak up and go instead of his dad. As he recoiled his rope he looked around and saw Wade already on his way to the barn. Anger rippled through the foreman. He caught Packrat clean the second throw.

His anger came back over him when the crew returned to the ranch for dinner. Another car was parked at Wade's trailer out by the barn. Matt could see two cowpunchers standing in the shade by the barn's front steps, watching Wade re-lace his stirrup leathers.

There wasn't any mistaking the men's Hollywood cowboy clothes. Cecil Bragg and Ed Gordon, Matt thought, spitting at fence post in disgust. They had come just the right time to mooch a free meal from Molly.

Matt gave them a curt nod as he walked up. Bragg eyed him warily, and Gordon slowly retreated around beside Wade.

"Just came out to see if Wade was ready for the rodeo, Mister Matt," Gordon said as if he thought an explanation was necessary.

Matt said nothing. There was a long uneasy moment, and even Wade, concentrating on his saddle, seemed to sense it. Finally Gordon resumed talking to Wade.

"Like I was saying, Wade, we could have us a real good time if we was to go on the rodeo circuit the rest of the summer. We could go to Arizona and Colorado and Wyoming—all them places like that. Just have us a good time."

A tension built up in Matt as he watched Wade studying his saddle, his brow knitted. Wade couldn't leave the country now, not with his dad in such bad shape. He just couldn't.

Presently Wade shook his head. "Aw Ed, I wouldn't feel right about leaving here for so long. Why don't you all just go ahead?"

Gordon objected vigorously. "We couldn't go without you, Wade."

Matt grunted. "Bet your life you couldn't. Who'd pay your bills?"

Wade looked up irritably. "I don't know why you've always got to insult my friends, Matt."

Matt felt his anger getting away with him, and he tried to hold it in.

"You'd find out just how good friends they were if you ever went broke."

Wade stood up, his eyes narrowed. "When I was a kid, Matt, you told me to never let anybody else pick my cows for me, or pick my friends."

Matt swallowed. "You've gotten to where you're a lot better at picking cows than you are at picking friends, Wade!"

He turned and tromped toward the house, fighting at the anger that surged within him.

Matt didn't try to get much work done while the rodeo was on. He turned the cowhands loose to go to the show. Matt himself didn't go until the last afternoon. The way he figured it, he had lived enough rodeo right out on the range the last forty-odd years.

Home again, Matt found Molly in a brand new dress, making pirouettes in front of a mirror and admiring the garment. It made her look like a million dollars, Matt thought proudly.

"It's for the dance tonight, Dad," she trilled. "I've got to take it up in a place or two, but isn't it lovely?"

Matt grinned. He hadn't seen her so happy in he didn't know how long. If she couldn't charm Wade tonight, the boy was blind.

Wade came to get Molly about dark. Matt's anger was forgotten as he watched the way the two youngsters looked at each other.

Old Foster came hobbling over just as the boy and girl left for town. A puzzled grin was on his face. "I just can't hardly believe it," he said, watching the car lights disappear down the town road.

Warm satisfaction spread through Matt. Just let

those two parasite friends of Wade's try to drag him off to the rodeo circuit now, he thought.

The slamming of a car door awoke Matt with a start. He threw back the cover a little and pushed himself up on one elbow to look at the clock. Hardly midnight. Doggoned early for Wade and Molly to be home from the dance!

In a moment the front door opened and closed again. Matt sat up in bed as he heard Molly sobbing. Uneasiness spread through him as he started to get up.

Turning on the light, he saw Molly sitting in a living room chair, dabbing at her eyes with a handkerchief. He stood there uncertainly. He had never been much help when a woman was crying. Finally he walked over to her and patted her on the shoulder.

"Now, now," he said soothingly, "it can't be all that bad. Where's Wade?"

"He's still in town," she said bitterly. "I hope he has to walk!"

She soon got control of herself. "It's not Wade, really," she said. "It's those people who always hang around him, like Ed Gordon and Cecil Bragg, helping him spend his money. If we could make him see what a worthless bunch they are, he might straighten out all right."

Matt's anger began to kindle up again. "What made you go off and leave him?" he growled.

"It was Gordon and Bragg. Wade and I were having a wonderful time together till those two came in. Wade invited them to sit down with us. They had a bottle with them. I told Wade I didn't like it.

"Finally Ed Gordon took a notion he wanted to dance. He grabbed me by the arm and tried to drag me out onto the dance floor. Wade argued with him, in a quiet kind of way, but Gordon didn't turn me loose. So I slapped him good and hard. Then Wade told me I ought to be ashamed, that Gordon didn't realize what he was doing. I got so mad I slapped Wade, too. I grabbed his car keys off the table, got the car and came home."

Matt sat down in another chair, his hands trembling, his face hot. "It's my fault, Molly," he said softly. "I thought we could change him. But all I've done is get you hurt all over again."

About the middle of the next morning, Gordon and Bragg brought Wade out to the ranch. Matt watched Wade get his own car and back it up to his horse trailer. The old foreman strode over to him. He shot a hostile glance at Gordon and Bragg. He noted the pair's bloodshot eyes and hoped they both had a headache.

"Looks like you're going someplace, Wade," he said evenly.

Wade nodded.

"I figured on going ahead with the branding," Matt went on. "We need your help."

Wade didn't answer, so Gordon piped in. "Wade's going with us to follow the rodeo circuit a couple of months."

Matt's heart skipped a beat or two. He felt a little of the color drain from his face.

"Wade's old daddy has got money enough to hire all the help he needs," Gordon went on. "He don't need Wade."

Heat roared back into Matt's face. He doubled his fists and said with anger, "Doesn't need him? You haven't got any idea how much old Foster does need him!"

Matt reached down and pulled Wade's hand away

from the trailer hitch. "You can just unhitch that trailer, Wade. You're staying here!"

Wade looked up in surprise. His grey eyes leveled on Matt's. "I'll go where I please and do what I want."

Matt thundered, "A few times when you were a kid I had to take my belt off and warm the seat of your britches with it. You're still not too big for me to wallop the daylights out of you!

"I hoped we could wake you up a better way. But wake you up I will, even if I've got to work the hound out of you. Now you unhitch that trailer and go find yourself some working clothes."

Wade stood staring at him, his mouth open. Surprise seemed to have knocked the argument out of him. Now there was a trace of a smile in his eyes.

"I'll stay and help you brand if you'll hire my two buddies here."

Dismay was in the two men's faces. Matt didn't like it. "They couldn't work their way out of a wet paper sack."

"If I stay, they do."

Matt gave in disgustedly. "All right. They're on till we finish branding. Regular day wages, seven dollars a day. And if they don't work, by dogies, they don't eat!"

The whole crew was up and out before daylight next morning. Foster Harbison came along despite Matt's protest. Matt didn't like the pale look in the old ranchman's face this morning.

The men stopped at the back side of the pasture to smoke and wait for daylight to make it light enough to work. Ed Gordon carelessly flipped his cigarette butt away. A moment later the grass began to crackle where it fell. Orange flames licked at the dry grass, and the pungent smoke bit at riders' nostrils.

"Put it out, quick," Matt shouted. "A fire in this dry grass could burn off a couple of sections."

Wade quickly swung to the ground, unbuckling his leggings. He and another cowpuncher used their chaps to beat out the fire. Gordon was on the ground too, but he stood helplessly, his mouth half open, as if he didn't know what to do.

When the last sparks had been tromped out and Wade had remounted, Matt said to him, "Tell your friends to watch their cigarettes from now on. We ain't firemen."

They got the cattle into the corrals, separated them and had the branding half done before Molly drove up in the ranch's second pickup, bringing their lunch. Matt noted sadly the uneasy way Wade looked at Molly and kept his distance from her. He noted too the way the girl avoided looking at Wade.

After the meal, Molly stayed around and watched the rest of the branding. Matt had a couple of cowboys drive the first pickup over to a windmill to fill the power sprayer, bolted to wooden skids fastened to the pickup bed. He mixed up a batch of DDT and poured it into the sprayer. He started the pump's motor, picked up the end of the long hose, and began spraying a heavy fog of insecticide over the cows and calves as boys pushed them through a narrow chute.

"This'll cut down on the flies and the tail switching this summer, Foster," he said happily. "Wish we'd had this years ago. But there'll be more beef to sell this fall."

Foster grinned. But Matt still didn't like the hollow look under the old man's eyes.

As soon as the pairs were sprayed, Matt had the two regular cowhands start driving them toward a new pasture. After a while the cows without calves had been sprayed.

"Gordon," Matt said, "you and Bragg drive these dry cows down the draw and put them out that gate over yonder a mile."

Matt, Wade and Foster finished up around the branding pens and cleaned out the power sprayer.

Gordon and Bragg had been gone perhaps thirty minutes when Molly yelled, "Fire, Dad! Down the draw!"

Matt's heart leaped right up into his throat as he saw the grey smoke curling upward from the draw. He started to curse the two careless cowhands. But there wasn't time for it.

"Wade," he shouted, "you fill up that power sprayer with water. We can use it to fight fire. Foster, you and Molly and me'll take the other pickup down there and get started on the fire."

Matt tore an old worn-out tarp into large pieces and quickly soaked them in a water trough. Then the three jumped into the pickup and bounced across the cow trails and ditches as fast as the thing would run.

Matt's heart sank when he saw the fire. It was already well out of hand. The wind was blowing right down the draw, carrying the fire rapidly in the direction of the windmills.

Gordon and Bragg were both swinging at the fire with their chaps. But about all they were doing was spreading it. Their horses, both loose, stood a long distance out on one side. The cows had scattered.

"Grab those wet tarps and get to working with them," Matt yelled. He told Foster to stay with the pickup, in case it had to be moved. But a minute later he saw the old ranchman right out front, beating at the fire as hard as he could swing. His heart couldn't take much of that, but how could you argue with a man like Foster?

Matt concentrated on the fire, and wished Wade would hurry up with that sprayer. The wind got stronger. The flames rose higher and spread swifter. They would hit the big mesquites and swoop up the dry grass clustered around them.

Sweat dripped from Matt's face and burned his eyes. Heat blistered him. His lips were dry as old leather. As he slapped desperately at the fire, he felt his breath getting shorter and shorter. It seemed the world was beginning to swing mad, fiery arcs back and forth before his seared eyes.

A scream brought him out of it suddenly. Molly! He looked around him but could see nothing but the wild, dancing scenes made by the blistering heat waves. Molly screamed again. Matt dropped his piece of tarp and went running toward her voice. Then he saw.

Foster had let the fire surround him. He stood in a small bare island out in the middle of a river of licking orange flames and wicked grey smoke. Molly was running toward him, dodging flames, jumping nimbly from one bare spot to another.

Matt called her excitedly but knew she never heard him. He saw Gordon and Bragg standing together outside the belt of fire, neither one making a move to help Molly or Foster.

Suddenly Matt saw Foster grip his shirt front painfully and slump to the ground. His heart!

Matt called again, panic seizing him. Forgetting the flames, he started running toward the girl and the old man. His foot caught between the forks of an old stump, and he felt the breath leave him as he sprawled out on the hot ground.

Black ashes choked him. He struggled for breath,

beating at the sparks that burned his flesh in a dozen
places. Pain and fear and desperation all grabbed hold
of him, and he hardly heard Wade's pickup come
bouncing to a stop.

Then he was painfully conscious of Wade bending
over him, helping him get his foot loose and slapping
the breath into him. "Come on and help me," Wade
was calling.

Gordon's scared voice sounded as if it was a mile
away. "And get burned up? Lord no!"

Wade was hastily helping Matt to the pickup and
beating at the flames that were burning the foreman's
clothes in places.

"I'll help you get up in back, Matt," Wade was saying quickly. "You'll have to handle the nozzle on that
sprayer. We're going on in to get Dad and Molly!"

Flames were already licking up at the pickup, but
nothing had caught fire. Almost automatically, Matt
grabbed hold of the sprayer. Then the pickup was
bouncing crazily through the flames. Matt held his
breath until it got to the little island in the middle.

While Matt kept a heavy spray of water going on
the flames, Wade jumped out. Matt didn't miss the
quick look that passed between the boy and the girl
as they stood together in peril—a look that told much
better than words ever could of love and thanks and
forgiveness.

They put Foster in the pickup. Then Wade swung
the pickup around and they were bouncing back out
again. The heavy grass smoke choked Matt and burned
his eyes until he could hardly see.

Outside the belt of fire again, Wade jumped out and
took a quick look under the pickup and beneath the
hood to make sure no flames had caught hold. Matt
blinked his stinging eyes and saw the two regular

cowboys spurring their horses as hard as they could run, coming to help.

Quickly Wade and Molly got Foster into the other pickup. Matt jumped off the fender and felt his sprained ankle give way beneath him, burning worse than the fire had.

"Molly and I are taking Dad to the doctor," Wade told the newly arrived cowboys. "You all take the power sprayer and hold the flames in check the best you can. We'll phone the neighbors and send out the county fire truck. Watch after Matt."

As an afterthought, he added, "Matt, get rid of Ed and Cecil, will you? Send them to town. Tell them if they're still here when I get back, I'm liable to kill them both."

The doctor let Foster come home Saturday morning. He would be all right, the medic said. It usually took one attack to show an old mossyhorn like Foster that the doctor was right.

Matt bedded Foster down in the Cooper house, where Molly could watch after him. With his sprained ankle bound up like a Christmas present, Matt wasn't getting around much himself.

Wade Harbison came in at noon, his face dusty, his clothes showing sign of hard work. Molly greeted him with a warm smile.

"Wade," Foster called irritably, "come make these people let me up. There's too much work around here for me to lie in bed."

Wade put his hand on his father's shoulder and gently pushed the old man back into bed. "You're staying there till the doctor says you can get up. From now on, if there's any work to do around here, I'll do it."

The irritation left the old man's face, and a pleased

smile replaced it. "What about that rodeo circuit your friends were talking about?"

Wade looked at Molly. "My friends? From now on I've got the same friends you have, Dad."

Wade stood watching Molly. Nervously he put his weight on first one foot, then the other.

"Molly," he said at last, "that sure was a pretty dress you had on the other night. I'd like to see you wear it again. There's another dance tonight."

Happiness shone in her eyes. "I'd love to go, Wade."

That night Matt Cooper and Foster Harbison sat on the front porch and watched as Molly and Wade went out to the car, arm in arm. Just like the old days, Matt thought, and he enjoyed the warm glow of satisfaction that began to spread within him.

"Matt," Foster chuckled, "I've decided I'm going to stay around a while. I've got a feeling we're going to have those grandchildren yet."

POISON

It was the prairie-dog law that brought Dev Leindecker to Old Man Edgewood's Long E outfit.

You don't find many prairie dogs in Texas any more.
But forty years ago the hole-studded dog towns spread
over so much of the state, crippled up so much livestock and ruined so much grass, that the legislature
passed a law requiring every ranch owner to extermi-
nate prairie dogs on his land.

Old Man Edgewood never would have hired Leindecker's kind if he hadn't been so tightfisted about
everything but whisky.

He liked to throw a big, long binge every now and
again, but otherwise he never squandered a nickel.

He was close-herding his money the day he rode
into Midland looking for a man to poison his prairie
dogs so the county wouldn't do it and assess him a stiff
price for it.

Leindecker was a big, brawling bear of a man, so
tall he had to duck to walk through a saloon door.
He had a broad, sun-darkened face with a flat mouth

and the coldest wolf eyes a man ever saw. Few ranches would hire him anymore. He'd generally last about a week or two before his mad-dog temper would bust loose and he left some cowboy beaten half to death.

The sheriff had been eyeing Leindecker pretty close for a day or two when Old Man Edgewood propositioned him, offering him ten dollars a month less than the going wage. Looking over his shoulder, Leindecker took it.

"I got a roundup crew goin'," Edgewood told him. "Any time you're workin' close to the wagon, just ride over there and eat. Otherwise, you camp and cook your own."

Then, hating roundup work like poison, the old man took the TP train for Fort Worth and a wine and wild women spree that was apt to last a month. That's how it was that nobody had the authority to fire Leindecker. And there wasn't anybody big enough to run him off.

Besides his black temper, Leindecker had another strong characteristic. He was as lazy as a hound dog in the sunshine. The first thing he did after he mixed up a batch of strychnine and grain and loaded it into the ranch's rickety old wood-hauling wagon was to hunt the roundup crew and chuckwagon. He didn't aim to cook any more than he had to.

The wagon cook was the first man to spot him coming. Old Cooney Peale spat disgustedly and wiped the biscuit dough off his gnarled hands onto the flour sack apron tied around his flat middle.

The kid horse wrangler missed that. Jinx Cavenaugh's blue eyes lifted in interest over the rim of his steaming coffee cup. "Stranger comin'."

Cooney's age-paled eyes narrowed. His voice had an

edge to it. "No stranger to me. Go see about your horses, boy."

The horse jingler drained his cup, lingering a little to satisfy a kid's curiosity about the man coming in the wagon. He stooped over an open Dutch oven and picked up a cold biscuit left from breakfast.

Cooney hollered at him, "And you quit feedin' biscuits to that paddle-footed sorrel of yours. He's a bigger pest than a pot-lickin' hound."

Grinning, the gangling button untied his sorrel from a thorny mesquite fifty yards out of camp. He took a bite out of the biscuit and fed the rest to the horse.

Swinging into the saddle, he hollered back, "Old age is ruining your cookin', Cooney. Them biscuits ain't got any more salt in them than you have."

Cooney hurled a chunk of firewood in his direction, missing him on purpose but coming close enough to make the sorrel spook and almost spill the kid. He chuckled as Jinx wildly grabbed leather.

Old Cooney never had married and had kids of his own. He often thought that if he had, he'd have hoped for a boy about like Jinx Cavenaugh.

Dev Leindecker halted his gray-horse team a respectful distance from the cook's fire and climbed down. Tying the reins to the wheel, he swaggered into camp. "Howdy, Cooney. If I'd knowed it was you a-cookin', I never would've hired." It was meant as a joke but sounded more like the truth.

He extended his big hand. Cooney didn't take it. Instead he wiped his hands again on the flour-dusty apron. Curtly he said, "There's coffee in the pot. It's two hours till dinner."

Resentment flicked in Leindecker's narrow eyes, then went back into hiding. He poured coffee into a battered tin cup and squatted on the run-down heels of his worn-out boots. This kind of hostility wasn't new to him. Seemed like he ran into it most everywhere he went.

Old Cooney Peale went on about his business, kneading dough or limping around the chuckbox lid to check the dried apricots soaking in water there. Now and then he stopped and leaned against the wagon, favoring his right leg. It was that leg which had taken him out of the saddle and put him behind a chuckbox fifteen years ago—that leg and an owl-headed bronc.

Cooney recognized the wood wagon Leindecker had been driving. "You workin' for this outfit now?"

Leindecker nodded. "Edgewood hired me to poison off his prairie dogs. Told me to eat at the chuckwagon as much as I could."

Cooney scowled like he had swallowed a half-raw mountain oyster.

"All right, but you better keep that wagon covered up. First time a horse sticks his nose in that poisoned grain, somebody's gonna' take an ax handle to you."

Before long a column of gray dust began a slow move across the buffalo-grass prairie toward the two wooden windmills where the chuckwagon was camped. The warm west wind brought with it the bawling of cattle. Cooking, Cooney could watch the cowboys working the herd out yonder on a tromped-off roundup ground along a barbed wire fence, half hidden by swirling dust.

Presently the main body of the herd was pushed into the big wire pens below the windmills. Three cowboys stayed behind with the cattle that had been cut out of the herd. Boyd Runnels, wagon boss, was with the first men who spurred their horses up to the wagon for chuck. Tying his horse, he glimpsed Dev Leindecker sprawled in the shade.

"Cooney," he muttered darkly, pointing his whiskered chin toward Leindecker, "what's he doin' here?"

Cooney told him. Runnels' jaw clenched.

"Hank McKee's out yonder with the cut," the boss said worriedly. "Apt to be trouble when he rides up here and finds Leindecker."

Cooney looked up sharply. "What's Hank got against him?"

"Leindecker prodded Hank's brother into a fight over at the 7B last year and beat him unconscious. He's a murderous devil when he cuts loose. Hank's brother can't hear thunder now, and the doctor says he never will."

It happened about the way the wagon boss figured. Hank McKee saw Leindecker the minute he rode into camp. His lips tightened, but he didn't say a word. He filled a plate and cup, then sat down cross-legged to eat. But he never ate much. He and Leindecker sat there smouldering, their angry eyes stabbing hate at each other till McKee jumped to his feet and flung his cupful of hot coffee into Dev Leindecker's wolf face.

Leindecker burst up at him with a roar.

McKee was big, but Leindecker was bigger. His huge fists relentlessly drove the strength from McKee until the cowboy was down in the sand, groggily shaking his bloody head.

Leaning down, Leindecker grabbed a handful of McKee's shirt and jerked the cowboy erect. His crunching fist swung. McKee's body jerked and fell limply. Ferocity gripped Leindecker. He fell to his knees on top of the half-conscious cowboy and beat him with his rocky fists.

Cooney Peale had seen all he could stand. He grabbed a heavy iron pothook from the side of his chuckbox and limped up beside Leindecker. "Stop it, Dev, or I'll brain you."

Leindecker ignored him until Cooney swung his arm up, the pothook whistling. Grudgingly then, he stood up, his fists still clenched and the wildness still running unchecked through his eyes.

His gaze flicked from one man to another, challenging. "McKee started it. You all saw him."

Cooney Peale's fists were still tight on the pothook. "You better go on out and see about them prairie dogs."

The cowboys moved Hank McKee under the shade of the chuckwagon, then melted away toward the hot, dusty branding pens. Cooney and the wagon boss gently washed off dirt and blood with one of Cooney's old flour sack cuptowels. The kid wrangler watched, his lips trembling in anger.

"He better not ever try that on me," Jinx Cavenaugh declared.

Testily Cooney raised his gray head. "You got no business here, boy. Git!"

McKee finally came around. His face was swelling, his lips bruised and cut. He muttered painfully that his whole body was raw and aching.

"You better ride back to headquarters and stay till you heal up, Hank," the wagon boss said. "You can find plenty to do there."

Cooney shot Boyd Runnels a sharp glance "You gonna' let Dev Leindecker stay here after this?"

The boss said angrily, "Don't see much I can do about it. It's the old man's orders."

"It'll happen again, Boyd," Cooney said. "Bound to."

Runnels helplessly shrugged his shoulders.

"I know it. And next time, Cooney, you use that pothook."

It didn't take Dev Leindecker long to decide he had done a day's work. By five o'clock he was back. Without looking in the wagon, Cooney would've wagered a right smart that there wasn't much of the poisoned grain gone.

The branding over, the cowboys were pushing the cattle out of the pens and back into the pasture. They would loose-herd them down there on the fence awhile to graze on the mesquite and buffalo grass and give the new-branded calves a chance to pair up with their mammies. It always took a while, what with the confusing new smell of dried blood, boneoil and burned hair and hide.

Dusty Jinx Cavenaugh came walking up to the wagon, spurs a-jingle on his patched-up boots. His hostile eyes met Dev Leindecker's and got a quick, contemptuous response. Then the horse jingler turned to Cooney Peale.

"Boyd's got him a fat yearlin' penned yonder for beef," he said. "Wants to know if you'll let him borrow your pistol."

Cooney grunted. On most outfits they'd just knock a beef in the head with the backside of an ax and be done with it. But the boys long ago had found out about the old .44 Cooney kept up in the chuckbox. It misfired sometimes, but it was still better than an ax, if a man's stomach was weak.

Cooney reached up and got it, handing it to the kid. "Tell Boyd the company's gonna' have to buy me some more shells if it keeps on usin' my artillery."

Forcing irritation in his voice, he pointed his crooked finger toward a loose horse which was nosing around at the edge of camp, looking for scraps. "And chase that sorrel away from here before I swat him in the rump with a shovel."

Jinx said, "Aw no, Cooney, it don't hurt to have a pet."

"Pet or pest, ain't a nickel's worth of difference. Keep him out of here."

Cooney grinned, though, watching the kid coax the sorrel away. Good button, that Jinx. He'd be a top hand one of these times.

Through the next week or ten days, Dev Leindecker didn't miss many meals at Cooney Peale's chuckwagon. Occasionally he would be gone all day, taking some cold biscuits and meat with him to tide him over till suppertime. But before dark, he always found Cooney's camp.

He might as well have missed it, no more recognition than he got. The cowboys never talked to him—would hardly even look at him. He stayed off to himself, a brooding resentment hovering over him.

"He don't hardly act human sometimes," Jinx told the cook one day. "I guess poisonin' prairie dogs is necessary, and a man has got to eat. But he shouldn't act like he was havin' so much fun at it. Yesterday I rode up on him after he had put out some bait. He was layin' there on the ground grinnin', watchin' them varmints sample the grain. Didn't even act human, I tell you."

So Dev Leindecker stayed around, and day by day the cow camp got to be more and more like a corked jug, with the pressure building in it.

The plug blew just after Cooney moved camp to Quitman's Mills. The cowboys rode in off drive near noon and caught up fresh horses from Jinx's remuda.

Jinx unsaddled his sorrel and roped himself a new mount.

The men were half through eating when someone hollered, "Jinx, get your horse away from that grain wagon!"

But it was already too late. The camp pet had shoved its nose under the loose tarp that covered Leindecker's wagon. By the time Jinx could run to him, tripping over his spurs, the sorrel was on its side, thrashing its legs in agony.

"Help me, somebody," the kid was bawling. "Somebody come help me!"

But there wasn't much anybody could do except stand there tight-throated and watch Jinx cry like a lost kid over the sorrel pony. Old Cooney melted some lard in a pan.

"Think that'll help?" Boyd asked.

Cooney shook his head. "But we can't have the kid thinkin' we never even tried."

Runnels held the pony's head up while Cooney forced the jaws open and poured lard down the animal's throat. If it helped any, it didn't show. In a little while the sorrel's thrashing was over.

One by one the cowboys straggled off toward the branding pens, their heads down and their boots dragging. Pretty soon the only ones left were the kid, old Cooney Peale—and Dev Leindecker.

Through it all, Leindecker had never moved. He hunkered just beyond the cook fire, near the woodpile. He had hunched his huge shoulders and drawn up within himself, putting a hard shell against the contempt of the cowboys.

Now the kid's brimming eyes lifted from the dead pony and fastened upon Dev Leindecker. Jinx Cavenaugh pushed himself to his feet. His kid shoulders squared, and his fists clenched hard as live oak knots.

"You killed him, Leindecker," he exploded in a shrill voice not his own.

Leindecker arose and waited, his hands flexing. Choking, the kid broke into a run and sailed into him with fists flailing. It was like trying to drive a spike with his bare hands.

Leindecker's left hand grabbed the kid and shoved him off to arm's length. The ox-strong right arm slashed across. Jinx staggered back, his hands defensively lifted over his eyes. A hard grin broke across Leindecker's dark face, tugging upward at the sweat-streaked beard. The big man closed in, smashing Jinx first with one fist, then the other. The wrangler sagged, his battered face smeared an ugly red.

Strong hands tugged desperately at Leindecker, hands gnarled and old, the veins standing blue.

"Stop it, Dev!" Cooney Peale was shouting. "Damn you, leave the kid alone."

Leindecker turned half around to shove the old man away. Cooney's horny fist smashed his nose and came away bloody, wresting from the big man a quick squall of pain. With a roar Leindecker whirled from the kid and grabbed at the old cook. Cooney managed to duck away and step back.

Then the tricky right leg betrayed him and he faltered.

Leindecker hurled Cooney backward into the woodpile, pinning the old man down to helplessness. His thin, hard lips curved in a crazy grin. There was no mercy in the wild gleam of his gray eyes. He was a slashing, killing wolf.

A shrill voice made Leindecker spin. Blood-spattered,

Jinx Cavenaugh poised there, a heavy singletree from the wagon arced over his shoulder. A bawl of fear tore from Leindecker's thick, whiskery throat as he tried vainly to jump away. The singletree snapped his head back, and Leindecker dropped.

Gently the hard-breathing kid helped Cooney to his feet. "He hurt you, Cooney?"

A dull ache throbbed all through Cooney's sparse frame, but he knew it would be nothing serious. "I'll make out."

Jinx still held the singletree. Worriedly he looked down at the slack body of Dev Leindecker. "Reckon I killed him?"

An ugly line of red oozed from a long slash across Leindecker's head. But the poisoner's back showed the steady rise and fall of his breathing.

"You weren't that lucky, son. Now you'll never be able to turn your back on him. Maybe you better clear out for a while." Jinx shook his head. "Nothing going to scare me out."

After washing, Jinx walked toward the branding pens to make a hand. Alone with Leindecker, Cooney went on with cleaning up the noon-day mess. But, glancing often at Leindecker's sprawled form, he made sure his old hands were never far from his heavy pothook.

How long Leindecker had lain there before he regained consciousness, watching him with crazy, hate-filled eyes, Cooney would never know. But when the cook took hold of his wreck pan and carried it off a ways to dump the soapy water out of it, Leindecker got to his feet and made for the chuckbox. Caught off guard, Cooney ran toward him.

But he was too late. Leindecker had the .44. And

when Cooney tried to wrestle it from him, the big man swung it up, then down again. He caught Cooney behind the ear and sent him rolling in the warm sand. Wildly Leindecker pointed the six-shooter at Cooney, and twice he squeezed the trigger. Both times it misfired.

Then Leindecker turned and weaved heavily out toward the branding pens. Painfully Cooney pushed himself to his feet and tried to follow him.

The dust that billowed up in the stifling hot pens was thick enough to cut with a knife. Two ropers on horseback were heeling calves and dragging them up toward the branding fire for the flanking crews to grab and hold down. Working hard to make up for lost time, the cowboys never saw Leindecker until he was in the pen with them.

Over the loud, steady din of bawling cows and calves, someone shouted, "He's got a gun!"

Young Jinx Cavenaugh, bruised and one eye swollen shut, was kneeling atop the neck of a struggling calf, gripping one foreleg with his left hand and pushing the calf's head down against the ground with his right. At the sharp voice, he looked back.

Leindecker towered behind him, the gun in his hand and a savage fury blazing in his dirty, black-bearded face. His dry lips pulled away from his teeth. He squeezed the trigger.

Jinx slumped forward. The calf broke loose and jumped to its feet, kicking the cowboy who had held its hind legs. Jinx lay limp, his fingers digging into the soft dirt of the corral.

Half a dozen cowboys surged toward the big man. But he swung the gun at them. They stopped.

Cooney Peale limped into the corral. A cry tore

from him at sight of the body lying still in the dust. Leindecker was watching Cooney. This last violent action had flushed the unreasoning anger from Dev Leindecker's narrow eyes. In its place was a cold determination.

"You," he said sharply to Boyd Runnels, "gather up them horses and bring them here. I ain't leavin' them so you can hurry no sheriff onto my trail. Shag it, I tell you!"

He whirled on Cooney Peale. "I'll need some grub. You, Cooney, go to the wagon and gather up the cold biscuits, meat, anything else you can shove into a sack."

Cooney hesitated, his stricken eyes still on the boy.

"Git, damn you," Leindecker bawled, "before I fire this thing again."

Cooney lifted his pale eyes to Leindecker's. They were two glittering chips of ice. "I'll git you what you need."

Boyd Runnels brought Leindecker the horses the heelers had been using in the branding pen. Hastily Leindecker chose one of them to ride. He led the others out the gate. Then, shouting at the top of his voice, he plunged toward the saddled horses tied along outside the fence, breaking them loose. He shoved them in front of him, leaving the cowboys afoot.

Leindecker reined in beside the chuckwagon.

"How about that grub, Cooney?"

Cooney Peale handed him a flour sack, bulging at the bottom.

"Don't let them forget I've got the gun," Leindecker warned. "I'll kill any man who comes after me."

Tying the flour sack behind his high cantle, Leindecker kicked the horse with his bare bootheels and loped out of camp, driving the saddled horses and Cooney's mule team before him.

The sheriff and his deputy changed to fresh mounts close to the wagon, then stepped up for a quick bite to eat. Silent, brittle as an old mesquite limb, Cooney showed them Leindecker's tracks.

"Headed for the New Mexico line, you can bet your boots," the sheriff commented darkly, biting a big chunk out of a piece of fried steak. "We'll sure have to ride fast if we're gonna' catch him."

Slowly Cooney shook his head, his pale eyes burning with a cold fire. "Take your time, sheriff. He won't make it to New Mexico."

The lawman's eyebrows lifted. "What's that?"

"He won't get far. Wherever he stops to eat, that's where you'll find him."

The sheriff's gaze touched the strychnine wagon. His jaw dropped in horror as he read the meaning in Cooney's grim old face.

"My God!" the lawman breathed. His tin plate and the food in it fell to the ground as he swung quickly into the saddle and spurred out onto Leindecker's trail, the deputy trying vainly to catch up with him.

They found Leindecker's body the next morning at a windmill where he had stopped to water his horse and eat a little of the food out of Cooney's sack.

Accidental death, the justice of the peace called it. Obviously, Leindecker had drunk some poison water somewhere along the way.

The roundup was over by the time the doctor let Jinx Cavenaugh go back to the ranch. Cooney's wrinkled old face lighted up like a camp lantern at the sight of that familiar gangling figure. Jinx was pale and thin, but his wide kid grin made up for it as he came swinging up the hard-beaten path to the cookshack.

"You lazed around town long enough," Cooney spoke, hardly above a whisper. "I begun to think you wasn't comin' back at all."

That was all he said, and it was all that was needed, for the stout grip of his rough hand said the rest.

Cooney led the boy out and down to a corral next to the red frame barn, where a little sorrel bronc watched with alert ears poked forward.

"Boyd Runnels picked him up down south. Thought you'd like to break him this winter, if you're able."

The kid was laughing and talking and crying all at the same time. Finally he managed, "Cooney, you reckon that if I went back to the cookshack . . ."

Cooney smiled, his hand tight on the boy's shoulder. "Sure, son. I saved them from breakfast, special. You'll find them in the warmin' oven."

RIDE A STRAIGHT ROAD

Coming in on the upper road, Toby Tippett slowed his dun horse as he started down the crest of the hill and came into sight of Patman's Lake. At first glance he thought the town hadn't changed much in four years. Pretty much the same—spread out a little more in the small Mexican settlement way down in the south. But when he got closer, he could see that there had been changes, a good many of them. A man couldn't be away from a place four years and expect it to remain the same.

There were three or four big houses up on Silk Stocking Street. Two-story houses they were, the kind a man saw in the prosperous cotton towns back in East Texas. Times must have been pretty good in the cow business lately, Toby decided. There were a few new buildings along the business street, too. They had torn down the old Mustang Saloon. Another one stood in its place, a big outfit with a conservative little sign up front that read Equity Bar.

A grin formed on Toby's face as his memory ran

back to things he had seen and done in the old Mustang. He had been too young to go in there, really, but the way people looked at things then, a man was old enough if he was big enough. And Toby had always been a stretchy, overgrown kid for his age.

They hadn't gotten around to building a new courthouse. The old frame one stood just as always on the big courthouse square. It was a couple of years late for a paint job. Saloons always did seem to do better than the county, when it came to taking in revenue.

Sight of the courthouse brought back some other memories, memories that made the grin fade. What had happened to him there would be with him as long as he lived. It showed in the lines, carved years early in a face that still was youthful in other ways. It showed in the solid maturity of his blue eyes, eyes which should still shine with mischief.

The homesickness came sweeping over him again, hard. He wanted to keep riding until he got to the ranch, until he had ridden through the last familiar gate and closed that familiar old door behind him. But the sun was dropping low over the cedar-covered hills west of town.

At the end of the street old Roper Finney's livery barn stood just as it always had. It never had had a coat of paint, and the frame walls were sun-bleached to a dull gray, the boards warped and cracked. Toby dismounted in front of it and stretched his long, saddle-weary legs.

A short, middle-aged man came out and squinted at him.

"What'll you have, cowboy?"

"Like to put up my horse. And I reckon old Roper'll still let a man make his bed in the hay, won't he?"

The little man peered closer at him. "You been gone

a long time, ain't you? Old Roper ain't been here in two years or more. Sold this place to me and went back to East Texas. Had an itch to farm some cotton."

Toby acknowledged the information with a nod. "Been a good year for cotton back there. Hope he's making a crop. How about that bed?"

"Sure," the stableman replied, "help yourself. Unsaddle, and I'll feed your horse."

Something was working at the little man. Toby could see it making a fever in his pale eyes. Presently, dipping oats out of a bin with a five-gallon bucket, the stableman spoke.

"You live here?"

Toby said, "The old home place is twenty miles out of town, south and west."

"Well, if this is your home, where you been so long?"

Toby hesitated, then shrugged. No use in trying to make a secret of it. The word would spread quickly enough, soon as anybody who knew him spotted him here in town.

"I've been in jail," he said. "For four years in the state penitentiary."

He thought the stableman was going to spill the bucket of oats. But the little man got control of himself and hurried on out the back door to the corral. There wouldn't be any more questions out of him, Toby knew.

The washstand was still where Roper had always kept it. Toby washed the trail dust off of his face and hands. He had shaved this morning. Feeling his chin, he decided that would do till he got home.

One big job was ahead of him right now. He dreaded it in a way. All the long ride across more than half a state, he had thought about it, and knew it was something he had to do. He worried over it now, wondering if he could find the words he wanted.

Toby started down the wheel-rutted street, afoot, toward the courthouse. It seemed to him that he could feel the eyes staring, the fingers pointing, and he knew it was his imagination running away with him. This had been one of the things he had dreaded most, his first time in Patman's Lake, not knowing how the people were going to receive him.

A cowboy came riding down the street toward him. Toby knew the face, although he couldn't tie a name to it. He knew where the puncher had worked four years ago.

Toby managed a smile and a quick howdy.

The rider slowed, and recognition brought shock to his face. He stared at Toby a moment, muttered something in answer, and hurried his horse on down the street.

No, Toby knew, it wouldn't take long for word to get to the Damon Frost ranch. They wouldn't be happy out there, some of them.

Toby half hoped he would find the sheriff's office empty, that he could put off the visit for a while.

A girl was seated at the rolltop desk. She looked up quickly as Toby walked in the door. She was nineteen, maybe, or twenty. She stood up, a slender girl, almost thin. Her oval face lacked a little of being pretty. But a man would never let that bother him. Her eyes made up for it. They were wide, gray, expressive eyes. And because of them, he knew who she was. Sheriff Cass Duncan had the same kind of eyes.

"I was looking for Cass," he said.

She was studying him with a quiet friendliness. "He's down the street. He'll be back in a minute. Won't you sit down, Toby?"

Her calling him by name brought momentary surprise. She knew who he was, all right. But more than that, it was the first time anybody had called him by his first name in years. Always it was just, "Hey, Tippett!"

Seating himself, he stared at her. It was pleasant to look at a girl, especially when he had seen so few for such a long time.

"You're Cass's daughter, aren't you?" he asked.

She nodded. "That's right. I remember when they had you and Dodd Parrish here, in the jail out back. I used to bake a cake or a pie every day or two and take it to you."

Toby smiled at her. "I remember, too. I haven't had any cooking like that since. But you've changed a lot. You weren't more than fifteen or sixteen."

Her gaze was level, appraising. "You've changed a lot too, Toby. And all for the better, I'd guess."

Heavy footsteps sounded in the hallway. Toby stood up as Cass Duncan walked in through the door. The sheriff stopped short.

"Toby," he said. "Toby Tippett."

He lifted his hand uncertainly. Toby stepped forward and took it.

"You're looking good, son," the sheriff said, the surprise fading.

"I had a chance to do outside work most of the time. You're looking good too, Cass."

The sheriff smiled. "My daughter's cooking. She doesn't believe in throwing anything away."

Cass Duncan was nearing middle age. His coarse black hair was shot with gray, and his mustache no longer was the raven black which Toby remembered from his boyhood. Cass had always been a kindly man. He could bawl out an unruly boy in a way that took the hide off. But there was always a grin and a handshake later, if it looked as if the boy deserved it.

He had always been able to handle men, too. Not many of the backtrail kind ever stayed in Cass's county long.

"You figuring on staying here, Toby?" he queried.

The young man nodded. "This is home, Cass. Folks may not take to me anymore. But I want to stay. I'm hoping they'll let me."

The sheriff's eyes appraised him. Toby felt the friendliness in them, yet he was still ill at ease.

"Depends some on how you take the folks, Toby. I hope you didn't come back with any grudges."

Toby shook his head. "No grudges, Cass. That's what I came to tell you. I wanted you to know that I've got no hard feelings for what happened. I'm old enough now to realize that I got what I had coming to me, and no more.

"I was just a wild kid then, young, dumb, and too well fed. I made my mistakes, and I've paid for them. What's more, I'm glad I did."

Now came the hard part. He dug deep for the words.

"You did me a big favor when you brought me in, Cass. If you hadn't, I might have kept going on the same way. I was just rustling cattle then. But later it might have been killing. You stopped me in time, and I'm grateful to you. Now the account's all squared. I intend to ride a straight road from here on out."

Cass Duncan's eyes studied him. A warm smile came up into them. "I believe you, son. You don't know how tickled I am to hear you say it." He hesitated a moment. "There's one thing that still bothers me, though. At the trial you and Dodd Parrish maintained all along that there wasn't anybody involved but just the two of you. Everybody knew there had to be more. But you two boys went on and took all the punishment. Maybe now you'd like to tell me the rest of the story."

Warily Toby shook his head. "No, Cass. Even if there had been anybody else with us—and mind you, I'm not saying there was—don't you think they'd have learned their lesson from what happened to Dodd and me?"

The memory of Dodd Parrish was always painful to Toby. He'd taken sick and died the second winter.

Cass shrugged, still smiling. "I reckon so, Toby. Leastways, the cow stealing stopped around here after you two boys went up."

Toby nodded. That was the way he had hoped it would be.

"Now, Cass, let's talk about something else. Tell me what has happened since I've been gone. How's Ellen Frost?"

Mention of the name brought a slow frown to the sheriff's face. "Ellen? Oh, she's doing fine, I guess. Got half the young men in the country after her—after her and her dad's money. You were going with her, weren't you?"

Toby nodded again. "Yes. We had sort of an understanding that someday we were going to get married. She wrote to me for a while, but the letters finally stopped."

There was pain in his face now. He had tried for a long time to reconcile himself to the idea that she was lost to him. But he never had been able to. The memory of her was as fresh as if he had seen her yesterday. It had always been so.

Something was troubling Cass Duncan. He frowned and tightened his fist, studying the toes of his old scuffed-up boots. The girl was watching Toby, her eyes saying nothing.

"Look, Toby," Cass said, "I know how you feel. But you better stay away from the Frost place. It'll only mean trouble for you if you go out there."

Toby peered closely at him. "Old Damon Frost?"

Duncan's eyes said yes. "He was awful bitter about you, son. He'd have gotten you two hung, if he could have. He'll never in a hundred years believe you've reformed. Give him the slightest excuse and he'll hound you till he's got you back in jail—or dead!"

Toby pondered that. "I don't want trouble, Cass. Not with old Damon or anybody else. I'll watch out, I promise you. Then he changed the subject. "You seen Dad lately?"

Cass nodded.

Toby said, "He never was much of a hand to write letters. I got a few from him, but they were always short. Looked like he sweated blood, just writing that much. I'm sure anxious to see him."

Duncan avoided Toby's eyes. "Toby, there's something else. You're going to find that your dad has changed some."

Fear hit Toby like the strike of a club. "He's sick or something?"

"Not sick, exactly. It's just that—well, he's had it pretty hard since you've been gone. It's taken less than that to break some men. And Sod Tippett's old."

Toby's throat swelled. He looked at the floor, and remorse burned in him like a banked fire. Toby had been the only son born to a man already in middle age, the son who had become everything to Sod Tippett after his wife died. Sod had drudged for years on the little ranch that was half his and half the bank's. He had done it for his son, and all he had ever asked in return was Toby's love.

And Toby repaid him for those years by leaving his father to face his old age alone, with nothing remaining to him but his smashed dreams and misery of soul.

The knowledge of this, and the bitter driving of his conscience, had been with Toby a long time now. They had done much to carve the lines in his face and burn the foolish gleam of kid wildness out his eyes.

"It may be too late, Cass," Toby said with sincerity. "But if there's any way I can, I'm going to make it up to him. I'll work till I drop in my tracks, if I have to. I'm going to repay him for all those wasted years."

Cass Duncan and his daughter watched through the window as Toby walked out the big frame courthouse and down the street.

The girl asked, "What do you think, Dad?"

Cass placed his hand on his daughter's slender shoulder. "I think he means it, Betty. I think he wants to go straight."

She frowned. "What about the people here? Will they let him?"

The sheriff shook his head. "I don't know, Betty. I don't know."

Ahead of him, bathed in the cherry glow of the newly risen sun, Toby Tippett could see the house where he had been born. His heartbeat quickened. His throat tightened to the quick rush of memories, and anticipation seeing his father again.

The thought of it had kept him awake all night, lying in the livery stable's hay and watching the twinkle of stars through the big open door. Sometime after midnight, unable to contain himself, he had saddled up and hit the road south.

He dropped the reins over a picket in front of the house. There was a sag to the fence, and the house had fallen into poor repair in four years' time. The barn is missing some shingles, too, he saw at a glance. Well, he'd fix that. Maybe it was a good thing. Lots of work was what he needed.

His hand trembled as he reached for the knob and pushed the door inward. He blinked at the sting in his eyes. Sod Tippett was faced away from him, stooped over the woodstove where bacon sizzled in a frying pan, and coffee boiled in a smoke-blackened pot.

"Hello, Dad," Toby spoke tightly.

The old man straightened a little and froze there. Then, slowly, he turned, his faded eyes wide in unbelief, his jaw agape.

"Toby!" he whispered. "Son!"

Toby took three long strides across the room and threw his arms around the stooped, frail shoulders.

For a long time no words passed between them. They just looked at each other, throats too tight for talking. Hunger had been gnawing at Toby for a long time, because he had never gotten around to eating any supper last night. Now, with breakfast in front of him, he was just content to sit and look at the man across the table.

Sod Tippett was old now, old even beyond his years. Toby had been expecting it, but the shock had staggered him, actually seeing the change that four hard years had beaten into his father.

"Son," the old man asked finally, "you're out for good? You're going to stay?"

"Yes, Dad. I'm here to stay."

He thought he could see the thin old shoulders

heave with controlled emotion, and he looked to the warped plank flooring that hadn't been clean in a long time.

After a bit, Sod Tippett had a grip on himself. "Son," he said, "I knew you'd be coming home soon. I could feel it. Just the other day, I was telling your mother, 'Toby's on the way home.'"

Toby's jaw fell, and suddenly there was ice at the pit of his stomach. Now he realized fully what Cass Duncan had been trying so painfully to tell him.

"I was telling your mother . . ." old Sod Tippett had said; but Toby's mother had been dead for fifteen years!

Sod had finally loosened up, and now he was talking freely. Toby sat there nodding, hearing little of what was said. He covered his face with his hand.

The riders came in the early afternoon. Toby was up on the house, checking the cracked shingles and trying to find the spots that would have to be patched. He heard the clatter of hooves and looked out across the big corral. He saw the four horsemen rein through the wide gate and head up toward the house. At the distance, and with four years' absence behind him, it was hard to recognize most of the men, but there was no mistaking the man who rode in the lead.

This was Damon Frost, and the grim set of his square shoulders made it plain that he wasn't here to say howdy.

Toby eased down off of the roof and waited in front of the house.

As the riders reined up, he stepped forward and held out his hand toward Damon Frost.

"It's been a long time, Mr. Frost," he said pleasantly. "You're looking good."

Frost made no move to grip Toby's hand. Instead,

he pulled his right hand even farther back, near his belt. His square face was set in a hard scowl. The years hadn't changed him much. A little more gray in his hair and his thick mustache, maybe, and a little more weight around his middle. Nothing like the changes in old Sod Tippett.

Toby glanced at the other three men. One was the cowboy who had seen him yesterday in town. Another was Marvin Sand. Sand was two or three years older than Toby. He had worked for Damon Frost a long time. Toby remembered lots of things about Marvin Sand, few of them with pleasure.

The fourth man was Damon's son, Alton Frost. Alton was just about as old as Toby. They had been friends since they had both been in the paint pony and marbles age.

"Howdy, Alton," Toby smiled. "It's sure good to see you."

Alton Frost glanced uncertainly at his father. Yes, old Damon still ruled his family with an iron hand. Or he tried to. Alton flashed a quick, uneasy grin at Toby. "How've you been, Toby?"

"Tolerable. How's Ellen? I'm sure anxious to see her."

It was Damon Frost who replied to that. "That's one reason I came over here, Tippett. Ellen doesn't want to see you. You'll leave her alone."

Toby tried hard to keep some trace of pleasantness in his face. But it was draining fast, and anger was seeping in. "Did she tell you to tell me that?"

Frost's face darkened. "I'm telling you, stay away from her. I'll have no cow thief even talking to my daughter."

"I've paid my debt, Mr. Frost. I'm a free man."

Frost's eyes bored into him. "To me, Tippett, you're a cow thief, and you always will be."

He waited to see if Toby was going to say any more to that. Toby didn't. Frost leaned forward on his saddle horn, his eyes like cold steel.

"I wouldn't advise you to stay here, Tippett. You're not wanted any more. They tell me a man has been trying to buy this place from your dad. You better get him to sell, and both of you move on."

In stubborn anger Toby replied, "This is our home place. I was born here, and intend to stay. I made a mistake. I've taken my whipping and learned my lesson. I'd like to be friends with you if I can. But friends or not, I'm going to stay!"

Hatred stood raw and deadly in Damon Frost's square face.

"No, you won't," he said in a quiet voice harsh as two rusty steel blades rubbing together. "I'll see that you go, or I'll see you dead."

He jerked his horse around and started him for the big corral gate. Just then old Sod Tippett came hobbling in from the barn.

"Howdy there, Damon," he said, beaming. "Been a long time since you were over here. My son's home. Did you see him?"

Damon Frost held up uncertainly, evidently not wanting to hurt the old man. They had been good friends a long time ago. "Yes, Sod," he said, "I saw him."

To Toby, Frost warned darkly, "You tell your dad what I told you. I'm giving you a week to clear out. After that, you better watch yourself."

He spurred away then, sitting straight and proud in the saddle, his broad shoulders squared. Without a backward glance, Marvin Sand and the cowboy rode out a length behind him. Young Alton Frost held back a moment, looking at Toby. He winked, then spurred on to catch up with his father.

Sod stared after them, not comprehending. "Damon wouldn't even light and talk," he murmured. "What's the matter with him, son?"

Toby's mouth twisted in bitterness. "I'm what's the matter with him. I didn't expect he'd ever like me again. But to hate me like that . . ."

The old man stood watching the riders trot their horses away on the trail that angled off across the flat toward the Frost ranch.

"I heard him tell you to leave, son. You figuring on going? You fixing to leave me again?"

Toby's jaw set grimly. He put his arm around his father's shoulder. "No, Dad. I'm not going to leave you."

Well past midafternoon, Alton Frost came back alone. He reined in at the front of the house and stepped down. Leisurely, he grinned up at Toby, who was on the roof, pulling out some bad shingles.

"Better climb down from there cowboy, before you fall off and mess up the front yard."

Grinning broadly, Toby climbed down. He clasped Alton's hand. "Say, you're a sight for sore eyes. I had a hunch you'd be back."

Alton laughed. "Sure. Had to wait till I could get loose from Pa. He's peculiar about some things, and you're one of them."

Toby's grin left him. "Alton, how come he's so bitter about me? I wouldn't expect him to greet me with open arms, but . . ."

Alton shook his head. "Like I said, cowboy, he's peculiar about some things. He's kind of a puritan, in a way. He hates anybody who steals anything. You were stealing from him; that makes it extra bad."

He grinned again. "Kind of funny in a way, ain't it? We all know how Pa got his start when he was our age. If it hadn't been for moonlight nights, a fast horse, and a wide loop, he'd still be working for somebody else, for wages. But nowadays, you let anybody steal something from him and he's like a grizzly bear caught in a trap."

Uncomfortably, Toby said, "You oughtn't to talk about your own dad like that, Alton."

Alton Frost shrugged. "It's the truth."

Toby frowned and changed the subject. "Tell me about Ellen."

"Oh, she's doing fine. She's got more brainless boys chasing after her than there are cattle in Tom Green County."

Toby hesitated with the question he really wanted to ask. "What about me, Alton? Reckon she ever thinks about me anymore?"

Alton smiled. "Sure she does. The minute Pa heard you were back, he laid down the law to her. Said he'd shoot you if he caught you near her."

"And what did she say?"

"She told him she would see anybody she had a mind to, and she would sure be wanting to see you."

Toby's heartbeat quickened. He sat down on the little front porch, trying to keep from grinning as foolishly as he felt.

"When can I see her, Alton? When had I ought to go?"

Alton shook his head. "She said tell you not to risk coming over there. She'll come to you."

Incredulously, Toby stared. "To me? That's even riskier."

"Not really. Our ranch adjoins yours on one side. She'll find some excuse to be riding in the next day or two. She'll slip across the east pasture and come over . . . Ellen's gotten to be a lot like us, Toby. She likes a little risk in everything she does. It's like the sweetening in coffee. Take it out, and the pleasure is gone."

Toby was disturbed by something in Alton's talk. He couldn't exactly put his finger on it; maybe it was the realization that the old wild spark still burned in his friend, unquenched by the years that had drained the last of it from Toby.

For a while Toby sat on the edge of the porch, staring past Alton, to the tall gate posts at the far end of the corral, and even beyond them to the rolling rangeland that stretched on and on until it disappeared out of sight in a vague green line of cedar.

"Alton," he said, "there's something been bothering me. Since I've been gone, have you been . . ." It was hard to say. The words were right on his tongue, but a man couldn't just come right out with a thing like this. He had to go at it from the side, and halfway cover it up. But underneath, it was still the same. "Have you been doing anything that you wouldn't want to tell Cass Duncan about?"

Alton laughed, but he didn't meet Toby's eyes for a moment. "Nothing serious, cowboy. Nothing serious." He looked behind him to be sure Sod Tippett was nowhere around. Then he leaned forward.

"Toby," he said excitedly, "we been hoping you'd get out soon, Marvin and I have. We've run upon a real good proposition. You ought to be in on it."

A coldness was growing in Toby.

Alton went on, "It's this, cowboy. You know they're building a new railroad down south of us. It's seventy miles away, but that's not too far. There's a man down there that'll take all the fat cattle we can drive to him.

Splits the profits with us and doesn't look at any brands. He comes up and meets us halfway. He butchers the cattle himself and sells the meat to construction workers on the railroad.

"It sure cuts down the risk, Toby. It's not near as bad as it used to be when we had to drive the cattle all over hell and half of Texas, and always take a chance on running into somebody. Now we cut out a few good ones here, a few there, make a fast night-and-day drive, and they're off of our hands."

Disappointment was like a cold, wet blanket dropped across Toby's shoulders. "You been doing this very long?"

Alton nodded. "A good while."

"Your dad's cattle along with the rest, I guess."

"He'll never miss them. He's got so much money now he doesn't know what to do with it. It makes him miserable, just thinking about it. In a way we're doing him a favor. Marvin and me have talked it over a right smart. You went to jail for us and never let out a peep. You've got something coming to you. How about it? The gravy's thick, and we've got a big spoon."

Toby stood up, stiff with the coldness he held inside him. He stared out across the pasture before turning back to Alton, his face clouding.

"You're not going to like this, Alton. But I wish they'd caught you. I wish they'd caught you and sent you up the way they did me."

Color leaped into Alton's face. His eyes glittered for a brief moment. "You don't mean that, cowboy."

"Yes, I do mean it. I hoped that what happened to me would be enough to teach you something. I learned, and now that it's over, I'm glad of it. But you never learned anything."

Alton stared in surprise and half anger. "That's the way it is, huh, cowboy?"

Toby nodded. "That's the way it is."

Woodenly Alton Frost walked out and swung up onto his horse.

"I'm sorry, Toby."

"I'm sorry, too."

Toby stood watching until Alton had ridden out of sight. An emptiness ached in him. There had been a close bond between them ever since they had been kids, playing together on a school ground and slipping over to the neighbors' ranches to rope their calves on the sly. Neither boy had had a brother, so they had been brothers to each other.

Now Toby sensed that this was all over, that it was being shoved behind him like the closing of a book.

He sat down once more on the edge of the porch, looking out across the ranch and not seeing any of it.

Ellen Frost came just as Alton had said she would. Toby's breath came short as he hurried out to help her down from her horse.

She was a beautiful girl, more beautiful even than he had remembered her, if that was possible. She had dark, laughing eyes and soft, full lips that made a man's pulse quicken. She wore a tight-fitting white blouse that swelled outward, then pulled in slim and narrow at the waist. She was the kind of girl who made men stop and look back, and she knew it.

Toby would have crushed her to him, but she pushed him back, smiling coquettishly. "Let's not be in too big a hurry," she said, looking into his eyes.

His heart was pounding. "I've waited four years, Ellen. Would you say that I'm in a hurry?"

Her only answer was another teasing smile. "Four years. That's a long time, Toby. Lots of things can change."

In sudden worry he asked, "Have you changed, Ellen? Do you feel different about me now than you did four years ago?"

She parried the question. "I took a big risk in coming over, didn't I?"

He replied, "Yes. And I'm glad you did. If you hadn't, chances are I'd have gone over looking for you. It wouldn't have mattered if your dad had been waiting with a cannon."

That pleased her. "That's one thing I always liked about you, Toby. You were bold. You didn't let anything scare you. A little risk never bothered you at all."

Toby started to frown.

She went on. "And that's something that has worried me. Surely at some time or other you must have had a chance to break out. Why didn't you?"

Surprised, he asked. "Break out? Why?"

"Why, to be free, of course. You must have hated it there."

A sudden darkness began to come over him, like the one he had felt talking to the girl's brother.

"You'd have wanted me to do that, Ellen?"

"Why not?"

Bitterly he said, "Because I'd never have been free. Loose, maybe, but not free. Everywhere I'd turn, I'd be looking for somebody with a gun. I couldn't have come home. All I could've done would be to run and keep running. Just like a coyote. It's better to wait. Now I can go to sleep at night and not lie awake wondering if they'll catch up with me tomorrow. I can look anybody in the eye and not have to flinch."

He looked levelly at her. "Isn't that a whole lot better, Ellen? Isn't it worth four years of my time?"

She smiled and touched his hand. "Sure, guess you're right."

The way she looked, he couldn't help himself. He grabbed her and kissed her, hard. She finally drew away from him, smiling teasingly.

"Four years have changed you, Toby."

He was almost pleading with her. "Four years haven't changed me in what I want, Ellen. I want you. I want to marry you and bring you here to live. This is a good place. We can make it good. You won't be sorry. Please, Ellen, what do you say?"

The same smile lingered. "Like I said at first, Toby, let's not be in too big a hurry. Let's wait and see."

Disappointment brought a slump to his shoulders.

"Come on," she said, "get a horse and ride back to the boundary fence with me."

He rode along beside her, hoping for her to break down and say at least part of the things he had dreamed of her saying through the four long years he had been away. She never spoke. Sitting straight in her saddle, she was only an arm's length away from him. Yet that lingering, teasing smile was like a barrier between them, making her as unreachable as a star.

They came to the fence that divided Sod Tippett's old place from the Frost ranch. Toby swung down and opened the wire gate.

Ellen said, "I'll be thinking about what you asked me. Watch for me. I'll be back to see you."

She leaned over then and touched her lips to his forehead, a kiss that wasn't really a kiss at all. It only brought an ache to Toby as he watched her ride away.

Another man was watching her ride away, too. Marvin Sand stood hidden in a thicket of mesquite, his face dark. He dropped a half-smoked cigarette and ground it beneath his boot heel. He stepped into the saddle and rode out of the thicket, angling across to meet Ellen Frost.

She pulled up in surprise, her face flushed. "Marvin! What are you doing here?"

His voice was flat. "Waiting for you to come back."

"You trailed me?"

He nodded. "And I saw what happened yonder by the gate. Stay away from him, Ellen. He's going to draw lightning."

She began to smile, the same teasing smile she had used on Toby. "Maybe I like the kind of man who draws lightning."

Marvin Sand edged his horse up against hers. "He's not your kind."

"And maybe you are?"

Angry color began to seep into his face. He reached for her, grabbing her arms. "You've seemed to think I was. I've stood by and let you run after other men because when it was over you always came back to me. But I'm not going to let you make a fool of yourself over some ex-convict."

Her tiny mouth dropped open. Her voice sharpened. "You'd have been a convict yourself, Marvin, only you never got caught."

In sudden fury Sand drew back and slapped her so hard that she reeled in the saddle. "Don't ever say that!"

Ellen's nostrils flared. She grabbed the quirt that was looped on her saddle horn. He threw up his arm to take the sharp bite of it. An angry cry swelling in her throat, she spurred away from him. She put her horse into a hard lope toward the Frost ranch headquarters.

Marvin Sand held back, the color still high in his

face. He glanced once back toward the gate, where he had seen Toby Tippett. His fists clenched. Then he swung his horse about and followed in a stiff trot along the trail left by Ellen Frost . . .

Toby Tippett was pleasantly surprised by the good shape his father had managed to keep the herd in. Toby spent a lot of time in the saddle, riding around over the ranch, looking at the cattle. It wasn't so much that they needed any care. The year was good. They were putting on a lot of tallow for the coming winter. And there was little doctoring to be done.

It was just that it felt so good to be riding out in the open, breathing the good air of the range country and knowing that he was free.

Riding back to the house late one morning, he saw the dun horse hitched out front, standing hipshot and switching flies. He read the brand as he rode by, but it was a new one to him. After unsaddling, he walked back to the house, curiosity working at him.

He recognized the gray-haired man seated in the house with his father. Paul English stopped puffing his pipe as he saw Toby enter. He stood up, leaving the big old rocking chair to rock by itself.

"By George, Toby," he said with genuine pleasure, "it's sure good to see you." He grasped Toby's hand.

Grinning at him, Toby warmed inside.

He would remember Paul English till the day he died. English had been Damon Frost's foreman for many years. Toby had hired out to him many a time for extra cow work. English was a good man, the kind a growing boy watches and tries to follow.

A lot of friendly talk passed between them. Finally English pointed the stem of his pipe toward the door, and Toby caught the hint.

Outside, away from Sod, English said, "Toby, I'd

like you to tell me something. Where were you last night?"

Toby frowned, puzzled. "Why, I was here, Paul. With Dad."

"All night?"

"Sure."

English nodded. "I'm glad. I asked your dad in a roundabout way, and he said the same thing. So I know it's the truth."

Toby asked, "What's the matter, Paul?"

Grimness crept into his gray eyes. "Somebody was trying to run off some Long S cattle last night. Just happened that a couple of cowboys were on their way back from town and jumped them. The rustlers lit out."

"Anybody see who they were?"

English shook his head. "Too dark. Never got that close, anyway. All they could tell was that there was two of them." He paused, drawing deeply on the pipe. "I was in town this morning, son. I imagine you can guess what people were saying."

A quick rush of despair hit Toby. "I reckon I can. But I didn't have a hand in it, Paul. I hope you believe that."

"I believe it. But not many will. Damon Frost will be calling for your scalp."

Toby clenched his fist. Damon Frost. The man's implacable hatred had long been a puzzle to him.

"Paul," he said, "you were just about the only one that ever spoke up for me during the trial. You even went in the face of Damon Frost to try to get me off light. I've always appreciated that. But I never understood it."

Paul English smiled. "Mainly, I reckon, because I knew there wasn't really anything mean about you.

You were wild, but that's the kind of thing that generally wears off in time. I was pretty wild myself, once.

"There was something else, too. I knew that you and Dodd Parrish were protecting Alton Frost."

That came as a shock. "You knew? But how?"

"Working with a bunch of kids like you were, a man gets to where he knows them pretty well. He can figure out lots of things for himself. That was another thing that made me try to hold Damon back. I knew that if he kept digging, his own son was going to be drug in, too."

"You still working for Damon?"

English shook his head. "No. It never set well with him, me talking up for you. Pretty soon I got a chance to buy the old Murchison place, so I quit the Frost outfit and went to work for myself."

"Then who's Damon's foreman?"

"Marvin Sand."

"Marvin?" Toby's eyes widened. A sudden, unpleasant picture came into his mind. As foreman, Marvin would know where to find the kind of cattle the butcher wanted, know when it was safe to get them, probably could even get by with false counts which would cover up the stealing.

English was eyeing Toby sharply. "Any reason Marvin shouldn't be foreman for Damon Frost?"

Evasively Toby said, "I don't know. I guess not."

But he could tell that he had planted a seed of suspicion in English. It showed in the man's face.

Beside his horse English paused a moment. "Toby, you've served your time. Don't let them get you sent back for something you didn't do. You better stop covering up for other people and think about yourself."

A knot of anger grew in Toby as he watched Paul English ride away. He had come home looking for a new start. He had asked nothing of anybody, except to be left alone and given a chance. Now he wasn't going to let a couple of careless cow thieves spoil the chance he had earned.

Sod Tippett came hobbling out to the barn as Toby saddled a fresh horse.

"I'm going to town, Dad," Toby said. "I don't know what time I'll be back."

The minute Sod spoke, Toby knew the man's mind had dropped back into a worried time that had been gone for years.

"All right, son. But you hadn't ought to be going so much. Paul English was just telling me you've been making a good hand over at Frost's. He'd like to hire you full-time, only he says you've still got a little too much wildness in you. You run around a lot. Maybe you ought to stay home . . ."

With a tug at his throat, Toby said, "I will, Dad. I promise you, I will."

Toby had no real plan. There wasn't much he could do except talk to Sheriff Cass Duncan, and lay the cards on the table. He wasn't going to implicate Alton Frost and Marvin Sand—not unless he had to. But he knew with a stolid certainty that he would do it, if it was the only way to keep out of jail.

He felt the brooding hostility in the faces of the men he rode past on his way to the big old courthouse. A nagging worry started. Maybe he had done wrong in coming here. Maybe he should have waited until they came after him.

But deep within him he knew he was right. He was sure he could make Cass Duncan believe him. And it would be better to convince Cass now than to wait until the suspicion had worked so deeply in him that it could not be dispelled.

Walking into Cass Duncan's office, he saw someone working behind a big shelf, cleaning out stacks of old papers.

"Cass," he called.

It wasn't Cass. Betty Duncan stepped out from behind the ceiling-high shelf. Her eyes warmed at the sight of Toby. It struck him again that they were beautiful eyes, gray and vital.

Flustered, he said, "Excuse me, Miss Duncan. I thought you were Cass."

She smiled. "So I gathered. But I'm not."

Her long brown hair, he noticed, was combed up and rolled into a tight, pretty bun at the back of her neck. "He went out to the Long S this morning with a bunch of men. He ought to be getting back pretty soon." Her eyes continued to smile at him. "I'm glad you came, Toby. Maybe you can help me put some of these papers back on the top shelf. It's hard for me to reach."

He climbed up onto a chair. She handed him some papers. Their hands touched, and a peculiar tingle ran through him.

Toby said, "You know what Cass went out there for, I reckon."

Her eyes told him the answer.

"I was home last night," he said urgently. It was suddenly important to him that this girl believe him. "I didn't know a thing about it till Paul English stopped by and told me. I came in to tell Cass I had no hand in it. I promised him I was going to stay straight. I meant it."

He looked down into her eyes and found them searching his face. He was glad he hadn't lied to her. He sensed that she would have known it.

"Dad'll be pleased to hear that from you," she said.

"He didn't want to believe what some of them were saying about you this morning. You really convinced him the other day, Toby."

Her words brought him relief. He relaxed. Looking down at her, he said, "How about you, Betty? Were you convinced?"

She looked past him, her eyes pensive. "You didn't notice me much four years ago, Toby. I guess to you I was just a little girl then. But I noticed you. I was pulling for you all the way, and I'm pulling for you now."

Then, a tinge of red color in her face, she turned away from him and busied herself with the stack of papers and books.

A sudden stirring inside him, Toby watched her wonderingly. She had seemed only a kid then in her starched, schoolgirl dresses, her long brown hair braided and tied behind her head. He had often wondered why she was so eager to bake cakes and pies for him. Now he thought he knew.

The knowledge left a warm glow in him. Betty Duncan was no little girl now. He could see how a man could lose his heart to her in a hurry, if he hadn't already lost it to someone else.

Cass Duncan returned about half an hour later. The heavy sound of his footsteps preceded him down the courthouse hall. He stopped abruptly in the doorway as he sighted Toby sitting there.

Cass pitched his big dusty hat at a rack and missed. He paid no attention to that. He settled himself heavily into his chair and looked across at Toby, his gaze steady and questioning.

"I've been listening to everybody else all day," he said. "Now I want to hear what you've got to say."

Toby told him about Paul English's visit. "I haven't

stolen anybody's cattle, haven't tried to, and don't intend to try to."

Cass Duncan stared at him, his gray eyes as inescapable as his daughter's had been. "You know something, Toby? I believe you. But you know something else? I believe you know who was trying to run off those cattle. You ought to tell me."

Toby looked away from him. "I've told you all I know."

The sheriff frowned. "All right, Toby, if that's how it is."

Then he gave the same warning which Paul English had made. "You're fixing to get hung on somebody else's rope, son. Don't let it happen."

It was seldom that Toby Tippett ever took a drink. He felt that he needed one now, bad. Stepping into the saddle, he swung around and angled down the street to the new place which was called the Equity Bar. He walked up the steps, then stopped short at the door. A good-sized bunch of men was inside, and among them was Damon Frost.

Toby knew he didn't want any trouble now, and stepping in there would be a sure way to get it. Slowly he started back down the steps, dismissing his need of the drink. He saw two men riding up the street toward him, and he hauled up short again. They were Alton Frost and Marvin Sand.

He swung into the saddle and pulled out to meet them. The anger built in him. He saw surprise flush into their faces.

"I want to talk to you two," he said shortly. "Let's ride out a ways."

Sand's gaze nervously swept up the street. "This isn't the time to do it, I don't think."

Angrily Toby said, "We'll do it now, and we'll do it

right here, unless you turn around and ride out to a better place with me."

Resentment smoldered in Sand's face as they rode out around a hill just south of town. Once he looked back over his shoulder.

"Afraid somebody'll see you with me, Marvin, and get the idea you might be a crook?" Toby asked acidly. Sand didn't answer.

Toby felt an old dislike swelling in him. He never had thought much of Marvin Sand, even when they had ridden together years ago. With Toby and Dodd and Alton it had been mostly just wildness that pushed them into rustling cattle. Wildness and a thirst for adventure.

But with Sand, two or three years older than any of them, it had been something else.

It had been the money that had attracted him, a love of money that amounted to greed.

And with it had been a mean streak that had sometimes frightened the other boys. That streak had made him kill cattle for spite once when a posse had closed in and the young rustlers had had to abandon their stolen herd. And another time it had been all Toby could do to keep Sand from shooting Cass Duncan from ambush. Malice had burned in Marvin Sand, a malice beyond Toby's understanding.

"This is far enough, I reckon," Toby said when they were behind the hill. He swung his horse around to face them. "You knuckleheads! Don't you know what you're doing to me? I don't intend to stand around here with my hands in my pockets while you two fools get me sent back to prison for something I didn't do."

Alton Frost stammered. "N-now, Toby, it wasn't our fault. There wasn't a chance in a hundred that we'd get caught. It was just bad luck. It's not going to happen again."

Furiously Toby exploded, "It better not happen again. There's something I want you two to get straight, right now. I covered up for you once, because I was as guilty then as you were. But I'm not going to cover up for you now. Get my tail in a crack and I'll spill the whole story."

Sand's eyes narrowed. There was poison in them. "You wouldn't, Toby."

"Yes," he said levelly, "I would."

Sand leaned toward him, grabbing Toby's shirt. "You ever say a word about us, Toby, and I'll kill you."

Toby's anger burst free. He drove his fist into Sand's ribs so hard that Sand almost fell out of the saddle. Sand took a futile swing at him. Toby hit him again, and this time Sand fell.

Instantly Toby was on the ground, just in time to see Sand get up. Sand rushed him. Toby faltered under the savage impact of Sand's hard fists. But he managed to hit Sand in the face, twice. Sand slowed a little.

Alton Frost had dismounted and was standing there helplessly.

He pleaded, "Let's stop this. You got no call . . ."

Rage boiled up in Marvin Sand's face. He drove into Toby again, his fists striking like sledges. Toby staggered backward and fell. Sand drew back a foot to kick him.

Alton grabbed Sand's shoulder. "Marvin," he cried, "you can't . . ."

In blind fury Sand smashed Alton in the face. Young Frost fell to one knee and stayed there, holding his hand to his bleeding mouth.

Sand whirled back on Toby. But the brief break had

given Toby time to get part of his breath back. He never gave Sand a chance to balance himself. He dived into him, punching, slashing, pounding until Sand went down on his hands and knees.

Toby stood over him, his chest heaving. "You boys just . . . remember what I told you. I'm not going to jail . . . for anybody."

Sod Tippett was asleep when Toby got home that night. Hungry, Toby found a few cold biscuits without lighting the lamp. He went to bed.

Next morning he ached from the fight, and the bruises and cuts on his face were burning like grass afire. He walked out by the cistern and hauled up a bucket of water to wash his face. The water cooled him, but the fire soon came back.

Sleepy-eyed old Sod saw the bruises first thing.

"Horse fell with me," Toby lied.

The old man didn't believe him. Over his coffee, Sod said quietly, "Not taking to you very well, are they, son? I was afraid they wouldn't. It ain't the same now as it used to be. It'll never be the same again."

He sipped long at the scalding coffee. "Son," he spoke again, "what do you say we just up and leave? We can sell this place. We'll find us something somewhere else, where folks'll leave you alone."

Toby studied his father closely. "You think we could ever find a place we liked as well as we do this one?"

Sod didn't answer that directly. "That ain't the point, son. The point is . . ."

Toby interrupted him. "The point is that we wouldn't. So we're not going. They may try, but they'll never chase me off. Don't you worry yourself about it."

He rode out again that morning. When he came in at noon, he found Ellen Frost waiting for him. She sat in Sod's old rocking chair on the front porch, impatiently rocking back and forth. At sight of Toby she stood up quickly. Toby heard the clatter of cooking utensils inside the house.

Ellen hurried out to meet Toby as he swung down and looped one rein over the fence. She took Toby's arm and headed him toward the barn.

"Let's get out there where we can talk," she said quickly.

At the barn, out of sight of the house, Toby turned her around into his arms and kissed her. She gave little response, but she didn't try to stop him.

Huskily he said, "I've been thinking about you ever since you left."

She smiled, reaching up to pinch his skin. He flinched, because the bruises there sent pain knifing through him.

Ellen laughed. "You don't look so bad," she said. "Marvin's face is half blue."

Displeasure stirred in him. "They told you?"

"Why not? There aren't any secrets between Marvin, Alton, and me."

He turned loose of her. "You know what they've been doing?"

"Certainly. Sometimes I have to cover up for them with Pa."

Toby's face fell. A sickness started in the pit of his stomach.

Ellen went on, "Why do you want to be so hard-headed, Toby? Why don't you go along with them? Alton told me he made you a good proposition the other day. As long as people are blaming you anyway, you'd just as well be getting something out of it."

A sense of disgust swept him. He turned away from

her. "I was surprised enough at Alton," he said. "But you . . ."

"Surprised to find out that I've got some nerve, that I don't just sit at home and be a proper little girl with a pink ribbon in my hair? Maybe that's the kind of washed-out girl you want." Her voice rose angrily, "Well, that's not what I want to be. You've seen my mother. A dried-up, miserable little woman who shivers in fear every time Pa stomps into the house. She's scared to death of him all the time.

"You think I want to be like that? God knows Pa has tried hard enough to whip me into being that kind of a woman. But he hasn't been able to do it. No man ever will."

In despair, Toby said, "I think you better leave, Ellen. And maybe you'd better not come back."

Anger flared in her eyes and settled into disgust. "You're a fool, Toby."

He nodded. "Maybe. But I'm not a thief."

She slapped him so hard he stumbled back against the barn wall. She turned sharply and struck for the house in a fast, sharp stride. He stepped out and watched her. And suddenly he wasn't very sorry anymore.

Rubbing his burning cheek, he wondered why it didn't hurt him more, watching her leave. She had shattered a dream that he had built through four long years. There was some regret, sure. But there wasn't the kind of ache he might have expected. Instead, there was almost a feeling of relief. Maybe the shock Alton Frost had given him helped inure him. Then his mind went back once again to a pair of wide gray eyes, and he thought he knew.

He had gotten no more than halfway back to the house when the horsemen came—Damon Frost, flanked by Marvin Sand and a dozen cowboys. With them they were bringing back Ellen Frost, her shoulders squared defiantly. Toby knew they had trailed her here. He sensed what was coming.

For a moment he considered running for the house and getting a gun. He might be able to make it. But he knew they wouldn't leave until they had him. And they might hurt old Sod.

They reined up in front of him. Damon Frost leaned forward, his face clouded. "I gave you a warning the other day, Tippett. I told you to leave my daughter alone, and I told you to clear out of the country. You've done neither. Well, I made you a promise then. And now I'm going to keep it."

Marvin Sand and two cowboys stepped down. They rushed Toby. He stepped forward to meet them, his fists swinging. But in the space of two quick breaths they had grabbed him. Marvin Sand was standing directly in front of him, hate smoldering behind the dark blue splotches on his swollen face.

Frost glanced severely toward his daughter. "I warned you, Ellen. Now sit there and watch." To Marvin Sand he said, "Go ahead with it."

Sand's first fist plowed into Toby's stomach. Nausea swept him. The second blow struck his bruised face and brought slashing pain. For just a moment he saw Ellen's face and he found no sympathy there.

Malice leaped into Sand's darkened eyes. Then Toby's own eyes were closed by the merciless pounding of hard, hate-driven fists. He struggled vainly against the strong arms that bound him. Each blow drove him back a step nearer the deep, dark pit that yawned just beyond the whirling bursts of fire.

He heard Sod Tippett's enraged voice, but then Toby slumped, falling backward into that great pit.

Sod Tippett rushed out and down the steps, his old .30-30 rifle in his hands. "Damon Frost," he shouted hoarsely, "you leave my boy alone." In fury Sod Tippett stopped and pointed the gun at the ashen-faced cowboys. It clicked harmlessly. Cursing, the old man fought at the lever. But the rifle had jammed.

He came running then, grasping the rifle by the barrel. The two cowboys made a rush for their horses. Marvin Sand stood there. Sod Trippett's gaze furiously fell upon him. He rushed Sand, swinging the rifle viciously. Sand caught the blow on his left forearm. His right hand grasped the barrel. For a moment he struggled with the old man.

Then he wrenched the rifle free and gave Sod Tippett a savage glancing blow on the forehead. The old man fell heavily. He got up on his knees again, blood trickling down the side of his face. Sand smashed the rifle against a rock.

Suddenly Sod Tippett was babbling incoherently. He swayed to his feet and staggered toward the unconscious Toby.

"Martha!" he began calling hoarsely. "It's our boy. Come help me with our boy."

Puzzled, Sand looked up at Frost. Damon Frost sat rigid in the saddle, his widened eyes on the staggering old man.

"Martha," Frost said, shaken. "That was his wife."

Sand swung into the saddle. "The old man's as crazy as a loon. Let's get out of here."

They reined their horses around and rode out in a stiff trot.

Pain awakened Toby; his head throbbed as if someone was pounding on it with a sledge. He pushed himself onto his elbows and tried to open his eyes. He winced at the sharp pain of the bright sun, but he managed to get to his knees. His eyes were swollen almost shut. He could see the vague form of the house ahead of him. He tried to get there, but he stumbled and fell weakly. Pain rushed through him with sickening force.

He heard Sod Tippett's voice. "What's happened to you, son?" the old man said, almost whimpering. "That old Socks horse throw you again? I told you to be careful about him. He'll really hurt you some day."

Toby realized vaguely that Sod's mind had gone astray again. Socks was a mean horse Toby had ridden when he was about ten years old, one that had caused him many a skinned face and bloody nose.

Sod got hold of Toby and helped him up again. With the old man's support Toby got to the house and swayed over to the cistern. He pulled up a bucket of water and doused his face in it. After a while he could open his eyes enough to see. He saw the dried streak of blood on his father's face, and the broken rifle lying out there. He could imagine the rest.

Tenderly Toby reached up and touched the wound on his father's head. "They hurt you, Dad?"

Sod shook his head. "You and your mother, always worrying about a man. It's nothing. Horse took me under a low limb is all."

But that wasn't all. From the tracks Toby could tell pretty much what had happened. And the excitement had been a little too much for his father. Toby saw him grip his chest. He managed to rush forward in time to catch Sod Tippett as the old man fell.

It was after dark when Toby pulled the heaving team to a halt in front of the doctor's house in town and climbed down from the wagon. He tried to lift Sod out by himself. But he was still too weak to manage it.

"Doc!" he called. "Doctor Will!"

In a moment Doctor Will Chambers came out onto his porch with a lantern held high.

"It's me, Doc, Toby Tippett. Dad's had a stroke."

Together they carried Sod into the house and eased him onto a cot. The physician took out his stethoscope and listened to Sod's heartbeat.

"I've been afraid of this," he said, "ever since he had that sick spell three years ago."

Toby had never heard about any sick spell. But his father wrote but seldom, and never much even then.

"It's all my fault, Doc," Toby said. "Maybe if I'd been here, if I hadn't caused him so much worry . . ."

The doctor glanced up at Toby. It was the first time he had really looked at him, and his eyes widened at the bluish, swollen face. But he never mentioned that.

"There wouldn't have been much you could've done about it, one way or the other. He caught pneumonia and it almost killed him. He was out of his head for a week. He hasn't been the same since, Toby. You've seen what that spell did to his mind. No, there wouldn't have been much you could do about it. He was old, and it just happened."

Toby sat in silence, letting that soak in. Somehow it left him feeling better. It lifted some of the guilt from his shoulders.

He hadn't been there long before Betty Duncan came in. She paled at the sight of Toby's swollen face. Then sympathy came into her eyes.

"I just heard, Toby. I came to see what I can do."

Toby shook his head. "There's not much any of us can do but wait."

She took hold of his hand. Warmth rose in him.

"I'll wait with you," she said. She sat down beside him.

It was two days before the doctor decided Sod

Tippett was going to pull through. During those two days Toby saw Betty Duncan a number of times. Each time he came near her, he felt a little lightheaded, like he used to when he'd been in the old Mustang Saloon too long. He knew what was the matter with him, and it wasn't anything the old saloon had had to offer.

Toby noticed something else, too. Cass Duncan was seldom around. He was always gone at night. Toby thought he knew the answer to that. The sheriff was staying out in the country, hoping to jump those cattle thieves if they made another try. So far as Toby knew, they hadn't tried. He hoped they had been scared for good. But he knew within reason that they would try again.

In town, Toby was conscious of the half-hidden hostility which followed him wherever he went. He felt it when men broke off their conversations as he walked by. He sensed it when women passed him on the street and kept their eyes averted.

Only with Betty Duncan could he put aside the growing bitterness in him. So he was glad to return to the ranch when the doctor told him it would be all right.

The sharp thud of hoofbeats brought him straight up in bed. He was wide awake in an instant, and one thought stabbed him.

It's gone bad with Dad, and they're coming to tell me.

He pulled on his boots and the pants which he had left hanging on a corner of the iron bedstead. He was fully dressed and waiting on the porch when the riders came up. His heart was pounding hard.

Silver moonlight splashed upon the men, and he saw that he had been wrong. They were Marvin Sand and

Alton Frost. Alton was slumped over the saddle horn, wounded.

Toby grabbed hold of him. He eased him out of the saddle and onto the porch. His hand came out from under Alton's back warm and sticky, and even in the moonlight he could see the dark smear of blood. The boy's throat rasped as he struggled to breathe. He was dying—there wasn't much time.

Sand never dismounted. "They jumped us over on Paul English's place. There was a bunch of them, and they were on us before we knew it. After they hit Alton, I managed to get him away. But they're close behind us. You can hear them now, if you listen hard."

Toby's heart leaped. Yes, he could hear the hoof-beats. Anger swept through him. "You led them here? You fool, don't you know how that'll look for me?"

He could feel the hard grin on Marvin Sand's hat-shadowed face. "Sure, Toby, I knew how it would look. That's why I led them here. Keep them company. I'm riding on."

Wheeling his horse around, he spurred away. In the first flush of helpless rage Toby dashed for the door, wanting a gun. But he stopped, realizing that it would be useless now.

He dropped on his knees beside Alton Frost. He could hardly hear the breathing now. Desperate, he knew he had to keep Alton alive, had to keep him alive until the posse got here. Only Alton's word could clear him of the implication which Marvin Sand's coming here had made.

The posse rode in cautiously, guns ready, a circle of men drawing a tight noose around the little ranch house. Toby waited quietly, standing in the moonlight where they could all see him.

"It's all right, Cass" he called. "Come on in."

Cass Duncan stepped down from his horse, the gun in his hand catching a glint of moonlight. "Better raise your hands, son."

Toby did. "I haven't got a gun on."

He pointed his chin toward Alton Frost. "You better see after Alton, Cass. He's about gone."

Someone exclaimed, "I told you we got one of them. I told you I saw him almost fall."

Instantly Cass was on his knees beside young Frost.

Toby said, "They rode up here just a couple or three minutes ago."

"They?"

"Alton and Marvin Sand."

Cass said, "There's nobody here but you and Alton. And we were chasing just two men."

Panic rising in him, Toby tried to explain. But he could see disbelief and disgust in the dark, shadowed faces that surrounded him.

"Alton will tell you the truth of it, Cass," Toby exclaimed in desperation. "Ask him. Ask him before it's too late."

Cass Duncan's voice was flat and hard. "It is too late. Alton has just died."

Riding in, he felt the sheriff's eyes upon him, hard as flint. "You oughtn't to've come back, Toby. Cattle stealing was bad enough. At least they couldn't do anything worse than send you to prison for it. But murder is something else."

"Murder?" Toby's chest tightened. "What murder?"

"You shot Paul English tonight. He got a little too close, and your slug caught him. We sent him to town in a wagon. But he looked like he didn't stand much chance."

Paul English! Toby slumped in the saddle. The only

man left who would have believed him, would have fought for him.

Toby became angry with himself. It needn't have happened this way. If he had told what he knew the first time Cass asked him, this wouldn't have happened. But he had held back. Minding his own business, he had told himself. Hoping Alton Frost would come out all right.

Now it was too late to talk, because there was no one who would listen, no one who would believe.

But he found himself wrong. Betty Duncan was standing in front of his cell door ten minutes after Cass had clanged it shut. Her gray eyes glistened. Her slender hands trembled if she did not hold them tightly together.

"Toby," she said, and then stopped talking because she could not hold down the tremor in her voice. But her eyes told the rest of it. He reached through the bars, and her hands came into his.

"Betty," he whispered, "they won't believe me."

"I believe you, Toby." Cass Duncan finally came back from the doctor's. Toby asked him, "What about Paul English?"

Cass shot him a hostile glance and turned his back, shrugging. "Fifty-fifty chance."

The sheriff sat down heavily in his chair, his shoulders slumped. He and Paul English had made many a cow camp together in years past. They'd gone off hunting together many a time.

Toby waited a while before he tried talking to the sheriff again. "Look, Cass," he said, "I feel as bad about this as you do. I didn't have many friends left, but Paul English was one of them. I didn't shoot him, Cass. Believe me."

Cass Duncan sat there for a time in thoughtful silence. Finally he said, "I wish I could believe you."

Toby pressed, "I've told you it was Marvin Sand who was with Alton last night. You don't have to take my say-so on it. Make Marvin prove where he was. He won't be able to do it. Then maybe you can find his gun and see if it didn't fire the bullet that hit Paul."

Cass Duncan swung around. His hard gaze probed Toby's face. "All right Toby. But you better not be making a fool of me this time."

He was gone all day. He came in late in the afternoon, when the reddening, bar-crossed sunlight that entered Toby's cell window was easing up toward the plaster ceiling. The sheriff's shoulders sagged, and weariness cut deep lines into his beard-shadowed face. But a dangerous fire smoldered in his tired eyes.

"You lied to me, Toby."

Heartbeat lifting, Toby stood erect.

Cass said, "I found somebody who vouched for him, Toby. He was at the ranch all night."

A cold numbness gripped Toby. He sensed the rest of it, even before Cass told him.

"Ellen Frost. She said he was with her."

The word came next morning. Paul English was going to live.

Betty Duncan was the one who told Toby. He turned away, standing in front of the window a long moment, swallowing down the tightness in his throat.

"He's not conscious yet," Betty told him. "But his heartbeat has gotten stronger. Doc Chalmers said he's sure Paul will make it all right."

Toby faced back toward the girl. "Betty, maybe Paul got close enough to know who it was that shot him. When he wakes up and tells, they'll have to turn me loose. They'll know I wasn't lying."

Suddenly a grim realization came to him. His face fell. "Marvin Sand will think of that, too."

Betty's eyes widened. "You think he might try to kill Paul?"

Toby said, "I know he would. You better get Cass, Betty."

Cass Duncan stared at him in cold disbelief. Contempt lay coiled in his eyes as he listened to Toby's desperate plea.

"You've got to get somebody over there to guard Paul," Toby cried. "Everything I've told you is the truth. You can't just stand by and let Marvin kill him."

Cass said flatly, "You've lied to me too many times, Toby. You're not going to make a fool of me again."

He turned his back and started to leave the jail.

"Cass," Toby called after him, "I swear I'm not lying to you. You can't just turn your back."

Cass whirled on him, his eyes ablaze. "Toby, I've got one solitary confinement cell back yonder, padded all around, without any windows. Say one more word to me and I'll throw you in it!"

He stomped out. Toby sank back onto the cot, face fallen in despair.

Cass Duncan's lean, stoop-shouldered deputy came in a while later. "Hungry?" Toby shook his head.

"Betty Duncan's bringing you some supper anyway," the deputy said. "Was I her, I wouldn't even give you a burnt biscuit. But then, I ain't her."

The deputy unlocked the cell door when Betty came in. She gave Toby a quick, half-scared smile, then uncovered a platter with biscuits, fried beef, and some dried fruit on it. She had also brought a small pot of coffee.

Toby's heart went into his brief smile. "Thanks, Betty." Then his chin sank. "I guess you know Cass won't listen to me. He won't put a guard on Paul. Marvin'll kill him, and there's not one thing I can do to stop him."

Betty touched Toby's hand, a quick, fleeting touch that left a warm glow.

"Maybe there is something you can do about it, Toby. Don't worry. Just eat your supper and drink all your coffee. All of it."

He soon had eaten all he could of the supper. He was pouring the third cup of coffee when he heard the metallic click inside the pot. Betty's words came back to him in a rush. "Drink all your coffee." He looked up quickly to see if the deputy had heard the faint noise. But if he had, he gave no sign.

Cautiously Toby took the lid off the pot. There, sticking up out of the remaining coffee, was one end of a long key. Toby fitted the lid back in place and looked up again, hoping his sudden excitement didn't show in his face.

After a while the deputy took a heavy old watch out of his vest pocket. "Well," he said, jokingly, "I got a few rounds to make. I won't be long. You just stay here till I get back."

Toby's heart was in his throat. He waited a long minute after the deputy was gone. Then, quickly, he took the key out of the coffee pot. He stepped up to the door and fitted it into the lock outside. He fumbled a moment, a choking fear rising in him that this wasn't the right key, that Betty had made a mistake.

Then he heard a click, and the door swung open under his weight. He looked longingly at the gun chest in a corner. But it was locked, and he couldn't afford to spend time in hunting for a key. There were no loose guns around.

Lamplight bathed the front door. He couldn't go out

that way. He hurried to the back door and tried it. It was unlocked. He knew he could thank Betty for that. He stepped out into the darkness.

"Toby!"

He spun around. He made out the shadowy form of the girl hurrying toward him.

"Betty," he breathed.

She came into his arms, and he held her tightly. He found her lips.

When they stepped apart, she put something heavy and cold into his hand. A six-shooter.

"One of Dad's," she said. "Now let's move away from here before John comes back and finds out you've left."

They kept to the shadows, moving quietly but hurriedly along at the backs of the town buildings toward the doctor's house.

Once somebody stepped out of a door. Toby flattened against a wall, holding his breath, while Betty held tightly to him. The man flung a panful of water out onto the ground and stood there a minute, biting off a fresh chew from a plug of tobacco while he looked around. But the lamplight inside evidently had blinded him against the darkness. He never seemed to notice the man and the girl.

In a few minutes they reached the back of the doctor's house.

Pointing, Betty said, "That's the room where Paul is. Your dad is in a room on the other side."

Toby studied the house. He figured what he would do in Marvin Sand's place. Safest thing would be to shoot from outside through a window. That way, he could get away in a hurry.

Next to the doctor's home was a house set up on wooden blocks. The bottom was boarded up, but a big open space was left unboarded beneath the high front porch, probably to let the family dog sleep under there. Toby motioned toward it.

"I'm going to wait under there," he said quietly. "It gives me a good view of Paul's window, and it's in range. It's dark enough that nobody can see me. You better get along now, before Cass misses you."

Betty shook her head. "I'm staying here with you."

Firmly he said, "I don't want you getting hurt. Go on."

She started to argue with him, but stopped as they heard a plodding of hoofbeats. Somebody was riding down the street toward them. Without hesitation Betty ducked under the high porch. There was nothing else Toby could do. He followed her.

The rider went on by. Then sounds of excitement burst over toward the courthouse square. Toby could hear running feet, and someone shouting. Old John had returned to the jail and found Toby gone.

It wasn't many minutes before searching riders and men afoot began working up and down the streets and alleys, nosing into all the dark places. Toby crawled farther back under the house, and Betty crawled back with him. He knew he ought to make her leave, but she didn't want to. And touching her warm, slender hand, he didn't want her to leave now.

Presently the search died down.

"I reckon by now Cass knows how I got out," Toby whispered. "You ought to've gone home when I told you."

She shook her head and touched her cheek to his arm. "I'm where I want to be, Toby, with you."

There was no warning before the shooting started. Toby and Betty knelt together, watching carefully where they thought the killer might come. But they never saw him before the two sudden shots shattered the night stillness. The man and the girl exchanged one swift, terrified glance, then both burst out from under the porch in a hard run.

More shots sounded from inside the house. A rider spurred out from the other side of the building. A quick shaft of moonlight touched him—Marvin Sand.

Heart hammering, Toby dropped to one knee and fired. Sand leaned low over his saddle horn. His gun came up, and dust leaped at Toby's feet. Toby squeezed the trigger again.

He saw the second flash of fire just as Sand's bullet sent him reeling, to sprawl in the sand.

Betty screamed and rushed to him. She grabbed up the fallen gun and fired futilely at the horseman who was spurring away. The darkness swallowed him up.

Toby fought for breath. The girl dropped to her knees beside him and sobbed, "Toby, where did he hit you?"

Toby pushed onto his knees, supporting himself with his left hand. His right hand felt along his ribs, searching for the source of the hammer-like throbbing.

"My ribs," he gritted finally. "Creased them a little. Knocked the breath out of me."

Running feet thudded on the soft ground, and from somewhere came the sudden clatter of horses' hooves. A shadow fell across the man and the girl. Cass Duncan stopped there, a smoking gun in his hand.

"You hit, son?"

Toby didn't answer the question. Instead he asked fearfully, "What about Paul? Did he get him?"

The sheriff was slow in replying. "No, Toby, he didn't get Paul."

Cass Duncan helped Toby to his feet. Betty's arm

went around Toby, supporting him. She was trying to keep from crying.

"This clears him, doesn't it, Dad?" she begged in a breaking voice.

Cass said, "Well, it does put a different complexion on things. It doesn't clear you all the way. But at least it shows you weren't lying about Marvin Sand. The funny thing is, I had a notion you were going to try to kill Paul yourself, when we found you had gotten out. I was in Paul's room, waiting for you to try it."

A dozen or more men were crowding around the trio. They made room as Cass, Toby, and Betty started toward the doctor's house. Toby felt his strength seeping back into him, and the pain in his ribs was easing down to a dull throbbing. Just a crease.

At the front door, Cass Duncan stopped. "Toby, before you go in, I better tell you Marvin Sand picked the wrong window, and he got the wrong man."

Toby choked, a sudden rush of panic sweeping through him. Betty's hand tightened quickly on his arm.

He whispered, "Dad?"

Cass nodded, his head down. "I'm sorry, Toby."

The first rush of grief passed, and in its place grew a burning anger. Toby sat motionless while the doctor bound his ribs. But his fists were clenched, and his lips were drawn flat and hard. With his returning strength came determination.

Betty Duncan laid her hand on his arm. "Lie down and try to get some rest, Toby. Dad has taken a bunch of men out to the Frost ranch. If Marvin tried to go back there, they'll get him."

Toby shook his head. "I'm not going to rest, Betty, till I've gotten Marvin Sand."

A nagging worry kept working at him. What if

Marvin didn't go back to the Frost ranch? He had seen his plan blow up in his face. Chances were good that he would not dare return to the ranch. Where would he go?

And suddenly Toby thought he knew. Marvin and Alton had been taking their stolen cattle to somebody down south who was selling the beef to railroad construction workers. The three of them were splitting the profits, Alton had said.

What if there were still some unsplit profits down there? Toby knew Sand's greed. He knew Sand wasn't the kind to go off and leave any money behind him.

The idea became a certainty with Toby. Half an hour later he was on a horse and heading south . . .

He found the railroad. There was still a shiny newness to the rails. Although the ties already were beginning to show dark stains from coal and dirt-laden steam, they were fresh and new, the ends not scored or cracked. Toby headed west, following the tracks toward a drifting trace of coal smoke far ahead.

Up near the end of track he found the settlement. There had been a little trading post and post office down here for years. They called it Faraway, because the man who first established it moved off in disgust, declaring that it was too far away from civilization ever to amount to anything.

Faraway now was a booming little construction town. Later on, it probably would die again. But right now it was living high. Tents, slapped-together shacks, and wheel-mounted business houses set off on side tracks had all but swallowed up the original old trading post. There were lots of men here. A good market for beef, Toby mused, watering his horse in a wooden trough and taking a wide, sweeping look.

A saloon would be the best place to pick up information. He sought out the crudest, meanest-looking one of the lot.

It was about as bad inside as it was outside. The saloon was really a big patched tent, the sides walled up with old warped boards which still had some loose nails sticking out of them. The bar was two more such boards nailed down across four empty kegs. And behind the bar slouched a bartender who likely hadn't had a bath since the last time he got caught out in the rain.

Toby ordered a drink and sat down at a crude scrap-lumber table with it. Nervousness prickled him. He didn't want to seem eager, but he didn't have any time to waste.

After a while he sidled back up to the bar.

"Say," he asked quietly, "where could a man sell some fat cattle around here? Who's the butcher for this outfit?"

The bartender scratched his chin under a mat of whiskers which could not properly be called a beard, even though they were long enough.

"Well, there's an outfit owned by John Pines that has a contract with the railroad. Then, there's a couple of old boys that do butchering to sell beef around the camp."

Toby looked back over his shoulder as if making sure nobody was listening.

"I need to find me a butcher who can keep his mouth shut."

The bartender's eyes lighted. "Stolen cattle?"

"Now," Toby drawled, "I wouldn't go so far as to say that. Just say there's a little room for argument about them, and I don't especially enjoy arguments."

The bartender grinned and poured Toby another

drink. "The man for you to see is Bud Spiller. He won't pay as much as the others, but he can't tell one brand from another. And he don't watch over his shoulder as you leave."

Bud Spiller's camp was south of the railroad, out in the brush, according to the bartender's directions. Spiller had some holding pens down there, and some Mexican workers to skin and dress the beef. He hauled it to the construction camp in a tarp-covered wagon.

The wind was out of the south, and Spiller's place wasn't hard to find. First thing Toby located was a Mexican dragging offal and cattle's heads away on a mule-drawn sled. At a rotting, stinking dump ground the man stopped, tipped the sled over, and headed back toward camp in a long trot, getting away from the foul stench.

At sight of Toby riding up to camp, a Mexican shouted something. A man stepped out of a big shack and strode forward. This, Toby guessed, was Bud Spiller. Spiller was a medium-tall, soft-bellied man with a stubble beard. His hairy arms were bloody most of the way to his rolled-up sleeves. Dried blood speckled his dirty clothing. He scowled darkly at Toby.

"What do you want here?"

"You Bud Spiller?"

The man nodded. "And I got lots to do. If you got business, get it over with."

Toby took his time, getting a good look at the camp. "I got some cattle to sell," he said. "I heard you might be the man to buy them."

Spiller grunted. "I ain't interested." He turned away. He took a couple of steps, then turned around again. "I might be, if they was cheap enough."

"I'd make them cheap enough," Toby said, "if I

knew you'd keep your mouth shut about where they came from."

Spiller's eyes widened a little. "They stolen?"

Toby rubbed his chin. "Well . . . I come by them awful easy."

He thought he saw a face behind a window in the shack. But as he squinted for a better look, the face disappeared. His heartbeat quickened.

Spiller's whiskered face frowned darkly. "Where'd you get the idea that I'd buy stolen cattle?"

Toby hesitated, then decided to throw in the whole stack of chips. "Friend of mine told me. Man named Marvin Sand."

In one unguarded moment the name brought a quick leap of surprise into Spiller's muddy eyes, and his mouth dropped open a little. He glanced quickly back over his shoulder, toward the shack. Then, as if realizing this had been a trap, he gripped himself. His face tightened.

"Get out of here," he snarled.

Toby's gun leaped into his hand. He swung to the ground, keeping the gun muzzle on Spiller. "I've got a hunch he's in that shack yonder," he said. "You're going to go in front of me. If he makes a wrong move, I'll kill you."

Spiller's jaw was bobbing. His throat swelled as he tried to force the words out. But fear choked them off. He turned woodenly and started toward the shack.

The Mexicans had all stopped work and were watching. Toby didn't think they would try to interfere with him. They were hired laborers, probably being paid just enough to eat. Chances were they wouldn't risk injury by interfering.

"Come on out, Marvin," Toby shouted. "Don't try anything, or I'll shoot Spiller."

There was no answer from inside. Toby repeated his order, and still he heard nothing. A doubt began to work at him. Maybe he was wrong. Maybe Marvin wasn't here at all. But he had to be.

Toby heard a sharp whirr, and he jerked around too late to dodge the hatchet flying at him. The flat edge struck the brim of his hat and flattened it against Toby's head. He saw a blinding flash of light, then dropped limply to the ground.

In a dreamy, half-real world, he sensed the tread of boots in the sand. He forced his eyes open enough to see the boots halted in front of him, swaying back and forth, back and forth. A voice broke through the fog.

"You've killed him." Fright lifted Bud Spiller's voice to a high pitch. "You'll get me hung, Marvin."

Even in half consciousness, Toby knew the other voice.

"He's not dead. But we better kill him. He'll talk, and you'll do a stretch where he just come from," Marvin Sand said.

"No," Spiller said, his voice wavering, "we're not going to kill him. I can stand a stretch for butchering stolen cattle, but I don't want to hang."

Sand shrugged. "Have it your own way. But I'm leaving. Give me my money. I'm getting out of the country."

They walked into the shack. His head clearing, Toby tried to push himself up onto his hands and knees. He could hear the voices inside the shack.

"Here's for that last bunch you and Alton brought me. I reckon you get his share now," Spiller said.

There was a brief silence, then a chuckle. "That's a right smart of money you got there, Bud. Ain't you afraid to keep that much on you?"

"There's no better place that I know of. I couldn't

leave it lying around this camp. I sure wouldn't take it to Faraway. Too many crooks around there. Best thing is to keep it on me. I always got a gun to . . . Marvin, don't point that thing at me."

Sand chuckled again. "I won't hurt you, Bud, not if you don't give me any trouble. Just hand over that money."

Spiller's voice was shrill with outrage. "It's mine, Marvin! My share of what we made together. We split the profits even, you and me and Alton."

Toby heard a sharp cry, then a clubbing sound like a butcher axing a steer.

A moment later Marvin Sand strode out of the shack, his pockets bulging. He stopped beside Toby. Toby's heart hammered in helplessness. He knew Sand was considering whether or not to shoot him.

Then Sand turned away. He walked out to a small shed and reappeared astride a horse. He touched spurs to the animal and swung northward in an easy lope.

Toby pushed himself up and swayed toward a bucket he saw on a bench by the shack. The bucket was half full of water, and he splashed some of it on his face, soaked a handkerchief in it, and held it to his swollen forehead, where the flat side of the hatchet had struck.

The cool water cleared his head. He went back to where he had fallen and picked up his gun. He heard a scraping sound at the door of the shack. Bud Spiller was dragging himself out. Blood trickled down his face from a ragged wound.

"Where was he going, Spiller?" Toby demanded.

Spiller sagged, bracing himself against the door. Despair was stamped in the heavy lines of his face. "Train. Going to catch the evening construction train east. Go get him, friend. He's all yours."

Toby lifted himself stiffly into his saddle and spurred

out, heading north after Marvin Sand. For a moment or two he thought he might fall, but he gripped the horn, and soon there was little weakness left. From the north he heard the whistle of a train.

He broke out onto a hilltop that gave him a long look down toward Faraway. And yonder, just starting to pull away, was the eastbound construction train. A cold certainty gripped Toby. Marvin Sand was on that train.

Toby slanted his horse a little eastward. It took a while for the train to begin working up speed. A mile east of town the road made a bend around a rocky hill that had been too mean to blast out. The train would travel slowly until it passed the bend, Toby thought. Counting on that, he headed for the bend.

He hauled up at the bend, moments ahead of the train. He held his winded horse alongside the track and waved his hat frantically.

The frightful racket of the engine bearing down upon them threw the horse into a frenzy. He fought back away from the tracks. In desperation, Toby kept on waving his hat. But as the train passed, the grinning engineer waved back. Some cowboy seeing his first train, he probably thought.

Still yelling, Toby touched spurs to the horse and broke into a long-stretching lope alongside the train. The cars were rapidly pulling away from him. He crowded in, trying to grab hold of something and pull himself up onto the train.

The cars were passing him, one and then another, and then a third. It was a short train, and there weren't many more left. Toby kept spurring hard, the rough ground flying by beneath him. One misstep could throw him under the wheels.

He caught a flashing glimpse of a face as an empty flat car went by. Marvin Sand.

The grade flattened out, and the train was picking up speed. Yelling at his horse, fighting at the reins, Toby crowded him in once more. He grabbed at an iron bar. It jerked out of his hands. He grabbed at another. This time he got a good hold. He kicked his feet free and let the train pull him away from the saddle.

His body slammed hard against the side of the car, and for an agonizing moment he thought he would fall. He glimpsed the railroad ties whisking by beneath. He held onto the bar, and found a foothold.

He pulled himself up onto the swaying car and looked behind him. Way back yonder his horse was still running, pulling away from the train. Another moment and he would have lost the race.

Toby drew his gun and started moving forward, crouched low. Marvin Sand must have been watching him, hoping he would fall. Now, he would be waiting.

A bullet tugged at his sleeve, and the sharp blast of a gunshot burst almost in his face. Without time to aim, Toby squeezed off a hasty shot at the hat which was ducking beneath the top of the next car. Splinters flew. Toby rushed forward.

Another bullet reached for him from beneath the roof of the car. Marvin was between two cars, holding onto a ladder and shifting positions for each shot. Toby sent a second bullet at the edge of the car and kept pushing forward. He jumped the space between the two rumbling cars, and then he was on the car behind which Marvin was waiting. Sand bobbed up. He fired rapidly, one shot, two, three. Toby sprawled flat, the bullets singing over him.

Sand stopped shooting then, and Toby knew why— his gun was empty. Toby lurched onto his feet and ran ahead, toward the end of the moving car. Sand was fumbling with his gun, trying to reload it. At the sight of Toby rushing toward him, he hurled the gun.

Toby ducked it. Sand climbed up onto the car and came rushing to meet him. He grabbed at Toby's gun.

Toby was aware that the train was slowing down. Aroused by the crash of gunfire, the engineer was putting on the brakes. Up ahead, just behind the engine, someone climbed onto a car and was coming on the run. He had a shotgun in his hands.

Toby's feet slipped, and he fell backward. Marvin crashed down on top of him. Marvin's knee drove into Toby's bound ribs. Toby cried out in pain. His hand involuntarily relaxed, and Marvin wrenched the gun from his fingers. Sand jumped back onto his feet. He brought the gun down into line, his face twisted in hatred.

Then the brakes grabbed hold. The car lurched suddenly and Sand's feet slipped. He struggled for footing, then he plunged backward between the two cars. His wild scream cut off short.

Ribs aching, Toby was down off the side of the car the moment the train stopped. He trotted back down the tracks toward the twisted form he could see lying there.

He stopped short, his eyes widening. His face drained white, and he turned back.

Two smoke-blackened train men came hurrying. One of them held the shotgun on Toby, but he paid little attention to it.

"What's this all about, boy?" one of the men demanded.

Toby motioned toward the body. "He killed a man over in Patman's Lake yesterday. I was trying to take him back."

The trainman lowered the gun. "Well," he commented, "there ain't hardly enough left now to take back."

Despair bore down like a leaden weight in Toby as he rode northward to Patman's Lake. Ahead of him was the grim task of burying his father.

Toby's consuming anger had burned itself out after the fight on the train. No longer was there any hatred in him. But the grief remained, and he had the whole trip in which to think about it. There was so much he had wanted to do for old Sod Tippett, so many wrongs to make up for.

Something else was eating at Toby as he rode back across seventy far-stretching miles of cow country. A cloud of suspicion would always hang over him now. Marvin Sand could have cleared him, but Sand was dead. So was Alton Frost. As for Bud Spiller, the man had cleared out, just as Toby had figured he would. Toby had ridden back to Spiller's slaughtering camp and taken Faraway's marshal with him, but Spiller was gone. The country was big, and Spiller had his start.

Toby never even went by the ranch. He rode on into Patman's Lake. His shoulders sagged, and his body ached all over. He paid scant attention to the men who watched him from a dozen porches and doorways. Stiffly he swung down at the courthouse square and walked to the big, open doors.

Betty Duncan was waiting for him. Her wide eyes shone as she rushed forward to meet him. He folded her in his arms, pressing his cheek to her soft hair while she buried her face against his chest.

Later Cass Duncan shook Toby's hand with a genuine pleasure. "We got the news from Faraway by telegraph," he said. "Sure glad you weren't hurt."

Toby nodded, murmuring his thanks.

"I didn't want Marvin to die, Cass," Toby said. "I wanted to bring him back to clear me. Now there's no way to do it. As long as I live, people will be wondering if I was with Marvin and Alton."

Betty shook her head. "No, they won't Toby. They know the truth."

Toby stared at her. For the first time he noticed the thin blue color that ringed one of her eyes, and the red-tinged, angry-looking mark that reached down her cheek.

"I had a hunch Ellen Frost could tell the whole story if she wanted to," Betty said. "So I went out there. We had a long talk. When we got through, she told everything, Toby. She cleared you."

Relief washed over Toby. Gratefully he squeezed the girl's hands. "How about Ellen?" he asked, smiling. "Does she look as bad as you do?"

Betty smiled back. "Worse."

"And Damon Frost?" Toby asked. "How's he taking this?"

Cass frowned. "Pretty hard. I think he knew all the time that Alton had outlawed on him. And Ellen had gone wild, too. Damon wanted to blame somebody for it, and so he blamed you. He never guessed about Marvin Sand. He took out all his vinegar on you, Toby. He tried to get you the stiffest sentence he could, hoping that what happened to you would be a lesson to Alton. He thought it had. But when you came back, he was afraid it would start all over again. He didn't know it already had.

"That's why he hated you so much, son. He wanted to blame somebody for ruining his son and his daughter. But I think he knows that it was really nobody's fault but his own."

Soberly Cass studied the floor. "I reckon we're

always fighting ourselves, never ready to accept our own responsibility."

"And that's where you're ahead, Toby. You can ride a straight road now and never have to look back," the sheriff said. He stood up then, placing his hand on Toby's shoulder. "You're tired, son. You ought to rest. Come on over to the house with us. We'll fix you a bed."

Toby nodded. "Just one thing first. I'd like to see Paul English, if he's conscious."

Cass said, "Yes, he's all right now. Funny thing, too. You might never have been cleared if Marvin hadn't gotten scared and tried to kill him. But he didn't need to do it. Paul never saw a thing that night we jumped the cow thieves. He never got a look at the man who shot him."

Together the three of them walked out of the courthouse and headed down the long, dusty street. Toby glanced down at Betty, and tightened his arm around her.

DEADLY HOMECOMING

Two riders come," Enrique said.

Kyle Rayford turned at the warning and squinted down the grassy slant of the hill. The horsemen were still only two black dots out on the broad prairie past the deep green line of trees along the creek. They hadn't wasted much time. His fist clenched near the gun at his hip.

Enrique Salinas spoke again, his voice almost casual. "Is still time, *hijo*. We can still go."

Kyle Rayford shook his head, a grim set to his square jaw. "We didn't come back to run."

Salinas shrugged, a great patience in his ageless black eyes that might have seen fifty years or seventy years—no man could ever guess their exact age.

Kyle turned back to what had been the Slash R headquarters, so long ago. Bitterness rode him the way a restless man rides a horse. There wasn't much left after four years. He found where the dugout had been, all tumbled in now and grown over with grass. It was now a rattlesnake den inside, more than likely.

Lying there, rotted on the ground, was the heavy ridgepole he had helped his father and Enrique haul in from miles down the creek. The mob had tied a rope to it that night four years ago. Then they had jerked it out to cave in the dugout and destroy what little home the Rayfords had.

The only thing still there was the set of corrals they had built. Somebody had added onto them and made them bigger. A Bar E iron had been burned into one of the posts, probably by some cowboy testing the heat of it.

Bar E. That was Ebeling. Kyle realized suddenly that they'd even built a corral over his father's grave. He swore softly to himself. He couldn't even be sure any more exactly where it had been.

"They wouldn't let him alone while he lived," Kyle Rayford said aloud. "You'd think they'd let him lie in peace now."

It was a long and bitter story, one hard to think about. Yet now he wanted to think about it. He wanted to keep the memory fresh and vivid and raw until he had evened the score, wiped the slate clean . . .

Hope had ridden high with Earl Rayford and his young son Kyle when they had come up to the high plains from the brush country of South Texas with a string of longhorn cattle, a worn-out wagon, and not much else. Up here, people said, a man could carve himself a place out of virgin range. He could do anything he felt big enough to. He could grow as big as he wanted to because there was room up here for everybody.

So they came and pushed out the buffalo and traded out the Indians. But in time there were too many people. The elbows got to rubbing a little too close, and some got careless with other men's range and other men's cattle. Accusing fingers pointed one way, then another. And more and more they pointed at Earl Rayford, his son, and the gaunt old Mexican vaquero who had come up the trail with them.

They had been wrong. One man who had come up with a hunger for land and cattle was Clint Ebeling. He saw what the Rayfords had and wanted it. So he saw to it that the fingers kept pointing.

It hadn't meant much to Kyle then because he was eighteen and full of beans and didn't give a damn what anybody thought. It had all blown up in his face the Sunday afternoon he had gone over to the Half Circle B to pay court to Jane Emmett, daughter of Brook Emmett.

Jane Emmett. Even after four years the picture of her was still bright and clear in his mind. He had courted her quite a while, and they'd begun making plans about building a place of their own up at the head of the creek. Eighteen wasn't too young in those days.

But that afternoon Jane didn't come out to meet him at the cedar picket gate the way she always had. Brook Emmett was standing there, and his huge shoulders were squared for trouble.

"Don't get down, Kyle," he had said. His voice was almost soft. But men had learned that when Brook Emmett talked soft, it was time to start backing up.

"Don't get down and don't come here anymore. If you ever speak to my daughter again, I'll kill you!"

The big explosion came a few nights later. Kyle was alone in the dugout, still worrying over the sudden change, puzzled by the way Jane had turned from him and walked away when he had slipped back after old Emmett had gone riding off.

Enrique was across the creek, helping their friend

Sam Whittenburg brand a bunch of calves. He wasn't expected back till the next day. But Pa had been due back hours ago, and Kyle was beginning to worry.

The sound of hooves sucking at the mud finally came to him in the dugout. He lit the lantern and stepped outside in the drizzling rain. The flickering yellow light splashed upon a dozen riders, sitting their horses in a half circle around the front of the dugout. In a glance, Kyle caught the grim purpose in their hard faces. He whirled away.

A gun barked. A bullet plunked into the rough-hewn wooden door. "Don't do it, Rayford," a rough voice said.

The lantern light winked against silver gun barrels. Uncertainly Kyle set the lantern down on the muddy ground at his feet. Only then did he see the horse outside the circle, and the slack body hanging across the saddle. A man pulled the horse up and gave the body a shove. It made a soft thump in the mud.

He didn't have to look at the face. He sank beside his father's body, his shoulders heaving.

"We caught him this time, kid," somebody said. The voice belonged to Clint Ebeling. "He was running his brand on a Bar E calf."

Kyle looked at Ebeling and saw a trace of a satisfied grin on the man's face. A terrible fury roared through him. He leaped at Ebeling, jerking him out of the saddle, driving at him with his fists. "It's a lie, a lie!"

A gun barrel slashed across the back of his hatless head, driving him to his knees. He rubbed a muddy hand across his face, trying to clear his head. One thing was clear. This was what Clint Ebeling had been working up to. He'd planned it. He'd framed it.

Desperately he tried to tell them that. Nobody listened. A fist struck him behind the neck and sent him face down into the mud. He heard the ragged voice of Benny Ahrens.

"Shut up, or I'll stomp your brains out!"

Wet and muddy from his fall, Ebeling said harshly, "Let's stop playing with him and get it over with, before we all die in this damp."

Benny Ahrens's feet clomped into the dugout, then out again. "Wonder where that Mexican is? We ought to hang him, too."

A big man, broad of shoulder and a little heavy, swung down from his saddle, grunting at the effort. "No, Ahrens. We're not hanging anybody."

It was Brook Emmett. They all listened to him because he was a man of strength and dignity. Emmett helped Kyle to his feet. Once Emmett had liked him, had liked the idea of hard-working Kyle Rayford for a son-in-law. Now there was only contempt in the big man's eyes.

"He's a kid, Ebeling," Emmett said. "We'll let him go."

But the big man's eyes burned into Kyle. "You'll bury your father, then you'll leave. If you ever come back, I'll not stand up for you again."

Kyle tried to talk, tried to tell him the truth, but Emmett wasn't listening. He turned his back and remounted his horse. He rode away, two of his cowboys with him. Only Ebeling was left now—Ebeling and his own two men, and some other ranchers who usually leaned on Ebeling's counsel.

For a moment now, with Brook Emmett gone, Kyle feared the others might hang him anyway. But Emmett carried a lot of weight in this country.

Benny Ahrens blurted, "If we ain't going to hang him, then we ought to leave our mark on him!"

Benny was Clint Ebeling's dog, trailing in Ebeling's shadow, lolling his tongue at everything Ebeling did. A coward in a fight, but a tiger when he knew nothing could hurt him.

They ripped off Kyle's shirt and tied him flat against the rough door of the dugout. It wasn't easy, for he fought like two men, and while he fought he tagged every man in the bunch. Not all their faces—it was too dark for that. There are other ways to know a man. There is the set of his shoulders, the way he sits his horse, the way he stands, the sound of his voice. Kyle marked every man.

Clint Ebeling dropped a coiled rope into muddy water to wet it. He handed it to Benny Ahrens and stepped back, that mean grin on his mud-flecked face again.

The doubled rope sang wickedly. Kyle choked off a cry and hugged the flat door. Again and again the lash sang and struck him, cutting, biting, searing.

Then someone cut Kyle loose and he fell in the mud, the world spinning crazily about him, his body afire.

"We'll, be back, Rayford," Clint Ebeling said. "If you're still here, we'll kill you!"

Kyle lay helpless in the mud while they tied onto the ridgepole and pulled it out, caving in the Rayfords' home. Out of his pain grew a burning hatred, a bitter purpose that was to drive him through the years ahead.

"You'll wish you'd hung me. Because now I'll get you—every one!" Kyle had said, making this a promise.

He lay in the rain an hour or more before he finally was able to crawl to a shed. The next thing he knew, Enrique was holding a bottle to his lips, and the fire of the whisky burned hotter even than the fire of the lash.

It all cleared up then. The rain was gone, and the full moon played hide and seek behind the drifting clouds. Kyle looked past Enrique and saw Sam Whittenburg standing over him, his friendly face full of concern. Kyle saw the body still lying where it had been dropped. Sam's slicker covered it.

"How did you—"

Sam Whittenburg spoke quietly. "Some of them came by my camp after it was over. They told me about it. I kept Enrique hidden."

The Mexican's face was without expression. The years had stretched his dry skin across jutting Indian cheekbones and given it the color of saddle leather. His face was patient and neutral. But his brown fingers moved restlessly, pulling at each other, tightening and loosening, tugging at the knees of his old trousers like angry dogs tearing at quarry.

"Ebeling?" he asked finally. "He was the leader?"

Kyle nodded. Enrique left him the bottle and hobbled to what was left of the dugout. He managed to dig out some supplies and some rain-soaked clothes and bedding. Somewhere he found a shovel.

They almost had to tie Kyle to get him into Sam's wagon. With the bottomless patience of his race, Enrique listened to Kyle's raging. When that had run out, he spoke half in Spanish, where his thoughts more easily were shaped into words:

"*Muchacho*. I am an old soldier. I have fought in many battles, in many places. I have learned long ago that one mark of a good soldier is to know when to pull away, when to give up a battle that one may live to win a war."

His long, slender fingers dexterously rolled a cigarette in thin brown paper. His black eyes touched Kyle as his tongue flicked across the edge of the paper to seal the cigarette.

"Our enemies are too many. There are only two of us. Me, I might be able to kill a few of them, but they would get me, in time. You, you are not yet a man, as they count a man in years. How long would you last?"

Kyle Rayford's eyes were dull and gray with pain and loss. But a fever burned in them. "I can last long enough to get Clint Ebeling. After that, I don't care."

Salinas shook his head. "That shows you are still a boy, *mi hijo.*"

For three days then, Sam Whittenburg kept Kyle and Enrique at his camp, risking the fury of his neighbors, risking the suspicion that this action was likely to cast upon him. Even before those three days were up, Kyle learned that Clint Ebeling had taken over the Slash R range, had begun rounding up the Slash R cattle and venting his Bar E brand on them. If the other ranchers objected, there was no sign of it. Few men spoke against Clint Ebeling.

Now Kyle Rayford was a boy no longer. Now he was a man, a bitter man with a gun at his hip. And in these four years he had learned how to use it. In South Texas men spoke his name with a touch of awe, for his name had become well known down there.

Enrique Salinas, the old *soldado*, had taught Kyle all he knew about a gun, and that was considerable. When Enrique had no more to teach him, Kyle had practiced and experimented and taught himself. Now he was the master, the pupil become better than the teacher.

The two riders were almost upon them now. Kyle stepped out away from the corral fence to be in the clear. He let his hands settle to his hips, the fingers not far from the gun.

His lips flattened in a dry grin as he recognized the men. Benny Ahrens, loud as a mongrel dog but without a bit of courage, and the other man was an Ebeling cowboy he remembered, a rawhide-tough rider named Thatcher. He, too, had been at the dugout that night.

Benny Ahrens reined up, his eyes worried until he recognized Kyle, grown taller and broader now, with tanned skin and the face of a man.

"The Rayford kid," he said. He relaxed, the bullying confidence coming back to him. "Thought we told you to never come back. You ain't going to like it here."

Kyle didn't worry about Ahrens, as long he faced him. But his eyes stayed on the other man. Thatcher wasn't a loudmouth.

"Like it or not, Benny, it's my ranch. I'm back to stay."

Ahrens sat straighter, beginning to feel a brush of worry at this show of defiance. "Looks like he forgot what we done to him, Thatch."

"I haven't forgotten anything, Benny. The rope scars are still on my back."

"You're asking for one on your neck."

"I'm not asking anything. I'm telling you. I'm taking back my land. Go tell Ebeling the Rayford kid's come back. He's here to stay. This time, I'm driving him out."

Ahrens laughed, but his laugh was hollow. He glanced quickly at Thatcher, asking him with his eyes what had gone wrong here, asking him what to do.

"Tell him something else, Benny," Kyle said. "Tell him I know every man who came here that night. I'm going to make every one of them answer for it. You, Benny. And you, too, Thatcher."

He saw fire leap into Thatcher's face. "Big talk, Rayford. But you're going to find it too tough to slice."

Kyle shook his head. He started baiting Thatcher, the excitement playing in him. "You were mighty brave in a mob. But you won't be any trouble one at a time, and that's the way I'm going to take you. Cut you off from the bunch and you're all cowards."

Thatcher's voice was strained. "You think I'm a coward?"

"A dirty, yellow coward!"

He hadn't planned to bait Thatcher, but he was doing it. He saw the warning in Thatcher's eyes as the man swallowed it. When Thatcher's hand darted, Kyle was ready.

The crash of Kyle's gun sent Thatcher rocking back in the saddle. For a second or two the cowboy clawed at the horn. He tumbled and lay quivering in the grass, his horse plunging away in panic.

For one brief fraction of a second, as Kyle had brought his gun up, he had looked at the spot just above Thatcher's belt buckle. That was where he intended to shoot him. But then he tipped the gun up just a little more.

Now Kyle stood with the smoking gun in his hand and looked down at Thatcher. The cowboy's face was twisted in pain, and his right hand was held to his left shoulder, where crimson quickly spread down through his shirt.

For a moment, Kyle was angry with himself. Why hadn't he killed him? That was what he had come for, wasn't it? He had all the reason a man would ever need.

Benny Ahrens's face was white as flour. His hands

were held high away from his belt, his eyes pleading as if to say, "I'm not going to draw. Don't shoot me!"

"Go catch his horse, Benny," Kyle said curtly. Benny nodded, greatly relieved that Kyle didn't intend to shoot him, too. He chased after the horse.

Kyle kicked Thatcher's gun away. Enrique knelt beside the cowboy and opened the shirt. He pulled a handkerchief from his pocket and put it against the wound, stanching the flow of blood.

"You don't die," he told the cowboy. "But that arm, she won't ever be much good."

Thatcher didn't reply. His face was drained white from shock. His teeth were clenched tight, holding down a groan. Thatcher had guts, Kyle had to give him credit for that.

But he didn't feel sorry for him. He remembered another man who had lain there four years ago, an innocent man. And Thatcher had helped kill him.

Benny came back. Kyle stood aside while Enrique helped put Thatcher on his horse.

Kyle said to Benny Ahrens, "Tell Ebeling what happened. Tell him I'll get him, too, by and by."

His eyes narrowed. "And I'm not through with you yet, Benny."

Benny Ahrens rode away as fast as he could go and still hold Thatcher in the saddle.

Watching them, Kyle was acutely conscious of Enrique's critical gaze.

"This was not good," Enrique said softly.

"It's what I came to do."

"I saw your eyes. It was not a good thing to see. You wanted him to try. If you had seen yourself, *hijo* . . ."

Kyle said subbornly, "It's what I've been waiting for, for four long years."

Enrique said, "Better we had never come back. This

hunger for vengeance is driving you the way a man drives cattle. Your father wouldn't know you."

A numbness spread over Kyle Rayford, and he didn't argue any more. It had started now. He had drawn first blood, and it was like being pulled out into the center of a roiling, flooded stream. It had started, and he couldn't stop it now until it was done.

"Come on, Enrique," he said. "We've got one friend left in this country. Let's go see him."

Sam Whittenburg's ranch had grown some. It wasn't so big as Sam used to dream it would be in three or four years. Kyle had used to like to sit and listen to Sam make glowing plans. Dreams, they had really been. He guessed the easy-going Sam had gotten over the dreams and become realistic.

Like I did, Kyle thought.

Sam no longer lived in the leaky dugout where he had sheltered Kyle and Enrique until Kyle's back had healed enough for travel. In its place was a picket house of cedar, chinked to keep out the howling winter of the high plains.

"Sam's come up in the world," Kyle observed. "There must be two rooms in it, it's so big."

The corrals covered more ground now, and there was a new picket shed. Sam had done a heap of work these four years. An old man stepped out into the doorway, flour sack around his waist.

"Looking for Sam," Kyle said. The old man was a stranger. Many people had come into this country since Kyle had left it.

"Gone out to where they're drilling the water well."

"Water well?"

"Fixing to set him up a windmill on the south end, back away from the creek. Good grass over there, only

Sam's never been able to use it much because there ain't been no water."

Growing, growing. Big enough to hire help and to drill wells. Good for old Sam, Kyle thought.

Following directions, they headed south. It took about three hours. The drilling camp was scattered over a lot of ground, the big wooden drilling rig in the center. The long mast-pole stood twenty feet up into the air directly over the hole. Off to one side, two horses trudged around and around in a circle, furnishing the power that lifted the drill bit at the end of the long well pipe and dropped it again to gouge the hole ever deeper into the ground.

Kyle and Enrique halted a bit to watch. In a few minutes the drilling crew hauled up the heavy steel bit from deep down in the hole. They carried it to a makeshift blacksmith set-up they had, with furnace and anvil. While one of the men prepared to forge a new point on the blunted bit, the others dropped a bullet-shaped slush bucket down into the well to clean out the mud and rock that the bit had broken loose since the last slushing.

Kyle recognized Sam Whittenburg's back. Sam eagerly watched the hoisting of the bucket. Sam caught hold of the bucket and swung it away from the hole, his fingers quickly sampling the mud.

He turned grinning, then spotted Kyle and Enrique coming down the slope. He stared a moment, unbelieving. The grin broadened across his friendly, sun-reddened face. He strode forward, rubbing the mud off his hands onto his pants.

"Kyle Rayford! Enrique Salinas!" Kyle swung down, a warmth inside him. They shook hands, Sam's grip as tight as a vise. Kyle felt a swelling in his throat. Not in years had he been so glad to see anyone.

He noted with pleasure that there hadn't been much change in Sam Whittenburg. Sam was crowding forty now, and a touch of gray glinted in his tousled mop of sandy hair. But his laughing eyes still showed the sparkle of a youthful spirit. He shook hands with Enrique, rattling at him in Spanish. Like Kyle, Sam had come from South Texas, and Spanish was second nature with him.

"By George, I'm glad to see you two." He pushed Kyle off to arm's length and looked at him. "You've sure changed. A man now, by jingoes. What is it, twenty-two? You look thirty."

There had been a lot to age a man in four years, Kyle thought without saying it.

Sam was jubilant. "Enrique doesn't look a particle different. He'll look just like this the day he's a hundred and six. Come to think of it, he may be, already."

Sam went serious then. "I think folks'll be glad to see you back, Kyle."

"Will they?" Kyle's voice held a raspy edge.

"They were wrong four years ago. Most of them know it. You've been riding on their conscience a long time now."

The irony of it brought a bitter twist to Kyle's mouth. "So now they're sorry. That makes everything just fine."

The sparkle had left Sam's eyes, crowded out by a sudden worry. "Kyle, it was mighty tough, what you went through. But after four years I thought—"

"You thought I'd forget? No, Sam, I didn't let myself forget."

Sam was fishing for words and having trouble finding them. "The country has changed. It's settled, and so have most of the people. They're not like they were when you left."

"Neither am I, Sam. Neither am I."

Sam's brow furrowed. He was silent a moment, thinking while he dug the mud out from under his fingernails. Unflinchingly, he looked up into Kyle's hard eyes. "What made you come back?"

"I told them I'd be back, and I told them what I'd do. Well, I'm here. And I'll do what I said I would."

Sam rolled a cigarette, frowning deeply and spilling some of the tobacco. "What do you figure on doing?"

"I'm going to put them off their land, the way they put me off mine."

"We still don't have any organized county here, but the Rangers come around now and again. They'll be on you, soon as you step out of line."

"No they won't, Sam. What I'm going to do will be legal. I'm working for a man who has bought deeds to just about every mile of creek and river country here, except for yours. These people are squatters. I'm going to move them off."

Sam's mouth dropped open. Kyle went on:

"The day of the open range is about over. Don't you know that, Sam? There's state, school and railroad land going on the market every day, and people are buying it. You, and everybody else up here are using free state land, just like Pa and me were. The land's been too cheap to bother with, and the state hasn't laid any claim to it, up to now.

"But it's beginning to get valuable. John Gorman's the man I'm working for. You ought to remember the name. He used to be spread out big, down in South Texas, using free grass. But then the twenty-cow nesters started coming in with a breaking plow and a land deed, and they finally squeezed him out.

"Now he's fixing to do up here what they did to him

down there. He got hold of some land promoters in Austin and bought up a bunch of land certificates.

"I helped him pick the sections, Sam. I got him those that are on the water. And I did it on purpose. Without water, these people will have to quit. The rest of their land won't be worth a dime to them. It'll be there for John Gorman to take, the way they took the Slash R land."

Kyle clenched his fists. "You see, Sam, I can square it for Pa. And the law is on my side."

Sam Whittenburg turned his back and stared a while over the rolling plains, the knee-high grass that waved like wheat in the wind.

"What are you getting out of it, Kyle?"

"Title to the land Pa and I had. But mainly I'm getting even. It's been a long time coming."

Sam turned back to him. "Do you really think you'll enjoy it, Kyle? You won't. Revenge is a mighty narrow thing to live for. Once you've had it, do you think you'll be satisfied? You won't. You'll hate yourself for it, the way these people hate what happened four years ago."

Warmth surged into Kyle's face. He hadn't expected this from Sam. "Let's go, Enrique." He turned back abruptly toward his horse.

"Kyle," Sam spoke quickly, "How about Brook Emmett? Are you taking his land, too?"

Kyle spoke firmly. "He was there the night they brought Pa home."

"Go see him first, Kyle. Maybe you'll change your mind. He's aged a lot. It's been conscience that's done it to him. Before you start this, go see what conscience can do."

"It's too late, even if I wanted to. Gorman has got the deeds."

"What about Jane, Kyle? Do you think about her anymore?"

Jane. He had thought about her every day for four years.

"No, I don't." It was a lie, and he sensed that Sam knew it. "I don't think about her," Kyle said again. "That was all finished four years ago. Done with."

Sam's eyes pleaded with him. "Before you do anything, go see her."

Kyle swung into the saddle and headed toward town. Gorman was bound to be there by now, waiting for them.

Enrique held back a moment, looking regretfully at Sam. Then he shrugged and followed after Kyle.

Before they had ridden a mile, Kyle began to bear to the north. Enrique rode with a puzzled look. Then after a while they topped over a rise and slanted down toward Brook Emmett's ranch headquarters, and the puzzled look left him. Enrique came about as near to smiling as he ever did.

From the moment he had left Sam, Kyle had known he was coming by here first, even though he had told himself he didn't want to. The first glance showed him that Brook Emmett's place hadn't changed much. It hadn't grown. Where Sam Whittenburg had improved his ranch and added to it, Brook Emmett evidently had stood still.

Kyle wondered at that. Old Emmett had been a man of drive and ambition. Kyle wouldn't have told Sam for a million dollars, but he had always thought Emmett to be the better ranchman, to have the better prospects. Down there was the rock house Emmett had built, having found a good rock out-cropping nearby as a source of building material. It used to be that Jane could see Kyle from half a mile away as he rode in across the open, rolling land. She would stand by the picket fence there and wait for him. He didn't see her now. But he could see that the fence needed fixing.

It was not that the place had gone to pieces, but it lacked the well-kept look it always had in the old days. It was as if Brook somehow had just kind of let go. A dog barked at the two horsemen. Kyle heard Jane before he saw her.

"Kyle!"

She stood at the gate of a small chicken yard, which had been net-fenced against the visitations of the coyotes which still roamed the prairie. Setting down the basket of eggs she carried, she walked hurriedly to meet him. He stepped out of the saddle and dropped the reins.

Two paces from him she stopped, her oval face pale from the sudden surprise of seeing him. The wind was picking up the curled ends of her long black hair, and it brushed softly against her slender neck. Her lips parted, and Kyle knew that to him she was still the prettiest girl he'd ever known.

"Kyle," she said again, almost in a whisper.

He wanted to step forward and sweep her into his arms, and he knew she wanted him to. But four years had taught him restraint.

Weaken now and he might jeopardize the whole purpose of his return.

But he knew he already had weakened it when he had ridden by here instead of going straight to town.

"I've always hoped you'd come back, Kyle," she said after a long moment of silence, while they stared at each other.

For a minute or two there, watching her, he had lost his bitterness. Now it began to come back to him.

"You gave me no sign of that."

"I didn't know where you had gone. I didn't know where to write, or where to look."

"You could have tried. Most anybody in South Texas could have told you about me, the last couple of years."

That wasn't a brag. It was a statement of fact.

She stared silently at him, and something in her eyes seemed to die. He realized that she had carried a hope with her for four years, and now it was gone.

He felt his heart tighten. Yes, he'd lied to Sam Whittenburg. He never had forgotten Jane Emmett. He wouldn't, if he lived to be a hundred. We could start it all over again, and try to forget, he thought hopefully.

But he knew it was too late for that. The die was cast. He still remembered his father, lying in a lifeless heap in the mud, and Brook Emmett had been there. Emmett would have to pay, like the rest of them.

"Is your dad here, Jane?" he asked.

Her voice was hollow. "He's in the house. I'll go with you."

She picked up her basket of eggs and walked ahead. Kyle followed, still fighting within himself, still wanting her.

A sense of shock stopped him in his tracks at his first glimpse of Brook Emmett. Emmett had aged fifteen years in the last four. His hair was almost totally gray. The big frame was still there, but he was no longer a heavy man. At sight of Kyle he leaned forward in his chair, starting to rise. Then he sank back again.

A hopelessness seemed to hang over him.

"I knew you'd come back someday. You were bound to."

He extended his hand. "Will you shake hands with me, Kyle?"

Kyle started to, then checked himself.

Brook sighed. "I shouldn't have expected it. I can guess why you've come back again. You want to even the score."

Kyle nodded gravely. "That's right."

"And what do you want of me? Do you want to shoot me, and get it over with?"

"I'm not going to shoot you. But I'm going to put you off this land."

Jane Emmett cried, "No!" and stepped up beside her father. Emmett patted her hand. "It's all right, Jane. It's less than I would have expected."

He smiled wanly. "It'll almost be a relief. For more than three years, I've lived with a shadow hanging over me, ever since I decided for sure that we'd been wrong about Earl Rayford."

Kyle demanded, "If you knew, why didn't you send for me? You could have found me."

Brook Emmett sadly shook his head. "A coward, I guess. Scared of you, scared of myself. I tried a long time to convince myself it wasn't so, that I hadn't been wrong. But I knew better, and it gave me no rest.

"Something else, too," he said. "I guess I was like the others. I didn't want you around, reminding me every day of the mistake I'd made, staying here close to me like a living conscience."

Emmett said wearily, "We'll let him have the land, Jane. It's little enough to pay for a clean conscience. I've had no heart in it anyway, the last few years."

Kyle stood openmouthed, taken aback by the old man's resignation. He had expected a fight out of Emmett. He had hoped for it. Emmett, who once had been their friend but had become an enemy. Emmett, who once had stood by the picket gate at the front of the house and told him he would kill him if he ever came back. Emmett, who had turned his back on him, refusing to hear the truth, and had left him to be whipped with the double of a rope.

Kyle's held breath eased out of him, and he felt a vague disappointment. There was no revenge in it if you didn't squeeze a man. Emmett didn't seem to feel any loss. If anything, he looked relieved.

Kyle said, "The man I'm working for has bought the sections along the creek. You'll have to move your cattle off of them."

Jane stared at him, anger and disbelief in her eyes. "Then we'd just as well move off all of it. The rest of the land is no good to us without water."

"I know," he said without sympathy.

Tears welled into her wide eyes. He couldn't be sure whether they were from hurt or anger—or both.

"This isn't you, Kyle. I knew you'd change some, you were bound to. But this—." She bit her lip. "You're not the Kyle Rayford I used to know. Get out, Kyle. Get out before I fetch a gun."

He backed up. "You don't need the gun. I'm leaving." To Brook Emmett he said "Five days, that's all I can give you. Get off the creek, this home and all."

From somewhere Jane Emmett brought a rifle. She swung it up and poked it at Kyle. "Get out!" she said. She followed him to the door and stood there watching while Kyle remounted and turned away.

Kyle found John Gorman waiting in town, just as he had expected. Gorman had been restlessly pacing up and down the hard-packed earth in front of the squatty adobe hotel for two days. His unlighted cigar was chewed down to about half its original length. He was a big-boned, restless ranchman with a drive and a ruthlessness about him that had made men in South Texas call him "the bull"—but never to his face.

Gorman saw Kyle and Enrique coming. It had been three weeks since they had parted in San Antonio. But there was no greeting, no handshake.

"Well, now, are you through fiddling around?" Gorman asked curtly. "Are you ready to go to work?"

Kyle Rayford eyed him levelly. He didn't like Gorman—he never had. To him, Gorman was only a means of getting done what he wanted to do. And he had no delusions. He knew that in Gorman's sight, he was nothing more than that, either.

Kyle said, "We've already started."

Gorman frowned as Kyle told him about Thatcher. The big man finally nodded. "Probably a good thing. It might have been better, though, if you'd killed him. It would've thrown a scare into the rest of them, and we wouldn't be so apt to have much trouble."

"I'm not afraid of trouble," Kyle said.

Gorman grunted. "So I've noticed." He motioned with his chin and turned back toward the hotel. Kyle handed the reins to Enrique and nodded toward the wagon yard. Enrique was looking daggers at Gorman's retreating back. Gorman had always treated him like a servant, and Enrique didn't like it. Enrique Salinas, the old soldier, the old *insurrecto* extraordinary.

Kyle followed Gorman to his gyprock-plastered room. Gorman waved his hand toward three men who lounged there. "You know the boys. Jack Dangerfield, Irv Hallmark, Monte Lykes."

Kyle nodded, resentment smoldering in him. They were strong men, gunslingers. He didn't need that kind for what he was fixing to do. He didn't want them. Then he asked himself harshly what he is turning up his nose for. *That's all I am, too. Just one of Gorman's gunslingers.*

Gorman said, "They're here to help you."

Stubbornly, Kyle said, "I won't need that kind of help." He caught the look of hatred from sallow-faced Jack Dangerfield. He had once shot a gun out of Dangerfield's hand when Dangerfield came into camp roaring drunk, looking for a fight.

"Maybe you won't need them, maybe you will. They'll be here, anyway."

Then Gorman said, "I've been listening a little while I've been here. I don't think we're apt to have a lot of trouble, except from this man Ebeling, maybe. He sounds to me like one who won't take it lying down."

Kyle said, "He'll take it lying down. Dead, I hope."

Gorman grunted again. "This Ebeling sounds like a man after my own heart. I almost wish I had him with me."

Kyle shot him a cutting glance. "You try to make a deal with Ebeling and you'll both be dead. I promise you that."

The color rose in Gorman's face, and he knew that Kyle meant it. Dropping that subject, he reached into a handbag and took out a map and a sheaf of land certificates. He handed them to Kyle.

"Which one do you figure on starting with?"

Kyle studied the map, seeing every ranchman in his mind's eye. Brook Emmett. Well he had already told Emmett. Lester McLeod. Lester might fight. Yes, he probably would. Milt McGivern, maybe? Thomas Avery? Ferman Olds? They weren't likely to fight. They would stampede easy, with just a little push.

His finger traced down the creek to Clint Ebeling's ranch. There it stopped. Ebeling. Kyle's fist tightened, crumpling the land certificates.

"Careful there," Gorman said sharply. "They're valuable." Then he looked at the map and saw the name penciled above Kyle's finger.

"Ebeling, eh? You're starting with him?"

Kyle shook his head. "I'll save him for the last."

Gorman shrugged disinterestedly. "Makes no difference to me where you start. I'm interested in the finish. We've got no time to fiddle. I've got a herd already on its way up from the Rio Grande. They'll be here in two weeks, three at the most. These people have got to be off the land. I'll need every acre they've got."

Kyle said, "They'll be off."

Gorman didn't offer to get them a room at the hotel. Probably because of Enrique, Kyle thought with a touch of anger. So they'd sleep at the wagon yard. Enrique didn't care, anymore. He had been at the top, and he'd been at the bottom.

As a boy Kyle had thrilled at Enrique's stories of his years as a rebel in Mexico. It seemed that whenever there was a revolution, Enrique was in it, always as a rebel. There was so much to fight about, a man could always find a reason. But mostly it had been the adventure, the wild freedom, that had called Enrique.

"*Insurrecto* or *bandido*," Enrique had once said. "The difference is not always a great one."

But time had tamed him down, and he had escaped across the Rio Grande one night with nothing but his horse and saddle, the clothes on his back, and an old hat with two fresh bullet holes in it.

He liked to talk about the old times, but to go back to them—that was no longer to be considered.

Enrique seemed always to be able to take it in stride when men looked down on him the way some were wont to do with a Mexican. But somehow it was different when the man was someone like John Gorman.

"Don't ever be bothered with what another man thinks or says," Enrique had advised Kyle a long time ago. "You live with yourself. Listen to your conscience, not to other men."

Kyle didn't sleep much that night, thinking about what he would do. In the morning, when he and Enrique shook the hay out of their blankets, he said, "We'll start with Lester McLeod."

He rode into McLeod's ranch yard shortly before noon. Enrique followed two lengths behind him, like a reluctant soldier following his lieutenant.

Kyle swung down and looked around for McLeod. A cotton-headed boy of seven or eight came poking out from behind a shed. He looked just like McLeod.

"I'm hunting your pa," Kyle said. "Where is he?"

"Out getting a horse. He'll be in directly," the boy answered.

Waiting, Kyle led his horse down to the creek and watered him. McLeod, like Sam Whittenburg, had done a lot of work since the last time Kyle had been here. There was a new house now, built of rocks hauled from farther down the creek. Out in back, a small irrigation system had been gouged out of the earth, and vegetables stood green and fresh. A woman's work, no doubt.

McLeod wouldn't want to leave this place, Kyle knew. That made it better. He had felt something of a letdown at the way old Brook Emmett had taken the news. There was no satisfaction in running out a man who didn't care anyway.

Kyle watched the boy playing with a matty-haired little brown dog. The boy was swinging a slingshot back and forth while the dog trotted ahead, testing every bush and weed. Presently he flushed a jackrabbit. The boy quickly fitted a rock into the sling, swung, and let fly. The rock kicked up dust at the rabbit's heels, and the dog kept on coming. Then the rabbit darted down a hole. The dog stood over it, barking furiously.

Then he gave it up and went trotting on after the boy, who was looking for fresh game. Watching them, Kyle was able to relax, at least a little.

Enrique saw it. "Like this, *hijo*, you are the boy who used to live up the creek. This way, I like you. But this bitter Kyle Rayford, this boy eaten up with hate—I don't know what to think about him."

Kyle didn't answer, but the spell was broken. He was frowning again when McLeod finally came riding in, leading a horse at the end of a rope. McLeod put the horse in a corral and slipped the rope off its neck. It wasn't until he was close that he recognized Kyle.

They stared at each other, Kyle afoot, McLeod still on his horse. Kyle could well remember, and a hard knot grew inside him. This was the man who had pushed his father's body out of the saddle, letting it fall in the mud. Kyle's voice was edged with steel.

"I've been waiting for you, McLeod." McLeod could see the smoldering in Kyle's eyes and misread its meaning. "I'm not armed, Kyle." He raised his hands so Kyle would see there was no gun at his hip.

"I didn't come to shoot you, McLeod."

McLeod loosened, letting out a long breath. "What did you come for?"

Kyle didn't answer directly. "How much land you running now, McLeod?"

"About thirty sections." McLeod's voice was wary.

"You've got about six sections along the creek, isn't that right?"

McLeod nodded.

"I'm here to tell you to get your cattle off the creek. That land belongs to another man now."

McLeod's face fell, then flushed red. For a moment he was obviously turning this over and over in his mind, desperately looking for a hole in it.

"I can't do that. The rest of my country would be worthless."

Kyle nodded grimly. "I know that."

McLeod sat numbly staring at him. "Look, Kyle, I know you got it pretty raw four years ago. I know you've got something coming to you. But not this. Everything I've got is here—home, cattle, years of work. I've even got folks buried up yonder on the hill. You don't think I'm going to pull up and leave all that!"

"You're going to leave it, McLeod. You've got three days. Get your cattle off the creek by then or we'll put them off. And if you're not gone from here, we'll put you off, too. The same way you did it to me."

Kyle turned his back then, stuck his left foot in the stirrup, and mounted his horse.

McLeod sat straight in his saddle. He was a tall man with a sharp, strong, determined face, a hard eye. Of all the bunch, besides Ebeling, Kyle knew McLeod was the most likely to fight.

McLeod said, "You'll have to kill me first."

Kyle answered evenly, "It's your choice."

He turned his horse around, glancing once back over his shoulder. "Three days, McLeod. We'll be back."

From McLeod's, he angled across to the Ferman Olds place. With Olds, it was much the same except that he could see the fear crawl in behind the man's eyes, and he knew there would be no trouble with him.

That day, and the next, he saw the rest of them. Thomas Avery, Milt McGivern, and the others.

Then Clint Ebeling.

Kyle's stomach drew up in a knot as he rode through the open gate that led to the Ebeling headquarters. It wasn't fear; it was an excitement that had grown from the long anticipation.

Even Enrique didn't seem to object to this visit. He had hung back on the others, taking no part except just to be there, and keep his hands clear. He would have helped Kyle if there had been trouble. But he had made it plain from the start that he didn't like it.

Now Enrique rode beside him, stirrup to stirrup. And early this morning Kyle had awakened to find the Mexican cleaning and polishing his old Colt.

Kyle smiled. This was the Enrique of old, the fearless *vaquero* who had helped Earl Rayford rear and train Kyle, who had taught Kyle how to hold and throw a rope, and more than once had busted Kyle's britches when Kyle had been thrown off a horse and didn't want to get back on. This was the old warrior, the old rebel, not anxious for battle any more, but ready for it if it came.

Clint Ebeling was waiting for them. He stepped out in front of his sod house and stood there, thumbs in his gun belt. He rocked back on his heels a little, defiant, evidently not worried. He was even grinning. Ebeling always had that grin. It used to remind Kyle of a wolf.

Kyle looked at him, and an ancient hatred seeped through him like the spread of a poison.

Warily then he glanced around him for sign of any of Ebeling's men. He saw only one, a dour cowboy who had worked for Ebeling a good many years. This man walked out from behind Ebeling and halted beside his boss, standing clear, his face tense.

"I've been looking for you, Rayford," Ebeling said.

"Heard what you've been telling the others, and figured you'd be here today."

"Then you know what I was going to tell you."

Ebeling nodded. "And you know the answer. I'm not leaving."

Gravely Kyle said, "Suits me. I've been kind of hoping you'd want to put up a fight."

Ebeling was still grinning. "The years haven't taught you much sense, have they, Rayford? You know that was just a lucky fluke with Thatcher. You couldn't do it again. You may bluff the others out with it; they're a bunch of runny-nosed cowards anyway. But you're not bluffing me."

"It's no bluff, Ebeling. Try me, if you think it is."

Out of the corner of his eye, Kyle saw Enrique's hand dip and come up. A split second after the blast, he heard a surprised yelp and a cry of pain from a window to his left, and a clatter of a rifle to the floor.

The man beside Ebeling started to move, then froze in place. Ebeling never budged, but his grin was gone.

Kyle's gun was out. He saw a movement and squeezed the trigger. Splinters flew from the corner of the picket shed. Benny Ahrens jumped out, terrified, his hands in the air.

For a moment they all froze there that way, looking at each other. A deep anger purpled Ebeling's face.

Kyle cocked the hammer of his gun back, the ominous click as loud as thunder.

"You see now it's no bluff, Ebeling. The old Slash R is mine. Everything else on the water belongs to John Gorman. Be off of it with your stock in three days, or we'll put them off. And we'll run over anybody who gets in the way."

They backed their horses a few steps, then turned quickly and left in a fast trot. Even when they were well out of six-gun range, Kyle half expected someone to send a bullet searching after them. It never came.

After they had ridden a while, Kyle turned to Enrique. "Thanks, *compadre*. I'm glad you were with me."

Enrique shrugged. "*Por nada*. The other places, I was not glad. This place, it is different."

The day of McLeod's deadline, they left town before sunup. Riding with Kyle and Enrique, somewhat against Kyle's will, were the three gunmen, Dangerfield, Hallmark and Lykes. John Gorman had not elected to go along.

"That's what I hired you for," he growled.

It was easy to see that McLeod had not attempted to meet the deadline. Riding to the creek, Kyle could see McLeod cattle up and grazing in the cool morning wind. The heat of midday would drive them to shade.

The corners of Kyle's mouth turned down. If that was the way the hand was dealt, that was the way he would play it.

"If he won't move them, we will," he said. He made a signal with his hand. The riders fanned out and began to push the cattle ahead of them.

By the time they reached McLeod's headquarters, they had three or four hundred head of longhorn cattle strung out in a dusty line, cows and calves bawling for each other, men shouting and pushing them on.

McLeod's rock house rose into view as they worked down a gentle slope. Kyle looked toward the sheds and pole corrals, and his hand dropped to his hip.

Several horsemen stood their mounts there waiting. Even at the distance, he knew them. In the center, squared and straight in the saddle, Lester McLeod sat with a rifle balanced in front of him. The other men were McGivern, Avery and two more who had been given their notice.

Kyle was not surprised to see them here. He had half expected them. But he hadn't expected to see Sam Whittenburg. Yet there he was.

Enrique pulled his horse up close to Kyle's. "It is as I told you. They do not go without a fight."

Kyle's lips flattened. "Then that's what we'll give them."

Enrique's black eyes narrowed. "Wait, *ichacho*. Hear me first." His voice was even and deliberate. "Too long I have ridden with you and kept the silence. Now you will listen. This is wrong. It has been wrong from the beginning. Will this mistake you are making bring back your father? Would he be proud of you today? He wouldn't be. I'm not proud, either.

"Look, *hijo*, it has been four years now—four years. These people have changed, what happened here is past. Leave the past where it belongs. Bury it with the dead."

Kyle started to pull away. Enrique pressed after him. "Sam is here. What if something happens to Sam?"

Kyle's fist clenched against the saddle horn. What business was this of Sam's? What did he want to come poking in here for?

"He shouldn't have come." Kyle turned away from Enrique and motioned to the nearest man, Jack Dangerfield. "I'm going on up to talk to them. If there's trouble, you know what to do."

Dangerfield nodded sullenly and turned back. Kyle said, "Coming, Enrique?"

In Enrique's eyes was the same look Kyle used to see as a kid when he hadn't done something the way

Enrique had taught him. But the old man touched spurs to his horse and came up alongside Kyle. Together they loped ahead of the herd, to where the horsemen waited. They hauled up ten feet from them, the dust swirling into the riders' faces.

Hostility passed like a spark between them. Sam Whittenburg was the first to speak. "You're making a mistake, Kyle."

Kyle shot him a quick, annoyed glance. "You shouldn't be here, Sam. This is none of your business."

"They're my friends, just like you're my friend. They made a mistake once. You're fixing to make a big one now."

"Looks like I'm entitled to it."

Sam leaned forward, grasping for words. "It won't right the wrong that was done before. It'll just add to the misery that's already been. You've still got time to stop it, Kyle. These men could be your friends. They could help you get back what you've lost, if you'd give them the chance."

Enrique touched Kyle's arm. "Listen to him, *hijo*. Sam talks good sense."

But Kyle could still remember four years ago. And he could hear the bawling of the McLeod herd pressing in close behind him.

He shook his head. "It's too late, Enrique. We've already made our deal."

McLeod said, "Then I'm going to stop you." His spurs tinkled as he touched them to his bay horse and started forward.

Kyle turned quickly in the saddle and waved his hand. The three gunmen fired their guns into the air and began to shout like uncaged demons. A shock wave of fear struck the herd like a bolt of lightning. In an instant the plodding cattle jumped into a run.

For the space of two seconds the five horsemen in front of Kyle stared, uncertain as to what to do.

There was nothing they could do. With that start, and the three men still chousing them like the furies, the cattle wouldn't stop running for anything.

Kyle caught the raw hatred in McLeod's eyes. Then McLeod jerked his horse away and made a run toward the cattle. The other men followed him, but it would be futile.

Sam Whittenburg held back a moment. "You won't be proud of this day, Kyle," he said regretfully.

Kyle and Enrique drew aside, letting the flood of cattle pour past them. They watched the five horsemen in front feverishly trying to turn the cattle. But they were like rocks in a flooded stream. The cattle poured around them, unheeding.

The drags passed. Gorman's men were still riding hard, shouting and firing their guns.

"Keep them running," Kyle said. "Don't stop till you've got them miles off the creek."

He saw McLeod coming back in a lope now. McLeod's face was purple with rage, and he had the rifle in his hand.

"Don't do it, McLeod," Kyle shouted. But McLeod jerked his horse to a stop and raised the rifle. There wasn't time to think. Kyle ducked low and grabbed at his own gun. He heard the heavy crash of the rifle and the whine of the bullet going past him. As McLeod levered another cartridge into the breech, Kyle raised his gun and squeezed the trigger.

McLeod jerked back, dropping the rifle, then slid out of the saddle. Instantly Kyle was on the ground, running toward him. He kicked the rifle aside, then knelt by McLeod. He saw the splotch of red where the bullet had smashed through, high in the shoulder.

In fury McLeod weakly swung at him with his left hand, then slumped over, moaning. Kyle caught him and eased him to the ground.

"What did you do that for?" Kyle said, reproach in his voice. "Look what you made me do."

From the house he heard a scream. A woman burst out of the door and ran toward him, her skirts flying. Another woman followed after her, trying to call her back. From somewhere McLeod's boy appeared. He had the slingshot, and he reached down for a rock. Kyle heard the singing of it, then the rock struck him in the chest, taking the breath out of him and almost knocking him over. The youngster came running, crying and cursing in the imitation curse words a boy uses.

Sam and the other men got there first. Sam gently took the slingshot and eased the boy away. Kyle heard the boy sob, and suddenly it was himself he heard, as it had been four years ago.

McLeod's wife got there then. She fell on her knees, crying and praying.

Kyle said tightly, "I didn't kill him, ma'am. He'll pull through that all right."

He stood up, looking into the faces of the two men, finding surprise and shock there. In Sam Whittenburg's face he saw a deep regret. Enrique Salinas looked at Kyle a moment, then turned his back. Enrique rolled and lighted a cigarette and stood there smoking it, his gaze on the ground.

Kyle heard a girl's voice behind him and turned sharply on his heel. It was Jane Emmett. "You've had your revenge now, Kyle Rayford. Does it give you satisfaction to shoot a man, run off his cattle, take the home from a woman and a little boy? Is that what you came back here to do?"

She didn't touch him, but her voice stung him like a whip.

"He was there when they killed my father," he said.

"He wasn't there," Jane declared tightly. "Neither was my dad, or any of these other men. Ebeling killed your father. Ebeling and his riders."

Kyle felt as if he had been kicked in the stomach. "He wasn't there? But they were all there. I saw them."

"You saw them after it had already been done. Ebeling sent riders to get them. Said he was about to catch Earl Rayford red-handed. When the men got there, your father was already dead. Ebeling had shot him. He claimed your father went for his gun.

"Sure, they condoned it, and that was wrong. But there was a calf tied down and half branded with a Slash R. Its mama was standing there. She had a Bar E on her. It looked like an open and shut case at the time. So they all rode with Ebeling and his men to your place.

"It was a long time before they began to see the truth, Kyle. Then it was too late to do anything. Nobody wanted to face Clint Ebeling. They all dread him."

Kyle turned away from her, suddenly sick inside. He had to get away, had to think.

Yes, he had done what he had come here to do. But there was no satisfaction in it. There was an emptier feeling than ever before. And there was the guilt, spreading through him like a burning infection. Guilt! Why should he feel guilty? They had done far worse to him.

"Come on, Enrique," he said tightly. "Let's go."

Enrique shook his head, his dark eyes firm. "No, *hijo*. The pupil has learned all the teacher can teach him, and more. Too much more. You do not need me now. I will stay here."

This was Kyle's moment of triumph. The culmination of four years of training and planning. And the bottom had dropped out from under him.

He swung into the saddle and turned away.

They pushed the McLeod cattle completely off the sections which Gorman had bought. They went ahead and cleaned out neighboring Avery sections as well, before darkness dropped down upon them and started them back to town.

Kyle rode along with his shoulders slumped and his gaze mostly on the ground. He wasn't much help to Gorman's three men.

Jack Dangerfield loped up to him once, looking as if he could bite a .45 caliber bullet in two. "What's the matter with you, Rayford, riding along like you've gone to sleep? Pitch in here and make a hand, why don't you?"

Kyle's eyes raked him like a hot iron, "Shut up and leave me alone!"

Next morning they started out again for the McGivern place to clear the creek sections there. But they found McGivern and some of the neighbors already doing that. McGivern rode out to meet them. Avery was with him. McGivern was a tall, graying man who had always reminded Kyle of a storekeeper, the kind who takes a lead in the community, a man with enough push and imagination to make himself a success. But he wasn't the kind to do much fighting.

Avery was short, nervous, a little fat. He was a hard worker when he had to be, but usually he had rather not. He had four kids and a strong-willed wife, and he wasn't a man to risk his life doing anything.

"You can take your gunhands and go, Rayford," McGivern said stiffly.

Kyle didn't see fear in McGivern's face. But he knew McGivern was a realist, too wise to sacrifice himself in a cause that was doomed at the start.

"We're moving my cattle off the water, just like you said. Everybody is—Brook Emmett and the others. We can't fight hired gunmen and land deeds."

Kyle nodded. "Suits me," he said. And it did. Since yesterday, somehow, he had lost stomach for this fight. He was glad to see it working out this way.

"How about Ebeling?" he asked.

McGivern frowned. "We don't know about Ebeling. He rides his own road—doesn't help anybody, doesn't ask any help. I imagine he'll fight."

McGivern pulled his horse around and went back to the herd, the other men following him. Kyle squinted at the herd. He could see Enrique Salinas there, pushing cattle beside Sam Whittenburg. Enrique saw Kyle, but he didn't come out.

Kyle winced. Then he shrugged. "Well, boys, looks like we're out of a job here. Let's head back to town."

Gorman took the news the way he took everything—with a dark scowl. He chewed on his cigar as if he were mad at it.

"I already knew it," he said. "Man came in this morning and told me."

Kyle straightened suddenly. "What man?"

Gorman didn't answer the question. Angrily he said, "You fools, don't you know what's taking place? Sure, they're moving their cattle off the creek sections I bought. They're moving them onto those I didn't buy."

Kyle demanded, "How can that be? You bought everybody's but Sam Whittenburg's."

"That's where they're going with them!" Gorman declared.

"That can't last long," Kyle said. "They'll have Sam's grass tromped out all up and down the creek."

"It won't have to last long," Gorman blazed. "I've got a herd coming in. Damn you, Rayford, why didn't you tell me Whittenburg had a well-drilling outfit?"

Kyle began to sense the rest of it.

Gorman said, "He moved it over to McLeod's place yesterday. They've already started drilling for water back away from the sections I bought. You can see what that means, can't you?"

Kyle nodded. Gorman went on, "Soon as they get water on McLeod's land they'll move the rig to Avery's, or McGivern's. They'll drill till they've got water enough and can get along without the creek."

Kyle sat down. Somehow the load which had been so heavy on his shoulders began to lift away. Somehow it got almost funny. He began to chuckle, and the chuckle became a laugh.

Gorman snarled at him. "I don't see what's so damn funny about it."

Kyle said, "Just thinking how I used to short-change old Sam. I liked him better than most anybody, but I never thought he was as smart as a lot of them. Now he's outsmarted the whole bunch of us."

Gorman paced the floor, raging like a caged lion. "It's your fault, Rayford. You didn't let me buy the creek sections Whittenburg holds. Good friend, you said. Sam'd be all right, you said. He wouldn't give us any trouble. Good friend, hell!"

Good friend. Yes, Kyle realized, Sam was a good friend. He had thrown a monkey wrench into this whole scheme, which had begun to turn sour to Kyle anyway.

Gorman kicked a loose boot out of the way so hard that it knocked plaster from the adobe wall.

"Trail herd is due in a few more days. These people have got to get off this land—do you understand that? They've got to get off or there'll be no place for my cattle."

He hurled his cigar to the floor. "I'll teach that Whittenburg to get in my way!"

A cold knot started in Kyle's stomach. "You'll leave Sam alone."

Gorman's eyes were ablaze. "Not to let him spoil this deal."

"We made a deal, Gorman, before we ever came up here. I helped you move the others off the creek, and you were going to leave Sam alone. I got them off the creek. I'm holding you to what you promised about Sam."

Gorman's eyes were like the muzzles of a double-barreled shotgun. "Our deal's off, Rayford. Your way didn't work. Now I've got a man whose way will work. Your old friend Clint Ebeling came to see me today. He wanted to make a deal. He's going to run those squatters out of the country."

Kyle jumped to his feet. "You know Ebeling's the main reason I came back here, Gorman. You're not going to cross me and make a deal with him."

"I've already made it, Rayford!"

Kyle leaped at him, knocking Gorman against the wall. He struck Gorman again across the mouth. The blood trickled down Gorman's lips.

Strong hands grabbed Kyle, spun him around. Jack Dangerfield jerked him away. Dangerfield's fist struck Kyle like a sledge. He staggered, then went after Dangerfield in a rush. His right fist flattened Dangerfield's nose, bringing a spurt of blood. His left drove high into the man's belly, and the breath gusted out of Dangerfield.

Irv Hallmark and Monte Lykes had been watching, stunned by surprise. Gorman cursed at them, and they jumped in. They grabbed Kyle's arms. He shrugged wildly, almost tearing loose from them, kicking the heel of his boot at Hallmark's knee and nearly folding him up. But they held onto him, twisting his arms, bringing him down.

Dangerfield was up again, wiping his bloody face, murder in his eyes. Kyle saw his fist coming but couldn't dodge it. He was locked in the grip of the other two gunmen. It was as if a charge of dynamite went off in his head.

Dangerfield's murderous rage drove him on and on, beating at Kyle, hammering at his head, his stomach. Kyle's struggling weakened little by little, and then there was none. He hung limp.

The two men let him drop. Dangerfield pulled his foot back to kick Kyle in the ribs.

"Hold it," Gorman said. "No use killing him. I got no use for killing unless it's necessary."

Hallmark said, "That Ebeling sounds to me like a man who'd do it, necessary or not."

Gorman grunted. "We're going out to Ebeling's ranch. Throw Rayford on a horse. We'll drop him off out there somewhere afoot. He can't hurt anything that way."

Hallmark frowned. "The whole town'll see us."

"Let them!"

Kyle was dimly conscious of being carried somewhere, lying facedown across the saddle. The pressure of blood on his brain made him struggle to straighten up. Someone hit him over the head, and he fell spinning back into darkness.

When consciousness finally did come to him, Kyle found himself alone, afoot, out on a wide expanse of rolling prairie. His head was splitting, and he ached all over from the beating they had given him. For a while it was all he could do to sit up. After a quarter of an hour he was on his feet, lurching about, trying to figure where he was. But it was no use. Out here on this open plain, the land all looked alike. He might have been anywhere.

He knew they had carried him here and dropped him off. He had no idea how far they had brought him. He found the tracks of the horses. No telling where they were going. He hadn't heard that. Wouldn't do any good to follow them. He had no gun. But by back-tracking, he would reach town, sooner or later.

Painfully he set out, following the tracks back toward their starting place. At first it was tough going. He would walk a couple of hundred yards, then have to sit down and rest. As he walked, however, his strength began to come back to him. Strength and a throbbing anger.

Before long it would be dark. He had to keep going. He cut down the rest stops until he was taking almost none. The sun sank low. And Kyle's heart sank with it.

Then he heard something. He stopped abruptly, listening. There it was again. A dog barking. The sound came on the wind, out of the north. A ranch. There had to be a ranch yonder somewhere. He started walking faster now. Hope surged back into him. If he could only make it. If he could only get word to Sam.

The sun dropped out of sight over the rim of the prairie. Dusk settled over him. *Hurry, Kyle*, he kept telling himself. *Hurry. Get over that rise yonder. Maybe you can see it then.*

He struggled up the rise, sinking to his knees in exhaustion as he reached the top of it. And there it was. Brook Emmett's place. Half a mile or more away. But he knew where it was now. He'd make it, even though it was dark.

A sudden fear struck him. What if they had already left? No, they hadn't done that, he'd heard a dog. But maybe the dog had slipped away and come back to the only home it knew, the way dogs will. That fear fastened itself to him as he kept on walking, fatigue bearing down on him like a two-hundred-pound weight on his back.

He was conscious of turning into a wagon road. It wouldn't be much farther now. *Keep on going, Kyle. Don't quit yet.* He tried to yell, but it wasn't in him. So he kept walking, dragging. He dropped in exhaustion at the picket fence. He sat there, unable to move, the dog warily walking back and forth in front of him, barking loudly.

Kyle saw lamplight in the house. Suddenly it winked out. He heard footsteps at the door. Jane Emmett's voice demanded, "Who's out there?" He heard the ominous click of a rifle hammer. The dog kept barking.

"It's me, Jane," Kyle said weakly. "Kyle Rayford." He was afraid she couldn't hear him. He said it again.

"Kyle?" She still didn't see him in the darkness. "Come on, Kyle, but keep your hands up."

Putting his weight on the picket fence, he pushed to his feet. "Help me, Jane. Help me."

For a moment she waited, fearing a trap. Then the rifle clattered against the door jamb, and she ran out to him. Leaning on her, he made it into the house.

"Is anybody with you?" she asked sharply.

"No," he said. "I've walked for miles."

Evidently believing him then, she lighted the lamp. She gasped at the sight of his bloody, battered face.

"Kyle," she exclaimed, "what happened to you?"

"I had a falling out. Gorman's thrown in with Ebeling. I tried to stop him." He paused for breath. "They're out to wreck Sam's drilling rig. They may kill Sam. We've got to warn him."

Jane had a teakettle of water on the big woodstove. She poured steaming water into a pan and dipped a cloth into it. "Do you know where the drilling camp is?" she asked him.

He shook his head. "Somewhere on McLeod's. That's all I know."

It struck Kyle suddenly that old Brook Emmett wasn't here. He asked Jane where he was.

"He's out with the cattle," Jane said in reply to his question. "He and a couple of men have pushed them over to Sam's. They're holding them there on the water."

"Jane," he said, "I've been wrong. Wrong about a lot of things. Enrique tried to tell me, and I couldn't see it."

"Don't blame yourself too much," she said. "A lot of people were wrong. Sometimes we have a hard time learning a lesson."

"Funny how it was," Kyle spoke. "Like a man wanting a drink. He wants it so bad he can taste it. He thinks about it, dreams about it. Then he gets to town and gets the drink, and it wasn't what he really wanted after all. It goes sour on his stomach. That's the way it was with me, Jane. For four years I'd looked forward to this. And somehow it went sour."

The wet rag was so hot that Kyle almost cried out. But Jane was quick and sure in the use of it. She cleansed the cuts and bruises on Kyle's face and hands.

Then she brought some antiseptic. Kyle flinched at the searing pain.

"I'm sorry," she said. "I didn't mean to hurt you."

"It's all right," he answered. "I've hurt you enough."

He touched her hand. The warmth of it, the nearness of her, brought a rush of blood to his face. "Jane, I—"

Suddenly he pulled her to him, crushing her as if to make up at once for four lost years. Kissing her brought a hammering of pain to his bruised lips, but he didn't let her go.

"Kyle, Kyle," she whispered, the flush high in her cheeks, "it's not too late for us, is it?"

"I don't know, Jane," he said. "I don't know."

He caught up the Emmetts' rustling horse and saddled him with an old rig he found in the shed. The stirrups were a notch too short, but he didn't have time to let them out.

The moon came up, only a half moon, but it cast enough light that he could follow the wagon down the creek toward the McLeod ranch. The place was dark as he approached but it wasn't vacated. He was still a hundred yards from the house when a woman's voice suddenly spoke behind him.

"Stop right there and put your hands up.

He raised his hands. "I'm Kyle Rayford," he said. "I've got to get word to Sam Whittenburg."

"Rayford?"

Kyle lowered his hands a little.

"Put them back up there!" He raised them quickly.

"I'm by myself," he assured the woman whom he hadn't yet seen.

"You better be. Get off easy and come in."

Inside the rock house he found it wasn't really dark. Blankets had been draped over the windows. Lester

McLeod lay on a bed in a corner. He raised up on his good elbow at the sight of Kyle.

"You're not welcome here, Rayford," he said. His voice was none too strong.

"I didn't expect to be. But I've got to find Sam. Somebody's got to help me."

He quickly explained about Gorman and Ebeling. It took a good while to convince them. It was his bruised face that finally did it. McLeod nodded. "I believe you're telling the truth. Johnny, saddle your horse. Take him to the rig."

McLeod's boy said grudgingly, "All right. But if he makes a false move, I'll pop him with my slingshot."

They rode about two hours. At times Kyle was afraid the boy would get lost in the dim moonlight. But the youngster knew the way.

"We ought to find it any time now," he said.

They found it, but too late. A sudden crackle of gunfire started ahead of them. They heard excited shouts, the screams of horses.

Fire leaped up in the darkness.

Kyle's heart sank. "Hold up, sonny. No use going in there now. I haven't got a gun and that slingshot wouldn't help much, either."

The gunfire stopped as abruptly as it had begun. A rumble of hoofbeats moved toward them. Kyle stepped down quickly and motioned the boy to do the same. They stood there, holding their horses' noses to keep them from nickering. The raiding party passed by no more than three hundred yards away.

The two rode on in after that. They had no trouble finding the camp. Even after the flames had stopped leaping into the air, the steady glow of fire lighted their way. Excited men were throwing water on the drilling rig, where stubborn flames clung, flickered low, then flashed bright again. But the last of them was snuffed out. Around the camp, the scene was one of almost total destruction. A burning wagon collapsed, sending a shower of sparks into the air while one of the wheels rolled down the slope twenty feet and came to clanking rest against a water barrel. The barrel was shot full of holes, the last of the water pouring out the punctures at the bottom. A short way from the rig, a mule lay screaming, threshing in agony. Rage roared through Kyle as he realized the raiders had shot all the animals.

One of the men put the mule out of its misery with a pistol bullet as Kyle and the McLeod boy rode up. Someone recognized Kyle and swung a rifle around. Sam Whittenburg's voice stopped him. "Hold on there! Let him come in." Kyle rode in with his hands well away from his sides, so they could see he carried no gun.

"What're you doing here, Kyle?" Sam demanded. His voice was grim.

"I came to warn you. But we got here a little late."

The boy piped in quickly. "Pa told me to come with him. Pa said he believed him. And it all happened just like he said it would."

"Ebeling was with your friend Gorman," Sam said. "I guess you know that."

Kyle nodded. "I knew it. That's why I came."

In the firelight Kyle saw the angry splotch of red on Sam's sleeve. "You better take care of that, Sam," he said, reaching to touch the arm.

Sam pulled away. "There's worse here. A lot worse. You better come with me, Kyle."

Kyle followed him to where a man lay on a blanket. Another man bent over him, working by lantern light, trying to stanch the flow of blood from a chest wound.

Kyle's breath broke off short. Enrique!

He fell to his knees, his throat tight. "Enrique. *Compadre*."

Enrique's eyes fluttered open. His lips moved, but no words came.

Kyle looked up quickly. "We've got to get to a doctor."

Sam shook his head. "It'd kill him to move him now. And we've got no wagons left. Buster McLeod, how's that horse of yours? Fresh enough to make it to town? Go fetch us a doctor. Hurry."

The boy left.

Even as the youngster rode away, Kyle knew it would be no use. A few hours, a day, maybe two days, Enrique was done.

The world came crashing down about him. He closed his burning eyes. His throat swelled and choked him.

Sam said, "You'd have been proud of him, Kyle. I never saw a man like him. He saw Ebeling, and he seemed to turn into a tiger. Ebeling rode in, and the old man jumped out after him. His gun was empty, but he went on anyway with a knife in his hand.

"They were all shooting at him at once, but just couldn't seem to hit him. He grabbed hold of Ebeling's leg and started pulling him out of the saddle. Ebeling shot him, then, in the chest. It wasn't till then that Enrique stopped."

Sam walked away, leaving Kyle alone with Enrique. Kyle bent low over the old Mexican, hoping Enrique could understand.

"You were right, Enrique," he said, almost pleading. "I was wrong. You tried to tell me and I wouldn't listen. Forgive me, Enrique."

Enrique's ancient, wrinkled hand lifted. It was a

terrible effort, but the old man managed to lift it and place it on Kyle's hand. Kyle felt a gentle pressure there, and he saw Enrique's lips pull into a thin, weak smile. He had to bend low to hear the whispered words.

"Once—I was young, *hijo*, just like you. That's why I understand you. You are Enrique—fifty years ago. Nothing to forgive, my son. Nothing to forgive."

Daylight came, and the word spread. The ranchers began riding in to look around, to take inventory and see what the others were thinking. The drilling camp was a litter of dead horses and mules, burned wagons and camping equipment. Every water barrel was shot full of holes. Oats were scattered all over the ground.

The well driller was talking to Milt McGivern, shaking his head. "The rig there, it's built out of oak, and it didn't burn bad. We got the fire put out. But we can't drill again till we get some new teams and camp gear, and some new rope, too. And we got to dig that drill bit out of the hole by hand. Weighs five hundred pounds."

He squinted. "Something else. We got to have better protection than we had, or we don't even start."

Thomas Avery, the family man, worriedly shook his head. "I don't know. It ain't worth it, risking our lives this way. Getting shot at for land that don't even belong to us. If Gorman don't get it, somebody else will buy it out from under us anyway."

Ferman Olds said, "What kind of a life is it when you got to live with your guns twenty-four hours a day, wondering when they're going to come next? It might last for months."

Riders came by during the day, and the news gathered. Gorman and Ebeling had raided several ranches after leaving the well site. They had burned buildings or caved them in. They had run off cattle from all over the range. Over at the Johnson place they had shot old man Johnson. He wasn't even in Gorman's original plan. And at the Hendersons', one of the horsemen had run over Mrs. Henderson and left her lying there with a broken leg.

Thomas Avery looked as if a mule had kicked him in the stomach. "That settles it," he said. "If they want it that bad, they can have it."

Ferman Olds nodded. "That's the way I see it, too."

But Milt McGivern still had some fight him. "Wait a minute, now. We're not going to tuck our tails between our legs and run off like mongrel dogs, without even putting up a fight. We've spent years building what we have. Are we going to let somebody take it away from us in one night?"

Jealous of McGivern's strong spirit, Avery said irritably, "What do you expect us to do? I'm not a gunfighter. I'm a rancher."

"You're a coward!" McGivern declared.

Kyle had been staying close to Enrique. Enrique had lapsed into unconscious last night, and he hadn't come out of it. Kyle knew he never would.

Still stiff and sore from the beating, Kyle stood up and walked over to where the men were arguing.

"Look," he broke in, "if you can hold out through the next couple of weeks, you'll have Gorman whipped."

They looked at him in surprise. "What you know about it?" Avery demanded.

Kyle explained about the trail herd Gorman was expecting.

"A week, ten days at the most, and it'll be here. It's a big one. Gorman has got to have your range for those cattle—all of your range. If those cattle come piling in here on him and he hasn't got it, he's sunk. He'll have to send them on north somewhere, west to New Mexico. Or even back to South Texas. Whichever he does, he'll have to do it quick."

Avery scowled. "How do we know you're not still with Gorman? How do we know you're not setting us up for a licking?"

Kyle said, "Gorman's got Ebeling with him now. And they've shot Enrique. You know I wouldn't ride with Ebeling."

McGivern had been eyeing Kyle critically. Now he said to Avery, "I believe him, Thomas. And I'm not going to quit. I'm going to stick, like he says."

Kyle felt the touch of McGivern's hand on his shoulder. "We've all made mistakes, son. I've made them, and you've made them. I don't blame you for yours. I hope you'll forgive me for mine. Let's call it square and see what we can do to set it right."

Avery's eyes were still hostile. They were still scared. "Stick if you want to, Milt. But I'm through."

He turned and started walking for his horse. Ferman Olds called, "Wait for me, Thomas. I'm going with you." Sadness was in McGivern's eyes as he watched them go. "I reckon we'll lose the rest, too. Let two pull out and the others will follow. Just like a row of dominoes falling down. One goes and they all do."

Kyle turned to Sam. "You were telling me the other day about the Rangers. Where are they?"

Sam shrugged. "No telling."

"Sam," Kyle said, "I think the law would stick with all of you now, whatever you did. Gorman had it on his side when he started. He owned those creek sections. But now he's over-reached himself, he and Ebeling. He's raided and burned and even killed.

"He's desperate for time now. That's why he cut the

dogs loose. He's hoping to get this thing wound up before the law finds out about it. He wants to get you all run out or buried. Once he's got possession of the land, even the law's going to have a hard time rooting him out."

Sam said, "So we send somebody to hunt the Rangers. What if it takes weeks to get them here? If the rest of the ranchers stampede like Avery and Olds, there's not much we can do. And they'll stampede, Kyle."

Kyle said, "Maybe we'll find a way. We'll just have to keep looking."

As Kyle had known he would, Enrique died the morning of the second day. Kyle sat beside him numbly, holding the red, wrinkled old hand that would never love again.

Brook Emmett and Jane were there. Ebling had made a lightning raid on Emmett, taking away in one sweep the cattle he and a couple of cowboys had been holding. Now McGivern was trying to talk Emmett into staying. Emmett was about ready to give it all up.

"It doesn't mean much to me any more, anyway," he was saying.

McGivern said, "I know what's been bothering you, Brook. Would it help you any if Kyle Rayford told you he no longer held anything against you? Would that wipe the slate clean?"

Emmett turned slowly to face Kyle, not knowing exactly what to expect. For a moment he stood in silence, the hope almost painful in his eyes.

Kyle said, "You asked me the other day if I would shake hands with you. I'd like to do it now."

Later Kyle turned back to Enrique. Jane sat down beside him. No words passed between them. None were needed.

After a long while she asked, "Where are you going to bury him?"

"He belongs on the Slash R," Kyle said. "I'm going to take him there, if you'll lend me one of your wagons."

Her hand touched his. "Sure, Kyle. I'll go with you."

He shook his head sharply. "No. We might run into Gorman or Ebeling."

She said, "I'm going with you, Kyle."

He didn't have it in him to argue. He shrugged. "All right. We'd better get started, or we won't be back before dark."

Sam was gone, trying to talk others into staying a little longer. So just Kyle and Jane went with Enrique's body. For an hour they sat together on the spring wagon seat, and not a word passed between them as the wagon bounced along. But Kyle could feel Jane's worried eyes upon him.

Jane said, "You're still confused, aren't you, Kyle? You don't know which way to turn."

He nodded solemnly. "For four years I was so sure what I wanted. And when I got it, everything blew up in my face."

An emptiness left a terrible ache in him. "Even the Slash R. I dreamed of getting it back. Now I don't know if I want it or not. There wouldn't be anything left there but memories—a lot of bad memories."

She took his hand. "You'll want it, when this is all over."

At the Slash R he picked a spot of high ground and took out the shovel. The summer sun bore down with a vengeance, and sweat soaked his shirt. But the ground was soft. The digging went fast.

While Kyle dug, Jane walked up and down the creek, among the trees which Earl Rayford had set out as soon as he had reached the place, and which now had grown tall and strong. Presently she came back.

"You know," she said, "there's a wonderful spot down there for a house. All that shade, and not far from the water. You could find all the rock you'd need just a little way up the creek."

Kyle stopped digging and wiped the sweat from his forehead. "I know. Pa had him a spot picked out down there. He used to always dream about the house he'd build someday."

"You'll build it, Kyle," she said. He didn't know. He didn't know if he'd ever want to see the place again.

Gently Kyle lowered Enrique's blanket-wrapped body into the grave. He stood with hat in his hand while Jane read from the Bible she had brought with her. She finished with a prayer. Kyle's throat was so tight he couldn't join in with her.

He wished, for Enrique, that he had had a priest. There wasn't one up here anywhere. Someday, maybe, he could find one and bring him here.

He picked up the shovel and let the first shovelful of dirt slide back into the grave. He blinked away the stinging in his eyes.

"Hold it, Rayford!"

The voice cracked like a whip from within the trees. Kyle grabbed at his hip and then remembered. He had taken off his gun while he was digging. It hung on the wagon, fifteen feet away.

Thatcher, Ebeling's man, stepped out from the trees. His left shoulder was bound because of the wound Kyle had given him, and his left arm was in a tight sling. But his right hand was all right, and it held a gun.

"I've been watching this place," Thatcher said. "Had a notion you'd be back over here, sooner or later."

Benny Ahrens was with him. Benny walked out behind him. Thatcher said something sharply to him, and Benny hurried up beside him. Benny also held a gun.

Thatcher's face was white and sick. He didn't seem strong on his feet. But his hand was firm, and the gun barrel held steady. That was what counted.

Thatcher's eyes still showed signs of fever. "Look at this shoulder, Rayford. Crippled. It'll be crippled as long as I live. You done it to me, and you're going to pay for it."

Kyle's heart was hammering. He glanced once again at the gun and knew he couldn't make it. His hands were beginning to tremble a little on the handle of the shovel, stuck down into the mound of fresh earth.

"What about her?" Kyle asked, nodding toward Jane.

"We're not here to kill women," Thatcher said.

Thatcher turned to Benny Ahrens. "Go pick up that gun on the wagon yonder."

Benny hesitated, his face a shade green. He had lost all stomach for this kind of thing.

Thatcher whirled on him in fury. "Go on, you sniveling coward. Get that gun or I'll kill you, too."

For a second, then, Thatcher's eyes went on Benny Ahrens. Kyle brought up the shovel and heaved dirt at Thatcher's face. It caught Thatcher in the eyes. The bullet whined past Kyle.

Kyle spun and raced for the wagon. But Jane was already there. She grabbed the gun and threw it to him. He whirled back as Thatcher rubbed the sand from his eyes and brought his gun into line again.

There wasn't time to aim. Kyle cocked the hammer and squeezed the trigger fast—once, twice, three times.

Thatcher doubled over and staggered two steps. The life was gone from him before he hit the ground.

Benny Ahrens quaked like a sapling in the wind. He dropped his gun. He had never fired it. His eyes pleaded.

"Please, Rayford, I didn't want to come. You got to believe me. I didn't want to come."

The sudden burst of action and its sudden end had left Kyle numb. He stared through Benny as if he couldn't see him. For the full space of ten seconds he had held his breath. Now he let it go. He relaxed, the gun still in his hand hanging at his side.

"I believe you, Benny. Only kick that gun out of the way. Where are your horses?

"Back in the trees."

Jane said, "I'll go get them."

Kyle nodded. "Benny, you take the shovel and finish filling the grave."

When Jane brought the horses, Kyle lifted Thatcher's body across the saddle and tied him on, facedown. He slipped the bridle off and gave the horse a slap across the rump. It would head home, he knew.

Kyle turned back to Benny Ahrens. "You want to go home the same way?"

Ahrens shook his head, his eyes wide and white.

"Then tell me. What are Ebeling and Gorman planning to do?"

Benny said fearfully, "I don't know. They ain't been telling me."

Kyle grabbed Benny's collar and shook him soundly. "That's a lie. You follow Ebeling around like a hound dog."

Tears brimmed in Ahrens's eyes. "He'd kill me if I told you."

Kyle took the rope off Benny's saddle and threw it out to full length, then drew it up again, doubled.

"Does this bring back any memories, Benny?"

Benny trembled. "Rayford, that was a long time ago."

"Not long enough for me to forget it."

Kyle swung the rope sharply, so that it wrapped around his boot with a loud slap.

Ahrens lowered his head, his fingers flexing rapidly. "Alright. They're making a sweep of the whole country. Rounding up every hoof they can get their hands on in a hurry. Throwing them together on that old lake over on the Bar E. Day or two, when they're finished gathering, they'll run the cattle west, back into the dry country."

Kyle swore lightly under his breath. "There's no water there except a few wet weather lakes. They'd starve to death."

Benny shrugged. "They ain't Ebeling's cattle."

Gloom hung like a cold, wet blanket at Sam Whittenburg's picket ranch house. Inside, Jane Emmett silently fixed a pot of coffee. Kyle Rayford sat on the front step, whittling on a stick, each stroke of the knife as savage as if he were cutting Clint Ebeling's throat.

Sam Whittenburg squatted on the ground beside him, drawing brands in the sand with a pointed stick and rubbing them out. Mil McGivern and Brook Emmett were there too, both grave.

"I don't know if we can do it, Kyle," McGivern was saying. "Not many of us left. McLeod's laid up. Thomas Avery and Ferman Olds have pulled out. They threw up their hands and quit. Smith's going, and I think the Callenders have left."

Sam jabbed the stick into the ground. "Together we could whip that bunch. They aren't that many of them. But we can't hold together. They've been afraid of Ebeling too long."

Kyle gestured with the knife. "There are still you, Sam, and Milt, and me. And you, Brook Emmett, if you'll go along."

Emmett squared his shoulders, and hope had come alive in his eyes again. Once more he seemed to be the proud Brook Emmet Kyle remembered from long ago.

"Three days ago I wouldn't have walked across the yard to save the whole ranch. Now I'll go where you go, Kyle—all the way."

Kyle nodded. "Glad to hear you say that, Brook. That's four of us. We can scrape up four or five cowhands."

Sam shook his head. "That's not enough."

Kyle said, "It might be, if we went at it right. If we aren't going to try, we'd just as well pull out like Olds and Avery."

Interest grew in McGivern's eyes. "What have you got in mind?"

"The same thing that worked for Gorman the other day, over at McLeod's. We're going to stampede that herd right over Ebeling's camp!"

At dusk they let Benny Ahrens out of the old dugout where they had been holding him. Kyle led him to where they had his horse saddled and ready. "Get up there, Benny. You're going to be our guide."

He shook down his rope and slipped the loop over Benny's neck. "If you let your foot slip anywhere down the line," he said bitterly, "I'm liable to jerk this thing."

They started out then, a string of nine horsemen working quietly down the creek in an easy trot, grim-faced, silent. It would be a long ride to Ebeling's. There was no way of knowing for sure where the cattle would be. This would all depend on Benny Ahrens. There was always a chance Benny might try a trick. But riding alongside him in the moonlight, Kyle could see the fear which clutched Benny's throat. No, he felt sure, Benny wouldn't try a thing.

It took more than three hours. Ahead, Kyle could see a flickering pinpoint of a burned-down campfire. He held up his hand. The other riders pulled in close beside him. Kyle dismounted, handing the reins and the rope to Sam. He walked ahead fifty or seventy-five feet to listen, where there would be no squeaking of saddle feather.

This late at night, the cattle had bedded down. There was no bawling. But listening a while, he made out a shuffling of hooves as some animals moved restlessly.

Returning to the others, he said, "Camp's on this side. We'd best circle way around."

He wondered worriedly where Ebeling's remuda of horses was being held. Let them smell these mounts and start nickering, and the lid might blow off in a hurry.

Quietly they made a wide circle around the camp, coming in at the far side of the herd on the edge of a huge natural basin which in wet weather made a fine lake of water. The water had shrunk back far from the outer edges of the basin now.

Kyle studied the herd a long while in the pale moonlight.

"There are three men on guard around the herd, near as I can make out," he said.

The nighthawks were slowly riding back and forth along the edge of the huge herd. Several thousand head were bedded down here. They belonged to Emmett, McLeod, McGivern, Sam Whittenburg, and many others.

"It's your deal, Kyle," Sam said quietly.

Kyle said, "Scatter out, and ease up toward the cattle. You know what to do. When you hear me start, then all of you open up."

He rode straight ahead, leading the quaking Benny Ahrens, while the other riders fanned out. Kyle stopped a hundred yards from the herd, giving the other men time. He reached up and took the loop off Benny's neck.

"You're on your own now, Benny. If I were you, I'd get clear of this country. If Ebeling gets away, he's liable to go looking for you."

Benny's voice was tight. "Don't you worry. I've always kind of wanted to see Arizona. I think I'll go take a look." Benny faded back into the pale moonlight. Kyle waited, giving the others a little more time. Excitement played up and down in him. What if it didn't work out? These men would lose everything they had.

But something had to be tried, or they would lose everything.

He drew his gun and touched spurs to his horse. Squeezing the trigger, he let go a rebel yell like his father had taught him a long time ago. Then noise rushed down upon the herd of cattle like an avalanche. Guns crashed, men yelled, and a herd of cattle jumped to its feet. In an instant the cattle were running, fear whipping the sleep-drugged beasts into a frantic dash for escape from the sudden thunder of men and guns and horses. The ground trembled beneath the gouging, grinding hooves of thousands of longhorn cattle.

In the near darkness and over the deafening drum of hooves, he couldn't see or hear the Ebeling-Gorman camp, but he knew what must be happening. The men would be scattering in panic, trying desperately to escape this sudden avalanche of horns and hooves and choking dust.

Kyle was at the edge of the herd now. Ahead of him he saw a man cutting across, fast as he could spur, trying to reach safety outside the path of the run. Another man went by. He saw Kyle. They were close, and Kyle recognized this one. Jack Dangerfield.

Dangerfield fired a quick shot at him. Kyle fired back. Dangerfield's horse fell, then the man was lost in the darkness.

Kyle knew then that it was going as he had hoped it would. Ebeling's and Gorman's men were scattering in every direction. They couldn't organize again tonight in any effective kind of force. Tomorrow it would be too late.

Ahead of him, Kyle saw another rider, spurring. It was a losing fight, for the man's horse was limping badly and dropping back. In a moment he would be swallowed up among the panic-stricken cattle.

The horse fell, and the rider went rolling. Kyle swung toward him. The man saw him coming and screamed for help. He was on one knee, and Kyle knew that his leg had been broken.

He swung in beside him, only then realizing that this was John Gorman. Gorman, in sock feet and without pants, just as he had rolled out of his bed, was more afraid of the cattle now than of Kyle Rayford. "Help me, Rayford," he cried. "Get me out of here."

Kyle pulled up beside him and reached down. Gorman gripped his leg, and Kyle took a fresh hold under the man's arm. With momentum from the nervous horse, he managed to swing Gorman up behind him.

Then he spurred up again as the cattle surged around them.

Before long the cattle began to run down. They had covered two miles or more in the first surge of panic. Now some were beginning to drop out. A few would run another mile or two, but without the speed or terror of the first few minutes. By morning they would be scattered out over much of Ebeling's land.

"It's going to be a real mess for somebody to straighten out." Kyle said.

Gorman groaned. "I've got to have help, Rayford. My leg is broke."

Kyle said, "I'll take you to camp, if there's any camp left. But it's a question whether they'll set your leg or stretch your neck."

At the demolished camp, the riders began drifting in. Three of the Ebeling-Gorman men were there, huddled for safety behind the ruins of an overturned chuckwagon. Most of the food had been trampled into the ground. The campfire was scattered all over the place. Bedrolls and clothing were beaten into the dust.

As the riders came, they brought several of the Ebeling-Gorman men they had picked up. These were herded into a bunch. Gorman's face fell at the sight of them.

He had lost. He could tell that now. More than half of his and Ebeling's force had been neutralized. And he, too, was a prisoner.

Gone was the driving bull force which Kyle had always seen in him. Gorman's shoulders slumped with defeat, and the pain of the broken leg was rapidly breaking him down.

"Somebody do something," he groaned.

Kyle scowled at him. "I should have left you. I ought

to shoot you now. We made an agreement, and then you fell in with the very man I came up here to get."

Gorman didn't try to rise too much of a defense. "You didn't go through with it. I had to get somebody I thought would do it."

"I went through with what I said I would do. But we both got outsmarted."

He felt along Gorman's leg until the big ranchman cried out in pain.

"That's it, I reckon," Kyle said. "Somebody come give me a hand."

By the time they had Gorman's leg set and bound in splints, the man was limp, clammy with cold sweat. "What're you going to do with me now?" he pleaded.

"Keep you till the Rangers come. Men have died here because of you. I reckon they could hang you for complicity in it."

Whatever courage the big man had had, it was gone now. In the shadow of a hang rope he was no longer the blustering, driving man who had controlled some of the biggest acreages in South Texas.

"I didn't kill anybody. I didn't tell Ebeling to kill anybody. He did it on his own. Listen, Rayford, let me go and I'll give you anything you want."

A sudden feeling of triumph swept Kyle. "I'll make you a deal. I'll sell you your freedom for those land certificates."

Gorman nodded quickly. "Sure, I always intended to give you that ranch of yours, Kyle. You know I always intended to."

Kyle shook his head. "Not just the deed to my ranch. The deeds to all the land you bought up."

Some of the fire leaped back into Gorman's face. "Lord, Kyle, I paid thousands of dollars for that land."

"And you've burned out a lot of people. You've destroyed homes and barns and caused the loss of cattle. Men have died here because of you. A few thousand dollars isn't much to pay for all that."

Gorman swallowed hard, looking away, "I won't do it."

"Then we'll wait for the Rangers."

For a little while Gorman sat there, nervously chewing his heavy lip in lieu of one of his cigars. At last he went slack.

"I have the certificates in town. Take me in, and I'll sign them over."

With daylight Kyle and Sam and McGivern and most of the others fanned out over the country, looking for the rest of Ebeling's men. They picked up two or three. Only one put up a fight. A bullet in his leg took it out of him in a hurry.

They found what was left of Jack Dangerfield where the cattle had overtaken him after his horse had fallen.

But they never found Clint Ebeling.

"He's finished," Kyle said. "He must know that the Rangers will be here, and that when they come, they'll be out to get him."

"Let's let him go," said Sam Whittenburg. "I think we've all had a bellyful of this anyway. The Rangers will find him."

Kyle shook his head. "They won't get him. He'll clear out. Besides, the Rangers can't square the debt I owe him."

Kyle caught up a fresh horse, checked his guns and rode off alone. Sam wanted to go with him, but Kyle had shaken his head. "This is my fight now, Sam."

He headed straight for Ebeling's ranch headquarters. After losing last night, Ebeling must be getting ready to leave the country, Kyle figured. He would be the rankest kind of fool not to.

But he would need food and a fresh horse or two, and chances were he had some money hidden away somewhere around the ranch. He was bound to go back for that.

Kyle made no effort at concealment. He wanted Ebeling to see that he had come alone. He knew the fear and the desperation and the loss and the hatred that must be chewing at Ebeling now, the same that Kyle had felt four years ago.

He felt sure Ebeling would come out to meet him, to try to kill the man who had precipitated this final disaster.

Boldly Kyle rode through the open corral gate and up toward the sod house. Hand on his gun, he halted fifty feet from the door and yelled, "I've come for you, Ebeling."

For a minute he sat there watching and listening. He heard nothing, saw nothing. He began to wonder if he had been wrong. Or if not wrong, if he had come too late.

Then the wooden door swung outward, and Clint Ebeling stepped out in front of the sod house. He left the door open.

"I'm here, Rayford," he said.

He kept his hand away from the .45 at his hip. For the space of a minute or more, he and Kyle stood watching each other. The range was a shade long for accurate pistol fire. Somehow Kyle was wary of closing it.

Ebeling said, "There was a job I should have finished four years ago, Rayford. If I had, there wouldn't have been all this trouble. Now you've ruined me. I hope you're satisfied."

"I am," Kyle said. "For four years I've worked and planned for it."

"Did you figure on dying for it too, Rayford?"

Kyle's mouth went dry. Why didn't Ebeling go ahead and reach for that gun instead of standing there talking? Ebeling was grinning at him, grinning with that supreme confidence of his.

Kyle caught the tiny flicker of movement inside the sod house. He threw himself from the saddle just as a rifle exploded and a streak of flame lanced at him from the darkness beyond the open door. He triggered a fast shot through the door and another at Ebeling, who was bringing his gun into line. Then Kyle sprinted like a jackrabbit, running desperately for the side of the house. Ebeling's .45 barked after him. Fire touched Kyle's leg, almost making him fall.

He gained the safety of the sod house. Above him was a small glass window. It shattered under a blow from inside, and the rifle barrel poked out. They were trying to get him in a hurry.

Kyle raised up, quickly shoved his gun through the window and fired. He heard a gasp, then a groan and the thud of a man falling to the floor.

Only one left now. Ebeling.

Kyle looked about him, his heart racing. He was exposed to fire from almost anywhere here on the open side of the house. He eased the window up and propped it with a stick. Then, the broken glass cutting into his hands, he lifted himself over the sill and into the house.

He paused to check the fallen man. Dead, all right. Kyle had gotten him through the throat.

There was no back window, and Kyle couldn't see out. But he knew Ebeling must be stalking him. Ebeling wouldn't know Kyle was in the house. He would be coming around, taking one side at a time.

Kyle waited just inside the door. The sun was behind

the house now. He watched the shadow for some kind of movement. Then it came.

Ebeling was creeping up the side of the house where Kyle had been. Kyle shrank back against the wall, gun leveled on the window in case Ebeling looked through. But he didn't. The shadow moved stealthily forward. Then Ebeling jumped around the corner, gun ready, expecting to see Kyle there.

Through the crack between the door and the jamb, Kyle watched the surprise in Ebeling's face turn to something else. The realization had struck Ebeling that he was no longer the stalker.

Fear crawled into the man's wide eyes. He whirled, looking behind him. He seemed not a bit relieved to see that no one was there.

He visibly began to tremble. His eyes darted to the door, and Kyle could read the desperate thought behind them.

Ebeling saw safety inside the sod house. A temporary safety, at least. Better to be hemmed into four protective walls than to be trapped in the open.

He made a dash for the door. He grabbed the door as he came through and pulled it shut behind him. Then he turned, breathing heavily.

He saw Kyle there waiting for him, and he seemed to sag. For a long moment that was almost eternity, he stared at death, his face blanched white. Then he raised his gun. Kyle pulled the trigger, and it was eternity . . .

Kyle finished the carving and carried the wooden cross up to the high point where he had buried Enrique. With the back of a rusty old axe he had found, he drove the point of the upright solidly into the soft earth.

The sound of a horse's hooves brought him slowly around. Such a thing a few days ago would have made him whirl about, gun in hand. Now there was no worry, no fear. The time for that was past, and need not return.

Jane Emmett pulled her horse to a stop. Kyle helped her down from the sidesaddle. He kept holding her hand even after it was no longer necessary, but he didn't want to let it go. She made no effort to pull her hand away.

She turned and looked back down the green blanket of grass toward the creek and at the trees which cast their deep shape along the banks there.

"It's really beautiful from up here, Kyle." she said.

He nodded.

She turned back to him, worry in her eyes. "You're not going to go away and leave it again, are you, Kyle? This is your home. This is where you belong."

He shook his head. "No, I'm not going to leave. There's too much here now to keep me—Pa, Enrique, all the work and the sweat and the fighting we went through. I can't ride off and leave that again. I thought I could, but I can't."

He picked up her bridle reins, and they started down the hill together, leading Jane's horse.

"Jane," Kyle said, "we used to talk about building a house, you and me. Where's that spot you found the other day?"

The grip of her hand suddenly tightened and the sunshine broke out in her eyes. Her pace quickened, and then she was almost running.

"Come on," she said. "I'll show you."

Forge

Award-winning authors
Compelling stories

· ·

Please join us at the website
below for more information
about this author and other great
Forge selections, and to sign up for
our monthly newsletter!

· · · · **www.tor-forge.com** · · · ·